ADVANCE ACCLAIM FOR
The HEIRESS of WINTERWOOD

"My kind of book! The premise grabbed my attention from the first lines and I eagerly returned to its pages. I think my readers will enjoy *The Heiress of Winterwood*."

—JULIE KLASSEN, BESTSELLING, AWARD-WINNING AUTHOR

"Oh my, what an exquisite tale! With clarity and grace, Sarah E. Ladd has penned a timeless regency that rises to the ranks of Heyer and Klassen, a breathless foray into the world of Jane Austen with very little effort . . . and very little sleep."

—JULIE LESSMAN, AWARD-WINNING AUTHOR OF THE DAUGHTERS OF BOSTON AND WINDS OF CHANGE SERIES

"Captivated from the very first page! *The Heiress of Winterwood* marks Sarah E. Ladd as a rising Regency star sure to win readers' hearts!"

—LAURA FRANTZ, AUTHOR OF THE COLONEL'S LADY AND LOVE'S RECKONING

"A delight from beginning to end, *The Heiress of Winterwood* is a one-of-a-kind regency that kept me sighing with joy, laughing, crying, and even biting my nails when the occasion called for it! A whirlwind of emotions captured in an exciting tale of intrigue, kidnapping, and bittersweet love. This is Ms. Ladd's debut? I can't wait to see she writes next! Remember the name Sarah Ladd because I'm sure you will be seeing much more from this talented author."

—MARYLU TYNDALL, BEST-SELLING AUTHOR OF VEIL OF PEARLS AND THE SURRENDER TO DESTINY SERIES

The

HEIRESS

of

WINTERWOOD

SARAH E. LADD

THOMAS NELSON
Since 1798

NASHVILLE   DALLAS   MEXICO CITY   RIO DE JANEIRO

Published in Nashville, Tennessee, by Thomas Nelson. Thomas Nelson is a registered trademark of Thomas Nelson, Inc.

Thomas Nelson, Inc., titles may be purchased in bulk for educational, business, fund-raising, or sales promotional use. For information, please e-mail SpecialMarkets@ThomasNelson.com.

All Scripture quotations are taken from the King James Version of the Bible.

Publisher's Note: This novel is a work of fiction. Names, characters, places, and incidents are either products of the author's imagination or used fictitiously. All characters are fictional, and any similarity to people living or dead is purely coincidental.

Library of Congress Control Number: 2013931019

ISBN: 978-1-4016-8835-6

Printed in the United States of America

13 14 15 16 17 18 RRD 6 5 4 3 2 1

For my husband, Scott. Your quiet strength and unconditional love inspire me daily. Thank you for believing in me.

PROLOGUE

Katherine was going to die. And Amelia could do nothing to prevent it.

Amelia Barrett dabbed at her dearest friend's brow with a damp cloth. A single tear, hot as fire, slipped unchecked down her cheek. Exhaustion pulled at her limbs. Fatigue pleaded with her to sit and rest. But she dared not stop.

Beyond Winterwood Manor's stone walls, icy rain pelted the earth, driven hard by the gusts from the moors. Not so very long ago, that wind had hummed soothing lullabies. Now, in dawn's gray light, its mournful wail whispered chilling omens.

From a distant chamber a wee infant's cry echoed through Winterwood's ancient halls. The babe, at least, would recover from the horror of the past three days. Katherine, however, would be fortunate to see another sunset.

Amelia rubbed her palms against her forehead, longing to erase the memory of a childbirth gone terribly amiss. Hours of anxiety had rolled into days of dread, and now her unconscious friend's breathing waned. Each shallow pant hinted another might not come.

The fire's dancing light cast shadows across Katherine's ashen cheeks. Perspiration trickled down her neck. Fiery locks clung to her damp forehead. Amelia immersed a cloth in a basin and drizzled cool water over her friend's fevered skin. At the touch, Katherine's eyelids fluttered. Amelia snatched back her hand with renewed optimism and fell to her knees next to the bed.

"Katherine!" Amelia clutched her friend's arm. "Katherine, do you hear me?"

A groan escaped Katherine's parched lips, followed by a shallow cough. "Where is the letter?" Her voice sounded dry. Raspy.

Eyes wide, Amelia nodded toward the letter on the writing table. "It's here."

"Promise you will give it to him."

"Of course."

"My baby." Katherine's weak whisper broke as a sob caught in her throat. "Please do not leave her. You will soon be all she has."

Deadening pain surged through Amelia's core, constricting her lungs. She squeezed her fingers around Katherine's clammy hand. "You have my word."

Katherine released a slow breath and closed her eyes.

The air thinned. The suffocating weight of death crept into the room. It lingered in the shadows, loitering like an unwelcome guest. Watching. Waiting.

Amelia's hands shook. She released Katherine's hand and curled her own into tight fists to prevent them from trembling. How could God let this happen? How dare he take away yet another person she loved? If she thought a prayer might help, she'd cry out in desperation. But she'd seen death's shadow too many times. Prayer had not saved the life of any she had cared for. She had no illusion it would avail this time.

She swallowed the dry lump in her throat and began to recite. Katherine would find comfort in her words, even if she did not. "The Lord is my shepherd," she began. "I shall not want."

Eyes still closed, Katherine's cracked lips mouthed a slow, faltering response. "He maketh me to lie down in green pastures: he leadeth me beside the still—"

Katherine's voice stopped. Her labored breaths dissolved into shallow gasps until she breathed no more.

Amelia stared unblinking at the lifeless body before her. Her limbs tingled, then numbed. Disbelief rendered her motionless. No tears remained for her to cry.

The infant's wail pierced the eerie silence and snapped her from her trance. With deliberate, reverent movements, Amelia pressed her lips to Katherine's forehead, then drew the linen sheet over her friend's pallid face.

Surely goodness and mercy shall follow me all the days of my life: and I will dwell in the house of the Lord for ever.

1

Amelia knew what she needed to do. In fact, she'd known ever since Captain Graham Sterling returned to Eastmore Hall.

Her plan would work. It must work. She had addressed every detail and anticipated every objection. Now nothing remained but to convince the captain.

Her only regret was sharing her intentions with her younger cousin Helena.

"This is madness. Absolute madness!" Helena's russet curls bounced in animated vigor with every syllable. "Whatever would possess you to even consider such a thing, let alone see it through?" She tossed her embroidery on the small side table and jumped up from the settee. "Captain Sterling will think you are a lunatic, and then where will you be?" Helena waved her hand in the air to silence Amelia's protest. "I will tell you where you will be. You will be without a husband, without money, and without prospects. That is where you will be."

"Oh hush. You are overreacting." Amelia shifted the sleeping baby in her arms. "You will wake Lucy with all of your carrying on. The last thing we want is for her to be out of sorts when she finally meets her papa."

Helena huffed. "Don't you dare change the subject, Amelia Barrett. The child is fine. It's you who is clearly daft. How could you even consider proposing to a man—and a veritable stranger at that? It's just not done."

Amelia lowered Lucy into a small cradle. "Captain Sterling is not a stranger. Well, not *really*. And as I told you before, I am resolved. Let us speak of it no more. Now, will you kindly hand me that coverlet?"

Helena snatched the yellow knit blanket and tossed it in her cousin's direction. "And what do you think Mr. Littleton will think about this, hmm? Five weeks, Amelia. Need I remind you that you are to marry in five weeks? Why, for you even to have a private meeting with another man, let alone—"

"Shhh! There's no need to get so excited." Amelia averted her eyes as she coaxed the conversation back to the captain. "There is no impropriety in my meeting with Captain Sterling. He has every right to visit his daughter. After all, she's nine months old, and he's never even laid eyes on her. And my proposal to Captain Sterling will be a business proposition, nothing more. If he refuses it, no harm is done. Edward need never know."

"No harm? No harm!" Helena's hazel eyes widened. "Do you not consider your reputation? I shudder to think what will happen when news of this reaches the gossipmongers. Edward could think—"

"He could think a number of things, Helena, and will no doubt do so. But I cannot stand by and say nothing. *Do* nothing. For if I did, Captain Sterling could take Lucy away from us forever, and that I could not bear. Furthermore, I will not break my promise to Katherine."

A pretty pout darkened Helena's fair features, and she tipped her small nose in the air.

"You and Mrs. Sterling may have grown close, but you had not known her a year before she died. I sincerely doubt she would expect you to go to such drastic measures to keep a promise." She leaned closer, not allowing Amelia to look away. "And need I mention that you have never even met this man, this *captain*? He could be a monster—a scoundrel who will take advantage of your giving nature. Why subject yourself to such a fate and risk your fortune when you already have secured such a fine match in Edward Littleton?"

Helena's warning resonated with Amelia. Had not those concerns crossed her mind? The thought of being bound in matrimony to a cruel man sent a shiver through her. But had Katherine not praised the captain's fine qualities? His gentleness? His upright character?

Amelia set her lips in a firm line. This was a risk she was willing to take. "He cannot be that dreadful, Cousin, else Katherine would never have married him. Besides, he is a captain in His Majesty's navy. You've heard the stories as well as I. He will be gone for months—nay, years—at a time, at least for as long as England is at war. No doubt we will live completely separate lives."

"But Mr. Littleton, Amelia. Consider Mr. Littleton." Helena's voice softened. "He loves you, I am certain. Why would you treat him so unkindly and risk a happy marriage for a child who is not even a blood relation?" Helena stepped toward Lucy, looked down at her, and smoothed the child's blanket. "It pains me to speak to you so bluntly, Amelia, but I love you too much to watch you proceed in such a fashion without at least speaking my mind. You have far too wonderful a future ahead of you to risk it now."

Amelia opened her mouth to protest but then snapped it shut. She could not deny that her cousin's point was valid. But how could she make Helena understand her dilemma? She would never have agreed to marry Edward Littleton had she not been genuinely fond of the man. Indeed, his handsome face and passionate nature still had the ability to stir her romantic sensibilities. But as their wedding drew closer, her hesitation mounted. His actions—including his refusal to allow Lucy to continue to reside at Winterwood after their wedding—had planted questions in her mind regarding his character and suitability as a husband. And the thought of her sweet Lucy being raised without a mother, as she had been, unnerved her.

No, she was certain she was taking the right course, difficult though it may be. She simply had to steel herself for the awkwardness of the coming interview with the captain.

A shout sounded outside the window, followed by the crunch of carriage wheels on the gravel front drive. The women locked gazes. Ready or not, the time had come.

Amelia dashed across the room and grabbed her cousin's hand. "Promise you will not say a word."

Helena offered a weak smile. "I do wish you would heed my words, Cousin, but since you are resolved, you have my word. Just, please, at least consider what I have said." With a sweep of her primrose muslin skirt, she quitted the room.

Amelia's slippered feet made little sound as she stepped over the Italian rug to the window. She lifted the corner of the green velvet curtain in time to see the back of the barouche, shiny and slick from the morning's rain, slow to a stop at Winterwood Manor's front entrance.

She smoothed a curl and forced a slow breath. Like it or not, her task was before her. She must not fail. She hurried to the teak writing desk and checked once again to ensure that Katherine's letter was in its place.

A knock echoed in the paneled room. The door unlatched and

swung open, revealing James, the aging butler. "Captain Sterling to see you, miss."

"Will you show him in? And please send Sally in with some tea."

Amelia waited for the mahogany door to close before gathering the sleeping Lucy in her arms. Footsteps echoed on the hall's planked floor. She straightened. James reappeared, but Amelia barely noticed. Her eyes fixed on the tall figure filling the door frame behind him.

Captain Sterling stepped into the light. She had expected him to be fair like his brother or stout like his father had been. He was neither. Sable hair curled over the high collar of his charcoal tail-coat, and his sideburns framed high cheekbones. Stormy gray eyes peered from a fringe of black lashes and darted from Lucy, to her, then back to the baby. His freshly shaven skin, bronzed dark from the sun, gave evidence of months spent on board a ship. She had half expected him to be dressed in uniform, but his dress was that of a gentleman.

At the sight of him, a nervous wave pulsed through Amelia's veins. For weeks she had anticipated meeting this man. She had practiced what she would say and rehearsed it at length. But she had never expected to be affected so by startling smoky eyes. With a deep breath she pushed her anxiety at bay, stepped forward, and forced her best smile. "We meet at last! I am Amelia Barrett."

He bowed and their eyes met once more, but his interest was not in his hostess. His attention fixed on the child nestled in Amelia's embrace. Amelia shifted to give the captain a better view, and at the movement, Lucy stirred and opened her eyes.

Amelia stepped even closer and lifted Lucy into her father's waiting arms. "Captain Sterling, I would like for you to meet your daughter, Miss Lucille Katherine Sterling."

A tentative smile tugged the corners of his mouth. The captain accepted the child in his arms and cradled her against his chest.

Father and daughter stared at one another for several moments, until Lucy lost interest in him and found the fabric-covered button adorning his tailcoat. He touched his fingertips to the copper curls that escaped her lace bonnet. "She has red hair."

She nodded. "Like her mother."

Lucy wiggled in her father's arms and released a shrill cry. The captain stiffened. "Whatever is the matter?" He extended the small body away from him, at which point Lucy's face scrunched and a wail escaped. His eyes widened in what could only be panic. "Why is she crying?"

Amelia masked a smile. Had the man ever held a child? "She is just getting comfortable, I am sure. Here, allow me."

The captain, all too eager to hand over the crying child, deposited Lucy in Amelia's arms and stepped back. She soothed Lucy until the child calmed. With a wave of her hand, she directed the captain to a wingback chair by the fire. "Please be seated."

Amelia placed Lucy in the cradle next to the captain's chair and looked up as Sally, the downstairs maid, appeared with a tray of tea and biscuits. Grateful for the distraction, she turned to direct the servant. But out of the corner of her eye she watched the captain lean over the arm of his chair and stare at his daughter.

As Sally fussed over the refreshments, Amelia feigned interest but kept her peripheral gaze fixed on the father and daughter. For the first time, the captain smiled at the baby, who promptly rewarded him with a grin. He reached into the cradle and pulled out a small wooden horse. Lucy grabbed it and stared in wonder before banging it against a nearby flower stand. Amelia's heart raced. The scene made her feel more like an intruder in her home than heiress to the estate. Desperate to keep her hands busy when she could find no words to speak, Amelia dismissed the maid and moved to stoke the dying fire.

"I must correct you."

Amelia turned from the fireplace, poker still in hand. "Pardon me?"

"You were mistaken when you said, 'We meet at last.' I doubt you remember, but we've met before."

The poker clattered as she returned it to the stand. "Have we?" Amelia pushed her hair from her flushed face and moved to pour him a cup of tea. The task should have been simple, but her hands trembled and the steaming liquid threatened to splash onto the saucer.

"I lived in Darbury for the first twelve years of my life. I remember seeing you when you were not much older than my Lucy."

Amelia handed the captain the tea, poured a cup for herself, and settled into the chair opposite him.

He looked over his shoulder. "Is your uncle not at home?"

Amelia shook her head. "Uncle George has traveled to Leeds on business. He should return tomorrow. My aunt is away also, calling on an acquaintance."

The captain stretched out a booted foot. His posture relaxed. "Well, as I understand from my brother, you are the person to whom I am indebted. Not your uncle."

Heat crept up from the neckline of her dress, and she looked down at her hands. "You are not indebted to me, sir."

"I cannot begin to thank you for the care you showed my wife. And for what you have done for my daughter—I could never repay you."

Uncomfortable under the weight of his attention, she jumped up from her chair and crossed to the window. She drew back the curtains, allowing a fresh wave of gray morning light to flood the room. "How long do you intend to stay in Darbury, Captain?"

"Just long enough to find suitable arrangements for Lucy. I must return to my duties within the month. I hope to have everything settled by then."

A month. She sank her teeth into her lower lip and moved to the desk. The letter lay right where she had left it. She tapped it lightly. If she waited too much longer, she might lose her nerve. "I think I may be able to help you find care for Lucy."

Interest flashed in his eyes. "I would be most grateful for any assistance. I have met with two nurses since my return to England. They were unimpressive at best."

At least he is open to a discussion. She took a steadying breath. "Before Katherine died, I made her two promises. The first was to give you this." Amelia picked up the letter and held it at arm's length.

Captain Sterling eyed the correspondence. As he reached to take it, Amelia noticed a wide purple scar that crossed over the top of his hand and disappeared under his coat's cuff. The scar looked fresh. She diverted her eyes and thrust the letter into his hand.

He flipped the sealed letter to read the inscription. His countenance sobered. He stood and took a cautious step in her direction. "This is from my wife?"

"Yes, written a few days before she died. She asked that I place it directly in your hand." When he failed to respond, she continued. "She was afraid it would never reach you if we sent it by post."

The captain stared at the letter, his square jaw clenched, his expression controlled. He looked from the unopened letter, to his daughter, and then to Amelia. But even as his eyes met hers, Amelia sensed his mind was far away. He seemed to look right through her.

He tucked the unread letter in his pocket and sat down again. "You said you made two promises, Miss Barrett. What was the second?"

Amelia returned to the chair opposite her guest. She paused long enough to regain control of her emotions before speaking. "I promised to stay with Lucy always. Never to leave her alone."

His dark eyebrows arched, but he remained silent.

"With your blessing, I fully intend to honor this promise, and I have had these nine months to consider how to do so. I have devised a plan that I think will work to the best interest of all involved."

He leaned forward and rested his elbows on his knees. "What do you recommend?"

Her clasped hands tightened in her lap. "Since you are from Darbury originally, you may be aware that I am to inherit Winterwood Manor."

He nodded, his gaze never leaving her face. He no longer looked through her, but at her.

"When my father bought this estate, many years before he died, it was in ruins. He dreamed of restoring it to its former glory, and now I share his dream. I am his only child, and there was no specified entailment, so Winterwood will pass to me when I marry. Until then it remains in the hands of my uncle."

Her next words flew from her mouth in a rush—not at all as she had rehearsed. "I would like Lucy to live here with me. She will want for nothing. She will have the best governesses, the finest clothes. And when the time comes, her dowry will be significant."

The captain's eyes widened. He stared at her as if she had grown a second head. Self-consciousness forced her to lower her gaze. She held her breath and waited for his response.

Finally he spoke. "I confess I had hoped you might offer some guidance in the matter."

Amelia exhaled. She straightened her sleeve, carefully smoothing the lace cuff. She must choose her next words very carefully. They were crucial to the success of her plan.

"Lucy is not—and never will be—a burden to me. Having said that, there is one barrier to her continuing to live at Winterwood. You see, in order to fully inherit, I must be married by the time I turn twenty-four years of age or the entire estate will pass to one of my distant cousins. If that happens, I will have nothing—no home, no money, no means of caring for a child . . ."

Her words trailed off. She leaned closer and lowered her unsteady voice. "I am currently engaged to marry Mr. Edward Littleton of Dunton. But Mr. Littleton has made it clear that once we are married, Lucy cannot continue to live at Winterwood."

No longer able to sit, Amelia jumped from her seat and stepped toward him. "Captain, I have raised Lucy these nine months. I could not love her more if she were my own. She is more important to me than a hundred Mr. Littletons and a thousand Winterwoods. Believe me when I say I will do whatever necessary to see her well cared for."

The captain stood to his full height. "You said you had a plan, Miss Barrett."

Amelia's hands shook. It was useless to even try to prevent her lip from quivering as she spoke. "In order to continue raising Lucy when you return to your duties, and in order to inherit Winterwood and have the resources to provide Lucy with what she needs, I would need to marry someone besides Mr. Littleton in the next few weeks."

His eyes narrowed. "What exactly are you suggesting?"

"You, Captain Sterling. You and I should marry. Immediately."

2

Uncertain if he had heard the slip of a woman correctly, Graham Sterling suppressed an incredulous chuckle. How is one supposed to respond when a lady—let alone an attractive stranger—proposes marriage?

"Are you always this direct, Miss Barrett?"

"The circumstances demand it, sir." Miss Amelia Barrett's gaze did not waver. "But I am sure you can see that the arrangement would be advantageous. You need someone to care for Lucy." Her hand flew to her chest. "Who better than I, the person who has loved her since birth?"

Graham could not have torn his eyes away from the animated woman even if he wanted to. Her cheeks flushed crimson, and her sapphire eyes sparkled with brilliant intensity. Mere minutes had passed since he first encountered this young woman. But already Graham knew with certainty that Miss Amelia Barrett was a force to reckon with.

He cleared his throat. "Do you not think marriage a bit . . . drastic?"

Lucy's whimper interrupted their conversation. Grateful for the distraction, Graham returned to his chair. Without a moment's hesitation, Miss Barrett leaned down, picked up Lucy from the cradle, and propped the child on her hip. Lucy peered at him from over Miss Barrett's shoulder. The child—his child—had brown eyes. Wide brown eyes.

Katherine's eyes. The fleeting thought stole the air from Graham's lungs. What would Katherine look like, standing there, holding their child? Guilt's familiar sting pricked his conscience. He'd been at sea for so long that his memory of Katherine's appearance had grown faint and grew more so by the day.

Suddenly desperate to be anywhere else, Graham jumped to his feet and wiped his palms on his buckskin breeches. What did he know about being a father? About fathering a girl?

His daughter smiled at him, drool trickling down her chin, and guilt assailed him once more. He might not be comfortable, but she still belonged to him. He reached for Lucy and forced words through a dry mouth. "May I?"

Graham did not overlook Miss Barrett's hesitation. But after eyeing him for several seconds, the woman relented and allowed Lucy to pass from her arms to his. The baby's mouth hung open and she stared at him, her large eyes full of wonder. Miss Barrett released the bow under Lucy's chin and pulled off her white bonnet, unleashing an airy mass of wispy curls.

An ache settled in the pit of Graham's stomach as the child melted against his chest. News that Katherine was with child had not reached him until she was a few months from giving birth, and by the time he'd received news of his wife's death, the child was already three months old. Lucy cooed and looked at him with Katherine's velvet eyes. "My dear Lucille Katherine Sterling," he told her, "I am very pleased to meet you."

Lucy pulled his nose.

He bounced her, and she squealed. Her tiny fingers tugged his hair.

"Curious little thing, is she not?" He scrunched his nose and squinted. The child giggled in delight. Graham smiled. Perhaps being around a child wasn't so difficult after all.

He glanced up at Miss Barrett and sobered as his eyes met hers. "How can I even begin to repay you for your kindness to Katherine and my Lucy?"

"I can think of the perfect way to thank me, sir. Consent to marry me."

Her pointed reply caught Graham off guard, and he stared at her for much longer than was proper. The answer was clear and staring him in the face. Miss Barrett had comforted his wife in her final days and cared for his child since birth. Surely there could be no better guardian for Lucy when he returned to his duties.

But marriage? The idea seemed preposterous.

Miss Barrett's voice interrupted his thoughts. "I know how this must sound, Captain Sterling. But I promise you my only interest is Lucy. I am determined to keep my promise to her mother and ensure that she is well cared for. And if I must endure the humiliation of asking a stranger to marry me in order to keep her with me, then so be it."

Graham picked up the toy horse Lucy had abandoned and handed it to her, attempting to buy himself more time. Miss Barrett's argument was persuasive. But had his experience taught him nothing?

No, he would deal with this now. "Miss Barrett, I am indebted to you, and I am at your service, but I've no intention of marrying again at present. I am sure we can devise some other arrangement."

His refusal seemed only to fuel Miss Barrett's determination. Though her chin trembled with every syllable uttered, her voice rang strong and determined. "Captain Sterling, if another arrangement were possible, I would never have proposed this one."

Perhaps she saw him wavering. She took a step toward him. "You need help, Captain. Someone has to care for Lucy when you return to your duties. I can provide that assistance. I will love and raise her just as Katherine would have done. Upon my honor, she will want for nothing."

Graham's high collar seemed to tighten around his neck. Lucy's happiness would have been Katherine's final wish, of that he was certain. But marriage? He could not. *Would* not. It was too soon.

Miss Barrett's words snapped him back to the present. "Please, at least consider the arrangement. What have you to lose? If we marry, you will be master of Winterwood Manor. You will be free to do as you choose, and you will be able to rest in the knowledge that Lucy's future is secure, regardless of what happens. All I ask, all I *need*, in exchange is your name."

Hazy thoughts raced through Graham's mind, each fighting for dominance. He prided himself on being a man of sure decisions and swift actions, but for this, he needed time to think. He swallowed hard. "I will consider it."

A cautious smile appeared on Miss Barrett's face, and an awkward silence enveloped the spacious room. The fire's warmth intensified, and Graham handed Lucy back to Miss Barrett before slipping a finger between his neck and cravat.

"What are your plans for Lucy while you are staying in Darbury?"

"I intend to take her to stay with me at Eastmore Hall. You've hired a nurse for her, correct? I was hoping to persuade the woman to stay on with us."

Miss Barrett nodded and adjusted the child in her arms. "Mrs. Dunne is an excellent nurse indeed. But would you consider allowing Lucy to remain here until your decision is made? She is familiar

with this house and the people in it." Miss Barrett tucked a way-
ward lock behind her ear and balanced the child on her hip. "It
might be difficult for her to be surrounded by new people, especially if her home might change again in a few weeks."

The hope in Miss Barrett's voice tugged at Graham, and he
realized she was right. He might be Lucy's father, but he was still a
stranger to her. And how could he expect the child to be comfortable in a house where he himself found little comfort?

"If you are willing to allow her to stay a little longer, then—"

"Then you must visit her as often as you can." A hint of lightness returned to her expression. "Every day, if you wish."

Outside, a fresh gust of wind slammed against the window-
pane, rattling the glass. Before retrieving his cloak and hat, Graham
pressed his lips to Lucy's curly head. He had hoped for another
smile from his daughter before he left, but she snuggled up against
her guardian and paid him no mind.

The unread letter in his breast pocket weighed heavily on his
mind. *If only there was another way.*

"Good-bye, little one." He bowed toward Miss Barrett, then
donned his hat and flipped the collar of his cloak up around his
neck.

There had to be another way. And he would find it.

※

Blast!

Graham kicked a rock, sending it tumbling through the carpet
of wet leaves.

Amelia Barrett had him at a disadvantage. And he hated to be
at a disadvantage.

Her outlandish offer had occupied his mind ever since he left
Winterwood, and it continued to bother him now as he stomped

across the grounds of Eastmore, spattering mud onto his polished boots.

What maddened him most was that the proposition almost made sense. Not only would it ensure a safe and loving home for Lucy; it would also free him to return to his duties with a clear conscience. But even so, how could he possibly agree to such an arrangement?

He shook his head. Miss Barrett's price was far too steep. He could not accept her offer.

Not even for Lucy's sake.

He snapped a twig from a branch and absently broke it in half as the image of his infant daughter took his mind captive. Haunting—her eyes were haunting. Pure and innocent, the child represented everything he had wanted to protect in her mother . . . but failed.

The insistent wind from the moors nipped and bit. The unread letter in his pocket smoldered. He had wanted to be alone when he read his wife's final words, and he knew of a place where he would not be disturbed.

The cast-iron gate to the Sterling cemetery loomed just beyond the hedge of holly bushes. Even as a child, he had hated entering those gates. Ghosts seemed to linger behind every tree, and memories crept amongst the gravestones. He hesitated, put a gloved hand on the rusting metal, and pushed. It creaked in protest, but the heavy gate eventually gave way and swung on corroded hinges. Before him, graves of generations of Sterlings stretched out in uneven rows.

To the left, under the protective boughs of ancient English oaks, stood two unfamiliar markers. Gerard Sterling and Harriet Mayes Sterling. His parents.

The site whispered for him to draw closer. The graves were overgrown. Shameful. He would speak with his brother, William, about it when he returned to the main house. He knelt and pulled a faded, stubborn ivy vine away from his mother's headstone and traced the carving of her name with his finger.

The span of eighteen years should have dulled his memory of the last time he saw her, but it had not. It had been late autumn then too. He could still feel the heated pressure of her grip on his arm as she clung to him before he left for the sea for the first time. He'd been little more than a child then—only twelve years old. The image of her tearstained face and the sound of her desperate pleas had burned themselves into his mind, never to be forgotten. The memories of his father's hard expression were equally memorable, but very different, and haunted him with equal fervor.

His father's decision to send him to sea had grown out of sound logic, regardless of the coldness behind it. Eastmore Hall, by law, would pass entirely to his older brother, so there had been a need for Graham to make his own way in the world, and indeed, he had done well for himself. He had grown to enjoy life at sea and excel at its requirements, achieving the rank of captain at a young age and amassing a small fortune in prize money for capturing both military and merchant vessels. At thirty years of age he had reached a level of success that few men would—and he still had the bulk of his career ahead of him. And now that England was engaged in war against America, his services to the Crown were needed even more.

A rustling nearby interrupted his thoughts. He jerked his head up and scanned the foggy landscape. *Was that a sob?* With silent steps he ducked below low-hanging branches to find the source. He spied the outline of a woman, shrouded in a dark cape, kneeling next to a headstone. The grave seemed fairly fresh. It had to be Katherine's. But who was the woman?

He battled to hear her voice over the wind.

"I'm so sorry, Katherine." Emotion broke the woman's words. "I will not lose hope."

The wind tugged at her gray woolen cape and pulled the hood free from her head, revealing an abundance of wild golden curls. As she reached up to re-cover her head, she turned. Graham ducked behind the tree, but it was too late. He stared straight into the eyes of Miss Amelia Barrett.

Feeling caught, Graham stepped out from behind the tree. She jumped to her feet and swiped her tears with the back of her gloved hand. Her azure eyes glowed in her pale face. Gone was the poise from earlier in the day.

"I'm sorry." He took a step closer. "I did not see you . . . I mean, I was not aware . . ."

She did not pause for his explanation. She brushed past him so quickly that he barely had time to step out of her path. "Wait, Miss Barrett, please, I—"

But she disappeared through the gate, leaving him alone with the wind and his memories.

He considered chasing after her. If he ran, he could overtake her before she reached Eastmore's outer walls. But if he caught up with her, what would he say?

Graham looked back to his wife's final resting place, and the sight of her name carved in stone made him momentarily forget about the woman running from the graveyard. *Katherine.* All these months, he realized, something in him had clung to the hope that it was all a mistake. That the letter was wrong, and his bride still waited for him in their little cottage on the grounds of Eastmore Hall. But now all trace of foolish hope departed. He would never again see Katherine's contagious smile or feel the warmth of her hand in his. Anger pulsed from his core. He'd always assumed that if one of them were to die, it would be he, so dangerous was his profession. How could a merciful God allow someone so pure to die so young?

He blinked away from the tombstone. He'd seen enough. But

even as he turned, something caught his eye. A small book rested in the grass next to the grave. He knelt to retrieve it. The brown leather binding was smooth beneath his fingertips. He flipped it to read the spine. *Psalms.* Miss Barrett must have just now dropped it.

He dried the volume on his outer coat and tucked it in his pocket, where his fingers brushed Katherine's letter. With the commotion of encountering Miss Barrett and the sting of seeing the tombstone, he'd almost forgotten about it.

The letter's dark red wax seal broke easily as he slid a finger beneath it. He held his breath as he unfolded the letter. The strokes were wide, the letters shaky, but the script was surely Katherine's.

My dearest husband,

My end is near. I am not frightened, for I am ready to meet my Saviour. My sadness lies in the fact that I shall never see you again nor live to see our daughter grow and thrive.

I have named the child Lucille Katherine Sterling and left her in Miss Amelia Barrett's care. Miss Barrett has been a loving friend to me since I came to Darbury and will ensure the child is raised in the ways of God. She will love our daughter, of this I am certain.

I admit to sorrow that our time together was so brief. But this I tell you truly: I have loved you as much as any wife could love her husband, and my sincerest wish is for your happiness. Do not let your heart grow cold. Open it to loving our child, and if the Lord brings you love again, do not hesitate on my account.

Grieve not for me, my dearest, for when you read this I will be amongst angels.

All my love, Katherine

Guilt weakened his arms. He lowered the letter and stared at the engraved stone slab. Had he really been so naive as to think he could be a husband? He was a naval captain, dedicated to his ship, bound to his crew, and sworn to serve the Crown. But now the sea seemed so very far away, and long-suppressed thoughts clouded his mind. Had he even realized how precious Katherine's love had been? He should have told her when he had the chance.

But now it was too late.

He folded the letter and tucked it away for safekeeping. Katherine's wishes seemed clear. She had wanted Amelia Barrett to care for the child while he was gone. But in order for that to happen, he would have to marry Miss Barrett.

Blast if he was going to make the same mistake twice.

3

Graham leaned forward, propped his elbows on his knees, and stared at his brother. William Sterling fumbled with the trigger on a pistol, attempting to polish gunpowder residue from the engraved casing. When Graham could stand it no further, he pushed himself up from the chair and stood to his full height.

"Who in blazes taught you to clean a pistol?" Graham snatched the weapon with one hand and the polishing cloth with the other. "At the rate you're going, this will take you the entire day."

William leaned back and balanced on the back two legs of the carved chair. "Ah, the great sea captain believes his weaponry skills are superior to those of his simpleton brother. You know I've always preferred horses to firearms. Annoyed Father no end."

Graham ignored his brother's taunt and turned the pistol over in his hand to examine the weapon's fine craftsmanship. Smudges of gunpowder provided evidence of recent use. He closed one eye and looked down the pistol's barrel, checking its straightness. "Where'd you get this?"

"Fine, isn't it?" William dropped the chair to its normal position and stood next to his brother. "Father bought it off a Frenchman. Not very patriotic, if you ask me."

Graham looked up from the pistol and studied the gilded portrait of their father hanging between two narrow windows. Even allowing for the difference in their builds, the resemblance between William and their late father was uncanny. Same cleft chin. Same sandy hair. Same light eyes, with a hint of mockery.

Graham sat down and began to polish the pistol. "Like this, see?"

William leaned over his shoulder. "I suppose you have use for a clean weapon in your line of employment, eh?"

"Indeed."

William laughed a deep, hearty laugh and slapped Graham's shoulder. "Good to have you home, Graham. How long has it been since you've been at Eastmore Hall? Fifteen years or better?"

"Eighteen." Graham could have told him the exact number of months, but he doubted William would care. Very few of those months had been spent on land. The sea had been his home for nearly all of his youth and into his manhood, and it wasn't until he achieved the rank of captain a few years back that he'd returned to England for any length of time. That was when he traveled to Plymouth to take command of the ship he'd been assigned—and when he met Katherine. Even now, though the *Miracle* had only been docked in Plymouth for a week, his life at sea seemed a thousand miles away.

He glanced up at his brother. "Place looks the same, mostly."

"Never changes." William flopped down into a wingback chair and propped his pointed boots up on the edge of a nearby mahogany desk. "Dull as tombs around here, most of the time."

Graham surveyed the room. The heavy, crimson curtains still flanked the tall casement windows, and family portraits of all sizes still adorned the cream-and-gold foliage-patterned walls. The only notable difference was the absence of his mother's portrait, which in his childhood had hung to the left of the intricate stone fireplace.

Graham nodded toward the empty space. "Where is Mother's portrait?"

"Father had it moved to the drawing room." William leaned his head back and folded his hands on his chest. "Why did you not return to Eastmore when you were last in England? I did not even hear of your marriage until that wife of yours arrived at Moreton Cottage. Quite a surprise, that was."

Graham stiffened at the comment. He didn't want to talk about Katherine, especially not with William. Their courtship had been swift and intense, the wedding quite sudden. No doubt, he should have notified his brother, his only living relative, of the union. But so many years had passed since he and his brother had spoken. Even their letters had become nothing more than a yearly update, and he'd found himself reluctant to share something so personal as his marriage in such a missive. He'd never imagined that Katherine would travel to Moreton Cottage alone and meet William without his being present to make introductions.

With all that in mind, he supposed he did owe his brother an explanation. Moreton Cottage belonged to Graham, of course, his only inheritance from the vast estate. All other assets had transferred to his brother upon his father's death. Still, it must have been a shock when she appeared, two servants in tow.

"I assure you, Katherine's move to Darbury surprised me as well. I met her in Plymouth when I returned to England to assume command of the *Miracle*, and we married shortly thereafter. When my ship sailed, the plan was for her to remain in Plymouth with her mother. But apparently her mother died unexpectedly, so Katherine left the coast to set up housekeeping at Moreton Cottage. By the time I heard of it, I was in Halifax."

"Halifax—in Nova Scotia, right? I had wondered where you might be now, with that rogue Napoleon finally in exile."

Graham shook his head. "Even with Napoleon conquered, brother, we are still at war, and I've got a battered ship to prove it."

As if poking a festering wound, his brother's questions continued. "What happened to your ship?"

Graham considered exactly how much to reveal. He scratched his forehead and rubbed his hand down his face before speaking. "It was a close-range battle with an American frigate. We sustained substantial damage but prevailed and sailed back to Halifax for repairs. But the resources there were sorely depleted. That is why we have returned to England. As soon as the repairs are complete in Plymouth, we will return to Halifax."

William nodded toward the scar covering Graham's hand. "The battle—so that is how you were . . ."

Graham followed William's gaze, then sucked in a breath. "No."

He said no more. William evidently understood, for he changed the subject. "What of your visit to Winterwood? They say George Barrett is in Leeds, due back tomorrow."

Graham held the pistol up to the fire's light to check his work, then resumed polishing. "I saw Miss Barrett and my Lucy, no one else."

"Ah, yes, my pretty little niece and her even prettier guardian." William removed his feet from the desk and sat up straight. "I must confess to some relief that Miss Barrett insisted on caring for your daughter. The situation seemed far more suitable, although of course I have tried—"

"No need for an explanation." Graham waved his hand in dismissal. "Miss Barrett seems an ideal caretaker. In fact, I have arranged for Lucy to remain at Winterwood until I can make other arrangements."

William chuckled and leaned with his forearm on his knee. "Speaking of Winterwood, do you recall how, when we were children, we would climb the stone wall separating Eastmore's south field into Winterwood's orchard and steal apples?"

Graham paused. A cloudy vision of himself and William climbing the gnarled elm materialized in his mind, but he could not recall an apple orchard—or climbing a wall with his brother, for that matter. "No."

William studied the toe of his boot. "I suppose that is what happens when one is out in the world, having adventures and sailing the seas." William's words grew pensive. "One forgets the happenings of sleepy country life."

Graham rested the clean pistol on his leg. Was that what William thought Graham's life was like? An adventure? If that were indeed the case, he should be so lucky as to lead a completely *unadventurous* life. He changed the subject. "What do you know of Amelia Barrett?"

William shrugged and stepped over to the sideboard. He uncorked a decanter of brandy and poured the amber liquid into the trumpet-shaped bowl of a glass goblet. "Want one?" Graham waved his hand in refusal, and William indulged in a long swig. "Miss Barrett? You've not fallen for her charms, have you? She'd be the one to pick, I'll tell you. Rich as Midas, that one. And lovely."

"I find it odd that a woman of her situation is not yet wed."

"'Tisn't odd if you know her uncle," William exclaimed. "Keeps her under lock and key. 'Tis no secret he handpicked the man she's to marry."

Graham frowned. "I don't find that strange."

William threw his tawny head back and laughed. "Not strange, he says. I have it on good authority that dear old Uncle George has his sights set on Edward Littleton—that's the scoundrel's name— joining him in the family business." William downed another drink and pointed his finger toward Graham. "I bet you ten to one that once the money from the Winterwood inheritance starts flowing into Barrett Trading Company coffers, things will suddenly get a little brighter for ol' George Barrett."

William's words simmered in Graham's mind. An engagement to a man of her uncle's choosing? The possibility of her inheritance being used to support her uncle's business ventures? No wonder Miss Barrett was dismissive about her engagement. And yet another reason why she might be eager to be free of it. A seed of suspicion planted itself in his mind. Could Miss Barrett have other motives for wanting to marry him besides her love for Lucy?

Graham resumed polishing. "Have you met Mr. Littleton?"

William nodded. "He visited here a fortnight past to inquire about Eastmore's west fields. Seems that once he's master of Winterwood Manor he plans to make a few, ahem, improvements."

Graham stopped polishing. "What did you tell him?"

"What do you think I told him? 'Sorry, my friend. Can't risk Winterwood getting any larger, nor Eastmore any smaller.'" William finished off his brandy and grabbed his coat off the chair. "I'm off for a ride. Care to join me? I just bought a new stallion in Birmingham last month. Capital animal—fast as blazes. Runs as if the devil himself is at his heels and takes a fence like a dream."

Graham shook his head. He needed to be alone. He needed to think. "Thank you, no. I need to see to some correspondence."

William shrugged. "If you want to meet Mr. Littleton, there's a dinner tomorrow night at Winterwood Manor. Did Miss Barrett mention it? I believe it is to celebrate their upcoming nuptials. I received an invitation. Wasn't planning to attend, but now I think the evening could prove entertaining. What do you say?"

Curiosity prevailed. Graham took the pistol by the barrel and extended the handle to his brother. "I would not miss it."

⚜

The sun had set, and night had descended upon Winterwood Manor. Flickering candles and a freshly stoked fire provided ample illumination for the expansive dining room, the yellow glow glittering off the silver service and gilded frames adorning the olive-green walls. Aunt Augusta and Helena sat near Amelia at the mahogany table, their upcoming move to London the topic of discussion for most of the dinner. But their cheery excitement just aggravated the heaviness of Amelia's heart.

The captain's refusal burned fresh in her memory, and every second that slipped past reaffirmed the consequence. Still, she harbored no regret for her actions. In fact, if she thought asking again could in some way sway the captain's decision, she would ask him one thousand times. But with pointed melancholy she recalled the firm set of his square jaw and the determination in his gray eyes. He did not wish to marry, not even to secure a new mother for Lucy or the fortune that would come from being the master of Winterwood Manor.

She studied the lamb fricassee and sweetbreads on her plate and pushed at the food with her fork. Her aunt and cousin's chatter continued. The sounds of their voices were so familiar, so much a part of her home. Ever since her father died twelve years past and named her Uncle George guardian over both her and the estate, Amelia had lived here at Winterwood with her aunt, uncle, and cousin. But in little more than a month, all that would change. Once she and Edward wed, her uncle's family would move to their new residence in London, and she would continue her life here at Winterwood—only as Mrs. Edward Littleton.

Aunt Augusta's head of fading hair bobbed with each word. The woman's words always spilled forth in a rush, like a waterfall of

31

unchecked thoughts. "Five weeks, dearest! Can you fathom it? I am counting down the days. Perhaps we should consider having new gowns made before departing—although of course the London seamstresses are far superior. By my word, Helena, this will be the season. Amelia has her match, and now you shall have your pick of suitors."

Helena's golden eyes flicked toward Amelia.

Now that Amelia has made her match. Amelia knew the words must have stung, and her heart went out to her cousin. When Uncle George first invited his colleague Edward to visit Winterwood Manor, he'd no doubt regarded him as a suitable match for either his daughter or his niece, and Helena's interest in him had been evident. But Helena, for all of her charm and beauty, lacked the single asset Amelia possessed and the one quality that would catch Edward Littleton's eye—a substantial inheritance.

Helena quickly turned her attention back to her mother. "I am eager for Father and Mr. Littleton to return."

"I, too, look forward to Mr. Barrett's return tomorrow, but I daresay our feelings are nothing to Amelia's anticipation for the return of her Mr. Littleton."

The weight of her aunt's attention shifted to her, and Amelia turned to see her aunt smiling at her as proudly as any guardian could. "Dear Mr. Littleton. You must be eager to see him."

Amelia's spine stiffened at the sound of her future husband's name. She pressed her napkin to her lips before returning it to her lap, refusing to look at Helena. "Indeed."

Her aunt continued. "I have instructed Cook to make pigeons *en compôte* for dinner. I have it on good authority that Mr. Littleton is fond of the dish."

Amelia forced words. "That is very considerate of you, Aunt."

Her aunt lowered her spoon to the table, surprise crossing her pointed features. "Why, Amelia, I should think you might show more enthusiasm. It has been more than two weeks since he last was here, has it not?"

Amelia nodded, her voice barely above a whisper. "Yes, Aunt. A fortnight."

"Two weeks is a long time to be separated from one's love."

Separated from one's love?

Did she love Edward?

At the beginning of their engagement, she had believed so. But now? So much had changed in the span of the past year that made her question the wisdom of her choice. And now, with Edward's refusal to allow Lucy to remain at Winterwood once they wed, she realized he was not the man she'd thought she knew.

"And what of the child?"

Amelia jerked her head up at her aunt's indifferent reference to Lucy. Immersed in her own thoughts, she had lost track of the discussion.

But before Amelia could formulate a response, Helena spoke. "Have you not heard? Captain Sterling has returned just yesterday. He is at Eastmore Hall with his brother."

Augusta dropped her fork and turned to face Amelia. "What is this? Oh, my dears, how did I miss this news?"

Amelia would have kicked her cousin under the table if the ornate table had not been so large. "Captain Sterling returned to Darbury yesterday, I believe. He paid us a visit this morning to meet Lucy."

Aunt Augusta pushed herself to her feet in a rustle of burgundy taffeta. "You girls should have told me of this immediately!"

Amelia thought she saw a hint of a smile flash on Helena's lips before her cousin looked down at her plate. "I am sorry, Mother. I thought you were aware."

Aunt Augusta tapped her forefinger to her lips. "I suppose no harm is done. After all, this is good news, is it not? Lucy's father will make arrangements for her, and you and Mr. Littleton will be left alone, as newlyweds should be."

Amelia felt faint at the words. She did not want her aunt—or anyone—thinking that Lucy would be leaving. She straightened her shoulders. "It is my desire that Lucy should remain here, even after we wed."

"Here? At Winterwood Manor?" Aunt Augusta's laugh echoed from the high plastered ceilings. "My dear Amelia, you need to focus on starting your own family now. Besides, has Mr. Littleton not forbidden it? You cannot go against his wishes. 'Twould not be right."

Amelia shook her head. "I am sure I can persuade him. Winterwood is a large estate. He need never even know she is here."

"I declare, Amelia, I do not understand you. Why can you not just enjoy your life with Mr. Littleton? The child's father has returned. He will see to her."

Her aunt gave a firm nod, calling a close to the conversation.

Amelia glanced at her cousin, who continued to stare down at her plate. She had hoped that Helena would come to her defense, help convince Aunt Augusta that she was right. It would hardly be the first time the cousins had allied themselves in such a fashion. But this time Helena remained silent.

Whether the room was indeed suffocating or it just felt that way, Amelia managed to survive dinner. It was clear she had more difficult decisions ahead of her. Her family might not understand her now, but she could only pray they would come to share her perspective. She still cared for Edward. But his refusal to allow Lucy to remain at Winterwood was forcing Amelia to choose between a future with him and her commitment to Lucy.

And that was really no choice at all.

4

The next morning every muscle in Amelia's body tensed as she waited once more in the drawing room, listening for the sound of carriage wheels. This time, instead of waiting for the captain, she waited for Edward Littleton. And yesterday's optimism had faded to a nervous melancholy.

Helena, dressed in a silk-embroidered gown of jonquil satin and with glossy hair coiled tightly to her head, rose from the settee with practiced poise and moved to stand beside Amelia. Concern creased her flawless brow as she laid her hand atop Amelia's arm.

"I do hope you are not upset with me for mentioning Captain Sterling's return to Mother. You know her disposition, and she would find out about the visit sooner or later. Far better it is for her to find out from you or me than from another source."

Amelia drew a deep breath and looked toward the window, fearing that if she looked her cousin in the eyes, her true feelings would be evident. Perhaps Helena's intentions had been innocent. But her cousin's behavior had been unpredictable since Amelia's engagement to Edward had been announced several months prior. Amelia had hoped that sharing her plan to propose to the captain might restore the closeness between them, but unease remained.

Amelia released the breath she'd been holding. Harboring resentment toward Helena would do nothing but steal her energy. "Think nothing of it."

As if content with Amelia's response, Helena patted her hand. "Good. Now, let us forget the entire thing." A pretty smile brightened her cousin's narrow face. "After all, the captain declined your offer, did he not? I shall never mention it, and the captain, if he is any sort of gentleman, would take it to the grave. So it will be as if your little indiscretion never happened."

Amelia fought to hold her tongue. *Indiscretion?* She turned away to reach for her shawl. Would she never be able to persuade Helena that she'd proposed out of pure necessity?

Did Helena's approval even matter?

At the sound of a shout and a carriage on the drive, Amelia lifted her head. Her uncle—and Edward Littleton—had arrived.

"Do you hear that?" Helena left Amelia's side and lifted the velvet curtain. "There, see! Father and Mr. Littleton are here. I'll have Mother call for tea. Amelia, be calm now."

Amelia smoothed her skirt and pinched her cheeks. Edward would be a guest at Winterwood for a little more than a day before traveling on to London for business. In that time she had to convince him to open their home to Lucy. She had little other choice.

The click of the door's latch echoed through the halls, followed by the sound of rain pounding the stone steps outside. Then Edward's hearty laugh filled the room. She eased at the sound. He was in a pleasant mood.

The moment Edward stepped into the drawing room, his eyes sought her. She could not help the girlish smile creeping over her lips or the flush rushing to her cheeks under the directness of his gaze. Even after the turmoil of the past weeks, she could not deny the pleasure his exuberant attentions afforded her.

He was certainly feeling exuberant today. He barely acknowledged Aunt Augusta or Helena before brushing past James, ignoring the butler's attempt to take his belongings. He simply peeled off his wet greatcoat and dropped his beaver hat on a wingback chair before hastening in Amelia's direction. His smile stretched wide as he grabbed her hands and pulled her toward him. The scent of rain still clung to his person. Amelia cast a quick glance over at her aunt. Aunt Augusta would never approve of such a blatant display of affection, but she was too engaged in welcoming her own husband home to pay heed to her niece.

Amelia attempted to remove herself from Edward's grasp, but he tightened his grip on her bare hands and pulled her even closer. His lips were so close that his breath moved a curl next to her ear. "Tell me, dearest Amelia, that you missed me, even a little bit, and I shall be put at ease."

She tried to tame her nervous smile and finally freed her hands, the intimacy of the interaction making it impossible for her to look him in the eye. She said what she knew he wanted to hear. "Of course I missed you."

"Well then, I am relieved." He straightened, his handsome smile continuing to light his face. "For not a moment passed that I didn't wonder what my dear little Amelia was up to."

His voice sounded devoid of hidden meanings, but guilt clenched Amelia's stomach. She hurried to change the subject. "Come over to the fire, Edward. You must be chilled through."

He did not object. Instead, he picked up her hand once again and looped it through his arm. The heat from the fire and the closeness of the man nearly suffocated her.

He kept his voice soft. "You wore the blue gown. Periwinkle, I believe the young ladies call it? You know how I adore you in this shade."

She had grown accustomed to his lavish praise of her appearance, but today his quick flattery made her blush. "You mustn't speak so. Aunt Augusta will hear you."

He leaned forward and smoothed the broad lace ribbon lining the outer rim of her neckline. "Let her hear me. What does it matter? I will shout it from the rooftops. I've nothing to hide."

"I know, but I beg of you. Propriety."

He stared at her for several moments, amusement tugging at the corners of his mouth. Then he allowed his hand to fall to the side. "Very well. If it is what you desire, then so be it."

Amelia exhaled and directed him to a chair—the very chair, she couldn't help but notice, to which she had directed the captain the previous morning. He sat down and adjusted his stark white neckcloth. The rain had darkened his hair to almost black, and with his hand he slicked the damp locks off his face. The long side-whiskers framing his high cheekbones accentuated the noble slope of his nose. His dark eyes, always alert, seemed able to delve into her very soul—a thought that made Amelia avert her gaze.

What if he learned of her proposal to Captain Sterling? She feared his reaction as a child fears an impending punishment. For all of Edward's winning qualities, his temper was no secret. Everything with Edward was an extreme. He was like a whirlwind: passionate and determined, impatient and headstrong. But his propensity to charm overshadowed any lapses of decorum. He could win the approval of almost anyone—and earn forgiveness just as quickly. Until recently, she had found him all but irresistible.

"Mr. Littleton." Amelia looked up. She had not noticed her cousin approaching. Helena's voice, as always, was steady and sure. "It is a pleasure to see you again."

Edward stood. "Ah, Miss Barrett!"

"What news from Leeds? Surely you saw someone of our acquaintance?"

Edward shook his head. "I fear I cannot satisfy your curiosity. The bulk of our trip was spent tending to business affairs. However, I am on my way to London in a day or two, and I hope to bring you news from there."

The overwhelming scent of rosewater signaled Aunt Augusta's approach. Before another word could be uttered on the matter, she rested her hands on Helena's shoulders. "Have you not told Mr. Littleton of our news here in Darbury?"

A sinking feeling pulled at Amelia, and she cast a desperate glance at Helena, hoping her cousin would be able to sway the conversation when she herself could not find words. But even that was too late, for her aunt's words tumbled forth. "While you were gone, we have had a most interesting development here." She leaned forward, clearly enjoying the game she was playing. "You will never guess who has returned to this county."

Edward, still standing, leaned back against the chair and crossed one booted foot over the other. "Well then, Mrs. Barrett, you will have to enlighten me, for I cannot even begin to guess."

The older woman fluttered her fan, raising a breeze that stirred the trim on her gown. "Why, Captain Sterling of course! Little Lucy's father."

Edward snapped to attention at the words, his features brightening. "You don't say!" Amelia winced as he directed his words toward her. "Why did you not tell me right away? This is truly a fortuitous development—and not a moment too soon! Now he can take responsibility for that child of his."

Amelia bristled. When would they see Lucy as someone other than a guest? "Actually, the captain is open to the possibility of Lucy remaining at Winterwood."

Edward's demeanor sobered. "We have discussed this, Amelia. The child is welcome to stay until we are wed. But not after."

Amelia stiffened at the finality in his tone but willed herself to hold her tongue. Pushing him too hard at this moment would get her nowhere. But she couldn't help wondering how Edward could love her, really love her, yet be so quick to reject the one person in the world who meant the most to her.

Oblivious to her agitation, Aunt Augusta began to chatter about tonight's dinner and the menu for the wedding breakfast. But Edward moved in so close that she felt his legs brush the hem of her dress. "Come, Amelia," he murmured in her ear. "There is no need to get upset. Everything will be fine, you will see."

So like Edward—eager to smooth things over with nary a commitment one way or the other. She was about to respond when his arm snaked around her waist and held a small wooden box in front of her.

Amelia frowned. "What is this?"

He circled around to look at her, a crooked grin on his face. "You will have to open it to find out. I was going to wait until later to give it to you, but I sense you could use cheering up now."

Amelia pressed her lips together. She was in no mood for gifts. But she took the box in her hand, the polished teak smooth and cool beneath her fingers. She unlatched the small clasp and flipped the lid open. Her breath caught. There, gleaming in a nest of fine white satin, was a sapphire pendant set in gold.

"Do you like it?" Edward reached into the box, his long fingers grazing her own. He lifted the necklace, the chain uncoiling with the action. "The color reminded me of your eyes."

She looked up. His own dark coffee eyes gazed intimately into hers. But to her, they were the eyes of a stranger.

※

Later that same afternoon Edward and Uncle George took a ride over the grounds with Mr. Carrington, Winterwood's steward.

With several hours left before their engagement dinner, Amelia wanted—needed—to spend time with Lucy.

She had asked Mrs. Dunne to bring the baby to her in the morning room—a smaller, warmer chamber with pale coral walls, white frieze and cornices, and a wide white fireplace with a cast-iron grate.

Amelia sat on a small sofa in a pool of fleeting sunlight, intending to bide her time with her needlework until Mrs. Dunne arrived. Try as she might, she could not keep her mind on the intricate pattern. Finally she sighed and set the frame down beside her. Patting her foot with impatience, she turned her attention to two familiar portraits flanking the fireplace.

On the left hung a portrait of her father as a very young man. It had been there for as long as she could remember. The portrait did not show the smile she had loved, but it perfectly captured the kindness in his eyes. Even though he had been gone for well over a decade, she recalled his face with vivid detail. What would he think of her engagement to Edward?

On the opposite side of the fireplace hung the only portrait of her mother. More than one guest had mistakenly assumed it depicted Amelia, so great was the resemblance. The artist's strokes had captured her mother with the bloom of youth, fair hair loosely gathered around a narrow face and large, watchful blue eyes. As a child, standing before the painted image, Amelia used to imagine that her mother could actually see her. How she wished she had a mother to guide her now.

Mrs. Dunne breezed through the door with Lucy propped on her hip. Amelia jumped from her seat, casting aside melancholy thoughts. "There is my girl!"

When the baby saw Amelia, her chocolate eyes grew wide. She waved chubby fists in the air and thrust herself toward Amelia, causing Mrs. Dunne to nearly drop her.

"Whoa, Lucy!" Amelia laughed at the child's enthusiasm. "You're going to fall!"

The child scrambled into Amelia's arms, and Mrs. Dunne laughed. "She's been out o' sorts all morning, lookin' for you all over."

The words, delivered with Mrs. Dunne's lilting Irish brogue, warmed Amelia to the core. "Oh, Lucy, I am so sorry."

The little girl giggled, showing her dimple. She squinted her eyes and batted her hand against Amelia's face. Amelia laughed, feeling the weight of uncertainty slip from her mind. Time seemed to stand still when she was with this child. When they were together, she could forget her worries.

Almost.

If the captain were to take Lucy from Winterwood, the baby would grow up as she had—motherless. Even with the presence of a doting governess and a loving father, something had been lacking in Amelia's childhood. When Aunt Augusta and Uncle George came to be her guardians after her father's death, Amelia had finally identified what it was. Though Aunt Augusta was never actively unkind, her relationship with Amelia was nothing compared to her bond with Helena.

Amelia freed her earring from Lucy's grasp and sat down on the floor. Mrs. Dunne produced three wooden blocks, and Lucy squealed and began to bang them together. Amelia smiled, trying to set aside the dread that had crept into her awareness. How much longer did she have with her? One week? Two? A month?

If Edward wouldn't relent, no more than five weeks.

"Bababa ba ba." Lucy's cheerful chatter filled the narrow room. Amelia wanted to memorize everything about her . . . the velvety skin, the soft copper curls, the plump, dimpled hands, that delicious baby smell. Amelia felt her chin tremble. Who would love her precious Lucy if she were taken away? Captain Sterling would be away at sea. Who else would sing to her? Read to her? Brush her hair? Teach her to mind? Teach her how to love?

Lucy lost interest in the blocks and scooted over to Amelia with loose, uncontrolled movements. Amelia gathered her in her arms, untwisting the child from the long white gown. Lucy wrapped pudgy arms around Amelia's neck and pulled herself up, babbling, "Mama ma ma." Without warning, tears sprang to Amelia's eyes.

Last week those sounds coming from the baby's lips would have thrilled her. Today they brought a joy laced with pain.

In the span of nine months, Amelia had watched the child grow and change. She herself had gone from being afraid of even holding the baby to loving her with an intensity she'd never thought possible. She could not—would not—willingly hand Lucy over. Not even to Captain Sterling.

She peeled a chubby hand from her hair and pressed it to her lips. She needed Lucy as much as Lucy needed her. She kissed the child's cheek, leaned her head against wispy curls, and whispered, "I will fight for you. You, my dear Lucy, will never be alone."

5

Y ou had better finish dressing." Helena cut her eyes toward her cousin, holding her head perfectly still so as not to disturb the lady's maid dressing her hair. "And for all that is good and holy, stop leaning against the wall. You will wrinkle your dress."

Ignoring her cousin's direction, Amelia pressed her body against the wall and bent forward, stretching her neck to watch carriages line the front drive. She strained her eyes to count them. "How many guests did Aunt invite?"

"Move away from the window, Amelia!" Helena waved a frantic hand, her head still motionless. "What if someone sees you?"

"Don't be absurd." Amelia's tone was sharper than she'd intended. The brocade curtain slipped through her fingers as she pulled her hand away. "It is far too dark in here for anyone to see in." She turned to pick up her dress, held it at arm's length, and tilted her head to the side, admiring the delicacy of the ivory Valenciennes lace and the way the pale azure silk shimmered in the candles' flickering light. Under any other circumstances, she'd be thrilled to be dressing in her finest for a formal dinner. But tonight was different.

"Not like that, Elizabeth!" Helena slapped at the servant's hand as the girl attempted to arrange a feather in her hair. Then she sent the maid on an errand and proceeded to adjust the brightly colored plume herself.

Once the lady's maid had quitted the room, Helena turned to Amelia. "Why are you so out of sorts tonight? Do not tell me you are still thinking about that captain."

The lie slid easily from Amelia's lips. "Of course not."

"Well, I should think not, especially tonight of all nights. I overheard Mother tell Father that the Simmonses are coming after all, and—" She paused midsentence and looked around, a frown darkening her face. "Have you seen my necklace? The one with the ruby pendant?"

Amelia nodded toward the jewelry chest atop the dresser.

"Ah." Helena retrieved the gold chain and held it up to her exposed throat. She pivoted, watching her reflection in the glass. "I do believe you have escaped catastrophe, dear Cousin."

Amelia adjusted her petticoat over her stays as Elizabeth returned to the room. "I do not understand."

Helena rolled her eyes and returned her attention to the feather. "It is early yet to tell, but I think you are going to come out of yesterday's episode unscathed. An entire day has passed. If Captain Sterling had planned to expose you, we would have already heard about it. Count yourself fortunate."

Amelia suppressed a groan. The interchange with the captain in the drawing room had been humiliating enough. Now, after the incident in the graveyard and today's interlude with Edward, she was practically at her wit's end. Feeling the need to defend herself once more, Amelia murmured, "As I told you before, it was a business proposition. Nothing more."

"Well, call it whatever you like." Helena took the dress from Amelia and handed it to the lady's maid. Elizabeth helped slide it on over the petticoat, careful not to disturb Amelia's meticulously arranged tresses. "At least Mr. Littleton hasn't discovered what you have done."

Amelia turned to allow Elizabeth to fasten the ivory buttons down the back of her gown. Glancing into the mirror, she straightened the silver netting adorning the bodice. There was no point in arguing. She needed to concentrate on what she would say to Edward, not on persuading Helena, who at any rate would not be swayed.

Once the buttons were fastened, Helena reached for Edward's sapphire necklace. She dangled the piece in front of her. "I do hope one day my betrothed gives me such lovely tokens of affection," she said, her voice wistful. The candles' flickering glow caught the intricate angles of the jeweled pendant, sending slivers of indigo light into the air. Helena draped it around Amelia's neck and turned her back toward the mirror. "Perfection."

Amelia's gaze lingered on the jewelry's reflection, and she touched it with uneasy fingers as she considered the imminent union the necklace symbolized and the man who had given it to her. Her stomach flittered at the thought of what she must do tonight. Now that Captain Sterling had refused her proposal, she had to convince Edward to allow Lucy to remain at Winterwood Manor. This would be her one request of him. But it would not be easy. Despite his mercurial temper, Edward was not easy to sway once he had made up his mind. Amelia would have to be intentional with her words.

But Amelia did have one advantage. Once she married and reached twenty-four years of age, which would be soon, she would be a very wealthy woman. That meant her husband, by matrimonial law, would increase his fortune too. And Edward was an ambitious man, with ambitious plans for building on his success in business. Had he not on more than one occasion referenced his plans to expand Winterwood once he was officially its master? Well, he needed her cooperation for that to happen. If necessary, she would remind him of this detail.

Amelia followed Helena from the dressing room. The voices of family and friends wafted up the curved staircase toward them. She bent her neck to see down to the main floor below and almost immediately spied Edward. Dressed in an impeccable black tailcoat and brilliant emerald waistcoat, drink already in hand, he stood laughing with a group of men.

She drew a deep breath. Until they could speak alone about Lucy, she would play the part of an excited and amiable bride. Straightening her shoulders, she shook out the folds of her dress and prepared to descend. But just as her foot was about to fall on the first step, she spotted another face, one she had not anticipated. A gasp escaped her lips, and she grabbed Helena's bare arm and yanked her back on the landing.

"Ow!" Helena snatched her arm away and rubbed it.

Amelia could barely squeak the words. "He's here."

"Whatever are you talking about? Who's here?" Helena craned her neck to look. After a scan of the main floor, she, too, jerked back from the staircase, eyes wide. "Oh. *He's* here."

Blood pounded in Amelia's ears. The tragedy that could ensue played in her mind's eye like a scene from the theater. Her words came in a pant. "He must have come with his brother."

"But William Sterling never comes to these things." Helena's eyes were wide. "Never!"

"Aunt always invites him, though. He is our neighbor. You know how your mother is."

Time froze. Amelia forced her breathing to steady. Not only would she have to face Captain Graham Sterling tonight, but she would have to face his older brother, the master of Eastmore Hall, as well.

Amelia had not spoken to Mr. William Sterling in months, not since he'd behaved shamefully toward her at a dinner party a year ago. She could still feel the grip of his bare hands on her upper arm, the smell of the claret on his breath, and the taste of tobacco as he forced a kiss on her. She shuddered. She had told no one save her friend Jane Hammond for fear that the incident would be misinterpreted as impropriety on her part. But she had also vowed never to speak to him again if at all possible. Mr. Sterling, if he even remembered the incident, had apparently utilized discretion and never spoken of it either, but that did not mean Amelia wished to be in his company.

But even more daunting than the prospect of an evening with William Sterling or an uncomfortable encounter with the captain was the realization that Edward and Captain Sterling would speak tonight. It would be unavoidable.

Helena's words were sharp. "This is a fine mess indeed."

"We need a plan. That is certain." Amelia paced the hall.

"*We?*" Helena shook her head, apparently forgetting about the carefully arranged tresses on her head. "No, no, *no!* I will not be a part of—"

"Please! Just . . . please. Everything will be fine, you shall see, but I need your help. You must keep the captain occupied. Stay by his side as much as possible. Prevent him from talking to, well, anyone else."

Helena planted her hands on her hips. "I have promised to keep your secret, Amelia, and keep it I shall. But I will not play a part in any of your schemes."

Amelia linked her arm through Helena's. "If not for me," she pleaded, "then do it for Aunt Augusta. She would be mortified should anything go amiss tonight."

Helena pursed her lips. "I am not happy, Amelia. Truly I am not. But you are correct. If anything should happen and word got out about what you have done, our family would be the laughing-stock of the entire county."

Amelia reached out and patted Helena's russet locks back into place. "I need you. Lucy needs you. And this is the last request I will make of you. You have my word."

"Oh, very well." Helena snapped her fan open and started for the stairs once more.

"Thank you, Helena." Amelia embraced her cousin and then smoothed her own silk skirt, forcing herself to ignore the guilt tapping in her mind.

⚜

Glass clinked. Gentle laughs and polite conversation rang through Winterwood Manor's dining room. The familiar setting and festive atmosphere should have put her at ease. But tranquility eluded Amelia.

She cast a sideways glance at her betrothed. Handsome and self-assured, Edward boasted a commanding presence. He sat so close to Amelia that if she moved her arm even a fraction, it would brush the black wool fabric of his coat sleeve. She remained uncomfortably still, not wanting to join his conversation . . . or any other.

She poked at the salmon on her plate and dragged her fork through the shrimp sauce, trying not to stare at the captain, who was seated directly across from her. She was grateful that etiquette forbade her from speaking across the table during dinner. At least she would be able to avoid conversation for now. The captain's brother, William Sterling, sat to his left. As if sensing her atten-tion, Mr. Sterling looked up, his forkful of stewed spinach hovering

49

in midair, and smiled at her. Amelia quickly looked away. Would the captain have told his brother about the proposal?

Amelia eyed the captain again. To his immediate right, Helena chattered on, doing her flirtatious best to ensnare his attention. Her dainty cousin threw her head back in a believable laugh, her cheeks rosy and her eyes bright. Amelia sighed. If only she could play as convincing a role. Captain Sterling smiled at something Helena said, his white teeth flashing in his sun-bronzed face. He appeared so at ease. How dare he be so calm when Lucy's future remained uncertain?

"That was a weary sigh, my dear."

The soft words coming from the guest to her left snapped Amelia back to the present, and she shifted to face her friend Jane Hammond. "Pardon?"

"Much too weary for a young woman so very close to her wedding day."

Amelia fussed with the napkin in her lap and suppressed a nervous laugh. "Forgive me. I'm afraid I was lost in thought."

Jane nodded toward Amelia's plate. "You have barely touched your dinner. You're not unwell, I trust?"

Shame crept over Amelia. For as long as she could remember, the older woman's nurturing manner had been a comfort to her. Jane, the wife of Darbury's vicar, had been her mother's dearest friend and, in the years since her father's death, had become her own friend and confidante. How Amelia wished she could seek her counsel about the past few days. But how could she? She could not risk the exposure.

Jane leaned close and wrinkled her nose. "Whatever is William Sterling doing here?"

Amelia glanced up at the captain's brother. "Aunt invited him."

"Tsk. After his actions toward you, I cannot believe he has the audacity to accept the invitation."

Amelia shrank back at Jane's words, regretting she had shared the details of William's indiscretion. Ever since, her normally kind and forgiving friend had all but shunned the older Sterling, all in the name of loyalty. Amelia hoped she would not reflect her opinion of William Sterling onto the captain. "I honestly do not think he recalls the encounter. He was full of drink. Besides, it is in the past, and no one but you knows of it. I would just as soon forget about it."

"Well, I certainly have not forgotten." Jane's composed face give little hint of the anger in her voice. "One would think a man in his position and influence would hold himself to a higher standard. It is indeed fortunate for him that your Mr. Littleton knows nothing of it."

Amelia winced at the reminder of the number of secrets regarding the Sterling family that she was withholding from Edward. She pushed them away. She had far too much on her mind to ruminate on the shortcomings of William Sterling.

Jane put down her fork. "Speaking of the Sterlings, I have been meaning to tell you about a very interesting visit I had earlier with Lucy's father, the captain. What a pleasant man he is—quite the opposite of his brother."

Amelia felt the tiny hairs stand up at the base of her neck. Had Captain Sterling told Jane what she had done? *Surely not.* "He does seem quite well spoken."

"Indeed. Mr. Hammond and I ran into him this morning outside Mr. Higgins's shop. We were so pleased to see him again, for the last time I saw him he was but a lad. What a pleasant man he has become—every bit as distinguished as one would expect a naval captain to be. And he spoke very favorably of you and the kindness you have shown little Lucy."

"Oh? What did he say?"

"Simply that he has no idea what would have happened if you had not stepped in."

With every word that Jane spoke, Amelia eased. Clearly, her

friend did not know of her proposal. She cut her eyes toward William Sterling before returning her attention to Jane. "I am sure the captain's brother would have seen to her well-being."

The older woman patted her lips with her napkin and returned it to her lap. "I doubt it. You know Mr. Sterling's disposition. He's of a selfish bent, and he would hardly be a suitable guardian for a child. I don't like to repeat rumors, but it is said he has lost his entire fortune at the tables. The lot of it. Mr. Hammond tells me he has heard reports that Mr. Sterling is trying to sell part of his land. Can you imagine?"

"And what of the captain?" Amelia leaned in closer to her friend. "Does he have the means to support Lucy?"

Jane nodded. "Indeed. Though he did not inherit his family's estate, I have it on good authority that he has done very well in his own right. Of course, Mr. Hammond knows a great deal more about these things than I, but I understand the ship under Captain Sterling's command has been integral to the blockade efforts along the American coast, and in addition to his military conquests he has overtaken several merchant vessels. Mr. Hammond said the spoils have made him quite wealthy. It's not for me to say, but it seems Mr. William Sterling would do well to hand over the running of Eastmore to his brother."

Amelia had to smile at that. Her friend seldom found herself at a loss for something to say and was always quick to share her opinion. She tucked her hands beneath her napkin. "Did the captain say anything to you about his intentions for Lucy?"

Jane lowered her napkin to her lap and smoothed the amber silk fabric of her gown. "He said he was in the process of interviewing nurses. He also mentioned visiting the Creighton School because it is so close, but of course Lucy is far too young for such an establishment." Jane hesitated and lowered her voice even further. "Is there no way you can continue to care for Lucy?"

Amelia's nose twitched with emotion. She didn't want to talk about this. Not now. Not here. She shook her head. "I want nothing more than for that to be so. But Mr. Littleton is adamant against it."

Why even try to hide emotion from Jane? Amelia didn't *want* to hide it. If it weren't for the company surrounding them, she would be tempted to tell her friend the entire story, right down to her proposal to the captain. She felt like a child again, hoping the woman could soothe her sorrows as she had so many times over the years.

"I do not understand why Mr. Littleton is so opposed to your caring for the child. Has he given any indication as to the source of his opposition?"

Amelia shook her head. "He has spoken of not wanting to use the funds to care for Lucy that will one day go to our children. When his father died, Edward was surprised that his inheritance was not what he had anticipated. It seems his father had given a large sum to support a local poorhouse. Edward has declared on more than one occasion that he has no intention of using our son's money to support another man's child."

"But that is ridiculous. Lucy is not a charitable cause. I am sure the captain would support her financially, especially given the success of his recent exploits."

"But Edward does not see it that way." Amelia blinked back tears. "What will I do? I really do not know how I can live without—"

The ping of a silver spoon tapping a goblet pierced the conversation. Amelia looked up. Uncle George stood at the head of the table.

Uncle George's thick hands hung in the air to silence the chattering guests. Edward had all but ignored her through the course of the dinner, but now he turned to her with a wide, boyish smile. Amelia's stomach knotted.

Uncle George dabbed his mouth with his napkin and let it fall to the table before clearing his throat. "I know my wife is eager to get the ladies off to the drawing room, but before you all leave, I have wonderful news to share."

A rush of whispers circled the table.

Uncle George's ruddy face flushed, a broad smile crinkling his eyes. "As you know, my lovely niece will soon be joined in matrimony to Mr. Edward Littleton, a first-rate young man. But what you do not know—what even my niece doesn't yet know—is that once he and Amelia wed, Edward Littleton will become a full partner of Barrett Trading Company." George Barrett held up his goblet in a toast. "Welcome to the family and the business, my boy."

A burst of conversation exploded from the guests. Edward, who could barely contain his enthusiasm, reached for Amelia's hand and squeezed, nearly knocking over his glass in the process.

More was said, but Amelia did not hear. Piece by piece, the puzzle came together. Her uncle's sincere yet emphatic insistence on the union. Edward's constant talk of expanding Winterwood's worth. Yes, Edward had professed his love—repeatedly. He had done it so often and so enthusiastically that at times she had doubted his sincerity.

Suddenly, she doubted it completely.

She needed air.

Amelia survived the next several minutes until the ladies were excused to the drawing room. At a moment when she was certain no one was watching her, she slipped away from the guests, made her way to the empty library, and pushed open the terrace door.

The cool November air welcomed her. She crossed to the railing, intent on a few moments of privacy before returning to the hustle of entertaining. But after several minutes of attempting to process what she had heard, the door from the library flew open.

"There you are." A grin flashed across Edward's chiseled features. His footsteps echoed on the stone beneath him, his unsteady walk explained by the goblet in his hand. "I've looked everywhere for you. Isn't this a nice turn of events?" He leaned next to her against the rail. "I do believe that we are headed in the right direction, dearest Amelia."

She nodded. The wool of his jacket rubbed her arm through the loose weave of her shawl. She drew the shawl more tightly around her. She wrinkled her nose at the pungent stench of brandy, surmising that his drinking had begun hours before the gathering. "You startled me. I thought you would stay behind with the gentlemen."

He ignored her statement, a habit of late. "Ah, you're wearing the necklace." He traced the chain with his finger, allowing it to linger on her skin. "Sapphires suit you. But in the future, they shall be diamonds." His breath brushed her neck.

Amelia shifted uncomfortably under his touch, then swallowed. She had better get used to his taking such liberties. "It is beautiful indeed."

"You must imagine my astonishment at our last-minute guest." The change of subject was abrupt. Edward dropped his hand from her and took a swig from the goblet before setting it on the railing.

"I assume you mean Captain Sterling?"

"Of course I mean Captain Sterling." Edward's nostrils flared at the mention of the name. "If he has returned, why is *she* still here?"

He did not need say more for Amelia to understand his meaning. "Lucy is just a baby, Edward."

A sneer tugged his full lips. "If it is babies you want, I can give you all the babies you desire. Just give me five more weeks."

Amelia ignored his suggestive comment. He was leaving tomorrow, and she needed to broach the subject of Lucy before it was too late. "I fail to understand why Lucy cannot continue to live with us. Once we are wed, that is. What is the harm of it? Winterwood is so large, and—"

Edward's string of curses interrupted her. "I've told you—I just won't have it, and I'm weary of you pestering me about it."

A creeping panic gripped Amelia. She had seen Edward under drink's influence before, but something was different about tonight. He had always spoken of Lucy dismissively, but the closer they came to their wedding date, the more intense his opposition became.

"How can you not see it, Amelia? How can you be so oblivious?" Something like a laugh gurgled from his throat, and he dragged his hand over his face. "It pains me to be so blunt with you, but someone must be. Captain Sterling is taking advantage of you, Amelia. He is playing you for a fool. The entire Sterling clan is. And I won't have it."

Momentarily stunned by the accusation, Amelia shook her head. "That is a falsehood. The captain never asked me to care for Lucy. It was my idea. I was the one—"

Edward silenced her by stepping so close that the warmth from his body filtered through the filmy silk of her gown. "The child has family, Amelia, or have you forgotten? She is not destitute. It was her uncle's responsibility to take her in after her mother's death, though apparently that never crossed his mind. Now her father is home, and his financial success is no secret. It is up to him to provide for her."

"But, Edward, I—"

"It is time, Amelia. Past time. You have more than amply fulfilled the promise you made to her mother, and it does you credit. Now it is time to move on to the next stage. Your life with me. With our children."

Amelia did not trust herself to look up into the eyes that were now so near to her own. She opened her mouth to speak, to defend herself, to share the arguments she had so carefully prepared. "I—I cannot help but disagree. You say I am being taken advantage of— well then, so be it. We have more than enough money, more than enough room, I—"

Edward grabbed her forearm. Startled, she snapped her mouth shut. "You may not care about it, Amelia, but I do. I care a great deal. I will not allow another man to prey on my wife's fortune or good nature, regardless of how he disguises it."

With a sudden jerk, he dropped her arm, straightened, and smoothed his cravat, which the wind had disrupted. His hard glare bore down on her, the wildness in his expression frightening her. "Consider your motivations, Amelia. You are acting on emotion, not reason. But I will not allow him to exploit you. Exploit *us*. My mind is made up. I will not subvert my children's inheritance to raise another man's child, especially when that man is fully capable of doing so on his own. I will not be taken advantage of like, like—"

His words stopped short. He cut his eyes away from her, lifted the glass to his lips, and tossed the liquid down his throat. His body swayed.

Amelia shrank back into the corner, hunching under the protection of her shawl, as if it could protect her from the bluntness of his words.

Even in cover of darkness, she could see the anger in his dark eyes. "I care not how it is done, but that child will leave my house."

He wiped his mouth with the back of his hand and nodded toward the door, a silent indication he was done with their discussion. "Do not stay out in this air. You will catch a chill."

Edward staggered back inside. Watching him go, Amelia could not help but recall the day she had met him. Handsome, self-assured, attentive, he had drawn her to him effortlessly. His every word had held tenderness and a promise.

How had he become . . . this?

How could she possibly marry a man who would treat her so? But what choice did she possibly have?

Tears threatened. Amelia stared into the black, starless night, pulling her shawl ever tighter around her, as if such a simple action could shield her from the uncertainty of her future.

6

G raham stepped into the broad hallway, determined to go unnoticed by the handful of guests who had gathered there. A quick sweep of the space confirmed Miss Helena Barrett's absence. He exhaled. The woman had babbled all evening. Her incessant prattling had kept him from seeking out Miss Amelia Barrett, his true reason for attending in the first place.

He made his way down the hall to the library in time to see Edward Littleton stumble in through an outside door. The inebriated man shuffled past without seeing him. Graham released a breath. He wasn't fond of Littleton. But if the person coming in had been Helena Barrett and he'd been forced to endure one more tale about purchasing Indian muslin or German lace, he would have thrown himself from one of Winterwood's towers.

He watched Littleton stagger past a side table and nearly knock a candle to the planked floor below. So far, what he had seen of Amelia Barrett's intended had been unimpressive at best. Graham had every intention of watching him more closely as the evening progressed, but first he needed a minute alone. He stole behind the couches, careful not to draw the attention of a small group of men who had gathered in front of the fireplace. Twisting the door's ornate brass handle, he stepped out onto a wide stone terrace. The breeze carried a hint of rain, and the frost's spicy scent invigorated his senses. He stretched and inhaled deeply. He still missed sea air, but this was preferable to the suffocating rooms within.

"Are you looking for something, Captain Sterling?" The voice was soft. Feminine.

He turned to find Miss Amelia Barrett standing behind him. He glanced back over his shoulder. She had been alone with Littleton. He bowed. "Miss Barrett. I wasn't aware you were out here."

"If I did not know better, I would think you were following me." Her words were an obvious attempt at lighthearted conversation, but her face told a different story.

"I deserve that. I apologize for my behavior in the cemetery yesterday. I had no intention to intrude or offend."

Miss Barrett stepped from the shadows. The yellow light filtering through the tall drawing room windows slanted over the gentle slope of her nose and highlighted the curve of her cheek. "It is I who should apologize, sir. It was impolite of me to leave so abruptly." She lowered her voice, as if taking him into her confidence. "You see, as a general rule, I prefer not to cry in front of other people. Especially people I do not have the pleasure of knowing well."

You will not cry in front of a stranger, yet you would propose to one? The words bubbled near the surface of his mind. But he said nothing.

The breeze carried strains of a pianoforte from somewhere in the house, and she glanced toward the door. "I should return. If you will excuse me?"

Without a thought for decorum, Graham reached out and touched her arm. "Wait."

She turned, her eyes flitting from his hand on her arm to his face. "Yes, Captain Sterling?"

He shifted uncomfortably. He was alone with her. Would not now be a good time to speak with her as he had intended? With his time in Darbury limited, he did not have the luxury of waiting. "I wondered . . . I have been meaning to ask . . . You see, I know very little about my wife's final days." He hesitated, pausing to interpret the shadow crossing her face. "Might I trouble you for a moment of your time to ask you a few questions?"

She hesitated, interlaced her fingers, then nodded. "Of course. You have my permission to ask me anything."

"I received only three letters from Katherine after she moved to Darbury. I have no doubt she wrote more frequently, but as you can imagine, the post did not always extend over the sea. How did you and Katherine become acquainted?"

After an awkward silence, Miss Barrett spoke. "We met after she moved to Darbury, to Moreton Cottage. That was almost a year and a half ago. Jane Hammond—that's the vicar's wife—told me that I had a new neighbor, and as I am sure you can imagine, we do not often receive new neighbors in Darbury. I called upon Katherine; we grew fond of each other and soon became fast friends. We spent nearly every day in each other's company. She was, of course, with child when she arrived, but a few months after her arrival, she fell ill. Since she was all alone at Moreton Cottage, with only two servants to tend to her, I insisted she stay at Winterwood for her lying in."

Graham could no longer hold back the question. "Did my brother not offer any assistance?"

Miss Barrett's lips parted in what could only be surprise at his directness. Heavy silence blanketed the space before she spoke. "If I remember correctly, Mr. Sterling was out of town for most of the time Katherine was in Darbury."

Graham masked his annoyance. He would deal with his frustration toward his brother at another time. Right now there were other things he needed to know. "What was it . . . That is to say, how did she . . . ?" He stopped himself and tried again. "What were the circumstances surrounding her death?"

Miss Barrett stepped to the railing, as if trying to put distance between them.

Graham closed the space she created by joining her at the balustrade. "I don't mean to upset you, but I beg of you . . . I must know."

She stared away from him into the blackness. "How much do you want to know?"

"Everything."

A sharp gust swept over the terrace, and Miss Barrett shivered. She gathered the hem of her shawl and ran the fringe through her fingers. He adjusted his stance, preparing to hear whatever might pass her lips.

"From the beginning of her confinement, it was clear that something was amiss. She was confined to bed early on. The midwife advised that if she was too active, she could lose the baby."

The wind calmed. Miss Barrett paced with slow, decided steps, her shimmering gown billowing behind her and glittering in the faint light from inside.

"When her time came, the midwife told us it was too soon. Katherine should have carried Lucy for another month, but she couldn't . . ." Amelia paused, her head lowered, as if gathering her thoughts or calming her emotions. She sniffed, fixed her eyes on the ground, then went on. "She labored for days. Then, after Lucy came, Katherine succumbed to puerperal fever." She pointed, directing his attention to a narrow window in a far wing. "There. That was her room while she was at Winterwood. She died in that room."

Graham rubbed his hand over his face and let it settle over his mouth. Katherine, *his Katherine*, had been in pain. Snippets of memories bombarded him. Her smile. Her hair.

He looked over at Miss Barrett. She had stayed with Katherine to the last. Without her, who would have been there for his wife? His indebtedness to this wisp of a woman ran deep indeed.

Graham forced words through his tightened throat. "That must have been very difficult for you, Miss Barrett. Thank you for your kindness. I am grateful she did not die alone."

Amelia fixed her eyes on her hands. "As I have told you, Katherine asked me to care for Lucy. I promised, and I do not give promises lightly. Ever since that day, Lucy has never been out of my care." She hesitated. "And forgive me for speaking on such a private matter, but I intend my words to be a comfort. Katherine loved you so very much."

Words failed Graham. The more details he heard, the more difficult they were to hear. To absorb. He had hoped that knowledge would soothe the unsettled ache in his chest, but the answers only caused further turmoil.

Drops of rain blew in with the wind. A shout echoed from inside Winterwood, and Amelia cast a nervous glance toward the door. "I must go now, Captain. Edw—Mr. Littleton—will be looking for me." She bobbed a curtsy, but instead of heading toward the drawing room door, she moved to the stone stairs leading down to the lawn.

"Where are you going?"

Her glance back at him was incredulous. "You do not suggest that I go back through those doors after being alone with you out here?"

He shook his head. "Do not be absurd. It's been raining for days! You'll slip and do yourself harm in all that mud."

"Captain Sterling, we have shared this terrace for more than a quarter of an hour, and there may be guests in the library. If some-one should notice that we walked in at the same time—no, I thank you. I will go around."

He trailed her as she moved farther into the darkness. "It's starting to rain. You will be soaked through. We'll go in through different doors, and surely no one will see."

She stopped and turned so quickly that he almost ran into her. "I do not think you understand." She fretted with the edge of her shawl. "Mr. Littleton is not a man to be crossed. If he should even think that you, um, I mean, that I . . ."

Her words faded, and she diverted her eyes.

Was she frightened of Edward Littleton, or were her words a warning? And if the latter were true, did she think the man intimi-dated him? Graham stifled a snort. "You don't know me very well, Miss Barrett."

Miss Barrett jutted her chin into the air. "And you do not know me, sir."

He stepped closer to her, almost enjoying the interchange as a welcome relief from the somber nature of their discussion. "Your Mr. Little-whatever-his-name-is is a pup compared to the men I deal with every day."

She matched his step with a backward one of her own. "Well, you do not have to live with the man. I am to be married to him in a matter of weeks. I would consider your discretion a personal favor."

"It's none of my business, but—"

"You are right," she cut him off. "It is none of your business. So if you'll pardon me . . ."

This was ridiculous. He could not, would not, let her or any other woman go stumbling blindly into the dark night.

The rain's intensity increased. The drops plopped on his cheeks and brushed his eyelashes. "Very well," he grumbled, waving his hand toward the door. "Go inside if you must. I'll go around."

She hesitated, but as a fresh gust of wind brought stronger rain, she ducked her head and looped her shawl over her hair. "Thank you, Captain Sterling. If you round the corner there, you'll find the kitchen entrance."

He covered sarcasm with a huff. "I think I can find it."

"I will see you inside."

She disappeared through the door. Staring at the empty door frame, he flipped up his collar and descended the stairs to the lawn.

Headstrong woman. Headstrong, determined, *intriguing* woman.

⁂

Graham slipped back inside Winterwood Manor and followed the sound of voices to the billiards room, where the men had gathered. The room was dim and close. The smoke from the fireplace escaped and curled toward the molded ceilings, obscuring the multitude of landscape paintings adorning the dark green walls. Laughter abounded. He took a seat next to the fire, hoping the warmth would dry out his soggy boots.

"Mr. Littleton is not a man to be crossed." Miss Barrett's words echoed in his mind. He stared at Littleton, who stood next to the billiard table, cue in hand, laughing a little too loudly. The man's arrogant manner irked Graham. So did his obviously drunken state.

"Well, well, where have you been?" William sauntered toward him with a glass in each hand. Another sight Graham had seen more times than he cared to admit. William handed him a goblet of port.

"Needed some air." Graham considered downing the drink, but instead swirled the tawny liquid in his glass and watched it splash against the sides.

"Why are you wet?"

"You would not believe me if I told you. What's going on in here?"

William leaned back and balanced himself on the arm of the sofa. "Billiards. You play?"

"Of course."

"Join us." With a chuckle, he pushed himself off the furniture. "If you think you can beat me, that is."

Graham slouched to the left and caught a glimpse through the open door of the drawing room where the ladies had gathered. The pale blue silk of Miss Barrett's skirts swirled past the threshold. He found it difficult to tear his eyes away. Like it or not, he was bound to the woman. Bound by grief. Bound by the love of a child. And now that he knew the full extent of the service she had done his wife, bound by honor. That connection posed no small amount of difficulty, since it was clear to him that Miss Barrett had no business marrying a man like Littleton.

"Graham!" William's voice carried above the laughter. "Get over here."

Rising from his chair, Graham headed toward the table to stand next to Littleton, whose height matched his own. He didn't speak to the man, nor did the man speak to him. Right or wrong, Graham judged character quickly. He had to. One such misjudgment on board his ship could spell disaster.

His instincts screamed for him to watch this one. And watch him he would.

❧

The morning following the engagement dinner dawned overcast. Settled at a small writing desk in the library, Amelia sought distraction. Her fingers traced the printed words in her father's worn Bible. She tried to concentrate, but the letters swirled on the page.

Blessed is the man that trusteth in the Lord, and whose hope the Lord is.
For he shall be as a tree planted by the waters, and that spreadeth out her
roots by the river, and shall not see when heat cometh, but her leaf shall be
green; and shall not be careful in the year of drought, neither shall cease
from yielding fruit.

If only she found it as easy to believe the words as to read them. As much as she hungered for the truths in them, her fear-laden heart and mind stubbornly refused to give them credence. She leaned her elbows on the desk and stared through the window's wavy glass at a vista of wide lawns, manicured gardens, and the moors beyond, still tinged with a remnant of fall's rich color.

The sun peeked golden from behind the waning clouds, bathing the page in sunlight. *Whose hope the Lord is.* The words called out to her. But somehow she couldn't bring herself to trust them. Not after all the sadness she had known—growing up motherless, losing her father, watching Katherine die, fearing that Lucy might be taken. In truth, Amelia was beginning to believe that those words were for people like Katherine and Jane. Not her.

Amelia sensed Edward's presence before she saw him. The fine hairs on her arm prickled as his footsteps approached. After their daunting interaction on the terrace the previous evening, she wondered what to expect in his demeanor.

A finger traced the back of her bare neck, the touch shooting shivers through her body. He rested his large hands on her shoulders, and his lips grazed the top of her head. "Good day, my darling."

Amelia tensed. His voice sounded as it always did: confident and agreeable. She kept her eyes fixed on the Bible's page. "Good afternoon, Edward. I trust you slept well?"

He swung around to lean against the desk. His leg, dressed in fine gray pantaloons, rested dangerously close to her arm. "I'll sleep better when I don't have to sleep alone."

She winced at his suggestive remark but decided to ignore it. She had other things to worry about.

Edward drew a deep breath and stretched. "What to do today." He said it more as a statement than a question. His tone of voice suggested that he either did not remember their curt interaction or did not care to discuss it.

So be it. Regardless of how she felt about Edward's behavior last night, she was plighted to marry this man in just a few weeks. She must make every effort to be civil.

"Care to take the horses for a ride?" she asked.

"No."

"Shall I read aloud to you?"

He laughed, his rich baritone filling the small space. He took the Bible from her and flipped through the pages. "Dear Amelia. Dear sweet, good Amelia. Read aloud if you think it will do some good, but I fear I am beyond help from that book or any other."

"Nobody is good of their own accord," she reasoned.

"Well then." He looked at her with eyes still red from last night's indulgences and all but dangled the Bible in front of her. "Perhaps you can reform me."

Vexed by his condescension, she snatched the Bible, pushed herself away from the desk, and crossed the room to the window. "A walk, then?"

He gave his head an impatient shake and began to pace. Edward Littleton was a man in constant need of amusement, never content to be still. In Darbury for but a day, and already his restless eyes beamed impatience.

She glanced from the shelves of her mother's books to her father's faded chair. She loved Winterwood. It was her home, the seat of her memories. She feared that Edward appreciated the estate purely for the fortune that came with it.

But was she any better? Had she not deceived him only two

days ago by proposing to another man? She bit her lower lip, aware of her wrongdoing. He, however, seemed blissfully unaware of his.

The mantel clock struck the hour. She looked out the window to the front drive. "Mr. Carrington will be here soon. That will be a nice diversion for you."

Edward studied his fingernails. "I have been meaning to talk with you about Carrington. When your uncle and I returned yesterday, we paid him a visit. I have relieved him of his duties."

"What do you mean, 'relieved him of his duties'?"

"Just what I said. Now that I am to be master, I do not need his assistance with our affairs. I will handle Winterwood's business on my own. I believe the man has already departed the estate cottage for his offices in Sheffield. He will send for his things later."

She whirled around from the window. Had he intended not to tell her? Had he thought she wouldn't notice? She forced steadiness to her voice. "Before he died, my father hand-selected Mr. Carrington to handle our affairs. He knows more about Winterwood's workings than you could possibly imagine. He knows all the tenants by name. *I* don't even know them all by name. How could you do something like that without discussing it with me first?"

"Calm down, Amelia." He stretched his hands out in front of him, attempting to settle her as one would a nervous horse. "You're getting upset for nothing. You are right that managing an estate like this is a complicated business, but I'm a competent man. There's no need for you to worry about it."

"You are missing my point," Amelia retorted. "Mr. Carrington is a trusted family friend. How dare you just cast him aside without even—"

"Your uncle and I spoke at great length about it. He agreed it was the best course of action for everyone."

For you, you mean. She bit back the words and focused on her argument. "My uncle is not Winterwood's heir. I am. That fact alone gives me the right to—"

"Egad, Amelia. Why would you worry about such things? Do not allow yourself to become agitated over something so insignificant."

"Insignificant? I—" She shut her mouth as a painful realization registered. Edward was patronizing her. Treating her like a child. She studied his dark eyes, hardly recognizing the man who was speaking to her now. Yes, he was still handsome and confident, passionate and energetic. But this other side of him, abrupt and self-serving, almost frightened her.

She could not guess his motives, for nothing about him lately was as it seemed. But suddenly she knew one thing for certain. If allowed, this man would destroy everything important to her.

For weeks she had teetered on the cusp of losing Lucy. Now the one person who understood her father's vision and cared for Winterwood as she did, Mr. Carrington, had been cut from her life. Once bound by marriage, Winterwood Manor would legally be more Edward's than hers, and she would have little choice but to do his bidding.

Did she have any choice now?

She glared at Edward and fought the nausea swirling in her stomach. Arguing with the man would not get her what she wanted. She had to be smart, to act wisely. She looked out the window to the grounds below. As she did, her gaze fell on the one person who held the power to change her situation.

Captain Graham Sterling.

7

Graham's headstrong mount stopped midtrot and veered sharply to the right. Again. Graham lurched in the saddle and yanked the leather reins, struggling for balance. The obstinate horse's uneven gait and strange penchant to change direction without warning would threaten to unseat the most experienced rider, let alone a man who had spent most of his days at sea.

"Need help controlling that beast?" mocked William, pulling his fine bay up next to Graham.

"Stubborn mule." Graham assessed his steed's crooked ear and squeezed his legs around the animal's belly. He'd never been much of a horseman, and his years at sea had not helped. He resented having to buy the animal on his journey from Plymouth to Darbury, but he had been forced to when unable to secure a post chaise for a leg of the journey. He'd been so anxious to arrive that he had purchased the first halfway suitable mount he'd come across. He'd been paying the price ever since.

"We should have taken the carriage."

William laughed. "Nonsense. Too fine of a day for that. Finally, an afternoon free of rain! Besides, 'twould be a bother to take the carriage for such a short drive." He nodded toward Graham's horse. "When the time comes to select a pony for that daughter of yours, I suggest you leave it to me. It appears you have little talent for it."

Graham ignored his brother's jab and tightened his grip on the reins. The feisty animal wouldn't gain the upper hand again.

"I, on the other hand, have an excellent eye for horseflesh," continued William, his light eyes twinkling. "Take Tibbs here, for example." He gave a low whistle, and the stallion's ears perked up. "Pity I must sell him."

"What? Sell that one?" Graham nodded at William's prized bay. "I thought he was your favorite."

"He is, but he'll also fetch a fine price at Abbott's."

"Eastmore seems to be doing well enough. Why worry about money?"

William shrugged. "Ah, you know, foolish decisions, bad bets. Nothing outlandish, but a few extra pounds lining my pockets could not hurt."

Graham masked his surprise at his brother's comment and followed William through Winterwood's iron gates. Tall elms lined the drive. Autumn had blown most of the gold and crimson leaves to the ground, leaving a brave few to hold their stead against the insistent wind. Beyond the drive, Winterwood's gray battlements jutted majestically into the crisp blue sky. The sun's brilliant glow reflected from the numerous bay windows and cast shadows below the cornices and pediments.

They reached the main entrance, and two adolescent stable boys appeared to take the horses. Graham swung himself to the ground and handed a boy the reins, grateful to have both feet back on the ground. He started toward Winterwood's heavy front door, then noticed that his brother hung back.

Graham paused. "Are you not coming?"

William removed his leather riding gloves and tucked them in his pocket. "Of course. Of course."

Why was he acting so strange? Graham decided to overlook the alteration in his brother's demeanor. Heading back to the door, he lifted the iron knocker and let it fall. The anticipation of seeing his daughter again brought lightness to his step. Would she remember him?

The butler answered the door and ushered Graham and William into the drawing room. Everything looked exactly as it had when Graham first arrived at Winterwood three days past. But how different everything seemed now.

"Captain Sterling!" Miss Barrett appeared in the doorway, her lemon-colored gown bright as the afternoon sunshine, Lucy in her arms.

"And Mr. Sterling." Miss Barrett's smile faded a little when she spotted William. A slight awkwardness hovered between them, and Graham made a note to ask William about it later. But right now he could think about little else besides his bonny daughter.

Graham stepped forward eagerly, remembering how easily she had come to him that first day. But today she shrank back against Miss Barrett, her eyes regarding him with trepidation. When he reached out to take her, she turned her head and clung to Miss Barrett.

"Come now, dearest," coaxed Miss Barrett, her voice soft and low. "Go to your father. He's come such a long way to see you." As she tried to pass the child to Graham's arms, Lucy shrilled with such vehemence that he had to keep himself from covering his ear.

Graham stepped back, alarmed that his own child should be so resistant to him. Lucy's face reddened, and his eyes grew wide. "It is all right, Miss Barrett. She is clearly frightened. She does not yet know me."

Miss Barrett's eyebrows drew together. "I apologize, Captain Sterling. She's been a bit out of sorts today. I am sure she will calm down after you have been here awhile." She cooed at Lucy and bounced her gently, casting another cool glance over toward William.

"Welcome to Winterwood, gentlemen." Helena Barrett's energetic voice pierced the uncomfortable atmosphere. "We saw you coming up the path, so we had the servants set us up on the side lawn for our visit. It is fine out, perhaps the last beautiful day before winter, so we should take advantage, do you not agree?"

Graham and William followed the ladies and Lucy through the drawing room, down the corridor, and through the library to the same terrace he'd shared with Miss Barrett the previous evening. How different it looked bathed in day's warm glow. Below them, on the lawn, two servants scurried about, setting tables and chairs for tea and spreading quilts on the fading grass.

The two women led them down the stairs to the lawn just as George Barrett rounded the south wall riding a great black horse and accompanied by a small pack of auburn and white dogs. He appeared every bit the country gentleman—cropped riding coat, dark brown breeches, and top-boots.

"Ah, there's Father." Helena Barrett looped her arm through her cousin's and waved at her father with the other.

George Barrett pulled to a stop next to the ladies. "And how are you today, my dears?" he asked, smiling down at his daughter and niece before acknowledging the men.

"We're very well, Father." Helena Barrett pointed across the lawn. "We're about to have some tea. You gentlemen can join us in a bit if you'd like." Arm in arm, the cousins ambled toward the tables.

"Good to see you, Barrett." William took hold of the horse's bridle. "Been out hunting already, have you?"

"No, just out for a ride. Good for the constitution, or so Mrs.

Barrett tells me." A smile crossed the round man's chapped face, and he cast a glance over his stooped shoulder to the preparations on the lawn. "I think the women expect us to take tea, but I have something a bit more robust in mind. Can I interest either of you in a man's beverage?"

"Uncanny, Barrett." William gave the horse's neck a pat. "You know my very thoughts."

George swung down and slipped the reins over the horse's head. "What about you, Captain? What say you to a little diversion? I am anxious to hear an account of the war against America and what our forces are doing to protect our interests in the region. As you know, we make our living in trade, much of it with the West Indies. I have had more than one ship captured by the scoundrel privateers. But I hear your journeys take you farther north? Closer to Halifax?"

Graham nodded, looking over George's shoulder to where Lucy played on a blanket spread on the grass. "Yes, sir, we were in Halifax before our recent return to Plymouth."

A look of approval brightened the older man's ruddy complexion. "Very good. I look forward to hearing all about it. Shall we go to the house for some talk and libations?"

In another time and another place, Graham would have immediately accepted the offer. Now something else occupied his thoughts. "I believe I will visit with my daughter for a bit; it's why I came. Perhaps I will join you later."

George tipped his hat in Graham's direction. "Don't mind us, then, if we take our leave."

Graham returned the nod and stepped to avoid the noisy flurry of dogs that swarmed around George and William as they returned the horse to the stable. The sun peeked out from behind silver clouds as he crossed the lawn, its yellow light streaming through the leafless branches and casting curved patterns on the browning grass. A lively breeze blew in from the north, and if he closed his eyes, he could almost be shipboard again, standing on deck with the wind on his face. But instead of a sharp aroma of salty sea air, the mossy scents of the moors greeted him. And instead of the crass voices of hardened sailors, he heard only the polite tones of gentle ladies.

How different life was on land. He'd grown accustomed to the sea; indeed, it was the only life he knew. He could not help but wonder how different his life would have been if he had never been sent away, if he had been born first and inherited Eastmore Hall.

Miss Barrett's words interrupted his thoughts. "Lucy loves the outdoors."

"She comes by that honestly." Graham bent to sit next to his daughter and then stretched out his legs. "I prefer to be out of doors any day."

Lucy crawled from Miss Barrett's lap and attempted to wiggle over Graham's boot to reach the adorning tassel, apparently forgetting any qualms she'd had about him just moments ago.

"Where are you going, little miss?" he asked, drawing Lucy into his arms. She giggled when he crossed his eyes at her, then rewarded him with a lopsided grin. Her tiny legs punched him in the stomach as she inched back down to the quilt. He picked some grass and spread it before her. She squealed and reached for the treasure with her fists. He stopped her just before she put the grass in her mouth.

Just days ago thoughts of a child had intimidated him. But with every moment spent in her presence, he desired more. Lucy squirmed and yawned, and he scooped her up and kissed her plump cheek.

Miss Barrett stood and brushed grass from her skirt. "I think Lucy may need a blanket. There is a chill in the air. I'll return shortly."

Her footsteps crunched on the dry leaves as she walked away. The soft call of the warbler mingled with a nightingale's song, and a red squirrel scurried to the tree line. The sounds conjured memories of a forgotten childhood, of long afternoons spent surveying the moors and cavorting amidst the purple heather and rocky terrain.

"Do you hear that sound, Lucy?" Graham said, recognizing a sound he'd not heard since his youth. "That's a sparrow's song." The child, now worn out from her bout of play, drooped sleepily. Her eyelids gradually shut, displaying her long, pale eyelashes against her fair cheeks. He drew her close and tucked her head under his chin, enjoying the gentle rhythm of her breathing and the soft lavender scent of her hair.

What sounds of childhood would his daughter remember? Would it be the whistle of the wind over open spaces and the swish of the cotton grass beneath her feet? Or would it be of noisy carriages clamoring over cobbled city streets? He surveyed the main house, the lawns. The majesty of the grand estate was humbling, its beauty even surpassing that of Eastmore Hall. Miss Barrett's strange proposal came to mind. If he accepted it, his daughter's memories would be of this beautiful place. She could live here all her days, if she so desired. The place would belong to him, to Lucy, if he accepted Miss Barrett's offer.

"Shall I take the child, sir?"

Graham looked up at the sound of a strong Irish brogue.

"I'm Mrs. Dunne, nurse to young Miss Lucy." The plump woman, white cap over dark hair, stood ready to take the child. He'd lost track of how long he'd sat with his daughter. Miss Barrett had said she would return right away. Where was she? Careful not to wake the sleeping cherub, he stood and gently handed the child to her nurse.

"Don't worry, sir. I'll take good care of this one, I will."

He smiled as she laid the child in a wheeled baby carriage,

then started along the path toward the house. As he watched, he thought he heard rising voices carried by the wind. He furrowed his brow and listened.

Graham scanned the surroundings. William and George Barrett were still on the far side of the lawn outside the stables, apparently having forgotten about their port. Helena Barrett and her mother, whom he recognized from the dinner, sat at the table, sipping tea. It wasn't them. Then he spotted a flash of yellow. It swirled out from behind the terrace wall and then vanished from sight.

Curious, he walked back to the terrace steps. As each silent footfall brought him closer, the muffled voices grew in intensity.

Littleton's deep voice reached his ears first. "I will not have this discussion again. I think I have made myself very clear regarding my expectations on this matter. As my wife, you will comply."

Miss Barrett's response was immediate. "I am not yet your wife. How can you presume so? Do not think I—"

Littleton's words crushed her protest. "I'll hear not another word about it. You heard what I said, and you know what I meant."

"Or what?" Her voice held a power that surprised Graham. It held a challenge, as if daring Littleton to continue.

"Of all the impudence. I should think—"

Miss Barrett's voice sounded strained, as if pushed out through clenched teeth. "So help me, Edward, I'd sooner see Winterwood Manor in a stranger's hands and be sent to the poorhouse than turn my back on someone I love."

Littleton laughed. "Someone you love? So you love Lucy more than you love me, is that it? Well, you're too late for that realization, Amelia. If you call this off now, what do you think will happen? Your inheritance will pass to another, and it will happen soon. What will you do then? Do you think your uncle will continue to care for you? Allow you to live in his house? He is as invested in this union as I. Don't think for a moment that—"

The tones were harsh and escalating, and Graham recalled the hint of fear in Miss Barrett's eyes when she spoke of Littleton. He had heard enough. He took the terrace steps two at a time and rounded the wall. Littleton held Miss Barrett's arm in an awkward grasp. The knuckles of Miss Barrett's clenched fist showed white, and her sapphire eyes were wide. Her chest rose and fell rapidly with each breath.

Graham stepped closer, his boots heavy against the smooth stone veranda. "May I be of assistance, Miss Barrett?"

With a surprised jerk, Littleton spun around and glared at Graham, his eyes no wider than tight slits. "What in blazes are you doing here?"

"I heard shouting."

"This is not your concern. I'll thank you to mind your own affairs and leave us to ours."

Graham took another step. "Be that as it may, Littleton, you make it my business when I see a woman being treated in such fashion. I must ask you to release her arm."

Amelia seized the opportunity afforded by Littleton's break in concentration and twisted from his grip. She stood rubbing her wrist, her eyes like those of an animal caught in a snare.

Edward forced a casual smile that teetered on a sneer. "She is not your concern."

Graham glared at Littleton, daring him to look away. "Miss Barrett, Mrs. Dunne is looking for you."

For a moment nobody moved. Asserting the authoritative tone that he used with his crew, Graham lied again. "Miss Barrett, Mrs. Dunne needs your assistance."

Without a word she gathered her yellow skirts and scurried from the terrace.

Littleton tugged at his cravat. A smug smile coiled his lip. "I know your angle, Sterling."

"And that is?"

"You are exploiting Amelia's affection for your child, sir." Edward stepped forward, his words suspending a challenge between them. "What is it that you want, sir? Her money? Her land? Or just . . . her?"

Graham's jaw clenched at the accusation. "Nothing of the kind. Miss Barrett has shown a great kindness to my family, and I am grateful. But mark my words. I will not stand idly by and watch you or any other man treat a woman, regardless of who she is, with such incivility."

Edward sneered. "I know you Sterlings. You are all the same— you and your brother, and your father before you. Conniving. Calculating. You may be able to worm your way into Amelia's good graces, but you will not take advantage of me. I want you and your daughter off *my* property, and I want you to stay away from my future wife."

Graham's temples pulsed. Part of him wanted to silence Edward by telling him of Amelia's proposal, but he held his tongue. He could not put the woman who had done so much for him in such a precarious position.

He kept his voice low. "It will be my pleasure. But you are warned, Littleton. If I see you with your hands on her, or any woman, I will have no qualms about striking you down. That would also be *my pleasure*."

Littleton's face deepened to a dark purple. More like a spoiled child than a grown man, he flounced through the terrace's door into the parlor, his coattails swishing behind him.

Graham relaxed his fists and pulled his waistcoat straight. In the distance, he saw Miss Barrett talking to Mrs. Dunne and bending over the baby carriage. She flashed a nervous glance in his direction, then returned her attentions to the baby. As he headed toward them, he no longer heard the sounds of nature or the whistling of the wind. Littleton's harsh words regarding his daughter, his family, and Miss Barrett echoed in his mind.

At the sound of his boots stomping across the grass, the women looked up. He had no desire to see the embarrassment that painted Miss Barrett's expression, but he knew what needed to be done.

"Miss Barrett, I am afraid my daughter and I can no longer trespass on your hospitality."

Miss Barrett's hand flew to her mouth. "Whatever do you mean?"

He could not look her in the eyes when he spoke the words. "I think it would be best for all involved if we make other living arrangements for Lucy."

She cried out and took hold of his arm. "If this is because of Mr. Littleton, please, do not give it another thought. I will talk to him. I can get him to change his mind. Please, I—"

He raised his hand to silence her. "Please, Miss Barrett, do not misunderstand. I am grateful for your generosity, but all things considered, I believe this is for the best."

She circled him, blocking the path to the stable with her small frame. Her rosy complexion had drained to white. "Captain, this is Lucy's home. Please, I beg you, sir, don't take her away."

He had no desire to hurt her, but he wasn't about to apologize for intruding on her conversation or removing Lucy. He cleared his throat, not accustomed to explaining his actions. "To my knowledge, there is no nursery at Eastmore Hall. So if you would be so kind as to allow her to stay on with you until further arrangements can be made, I would be in your debt." He hesitated, then looked down at his daughter sleeping in the carriage. Emotion tightened his chest, and he drew a deep breath. "Good day, ladies."

He bowed, tipped his hat, and moved past the women. The sooner he could free himself from Winterwood and the insanity brewing within its walls, the better he and Lucy would be.

8

Please be home. Please be home. Please be home.

P lease be home. Please be home. Please be home.

With every step, the words thumped in Amelia's head. Faster and faster her feet carried her along the path from Winterwood's west wall to the vicarage.

Heart pounding, she abandoned the path for a shortcut through a copse of trees that bordered the moors. More than once she almost lost her footing on wet leaves and grass. A branch caught her hair and pulled it free of her ivory comb just as she reached the clearing where the vicarage stood. She sprinted toward the house and pounded on the door.

The moment a servant opened the door, Amelia pushed her way in. "Jane!" she cried. "Jane!"

Her friend flew around the corner. "For goodness' sake, child, whatever is—" She paused midsentence, her mouth falling agape at the sight of Amelia. "What on earth has happened to you? Come in, dearest."

"He's going to take her away!" Amelia gulped for breath.

"What? Who? Here, come in and sit down. Over here by the

fire." Jane wrapped her arms around Amelia's heaving shoulders and guided her to a chair next to the fireplace. "There, there. I want to hear all about it, but you must calm down first. Fainting dead away will not help."

Amelia stared into the fire, her tears blurring the dying embers' light. Her teeth chattered, but she wasn't cold. She inhaled and exhaled, willing the rapid breathing to subside.

Jane removed the comb hanging from Amelia's hair and brushed the locks with her fingers. "There now. What is wrong?"

"Captain Sterling. He said he plans to make other arrangements for Lucy." Amelia's pitch elevated. "He's taking her from Winterwood! What am I to do?"

Jane's voice was calm and controlled. "Where is Lucy now?"

"She is still at Winterwood, but the captain was very clear. He is making other arrangements."

"Tell me what happened."

Amelia hesitated. "I am not certain, to be honest. The captain and his brother were visiting Lucy. While they were at Winterwood, Mr. Littleton and I had a bit of a . . . disagreement. Captain Sterling intervened. I think the captain and Edward had words."

Jane grabbed her own lace shawl from the sofa and draped it around Amelia's shoulders. "If that is the case, then the captain's decision likely has more to do with Mr. Littleton than you." She reached out to pat Amelia's hand, but when she saw the red marks from Edward's tight grip, she pulled the hand closer. "Mercy's sake! How did this happen?"

Amelia drew her hand back and tucked it under the shawl. She should take this opportunity to tell Jane everything. About the changes in Edward's personality and her doubts about his motivation. About her proposal to the captain. About her heartbreak over losing Lucy. But the words just would not form.

Jane didn't push her. "This must be very distressing to you. I know how much you care for Lucy. But sometimes things happen that are beyond our control. But God has a plan, dearest. He has a plan for you and for Lucy."

Amelia sniffed and shook her head. "I don't believe it. How could that be so? God would take a child away from the one person who loves her?"

"You assume Captain Sterling doesn't love Lucy?"

"How could he?" Amelia retorted. "He's barely met her. Besides, he'll be gone for months—years—at a time! Katherine knew that. That is why she had me promise—"

"This is where trust comes in. You have done everything you can possibly do. You must accept that God's hand is in all things. He will not leave you nor forsake you, Amelia. He will not leave nor forsake Lucy."

Amelia bolted from her chair and crossed the room. She wanted to believe Jane. She did. Her Bible reading from earlier in the day rushed to the forefront of her mind. But what if she did trust God and Lucy was still taken from her? She could not take that chance.

Jane stood and crossed after her. "Calm yourself, dearest. Things may not be as dire as you think. The captain, by all accounts, is a fine, respectable man, and he seems to be a good one as well. I feel certain he will listen to reason." She produced a lace handkerchief from a drawer and handed it to Amelia. "Dusk will fall soon. You need to go home, get a good night's sleep. Then we will sort this out together. All right?"

Amelia nodded and allowed Jane to fold her into an embrace.

"Have faith, dearest," Jane whispered. "You are not alone."

❧

It was not a falsehood. Not exactly.

Aunt Augusta crossed her arms over her ample bosom and

glared at Amelia. The last rays of the setting sun filtered through the drawing room's west window and sparkled on the topaz pendant about her aunt's neck. "A headache?"

Amelia nodded, resisting the urge to look at the ground.

Aunt Augusta shook her head. "I declare, I do not know what has gotten into you the past few days. You're as flighty as I don't know what. And sullen. Poor Mr. Littleton has traveled all this way to see you, only to be told you will not be at dinner because your head aches?"

Amelia clasped her hands behind her like a child being scolded. "I suppose nerves are getting the best of me."

Augusta tapped her long fingers on the gossamer overlay on her sleeve. "Very well. Against my better judgment I will give Mr. Littleton your regrets." She turned to leave but paused at the threshold. "I've never attempted to mother you, Amelia. Perhaps I was wrong in that. But I'd be remiss if I did not remind you what a fortunate young woman you are. Mr. Littleton is well worth having, not to mention well connected. You're close to changing your situation for the better. Consider your actions. Do not give him cause for doubt."

And with those final words, her aunt disappeared in the hall.

Amelia almost laughed. Consider *her* actions? Not give *Edward* cause for doubt?

She had no fear Edward would break the engagement. He would not risk the scandal . . . or the money. But her aunt's words held truth. Whether Amelia liked it or not, time was running short. She would turn twenty-four in just shy of two months, and if she was not married by that time, Winterwood would pass to another. At this late date, she had little choice but to marry Edward.

Amelia moved to the desk, thinking of Jane's advice. *"Accept that God's hand is in all things."* But it had never been that simple for her.

She retrieved her father's Bible and moved to pick up her book of Psalms, but the smaller book was not in its normal place. She felt around for it deeper in the drawer but could find it nowhere. Assuming she had left it in her bedroom, she tucked the Bible under her arm and took the servants' stairs to the second floor.

The day's sun had warmed her bedchamber, and the warmth remained as night descended. She flung herself on the high bed and stared at its elegant draped canopy, trying to sort out all the thoughts and feelings that bombarded her. Nothing came clear, so she sat up again and picked up the Bible. The worn pages fell open, and she pictured her father sitting at his desk, poring over the same words that now stared up at her.

"*Have faith, dearest.*" She attempted to thrust Jane's words from her mind. They refused to be ignored.

But hadn't she asked God repeatedly for his help? He either had not been listening or cared not. She slapped the Bible closed and flung it down beside her. How could trusting in a plan that might or might not exist bring her anything but heartache?

Tears welled. She'd considered every detail. But was she any closer to getting her way? Fighting for control had only cinched the noose tighter. Weary of fighting and planning, she wanted rest. She wanted to feel peace. Could it really be as simple as trusting God?

A rap on the door interrupted her thoughts. She bolted upright from the bed.

"Amelia, it is Helena!" Knuckles tapped the door again. "Open the door!"

Amelia did not move.

"Whatever's the matter with you?" Helena's voice held urgency. "Mr. Littleton is in a terrible state. I've not seen him like this before."

Amelia pressed her hand to her mouth, willing her cousin to leave.

"Amelia? Are you awake?" Helena jiggled the door's handle. A few long seconds of silence ensued, then Amelia heard the soft pat of Helena's slippers moving away from the door.

Amelia waited until she was sure Helena was gone before drawing the curtains for the night. Outside, clouds were gathering.

"I want to trust you, God. But I don't know how." Amelia's chin trembled. "If you have a plan for me, please make it known. I cannot do this alone."

⁂

William poured himself another glass of brandy and leaned his arm against the library mantel. "I'll tell you what you need, Graham, and that is a distraction."

Graham looked up from the letter he was writing and frowned. "No, what I need is to find a nurse for Lucy."

"Doesn't she have a nurse already? That Irish woman?"

"I can hardly hire Mrs. Dunne while she's employed by Miss Barrett. And I need to have someone in place before I bring Lucy here. The situation at Winterwood Manor is becoming untenable."

William took a long swig and shook his head. "Never did care for Littleton. Now I care for him even less. And to think I was even considering selling him the west fields."

Graham lifted an eyebrow. "I think you'd be wise not to enter into any agreement with that fellow."

"No doubt you are right." William dragged his fingers along the fireplace's fluted lintel, then pushed himself away from the mantel. "But back to the distraction I was speaking of. Jonathan Riley over at Wharton Park is hosting a hunting party on his grounds. Nothing extravagant, just gentlemen who like to follow the hounds and fancy some cards and a drink or two afterward. I depart in the morning and will likely stay a few days. Riley's estate is only an hour or so away by horseback. Join us."

Graham considered the offer. The idea of a few days spent in mindless diversion tempted him. But too much of his youth had been wasted away in "distraction." He had left such pastimes locked in his past, and he was not about to revisit them. "Thanks, but no. I've things to do."

"Suit yourself. I still think it would do you good."

William moved to exit the room, but changed his mind and dropped into a chair. "Of course, it is none of my business, but it seems a shame that Miss Barrett's marrying Littleton. She's so attached to Lucy that she would probably marry you just to keep the child with her. If Littleton was as disrespectful as you claim, she'd probably be grateful for it."

Graham turned toward William, suspicious that he might have somehow heard about Miss Barrett's proposal. But William's expression was innocent. "You think a woman would marry a man just for a child?"

William shrugged and propped his boot over his other leg. "Maybe not most women. But Miss Barrett is wealthy in her own right, so she has no need to concern herself with the sorts of things that motivate other women." He brushed at his coat. "I would've asked her myself, but I believe at one point in the not-so-distant past, she referred to me as a self-absorbed blubbering idiot. Not exactly a match ordained in heaven."

Graham chuckled. Miss Barrett was indeed a woman who would speak her mind. He could almost hear the words slip from her lips. "Well, she's engaged to Littleton, and I've no intention of marrying. So that is that."

William slapped his knee. "Wise man. I've no desire to be saddled, myself. Well, maybe for the fortune that would come with the likes of Miss Barrett, but you understand." He stood and grabbed his riding crop from the corner of the desk. "I'm leaving after breakfast, should you change your mind about Wharton."

"I've no intention of marrying." Graham's own words resounded in his head as his brother took his leave. Was that the truth?

He refused to leave Lucy in a questionable environment when he rejoined his crew. So far, every option he had tried had proved unsatisfactory, and he would need to report back to his ship within the month. The only person he trusted with his daughter at the moment was Miss Barrett. And she had named her price.

Graham studied the edge of a book on the desk without really seeing it. Amelia Barrett. Headstrong, determined, intriguing Amelia Barrett. Her passion was contagious, her dedication admirable. And the thought of Edward Littleton harming her sickened him.

He opened the desk for a piece of paper and grabbed the quill from its holder. He prided himself on being a man of swift, sure decisions. Once his decision was made, he would not waver.

He flexed his hand, dipped the quill in ink, and began to write. "Dear Miss Barrett . . ."

9

Edward's hot breath grazed Amelia's cheek. "My temper got the better of me, dearest." He cupped her shoulder, then ran his hand down her arm, smoothing the thin cambric sleeve. He paused at her wrist and then lifted it to his lips. "I'm sorry. You forgive me, do you not?"

Amelia didn't move. His eyes, dark as coffee, bored into her, as if spying on her soul. A few months ago she would have believed his repeated attempts at contrition. Now his empty pleas echoed hollow.

"Come, let's not quarrel." He caressed her cheek. "We'll be married soon, and none of these petty details will matter."

What choice did she have? He was bigger, stronger, and would soon be Winterwood's master. She squeezed the lie through her teeth. "I forgive you."

A triumphant smile lit his handsome face. "Good."

She eased away from him and pretended to study the view out the window. Sounds of the servants packing the carriage carried from the drive. "How long do you intend to stay in London?"

"Eager for me to return, are you?" His grin was almost a smirk. "I plan to be gone a fortnight, give or take a day or so. Then I shall be here for good."

Thunder growled. "You'd best not delay here too long. I fear the heavens will open up on you."

Uncle George's voice entered the drawing room before he did. The older man slapped a heavy hand on Edward's shoulder. "Are you off, my boy?"

Edward bowed slightly and then turned to acknowledge Aunt Augusta as she sauntered in behind her husband. "Yes, sir. Best be off before the rain starts and the roads get muddy, eh?"

Uncle George's raspy laughter filled the room. "To be sure. Blasted rain."

"We'll miss you at the morning service, Mr. Littleton." Aunt Augusta's lips curved in a trite smile as she handed Edward his scarf. "Our family's pew will not be the same without your company."

James, the butler, stepped forward and extended a black beaver hat. Edward took it and tucked it under his arm, then led the way out to the carriage. The servants lined the drive to see their guest off. Edward barked instructions to the driver and then turned back to his soon-to-be family. He bowed. "Farewell, then."

A sigh of relief slipped from Amelia's lips as she watched the carriage start down the drive. She had never been quite so happy to see a carriage depart.

❧

Graham tapped his fingertips against the oak pew. The very sight of the worn wood summoned long-forgotten memories.

White. His mother always wore white on Sundays. He shut his eyes, forcing the recollection to subside.

Cold air rushed through the window across the aisle, carrying with it the scent of impending rain, and a rare shiver shook him. He shouldn't have come to this service. He was a relative stranger in the area. He didn't belong to this parish. But something had drawn him to church on this November Sunday.

Something . . . or somebody.

As the vicar's voice echoed off the stone walls and stained glass windows, his gaze drifted toward the Barrett pew. Littleton was absent. Next to Amelia Barrett sat her cousin and aunt and uncle. And nestled in Miss Barrett's arms was his little Lucy. Her eyes were closed in slumber, and even from this distance he could see the soft flush of her cheeks and the pink of her parted lips. Downy titian hair curled from under her bonnet in bright contrast to her pale skin. There was no doubting Lucy was Katherine's daughter.

Graham's chest tightened. The babe did not yet recognize him as her father. The reception she'd given him during his last visit to Winterwood was evidence of that. But perhaps over time she would grow to accept him, perhaps even love him.

He should have been listening to the homily, but his eyes drifted to Miss Barrett's face. He studied the creamy smoothness of her skin, the becoming slope of her narrow nose, and the luster of the golden curls that framed her face. A gown of buff cambric with a gossamer overlay hugged her shoulders, and a lace chemisette gathered at her neck. Her startling bright eyes were fixed firmly on the vicar. She was a beautiful woman indeed.

Not wishing to be caught in his stare, he returned his attention to the vicar as well. Graham had arrived late and barely made it to his family's pew before the sermon started. Miss Barrett had nodded a greeting, but no smile had curved her lips, no warmth had lit her eyes.

How would she react to the letter?

He pulled out Miss Barrett's book of Psalms from his breast pocket and set it on the pew. He slipped his finger under the cover and flipped it open, making sure his letter was still tucked inside. He would give her the book after the service, and then what would be would be.

After the dismissal, Graham stood up quickly to leave, but two elderly ladies who had been friends with his mother wanted to speak to him. By the time he said good-bye, the Barretts were gone. He wove through the pews and then, once outside, the headstones, his boots sinking into the soft turf as he hurried to catch up. Miss Barrett's back was to him, and Lucy, now awake, eyed him warily over her guardian's shoulder. Graham believed he saw a flash of recognition in the child's eyes, and she waved a fist in the air. At Lucy's movement, Miss Barrett turned around, her expression unreadable.

"Captain Sterling."

Graham bowed to the women and nodded at Mr. Barrett. "I see Lucy is well."

"Indeed." Amelia adjusted the child on her hip.

Graham extended a hand toward the child and caressed her cheek with his fingers. She smiled at him, giggled, and buried her face into Miss Barrett's neck.

Suddenly aware of all the Barrett eyes on him, he pulled the book from his pocket.

"My Psalms!" Miss Barrett's countenance lightened, and she adjusted Lucy in her arms before reaching for it. "I have looked everywhere for this! Wherever did you find it?"

"Next to Katherine's grave. Your name is written in it."

She rewarded him with a smile. "Thank you for returning it. This was my mother's. I would have missed it profoundly."

An awkward pause followed her words, and he shifted his hat from one hand to the other. "Well then, I shall be by for a visit tomorrow. If that is agreeable to you, of course."

He bowed, smiled at Lucy, replaced his hat, and turned back down the pebble path.

Would she notice his note tucked in the book? He had no way to know. But if all went well, he would not have to wait long to find out.

⸖

Amelia peered out through the carriage's clear pane as Captain Sterling's tall form cut through the cemetery toward Darbury's main road. She'd been surprised to see him at church. His brother never attended services. She'd assumed that the captain held similar views.

Even more surprising, despite her lingering anger over his plan to remove Lucy from Winterwood, was the peculiar quivering of her heart. Part of her wanted to call out to him, "Wait! Do not go!" But a curious peace settled over her as the memory of her brief prayer the previous night filled her mind.

Her aunt's commentary on Mrs. Mill's Sunday attire filled the carriage on the short ride back to Winterwood Manor. Rain now fell in waves and pounded the sides of the carriage. She and Lucy had nearly pitched forward out of her seat when the storm hit and a gust of wind slammed the back of the carriage. But the rest of the ride proved uneventful. Lucy slumped comfortably against her arm while Amelia thumbed through the pages of the book of Psalms, happy to have her treasured item back. But as she did, her finger caught on something. Tucked among the pages was a folded piece of parchment.

A letter! Amelia snapped the book shut. She cast a glance to her cousin and then her aunt to see if anyone had noticed. Her ears rang. Her pulse raced.

The carriage drew to a painfully slow halt in front of Winterwood. Amelia muttered something about delivering Lucy to Mrs. Dunne, and once she had done so, hurried to her bedchamber. She flung the door closed behind her and dropped to the bed.

Her fingers, cold and shaking, couldn't work fast enough as she broke the seal and devoured the words.

> *Dear Miss Barrett,*
>
> *Forgive my indiscretion. I must speak with you privately. Please do me the honor of meeting with me at the Sterling cemetery Sunday evening at dusk.*
>
> *Respectfully, Graham Sterling*

Amelia's mind reeled as she dropped the letter to her lap. No real gentleman would dare invite a woman to a private location unchaperoned. She caught her breath. Unless, that is, he had decided to accept her offer.

Anticipation swelled within her. Could this be an answer to her feeble little prayer? She swung around her room in a sudden burst of energy as every possible scenario flew through her mind. What if Captain Sterling had found another home for Lucy and wanted to tell her in person. What if he was taking Lucy with him to Plymouth? Amelia stared at the letter for so long that his strokes no longer made sense. The words were just scratches, their fine lines and marks nothing more than the drag of a quill over the rough paper.

The hours before sunset crept by at an eternity's pace. Amelia sought amusement, but the tasks that typically would bring distraction—reading, watercolor, needlework—failed to hold her attention. Even playing with Lucy failed to calm her restlessness. While the baby napped, she had walked through Winterwood's dormant gardens, glad for the solitude they afforded her.

Finally the sun peeked from behind parting clouds and began its descent behind the moors, and mauve streaks painted the evening sky. If she intended to meet the captain, now was the time to take her leave.

Calm. She must stay calm. She pulled a heavy burgundy cape from her wardrobe and paused at the looking glass. She smoothed her hair and pinched her cheeks, then stopped short when she noticed her father's Bible still lying on her desk.

She couldn't deny the irony. Last night she had lain on her bed, all hope gone. She had cried out to God, and today hope had returned.

She hesitated. It could be coincidence. Or it could be something more.

She dragged her fingertip over the Bible's worn cover. What if God said no?

But what if he said yes?

She let the cape fall to the bed. Today's prayer came more easily than last night's. *God, I felt your peace today. My faith lacks strength. I fear it may never be like Jane's or Katherine's. But I would like to try. Please help me learn to lean on you. To trust in your plan, and not my own.*

10

Black trees lined the east meadow, separating it from the Sterling cemetery. Their gnarled limbs, like bony fingers, reached into swirling fog. Wind whistled through their bare branches, urging Amelia on. Moisture dripped down from the branches and soaked the hem of her gown. She clutched her cape and squinted into the deepening darkness, keeping close to the tree line.

Upon reaching the cemetery gate, Amelia paused to make sure no one watched her, then pushed her way through the entrance. She spotted the captain immediately, sitting on the bench next to Katherine's grave. His hat was pulled low over his eyes, and even through the bulkiness of his greatcoat, his shoulders created a strong silhouette.

"Miss Barrett." He jumped to his feet and swept his hat from his head.

Had shadows not hidden his features, she might not have noticed the rich timbre to his voice. Scents of sandalwood and leather surrounded him. "Captain."

He motioned for her to sit. "Thank you for meeting me. I know these circumstances are unusual. Forgive me."

Amelia lifted the hood from her head and let it fall back against her cape. "It could not be helped, Captain. I was most grateful to receive your message."

She waited for him to speak, straining to hear above the whistling wind and the wild pulsing of her heart.

"I need to speak with you about Lucy." Captain Sterling sat down beside her. "I have decided where she will live when I return to my duties."

Amelia held her breath.

He leaned his elbows on his knees and looked at her with intense gray eyes. "She must live with you."

Had she heard him correctly? "Are you saying—"

He lifted a gloved hand. "Before we go any further, I need to know that you fully understand the implications."

"What do you mean?"

He tented his fingers and stared at them. "Your uncle is a proud man, Miss Barrett. Have you considered the consequences of going against his wishes?"

She lowered her gaze, now grateful for the darkness.

He continued, his voice low. "I don't mean to upset you, but I must, in good conscience, advise you to consider all outcomes. I must leave in a few weeks. You will be on your own to deal with any repercussions at Winterwood."

She chose her words thoughtfully. "You must believe me that I have played this out in my mind many times. I certainly do not anticipate an easy transition. My uncle, no doubt, wishes to maintain some control of my inheritance. I imagine my aunt is more concerned with what damage this might do to Helena's chances of finding a suitable match than with my happiness. So I do not doubt there will be uncomfortable moments between us, but I believe they will come around in time. They are, after all, my family, and Helena and I have been like sisters."

He stepped closer to the bench, rolling his hat in his hands. "It's not just your family, Miss Barrett. Edward Littleton is a volatile man. Are you prepared for his reaction?"

Amelia drew an unsteady breath. This, indeed, was what concerned her most. She'd once believed, despite Edward's ambition and his unpredictability, that he was a kindhearted man. Only recently had she seen his cruel side, his selfish disregard for anyone's desires but his own.

A sharp wind gust swept in, catching the folds of her cape in its billows. She settled her cape and wrapped it tightly. "I thought that Edward Littleton loved me, but time has opened my eyes to his true motivations. My inheritance, Captain Sterling, is no secret. Edward will be livid, to be sure, if I break our engagement, but it will be because he lost money, not because he lost me. And to answer your question, I do fear his reaction, initially at least, but he is a proud man. I believe, knowing Edward's nature as I do, that he will prefer to avoid scandal and will not publicize the news."

Captain Sterling studied her face. His presence did not unnerve her as it once did. But even under the cover of darkness, she feared too many of her thoughts would write themselves on her expression.

He sat down next to her on the bench, so close she could feel the warmth radiating from his body. "And the money?"

Reality returned with a vengeance. The money. "What of it?"

"If we proceed with this course of action, I am well aware of what will be said. But let it be known that I do not need your money, nor do I desire the trials that can accompany a large fortune." He lowered his voice. "I do not tell you this out of pride, Miss Barrett. My profession is a dangerous one. I may very well leave Darbury and never return, so I need to know my daughter will be cared for.

That she will be loved. I trust you in this regard, but it is important that you trust me in return. Your money is yours. I will not touch it. Just care for my daughter."

Her eyebrows shot up. Had she heard him correctly? For as long as she could remember, she'd been told her fortune was the key to finding a suitable match. She could only mutter, "Thank you."

He stood up from the bench and looked at her for a long moment. She shifted under the weight of his stare. A smile finally crossed his face.

"Well then." Captain Sterling knelt and picked up her hand from her lap. She jumped at the intimacy of the touch.

"Amelia Barrett, would you do me the honor of becoming my wife?"

⚜

Amelia closed the door without a sound and stood perfectly still, listening to make sure the servants were not about. Once certain that she was alone, she leaned her forehead against the door's rough wood and squeezed her eyes shut.

Her body shivered from cold, and her wet cape clung uncomfortably to her limbs. Was this really going to happen? Renewed excitement surged through her body, dancing in her stomach. She would marry Captain Sterling and be free from Edward. Most importantly, Lucy would be with her always. She whirled around in the shadowed vestibule and allowed her hood to fall to her shoulders. Not even the dampness of her clothes or the chill in her bones could quench the joy in her heart.

Faint moonlight slid through a tiny window on the staircase. She gathered her skirts and started up the stairs, pausing at the narrow window and peering through the wavy glass. She watched the captain's black silhouette stride toward Sterling Wood and disappear into the night's murky mist. A strange sensation danced in her stomach. Despite her protests, Captain Sterling had insisted on seeing her back to Winterwood. Never before had she walked alone with a man, let alone in the quiet of dark. She knew it was improper. But it didn't *feel* improper.

As quietly as she could, she continued up the servants' staircase. Every creak in the ancient wooden stairs made her pause. Amelia considered climbing higher still to Lucy's chamber. How she wanted to scoop the child in her arms and never let her go. Now she could be certain that Lucy would never be alone and would be loved always. She would not know the pain of a motherless childhood. Amelia just had to wait a little longer, until the captain returned from obtaining the license for them to wed. But she reminded herself to remain cautious. Much could happen in that time.

Deciding against waking the baby, Amelia stopped at the landing next to her bedchamber and peeked down the hall. Quiet. All of Winterwood was asleep. She moved to her door and cracked it open just far enough to slip through. The fire the maid had laid earlier had died down to embers, and she blinked, allowing her eyes to adjust to the faint glow. Tossing her cape on the chair next to the door, she turned around toward the bed and jumped to see a dark form sitting there.

"Where have you been?" hissed Helena. "I had a devil of a time trying to come up with a believable excuse for you. Are you even aware of the hour?"

Amelia jumped. "Helena, you frightened me. What on earth are you doing in here, sitting in the dark? You should be asleep."

"As should you, dear Cousin." Helena's dry tone hinted at emotion simmering just below the surface. She crossed her arms over her chest. "You failed to answer my question. Where have you been?"

Amelia's elation faded to discomfort. She reached for a candle on the small table next to her bed. A halfhearted excuse would not satisfy Helena, and the captain had asked her to keep their agreement secret until they could speak to her family together. "I needed some air."

"Air?" Helena prodded. "It's raining. It's cold. You have been out in the weather this entire time? Alone?"

Awkward silence hovered between the women. Amelia leaned down to the fireplace to light the candle from its dying embers. "Damp air is the best."

A flame flared on the tallow candle's wick, and Amelia rose. As she turned to place the light on its stand, Helena lifted her hand. A small parchment letter rested between two fingers.

The captain's note!

Amelia lunged forward and snatched it. "Where did you find this?"

"It appears you weren't entirely alone."

Amelia could not mask the defensive tone of her voice. "I don't know why you act so surprised. I made you fully aware of my intentions, and now you are surprised that I am following through with them."

"Yes, you told me your intentions, but I never in my wildest dreams expected you to act on them, especially after what happened in the drawing room the first day Captain Sterling arrived. Have you no shame, Amelia? How could you do this to Edward? He loves you, and this is how you acknowledge his regard?"

"Loves me? Quite the contrary, Helena. Edward loves Winterwood, and the fortune that goes with it." She paused, carefully choosing her words. She'd been mistaken to take Helena into her confidence on this matter. How she missed the old Helena, her beloved companion. "This situation, and whom I choose to marry, is not your concern."

A pained expression flashed across Helena's delicate features, but she straightened and lifted her chin. "Is that so? Well then, I fault myself entirely for the misunderstanding. I'll not deny our relationship has changed over the past several months, but I thought you might care to know my thoughts on something as important as your future husband."

Helena's argument fanned Amelia's frustration. Nobody knew better than Helena how to twist words to their advantage. How could she make Helena see beyond Edward's façade? "Helena, don't be absurd. Of course I value your opinion. But you must trust that I know Edward's character better than you do, and I am acutely aware of the possible repercussions of my actions."

Helena tossed her russet braid over her shoulder. "Have you really considered what will be said if you cut Edward loose now? Father will be furious. Surely you don't expect me to lie to him and pretend that—"

"I'm not asking you to lie. Can't you see what I am trying to do? Can't you see why this is important? I promised Katherine—"

Helena jumped up from the bed, her fists balled at her sides. "Will you stop falling back on that excuse?" Helena's sudden passion on the subject caught Amelia off guard, rendering her almost speechless. "Are you prepared to throw away your reputation, your chance at happiness, your very future, for someone else's child? For a promise made when your sensibilities were weakened with grief?"

Amelia took Helena's hand in hers, half expecting her to pull it away. She did not. "I know you don't understand what I am doing, but trust me. And as far as Edward is concerned, believe me when I say that he is not the man he professes to be."

Now Helena jerked her hand away. "Unbelievable. How quickly you turn on those who care for you." She pushed past Amelia and headed toward the door.

"Where are you going?"

"To bed." She stopped at the threshold, placed her hand on the knob, and turned back to Amelia. "But know this, Amelia Barrett. I will no longer be party to this misguided plan of yours. You are on your own."

Amelia put her hand on the door. "You must tell no one of this, Helena. Not yet. Please."

Helena hesitated. "I will not, for I hope you will have a change of heart. But do not forget, Amelia, that I, too, hope to marry one day soon. What will happen when news gets out that my own cousin called off her engagement so close to the date? We—I—will be the joke of society. I'll have little chance of an advantageous match if my family is involved in such scandal."

Without waiting for a response, Helena left.

Amelia's ears rang. She didn't know whether to be angry or hurt. But as Amelia stared at the empty space where Helena had been, she realized the truth to her cousin's words. The repercussions would certainly extend to those closest to her, and Helena might well suffer most from the consequences of Amelia's actions. The thought of causing her cousin pain brought a pang of regret, but Amelia was too far down the path for a change of heart now. She had no choice but to marry the captain.

After returning Captain Sterling's note to her book of Psalms, she peeled the damp dress from her body and pulled her nightdress over her head. She curled up next to her fireplace and, with her poker, prodded the fire back to life. Unease and uncertainty pushed at the joy in her heart. She stared unblinking at the leaping flames.

Dear God, I have done the right thing . . . have I not?

11

With buoyant steps, Graham strode out of the Doctor's Commons building in London. His journey had been long and tiring, but well worth the effort.

The need to minimize scandal and the delicate time frame made it impractical to wait for wedding banns to be read, so a special license from the Archbishop of Canterbury was the only viable option for marrying Miss Barrett. Unfortunately, Edward Littleton had announced plans to obtain a special license for himself within the next few weeks, and Littleton was currently in London on business. Concern that the man might already have applied for the license had nagged Graham every mile of the journey from Darbury. But the application process had proceeded without a hitch. He had beaten Littleton to the punch.

With the special license in hand, Graham and Miss Barrett could now be wed at any time, by any member of the clergy. He only hoped he could return to Darbury and marry Miss Barrett before Mr. Littleton paid his own visit to the Archbishop's offices and learned what had transpired.

Graham waited for a barouche to pass before stepping into the cobbled streets, dodging a heap of straw that had fallen from a passing wagon. London's labyrinth of avenues stretched out in unfamiliar twists, but he'd memorized the way to his hotel. It was just a short distance away. He'd walk.

Rounding the corner to Bracket Street, he nearly tripped over a small boy. Soot smudged the child's cheek, and ragged clothes hung limp on his scrawny frame. He stopped Graham with his expressive brown eyes and extended his cap. Graham stared at him for several seconds before realizing he wanted money.

Three weeks before, Graham might have walked past the urchin with little thought. Today thoughts of Lucy made him pause. This boy was someone's child. He fished in his pocket, pulled out some coins, and dropped them into the hat. The boy peered in, and a smile spread ear to ear. He turned and, like a shot from a cannon, disappeared into the sea of horses, carts, and people.

Graham allowed himself a gratified smile. He had helped a child and found a satisfactory arrangement for his own little one as well. All was going well. In just a short time—a week or two at most—he could return to his ship with a clear mind.

Graham wove through the throng of people who had braved the chill of the day, pausing once to allow a group of ladies to pass. His thoughts transitioned from his daughter to his soon-to-be bride and from there to his late wife.

Eighteen months had passed since he last saw Katherine, and even then, their time together had been brief. He had loved her with unequaled passion, but if he were to add up all the time he spent in her company, it came to less than six months. Indeed, the passing of time had made her seem more like a lovely memory than flesh and blood.

During those many months at sea, he had often imagined the

life they would share—a life free of war and struggle. He had feared that battle might claim his life before then, never dreaming that hers would be cut short. But she was gone, along with all his hopes for their life together. Lately when he envisioned his future, he saw Lucy. And now, Miss Barrett.

As the days crept by, he was growing accustomed to the idea of marrying once again. But he still must guard himself. As Amelia had reminded him many times, this was an arrangement, not a romance. He could not—would not—begin to think of her in such an impractical way.

He straightened his hat and turned down Binkton Street. He needed to rest well tonight. It was a long way back to Darbury. And he had a stop to make along the way.

⚜

Weary from days of travel and lost in the unfamiliar streets of Sheffield, Graham almost passed Henry Carrington's door completely. He backtracked and rapped on the door. Within seconds an elderly man appeared.

"Captain Graham Sterling to see Mr. Carrington."

The butler ushered Graham through a narrow hallway to a small office. Graham ducked to miss the library's low threshold and sidestepped to miss a haphazard pile of empty crates. Burgundy paper covered the walls, and thick brocade drapes blocked out the day's light. Only a single sliver of light pressed through the curtains, illuminating tiny specks of dust hovering in the air.

At the butler's announcement, Mr. Carrington looked up from behind an untidy stack of papers and fixed startling blue eyes on Graham. The old man's gaze traveled from the top of Graham's head to the brass buttons on his tailcoat to his gray pantaloons and Hessian boots. He pushed his spectacles down on his nose and squinted, making no attempt to hide his assessment. His gruff voice cracked the silence. "Captain Sterling. Come in."

Graham stepped over a sleeping bloodhound and moved to the desk. "Thank you for seeing me on such short notice."

Carrington nodded toward a carved chair. "Pay no heed to the crates. Moving from one town to another is maddening business. Sit down there."

Graham followed the man's instruction, removing a dust cloth from the back of the chair before sitting.

Carrington leaned back in his chair and folded his arms across his chest. "What can I do for you?"

"I'm here to discuss Winterwood Manor."

Carrington waved a dismissive hand and dropped his spectacles to his desk. "Any discussions related to Winterwood Manor will need to be addressed to George Barrett or Edward Littleton. I no longer manage its affairs."

"Actually, Littleton is one of the reasons I am here." Graham waited for the man to look back up from his papers before proceeding. "There's been a change of plans regarding the future of the estate."

The man's unkempt eyebrows lifted. "You have my attention, Captain Sterling."

Graham slid the letter confirming his license application from his leather satchel and held it in the air. "I've just applied for a marriage license."

Carrington chuckled. "Getting married, are you?"

"Yes. To Miss Amelia Barrett."

The old man jerked. His smirk dissolved. He pushed himself back in his chair, and a very different sort of smile crossed his round face. "Well, this is interesting. Interesting indeed. What happened to Littleton?"

Graham opened his mouth to speak, then snapped it shut. The less said, the better. "Let us say that circumstances intervened."

Carrington slapped his hand on the desk. "I'm glad to hear it. Littleton's a rogue." His proclamation echoed off the plaster ceiling and caused the bloodhound to lift his head. "A blackguard, he is, not fit to muck Winterwood's stables, let alone be its master."

Graham would have enjoyed nothing more than a thorough discussion of Littleton's shortcomings, but he held his tongue and returned the letter to the satchel. "Miss Barrett and I will wed as soon as possible, and I will return to my duties shortly thereafter. We will need someone to manage Winterwood's affairs, and Miss Barrett trusts you. I'd like to reinstate you as steward. You will, of course, be able to take up residence again at the estate cottage whenever you are in Darbury. Is that satisfactory?"

"It is, sir. I must say I am gratified to hear of these developments. You will of course let me know if there is anything I can help you with in the meantime."

Graham stood and held out his hand. "I'll not keep you any longer. I'll be in touch in the next few days with further instructions."

Carrington stood, stepped over the sleeping dog, and completed the handshake. "Of course."

"Good." Graham turned to leave, then turned back. "This is not public information yet. It's crucial you keep this news to yourself for a few days."

"Will do, Captain. I am at your service."

12

Graham quickened his pace as he rounded the corner to Winterwood's east lawn. Skeletons of rosebushes lined the walk, and his tailcoat caught on the bare, spindly branches. Shells of leaves crunched beneath each footfall as he approached the massive house. He allowed his mind to settle on a thought he had not yet dared to entertain: within the next couple of weeks, he would become master of Winterwood Manor.

The magnitude of such a role had yet to sink in. Ever since he left Eastmore Hall as a lad to make his way in the world, he had accepted that his profession would center around life at sea. He excelled at it and, yes, he enjoyed it. His plan had been to earn enough so that he and Katherine could live out their years comfortably. He had done well enough for himself, but the fortune connected with the Winterwood estate made his wages and prize money pale in comparison.

For the time being, honor and experience bound him to his ship. But should he survive the war, would he continue in his profession or return here—to Lucy, to Amelia Barrett, and to this magnificent house?

A quick glance up at the rolling sky and a threatening clap of thunder made him regret his decision to leave his oilcloth coat at Eastmore Hall. With his still-nameless horse in the care of a groomsman, Graham was eager to get inside. At the main entrance, the butler took his hat and gloves and showed him to the library. No fire blazed in the black marble fireplace—odd for this time of year.

Miss Barrett's smile, however, more than made up for the lack of warmth afforded by a fire. "Captain Sterling!"

Graham bowed toward Miss Barrett before turning his attention to Lucy, who perched on her nurse's hip. He smiled at Lucy, who regarded him with indifference. He straightened. At least she did not cry. Then she grinned and waved a paintbrush in the air.

He laughed. "Been painting, have you, Lucy?"

She waved it again and held it out to him. He went to take it from her, and she snatched it back, giggling and looking proudly at Miss Barrett.

"You tricked me." He chuckled. "Will you come to your papa today, or is it still too soon for that?"

He expected the baby to grab on to Mrs. Dunne in protest, but she did not withdraw as he closed the space between them. "Well, this is progress!" He lifted her from her nurse's arms. "See now, I'm not quite as bad as all that, am I?"

Graham bounced his daughter and kissed her cheek. He looked up, suddenly aware of the two women's eyes on him. "Miss Barrett, I was hoping to speak with you further about Lucy's living arrangement."

"Oh yes, of course. Mrs. Dunne, would you be so kind as to take Lucy to the nursery? I will follow soon."

Mrs. Dunne dropped a wordless curtsy, her prominent brown eyes assessing him boldly as she took Lucy in her arms.

Once the pair left, Miss Barrett stepped to the door, popped her head out in the hall, and then pushed the door closed before returning. She turned, her face flushed. "We shan't be disturbed. Uncle George is out, and Helena and Aunt Augusta are calling on the Mills."

"And Littleton?"

Her lovely smile faded. "He is still in London, or so we presume. We expect his return within the week."

Her pink gown made her cheeks appear even rosier than normal, but that was not what first drew his attention. A baggy canvas smock protected the front of her dress, stained with paints of every shade. Was his betrothed an artist?

Her easel faced away from him, so he sidestepped her to view her work.

No, definitely not an artist.

He nodded toward her smock. "It appears you managed to get more paint on your smock than on your easel."

She giggled, an unguarded, happy sound that he had not heard from her until now. His gaze drifted from her golden tresses to her sparkling sky-blue eyes to the curve of her neck. After months at sea with only men for company, one tended to underestimate the effect a beautiful woman could have on a man. The weight of her gaze rendered him a fool and momentarily speechless.

She frowned at the easel. "My painting leaves much to be desired, I fear."

"Perhaps a little."

"Captain Sterling!" she exclaimed with mock offense. "How can you tease me so?"

He laughed. It had been so long since a genuine laugh rumbled his chest that he'd forgotten its releasing power. "What is the subject of your painting?"

"You cannot tell?" She pointed out the window. "See that grove of elms and aspens just beyond the box hedge?"

"Oh. I see." The uneven strokes on the page bore little likeness to the vast landscape framed by the window. "Hm, where's your brush?"

She blinked at him. "What?"

"Your paintbrush." His gaze swept across her collection of watercolors and rags. A brush rested on the easel's edge. He took it in his hand.

"Why, Captain Sterling," she said. "I didn't know you were a painter."

"I'm not."

She stood very close to him, so close that the sweet scent of lavender danced around him. He adjusted the brush. It seemed too tiny for his thick fingers to maneuver, but he dipped it in green paint and pressed the bristles against the canvas. For a brief moment, Amelia's gaze fell on the scar on his hand. His jaw relaxed when she looked away again.

He cared little for painting. In fact, he hadn't stood before an easel since school days. But if pretending to be interested in art kept a genuine smile on Amelia Barrett's face, he would learn to like it.

A long, curly lock of Amelia's hair slipped from its comb. She lifted a hand to return it to its place, and as she did her arm brushed his. The realization that he was enjoying his time with her made him almost uncomfortable, as if he were breaking a code of honor.

He was grateful for her abrupt change of topic. "How was London?"

"Productive. I stopped in Sheffield on the way back and spoke with Carrington."

She looked up. "What had he to say?"

"He has agreed to resume his duties of steward and will change his residence—for the second time in a fortnight—back to his cottage here on the grounds. Good thing. I'd be no help in any matter related to running an estate."

Amelia untied her smock and hung it on a small peg near the easel, her eyes diverted. "And the special license?"

"I have it in my satchel."

She bit her lip as if calculating the significance of his statement. "So that means, um, that we can, well—"

"Be wed?" he finished her sentence.

A vibrant, becoming hue colored her cheeks.

"Yes." He leaned down to the leather satchel at his foot, amused at her sudden display of shyness. After all, had she not been the person to suggest the union in the first place? He pulled out the document and placed it in her ungloved hand. She balanced the weightless vellum on her fingertips and read the words. Her full name, Amelia Jane Barrett, on one line. His full name, Graham Canton Sterling, on another.

"We may be married any day, anytime, by any member of the clergy. And in my opinion, the sooner the better." Graham adjusted the satchel at his foot and then straightened. "Have you given any thought as to when we will inform Littleton?"

Her head jerked up. "We?" She lowered the license. "No, no. If it is all the same to you, I think I should be the one to tell him. Alone."

"Nonsense." He assessed her face, certain she must jest, but the firm set of her jaw told him otherwise. "I'll not allow you to bear the brunt of such an interaction alone. After all, this is as much my decision as it is yours. He will be angry, to be sure, but he can take the matter up with me, not my betrothed."

Graham snapped his mouth shut as the last word slid from his lips. *Betrothed.* The word echoed in the paneled room. He cleared his throat before speaking. "We'll need two witnesses."

Gone was the unguarded Miss Barrett. She appeared distracted, her eyes not leaving the license. "Witnesses? Yes. Of course. Mrs. Hammond, the vicar's wife."

"My brother can be a witness as well." He stood up. "We'll need to explain things to the vicar. What's his name?"

"Thomas Hammond."

He retrieved the license and slung the satchel over his shoulder. "I think it is best if we talk to your uncle first thing in the morning and let him know of our plans. Then we'll go explain the situation to the vicar. We'll deal with Littleton when the time comes."

Graham's eyes narrowed on her face. The sudden change in her demeanor concerned him. "Are you having second thoughts?"

"My dear Captain Sterling, I have never been more certain of anything in my life."

⚹

What exactly did William Sterling do all day?

Graham lowered the unread letter to his brother's desk, leaned back, and rubbed his hand over his chin. Silence engulfed the room. He was alone, and William was nowhere to be found.

Outside the library's only window, Graham's nameless horse pawed at the earth. The stable boy had saddled the animal and brought him around in anticipation of the ride Graham and William had planned for the afternoon.

Graham chuckled. What the beast lacked in elegance, he made up for in spirit. The animal's ears twitched. His restless tail swished from side to side.

I really should give the animal a name.

At that notion, he shook his head. He only planned to own the horse until he returned to Plymouth, where he would sell the animal before returning to sea. Or perhaps, once he was master of Winterwood, the animal could stay on there. Either way, the two of them would soon part ways.

He returned his attention to the letter from his first lieutenant.

He spread the wrinkled paper flat against the desk's leather insert and read the account of the ship repairs. Foster had written that everything was progressing according to plan, but that damages exceeded the initial estimations. An extra three weeks would be needed to repair the hull and the first deck before the battered vessel would once again be seaworthy.

Graham leaned his head against his laced fingers, attempting to push the memory of the battle—and the accompanying guilt— from his mind. Oddly, it was not the battle that had crippled his ship that haunted him, but one from well over a year ago. The American frigate had emerged from behind a curtain of misty fog, catching them off guard. Before he and his crew realized the ship was upon them, cannon fire sliced the hull. Water poured into the ship. The mast roared in flames.

Graham forced himself to look at the scar, now purple and tight, crossing the top of his hand and arm. He had been fortunate. Many members of his crew had not. And it had been his fault. All his fault.

He needed to respond to the letter. He glanced around the library, looking for paper. He pulled the top desk drawer open and rummaged through old letters. Nothing. He pushed the drawer shut and pulled open the one beneath it. Inside, a large book rested on top of loose papers.

Graham lifted out the leather-bound volume. The expert embossing adorning the cover reminded him of his father's ledger book. Memories of his father sitting at this very desk flooded his mind. He placed the book on the desk and lifted the cover. But William's writing, not his father's, covered the pages. Numbers. Figures. Names.

He flipped the parchment pages and skimmed the information. Never would he have guessed that such large sums of money flowed in and out of the estate. As he browsed the columns of more recent pages, it appeared that much more was streaming out than came in. He read down the list of names. James Creighton. Ernest Timmer. Who were they?

The nameless horse let out a loud whinny as raucous laughter wafted in from the front drive. Graham jerked his head up and slammed the book closed. *William.* He stuffed the book in the drawer and within seconds was out of the library and walking into the brisk afternoon air.

"There you are. I thought—"

Graham stopped short. William's bloodshot eyes glowed against his pale skin. A lopsided smile slid across his unshaven face. The smell of spirits drifted on the wind.

William piped a lazy laugh. He slipped from his horse's back, stumbling as his boots hit the ground. He patted at the horse. The animal sidestepped as William leaned his weight against the saddle.

Two mounted men accompanied William. They snickered, as if amused at their comrade's difficulty in the simple task of dismounting. From their slack posture and the disheveled state of their attire, Graham assumed they were involved in whatever his brother had been up to.

Graham grabbed the horse's bridle to steady the animal and waited for an explanation.

William giggled like a child as he found his footing and then straightened in an obvious attempt to hide the extent of his altered state.

"Gentlemen, meet my esteemed brother, Captain Graham Canton Sterling." William flung a wobbly arm in Graham's general direction. "He is the man defending the Crown while you and I keep commerce afloat on this hallowed isle." Then, in a sudden burst of amusement, he thrust his fist into the air in mock triumph. "Hail, the conquering hero!"

The men dissolved in laughter. William crumpled to the ground, still chortling hysterically.

Graham's nostrils flared at the blatant disrespect. On more than one occasion he'd come close to losing his life, and dozens of times he'd watched while men perished—all in pursuit of "defending the Crown."

Graham pitched William's horse's reins to the stable boy who had come round. He stepped into No-Name's stirrup and swung his leg over the saddle. He would not stay and watch this ridiculous display of intemperance. He didn't tolerate it in his crew, and he certainly wouldn't stand by and watch it in his own brother.

By the time William noticed his brother wasn't laughing, Graham had already circled No-Name around and was headed in the opposite direction. "Where you going?" William bellowed.

Graham ignored the jeers but did not attempt to hide his anger. How exactly was William keeping "commerce afloat"? He would reprimand his brother if he thought it would do any good. He'd pull him down from the horse and force him to listen, but to what end?

Graham clenched his jaw. He'd spent too many years in similar fashion. The price had been significant. By God's grace he had been able to conquer the vice of drink, but it appeared that William followed their father's footsteps in more ways than one.

He urged the horse into a canter and followed the tree line of Eastmore Wood. What he would give to be at sea again. The seafaring life held danger, true, especially in times of war, but at least on a ship he knew his place. His role. He knew who he was and where he belonged.

Being in Darbury reminded him of his childhood, which he wanted to forget, and Katherine, who would never be his again. Why would he ever want to stay here?

But as quickly as the thought entered his head, another thought, equally as persuasive, accompanied it.

Now the shore held Lucy. *His* Lucy. And Miss Amelia Barrett.

13

Amelia awoke with a start to the sound of shouting.

She threw off the thick quilt and paused, allowing her eyes a moment to adjust to the dying fire's faint light. She held her breath and listened.

Deep voices sounded from somewhere inside Winterwood's stone walls. She stood up and grabbed her dressing gown from the end of her bed.

Every sense tingled as she scurried across her chamber. Now fully awake, she cracked the paneled door to better hear the conversation's echo.

"Do you expect me to believe that?"

"Upon my honor, I had no idea, sir."

"Where is she?"

The words registered. Dread seized her and refused to allow her heart to beat. Her feet stayed fixed to the ground.

Edward!

She tried to force her mind into action, but her thoughts

sputtered. The patting of Helena's bare feet coming down the hallway snapped her from her trance.

"Whatever is going on?" Helena rubbed her arms over her shawl. "It's the middle of the night. Who is here?"

Now wasn't the time for secrets. All would be made known within hours—maybe minutes. "It's Edward. Who else could it be? Help me, Helena!" Amelia flew to her wardrobe and pulled out a gown. "Button this for me, will you?"

Before Helena could even respond, Amelia found her stays and draped her dress over her arm. Helena stared at her in rare silence.

"Helena, please! I can't lace this myself." She turned her back toward Helena and waited for her assistance.

Helena squeaked in protest, but as the yelling intensified, she complied. When Helena finished, Amelia flew to her writing desk and stood so her body blocked Helena's view. Her hand shook as she wrote.

Edward Littleton is here. I think he knows. Please come quickly. —AB

"What are you doing?"

Amelia barely heard Helena's words over her own thoughts. She folded the note, tucked it up her sleeve, and headed toward her chamber door. But Helena stepped in front of her, blocking the exit.

"I said, what are you doing?"

Amelia's shoulders tensed. "Very well. You might as well know. Captain Sterling and I are going to be wed. Apparently Edward has found out."

Amelia braced herself for Helena's dramatic retort, but one did not come. Instead, her cousin's voice sounded almost sad. "This is a mistake. You know it is. But maybe it's not too late. Mr. Littleton is not an unreasonable man, and—"

"No. I am resolved." Amelia reached for her shawl and turned to face her cousin. "You would not happen to know how he learned of the engagement, would you?"

Helena tightened her shawl around her shoulders, eyes wide. "How could you insinuate such a thing? Of course not. Where are you going?"

Amelia did not answer. She flew down the servants' stairs, leaving Helena standing in the hall. Blackness shrouded the lock of the servants' entrance. Her fingers shook and she fumbled with the key. Eventually the door opened, and Amelia sprinted toward the stables.

The lawn had never seemed so wide. Her bare feet slipped several times on the dewy grass. As she rounded the back corner of the mansion, she lost her footing and fell hard on her stomach, sliding over the wet turf. She ignored the pain, pushed herself up, and continued.

She arrived at the stables, gasping for air. A lantern lit the front half of the stable, where two stable boys were tending a gray gelding. *Edward's horse.*

"Peter!" She needed someone who was fast, and the younger of the two stable boys seemed the best choice. Obviously shocked at seeing his mistress in the middle of the night, he swept his hat from his head and stepped forward. "Yes, miss?"

She held the note out to the boy. "Take this as fast as you can to Eastmore Hall. Give it to Captain Sterling. Do not leave until you place it in his hand yourself. Do you hear me?"

The boy nodded his head emphatically. "Yes. Yes, miss."

She shooed him on. "Go. Go quickly, and be smart about it!"

Without another word, the boy pulled a horse from a nearby stall. Flinging himself on the animal's bare back, he disappeared into the black night.

She turned back to the house. From where she stood, she could barely see into the drawing room window. Faint light trickled from the opening, and a black figure moved across the space. Her heart thudded as she ran back across the lawn to the servants' entrance.

As soon as she opened the door, animated chatter reached her ears. She didn't see anyone, but it was clear the commotion had awakened the staff as well. She took the stairs at a very unladylike two-at-a-time pace until she reached her landing.

What she heard made her heart freeze. Footsteps stomped on the main stairs.

As if in a race, she bolted to her chamber. She dropped her wet shawl and grabbed a dry one, only now noticing the wet mud smeared across her front from her fall.

She didn't even have time to groan, for a knock on the door demanded her attention. "Amelia Barrett, open this door this instant."

Only Aunt Augusta. Amelia forced her breathing to slow before opening the chamber door. Her aunt pushed her way inside and grabbed Amelia's arm.

Amelia yanked free. "Let go of me!"

"Edward is downstairs. What have you done, you foolish girl?" Aunt Augusta pinched her lips together, waiting for Amelia's response.

Amelia straightened her spine, determined to stand her ground. "From your demeanor, I believe you already know the answer to that question."

Her aunt's rheumy eyes narrowed on her. "I do not know what you are trying to accomplish, but you listen to me. I will not allow you to ruin the future of this family. Of all the insolence! You will marry Edward."

Amelia bristled at the words. Of course her aunt had every right to be surprised and even angry, but the accusation in her tone only fueled Amelia's determination. "I've made no decision out of spite, Aunt. Lucy is my top priority, and I've made that clear since the moment she was born. I apologize for the effect that this has on you and Uncle and Helena, but I must consider my future. Lucy's future. And if you knew Edward as I do, you and Uncle would think twice before trusting him with any matter of significance."

Aunt Augusta's lips quivered with anger. "I am grateful for one thing and one thing alone. Praise the Almighty that your father is not alive to see the type of person you have become."

Those words stung more than Amelia cared to admit. What *would* her father think of this?

Her aunt's rant continued. "Regardless of whom you have so recklessly decided to marry, the sooner you are no longer a part of the Barrett family, the better."

Amelia forced her expression to remain stoic. She would not allow Aunt Augusta the satisfaction of seeing any emotion. If she allowed herself to become flustered, she might lose her composure when speaking with Edward.

"And look at the state of you, Amelia." Her aunt's gaze raked down the front of Amelia's gown. "What have you been doing?"

Amelia searched for an excuse, but none came. How could she admit that she had slipped in the mud to beg assistance of the stable boy?

Her aunt didn't wait for an explanation. "Well, you can't see Edward dressed like that. Heaven already knows what the man thinks." Her voice echoed flat. "Change your gown quickly, then come downstairs. You have some explaining to do."

A welcome silence settled over the room with her aunt's departure, and Amelia turned to the wardrobe to get a clean dress. When she turned back around, Helena stood in the empty space where her mother had been. Without a word, the younger cousin stepped forward to unbutton Amelia's soiled dress. Even with only the light from a single flickering candle, Amelia interpreted the sorrow on Helena's face.

As girls, Helena and Amelia had been inseparable. They had shared a governess, shared secrets, shared each other's company. Only in the last year had their relationship changed, for reasons Amelia still did not completely understand. "Please, Helena," she whispered, "don't hate me."

Helena buttoned the last button and rested her hand on Amelia's trembling shoulders. "I don't hate you." Emotion hung in her voice. "I don't understand you, but I could never hate you. Just remember, Cousin, that what we think we want may not always be best."

Helena offered a weak smile and stepped toward the door. Not convinced it would help ease the situation, Amelia breathed a desperate prayer, hoping that by some miracle she would find the right words to say to Edward.

"Fear not. I am with you."

Amelia's head jerked up. "What did you say?"

Confusion clouded Helena's features. "I didn't say anything. You'd better hurry. Mother is furious."

Amelia smoothed her dress and ran shaky fingers through her tangled hair. Her gaze landed on the Bible on her bedside table. Could it be?

"I am with you."

❦

Helena squeezed Amelia's hand as they descended the wide staircase. Below them, Amelia could hear her uncle and Edward speaking, but at least they were no longer shouting.

Amelia willed herself not to buckle under her mounting fear of what Edward was capable of. She was resolved in her decision and would not waver, but confidence in her ability to convince anyone in her family had waned. She could no longer rely on their support.

She breathed a prayer, then repeated it, desperate to believe God would answer. And in spite of her uncertainty, she felt her tense muscles relax. She lifted her chin, feeling stronger and more determined than she had in days.

Flickering light spilled from her uncle's study. Moving figures within the room cast animated shadows on the oak floor of the vestibule. She paused and listened.

Edward's voice reached her ear first. "What of Winterwood, then? Surely there is something to be done."

Her uncle's hushed response echoed from the stone walls. "Legally, everything—the land, the assets—will all be in her husband's name once she marries. Up until now I've barely been able to buy a horse without running it through Carrington."

"But Carrington's gone now. Remember?"

"Doesn't matter. It's an issue of how the will was written. My brother may have been an impudent fool, but he rarely missed a trick where business was concerned. How do you think he amassed all this property?"

"That notwithstanding, we need the funds. Surely something can be done."

"If she decides to marry someone else, there is nothing that I—we—can do to prevent her from doing so."

"Don't be ridiculous. Something can always be done. We just need to make certain that she doesn't marry anyone else. Then our problems are solved. Am I correct?"

Helena and Amelia exchanged glances and tiptoed to the threshold. Helena whispered in her ear, "What are they talking about?"

"My inheritance."

"Your inheritance? But I thought . . ." Helena's voice trailed off.

Helena's naïveté baffled Amelia. How could such a clever woman not see the clearest deception right in front of her? "I have been trying to tell you. Edward does not love me, Helena. He desires only Winterwood and the fortune that accompanies it."

"I think—" Helena's foot caught the leg of a side table and scooted it across the floor. The resulting sound ricocheted, and the voices inside the study halted. Helena's eyes grew wide, and her hand slapped over her mouth.

In a split second Uncle George appeared in the doorway, wrapped in a crimson dressing gown. His angry eyes flicked from his niece to his daughter, then back to his niece.

"I've underestimated you, Niece." He nodded toward the library, his voice devoid of any fatherly affection. "There is someone here who wishes to speak with you."

The room's stifling heat slapped her as she stepped in.

Edward stood in front of the roaring fireplace, broad shoulders silhouetted against the flames. His dark eyes locked on hers.

Amelia drew closer and prepared herself for battle. The scent of damp horse and the outdoors clung to Edward's person and prickled her nostrils. She mustered every ounce of energy to combat the desire to shrink away. She knew Edward's game of intimidation all too well, but this would be the last time she'd have to endure it.

His deep voice pierced the silence, and he pulled at his disheveled cravat as if it were a noose. "I'm desperately waiting for you, dear Amelia, to tell me there's been some mistake."

Amelia lowered her chin but refused to break eye contact. "I cannot."

Edward's face reddened. "When exactly were you planning to inform me of your change of heart? After all, our wedding is—should have been—just weeks away. So when? A week before? The day before?"

His tone sliced her confidence. She squared her shoulders and straightened as tall as her frame would allow. "This happened suddenly. I did not intend to deceive you."

A snide chuckle escaped him before he released his words through gritted teeth. "Imagine my surprise, my utter humiliation, when I went to apply for the license, only to be told by the snit of a clerk that my intended's name is already on a license." His words climbed to a shout. "With another man's name!"

Amelia's chest burned. Every breath felt shallower than the last. She cast a nervous glance at her aunt and uncle, for once grateful for their presence. "You must know within yourself that this marriage would have been a mistake, and I—"

His cry cut her off. "A mistake? I love you, Amelia. There is no mistaking that. My love has not wavered. What a fool I must be! All this time, these many months, I believed you returned my affection. And now I find you have deceived me in the most debased manner!"

Amelia squelched a stirring of guilt. She had given Edward repeated opportunities. His utter disregard for her concerns had left her no choice. She would not apologize for her actions. "I have told you from Lucy's birth that I intended to raise her. I made this abundantly clear, have I not? I will not allow that child, whom I love like my own, to be raised without a mother. Furthermore, it has become evident that your interest is in Winterwood, not me. I could never be happy married to a man who used me for my father's fortune."

"And you think this sea captain person has any other designs on you besides your fortune?" Edward's shouts echoed from the plastered walls. "Wake up, Amelia! He is using you in a most obvious fashion." He rushed forward, grabbed her hands, and pulled her to him with such fervor she almost lost her footing. "I want to protect you, Amelia. To give you my love. Why are you turning it away?"

His hands threatened to crush hers. He stood so close that his breath, laced with the ever-present scent of alcohol, grazed her cheek. Her strength faltered under Edward's overwhelming presence, and she fought the overwhelming urge to flee. She needed to stay calm, to fight the runaway beating of her heart, to remember why she was doing this.

Lucy.

A wild, frantic prayer raced through her mind. Days ago she'd felt God's presence. Mere minutes ago she'd thought she heard him speak. Would he help her now?

And where was Captain Sterling?

14

Graham climbed the stairs to Winterwood Manor with one goal: to rid it of Edward Littleton.

He should have arrived earlier. But dark clouds blotted out the moon's faint light, forcing him to rely on a newly sober William to show him the shortcut through Sterling Wood. Graham hated to rely on anyone. But his brother's help would make it possible for him to deal with Edward Littleton once and for all.

Graham reached the top of the stairs and grabbed for the iron handle on the massive wooden door.

"Wait!"

Annoyed with the further delay, Graham stopped at the sound of William's voice. His brother was fumbling with the horses' reins, attempting to tether the animals to a post. "You want this beast of yours to wander off? Where are the stable boys, anyway?"

"I've no idea. Hurry it up, will you?"

William tested the tether on No-Name before jumping up the stairs. "You have a plan, I assume?"

"No." Graham stepped through the main entrance into the darkened vestibule. Heated voices echoed on the stone walls and plaster ceilings. James and a footman hovered in a corner as if unsure what their duties were in such a circumstance. Littleton's angry shouts thundered above all.

William grabbed Graham's arm and pulled it back. "Whoa, whoa. Will you stop? Listen to him. He's mad as blazes!"

Graham returned the whisper. "Just stay quiet." He swept his hat from his head, tossed it in James's direction, and stepped through the library's threshold. William trailed closely.

A red-faced George Barrett came into view first, then his wife and daughter. Graham scanned the room for Miss Barrett and found her standing too close to Littleton. His breath caught at the sight of her. Never before had he seen Miss Barrett with her golden hair loose, blanketing her shoulders. He did not like the fearful expression on his intended's—*Amelia's*—face.

Graham forced his eyes away from her and onto Littleton. He assessed him as one preparing for a skirmish. Same height. Similar build. Graham flexed his hand at his side. He prepared his mind, just as he did before any battle.

Perspiration trickled down Littleton's face. His disheveled hair fell in damp clumps on his forehead, and his eyes boasted wild rage. "Well, there he is—*Captain* Sterling," he mocked. "Come to claim your bride, did you?"

Graham cast a glance at Amelia. Her face blanched as white as the wool shawl around her slender shoulders. "Take your leave, Littleton."

Littleton's lip lifted in a sneer. "Ah, he already speaks as if he is Winterwood's master. It didn't take long to assume that role, did it, *Captain*?"

"She's broken no law. You will respect her decision."

"She's broken a vow."

"She is entitled to change her mind."

"Change her mind? Women change their minds about what gown to wear. What novel to read or what bowl of fruit to paint." Saliva sprayed from Edward's mouth with each pointed word. "What exactly did you do, I wonder? Enlighten me. Did you bribe her?"

Amelia stepped forward as if preparing to say something, but Graham stepped in front of her. "Accept it, Littleton. I daresay you shouldn't be surprised."

"Oh, should I not?" Littleton's voice climbed. "You are here for a few days, and you think you know how my betrothed should think and act?"

"I saw enough." Graham didn't like the desperation in Littleton's expression. Desperate men were capable of desperate things. Graham squared his stance. "You can leave on your own, or William and I will show you off the estate. Take your choice."

George Barrett stepped forward, outrage in his voice. "You've no right to throw anyone out of Winterwood, Sterling. I am master here. I should be ordering *you* off the property."

Just as Graham opened his mouth in response, Littleton flung himself at Graham and swung a fist toward his jaw. Graham ducked, but not quickly enough. He staggered back from the blow, warm blood trickling from his lip.

Like a shot from a cannon, fire surged through his veins. Without hesitation he rammed his full weight into Littleton, hurling him against the wall. He thrust one forearm against the man's throat and the other across his chest, pinning his foe against the cold plaster.

Littleton flailed, throwing angry blows and spewing curses. Behind him, George Barrett clawed at Graham's shoulder. With a sharp jab of his arm, he freed himself from the older man's grasp, relieved when William finally stepped in and pulled Barrett from his back. He pressed harder, consumed by rage. All he could think about was dominating Littleton and keeping him away from Miss Barrett. Away from Lucy. Away from Winterwood.

Someone screamed, but Graham paid no attention. All his force and concentration was required to keep Littleton against the wall. He braced his feet and tightened every muscle and waited until the other man expended his energy and began to slow.

Littleton finally slumped in surrender. Both men huffed. Sweat dripped from Graham's forehead and rolled to his chin. He leaned in close to his opponent, his face just inches away. "I'll not repeat myself. Leave now." Then he stepped back.

Littleton's dark eyes raged with fire, but the man's physical strength did not match his passion. His chest heaved, and his stare moved from Graham to Amelia. He pointed at her. "Is this what you want? Then you shall have it."

Graham didn't dare break his stare. "Are you quite finished?"

Littleton snatched his hat from a nearby table, jammed it on his head, and hissed a warning through clenched teeth. "If you think for a moment I will give up easily, you, sir, are sadly mistaken."

The man stormed from the library, clipping William with his shoulder as he passed.

The room stood silent. Graham wiped the blood from his chin, noting idly that crimson stained his sleeve. He looked up to see Amelia by his arm, tears welling in her eyes.

George Barrett rushed toward him, his jowls trembling with rage. "Are you pleased?"

Graham pressed his lips together. One altercation was enough for tonight.

Barrett's face had gone purple. "What kind of a man preys on a young girl the way you have? Look at what you have done. And why? Because of her money? Because you needed her to care for your daughter so you can return to your ship?"

Amelia hurried over to them. "But it's not like that at all. I—"

"Quiet, girl!" Barrett pushed her away and addressed Graham. "You'll receive the punishment you deserve for bringing such scandal to our family." He spun around and took his wife's arm. "Helena, Augusta, return to your beds. We are finished here."

Helena jumped forward. "But what about Amelia?"

Barrett turned to stare at Amelia as if he had forgotten she was in the room. "You. You agree with this? You agree to marry this man and go against the solid guidance your aunt and I have given you all these years?"

All eyes were now on Amelia. She met Graham's eyes, then jutted her chin in the air. "I do."

Barrett slammed his palm on a round side table, sending the urn atop it crashing to the ground. "So be it. Then you are no longer a niece of mine."

She flinched as if struck. "I hope in time, Uncle, you will understand why I have made this choice."

Barrett made no answer, just grabbed his wife and daughter by their arms and yanked them from the library, glaring at Graham all the while. Graham let them go. Now was not the time to talk with the man. Maybe he could explain himself sometime in the future, but not tonight.

Graham rubbed his jaw and wiped his face, vaguely aware of his brother and betrothed walking toward him.

"You're bleeding." Amelia's voice trembled. She reached out to touch his wound but hesitated, letting her hand land briefly on his shoulder before falling to her side.

Graham didn't want her to withdraw her hand. He wanted to feel her touch. His chest still heaved with the effects of exertion and his jaw ached, but he refused to look away from her. She was beautiful, like an angel, with her untamed tresses and her gentle voice. Her very presence soothed him like a balm. His breathing slowed, and he wiped his chin again. "I'm fine."

Amelia pushed her hair out of her eyes, the firelight dancing on each long strand. It looked like gold. "Thank you for coming," she said softly. "If you hadn't arrived when you did, I . . ."

Graham nodded but said nothing. He prided himself on being a wise enough sailor to know when he'd entered uncharted waters. This woman touched something deep in him. Be it from the blow he received or the adrenaline from the fight, he didn't trust his words. Not just yet.

He had almost forgotten William was in the room. His brother hurried to the window, pressed himself against the wall, and lifted the curtain just enough to see outside. "Littleton's gone. Good riddance." He dropped the curtain and walked over to study Graham's bloody lip. "You should have ducked."

Graham nodded, grateful for the attempt at humor. "Thank you for your advice. I'll keep that in mind next time." He met Amelia's eyes and a look of triumph passed between them. Littleton was gone—for now. But how long would he stay away?

William slapped Graham's shoulder, sending sharp pains up his neck and through his injured jaw. "My little brother, master of Winterwood Manor. Impressive." He stared dramatically at the ceiling. "Does this mean you will be keeping your feet firmly planted on land now that you have a beautiful bride to cherish and love?"

The words *cherish* and *love* hung awkwardly between them. Amelia looked down at the floor. Graham straightened his jacket. "I'll return to the war as soon as the ship repairs are done, as planned."

"Seems a shame." William moved toward the door and then turned back to Amelia. "It's late. Miss Barrett, it was a pleasure to see you, even under these peculiar circumstances." He bowed. "Graham, are you coming?"

"I'll be there straightaway."

"Then I'll get the horses. That is, if your beast of an animal hasn't managed to wander off."

Graham shifted his weight as the heavy front door closed behind William. "Will you be all right?"

The trembling in Amelia's lips belied the confidence in her voice. "I should think so. Winterwood is my home, after all."

"I doubt you shall see any more of Littleton tonight, but perhaps it would be more prudent for you to stay at Eastmore Hall for the time being."

Amelia raised a blond eyebrow. "Me? At Eastmore Hall? Thank you, no. What would people say?"

"I would think it is a little late to consider the opinions of others."

She flinched at his comment but said nothing. She gathered her hair and absently wrapped her hand around the thick locks.

"Your cousin would be welcome to accompany you, of course."

She shook her head no, so Graham headed for the doorway, where James had appeared with his hat. He didn't want to leave her, not just yet, but he could hear William with the horses on the front drive and weary shadows smudged Amelia's smooth cheeks. "It's been a long night. You need rest. I will be by first thing in the morning and attempt to settle things with your uncle."

"Thank you, Captain Sterling."

He tucked his hat under his arm, bowed slightly, then lingered in the doorway for a moment, memorizing the look of her—the long, lustrous hair, the gentle mouth, the sapphire eyes. He suspected those eyes would haunt him from that moment forth.

❧

Graham didn't know if his throbbing jaw or the awkwardness of his position awakened him. With slow, deliberate movements, he pushed himself off the brocade cushion. Every muscle ached, and salty dried blood lingered on his lip.

When had he finally slept? Last he remembered, he'd returned from Winterwood in the black of night, opened Eastmore Hall's library window for some air, and sat on the plush settee to nurse his wounds. Now the sun's long morning rays reached into the room, bathing the space in a yellow glow.

Graham shook sleep from his limbs. He distinctly recalled explaining his and Amelia's engagement to William, careful to withhold any indication that she had proposed to him. He must have dozed off after that, and apparently his brother had done the same, for William's lanky frame slumped in an overstuffed wingback chair across the room.

Graham was like that too—able to sleep anywhere. Hammock or wooden deck, inside his cabin or under the stars, it didn't matter. His old captain, Stephen Sulter, always said that easy sleep was a sign of a clear conscience. Graham wasn't so sure.

He yanked off his boot and flung it in William's direction. It bounced off his brother's knee and thudded to the oriental rug. William didn't budge.

Graham removed his other boot and stood, grimacing as he stretched the kinks in his back and shoulders. He walked over to the open window, where heavy emerald drapes billowed in the wind, and closed it. Then he stepped over one of William's sleeping hunting dogs to stoke the pitiful fire. His muscles protested the movements, and he rubbed a protective hand over his ribs. Judging by the sensitivity, he must have taken more blows than he remembered.

It had been awhile since he'd engaged in a fight like that—many years, in fact. In his youth, however, a fiery temper and love of drink had plopped him right in the middle of brawl after brawl. Then Stephen Sulter led him to the Lord and helped Graham put an end to his dissolute ways. But now, after years of loss and disappointment, he found himself wondering about the God who rescued him from a life of rebellion. He did not actually doubt the Father's presence, but he hadn't felt it in a long time.

He rubbed his hands together and blew warm air against his cold palms. He needed a hot drink to dull the effects of the chill in the room. Graham turned from the fireplace and looked for the bell to call the servants.

He shuffled through the strewn papers and letters on his brother's desk in search of the elusive bell. How could William ever find a thing with this mess? He had begun to pile the papers when words scrawled across the top of a parchment caught his eye. *Receipt of sale.* He picked up the paper and read further. He glanced over at William, who still snored in the corner chair, then returned his attention to the document. At the bottom were two signatures: William Sterling and Edward Littleton.

The sight of Littleton's name hit with the power of another fist to the jaw. Hungry for the meaning, he skimmed the document, unable to read it fast enough. He forced himself to read it again. Could this be true? Had William sold part of Eastmore to that scoundrel?

The room's chill vanished. His arms and chest burned with exasperating intensity, and a million thoughts bombarded him. Did Miss Barrett know about this purchase? When had it happened? Was there a way to revoke it?

He stepped over to William and nudged his foot. "Wake up."

At the gesture, William drew a deep breath and opened his eyes, squinting in the sun's light. He covered his eyes with his hand and frowned. "Go away."

"What's this?"

William's face scrunched. "What's what?"

Graham held the document in the air. "It says 'receipt of sale.' It's signed by Edward Littleton."

William groaned and scratched his scalp as he pulled himself up to a seated position. "I sold the west fields to Littleton about a week ago. Leave my personal affairs alone." He lay his head back and closed his eyes. "Now go away and let me sleep."

Graham kicked his brother's foot again. "Were you going to mention this? Or just let me wake one day to find Edward Littleton practically in my lap?"

William opened his eyes again. With a sudden burst of energy he jumped up from his chair and grabbed the document from Graham's grip. "Yes, I was going to tell you," he spat. "Call me inconsiderate, but I didn't think last night would be the most opportune time to enlighten you, what with all of the yelling and punching."

"You told me you had no intention of dividing Eastmore."

"Of course I didn't want to. What fool would? But I did what I had to do. I needed the money, and Littleton wanted to buy the land. So I sold it to him."

The snippet of conversation from a few days ago about William selling his horse flickered in his mind. "Why do you need money, anyway? What happened to all of it?"

"Do you mean Father's money," William huffed, "or mine?" He stuffed the document in a desk drawer. "Either way, it is none of your business. I did what I needed to do."

"Why didn't you come to me?"

"What, go crawling to my baby brother? I can handle the affairs here on my own."

"That's preposterous."

William slammed the drawer shut. "You think it's easy, managing an estate this size?"

"I think it's easy to make foolish decisions."

"Ah, I see. Any financial trouble that has befallen the great Eastmore Hall must be of my own doing. Perhaps you forget that I inherited this monstrosity and all the worries that accompany it.

You, on the other hand, have been conveniently absent from any family issue, small or great."

William's sharp retort sounded suspiciously like an accusation. Graham squared his stance. "It was not my choice to leave. Or have you forgotten?"

William whirled to face his brother. Gone was his customary lighthearted nature. His response was one of a cornered animal, ready for battle. "You think you could have done better? I did the best I could with what I had, and I'll not apologize for it. When someone wanted to buy some of my land—*my* land—especially the man I thought was to be my neighbor, I was well within my rights to do so. How was I to know you were going to sweep his betrothed out from underneath him?"

Graham shifted his weight as he contemplated his response. A million retorts fired in his head about responsibility and discipline. But now wasn't the time. "Eastmore, and what you do with it, is your business. I have no say in it. What matters to me now is keeping Littleton away from Winterwood."

William leaned against his desk. The hunting dog rose and trotted to her master, and William scratched her ear. "You know, there is a very simple solution."

Graham snatched up his boot. "And what is that?"

William shrugged. "You will soon be marrying the answer to both our problems."

Graham glared at his brother. "What are you suggesting?"

"Oh, come on." William rolled his eyes. "Toss a little money at Littleton and buy the land for yourself. Make Littleton an offer he cannot turn down, and he'll sell you the land." A twinkle shimmered in his pale eyes. "And as for Eastmore, when you marry, we can use Winterwood's money to set Eastmore's finances right. All of our problems will be solved."

Graham didn't need time to consider his response. "No."

William's eyes widened in shock. "No? Why?"

"It's not my money to give. I promised Amelia I'd not touch Winterwood's money."

A short laugh burst from William. "What are you, a fool? Well then, buy the land yourself. Your prize money is no secret. Surely you have such funds. And while you're at it, perhaps you can help me a little."

Graham snatched up his other boot and tailcoat. The dark blue wool wrinkled under his grip. "How significant is your debt?"

"Significant enough that I had to sell the west fields. That I am selling my best horse. Who knows what's next?"

Graham paused and looked out the window. "If you want me to help, then I need to know a number, William. How much do you owe?"

William's face blanched, but he set his jaw. "Seventeen thousand pounds."

"Egad, William, how did you get yourself into such incredible debt?"

William's eyebrows twitched. "You don't know how it's been. I—"

Graham shot his hand into the air to silence William, but he lowered it immediately. "Don't tell me. I don't want to know, and quite honestly, I don't care."

An awkward silence hovered between the men. Graham tucked his coat under his arm. "I'm going to Winterwood to talk to George Barrett. We'll discuss this later."

William stepped forward, blocking the threshold. "Like it or not, this is your family home too."

Brother stared at brother. Unspoken words balanced in the empty space between them.

"I'll help you if I can," Graham finally said. "But Winterwood's funds are off the table."

15

The fresh scent of toasted bread, plum cake, and coffee met Amelia as she descended the stairs to the main hall. Whispers and clinking silver swirled in the morning air. The normally inviting smells of breakfast turned her stomach, and the tone of the voices tempted her to run back to her bedchamber.

When had her beloved Winterwood grown so cold?

Resolved to at least attempt to mend the rift between her and her family, Amelia forced one foot in front of the other. Her kid slippers made little sound as she stepped toward the breakfast room's threshold. Her deliberately slow steps afforded her precious moments to attempt to hear the conversation. Uncle George's strained voice reverberated from the room, but his words were undecipherable. She smoothed the pale pink sarsnet gown and adjusted the ivory fichu around her neck before stepping over the threshold. The sun's bright light flooded through the window and bounced around the breakfast room, reflecting from the gilded mirror to the silver service to the sparkling ruby at her aunt's neck.

Amelia squeezed a greeting through her constricted throat. "Good morning."

Her uncle didn't acknowledge her. Her aunt glared at her. Sympathy balanced in Helena's red-rimmed eyes, but she said nothing. Amelia sat down in her chair, and immediately Sally was at her elbow with tea. She sipped the steaming liquid, hoping its warmth would soothe her mounting anxiety.

Tension hovered in the air, daring someone to be the first to speak. Finally, her aunt's biting voice stopped Amelia midsip. "Since no one will address what has transpired, I shall." She turned and thrust the full brunt of her glare onto Amelia. "I hope you are satisfied. In one night you have destroyed everything your uncle and I have worked so hard to create for this family. Everything!"

Uncle George snapped his paper closed and let it fall to his lap. "Don't bother, Augusta. She has made her decision."

Amelia snuck a glance at Helena, hoping to garner support, but Helena stared at her lap.

Aunt Augusta's face reddened and trembled as she spoke. "Indeed she has, with little concern for the welfare of those who have sacrificed for her."

Amelia's Wedgwood teacup clattered against the saucer when she set it back down. Her shoulders slumped. How many times must she defend her cause? Would anything she said make a difference? She forced strength to her voice. "I hope that one day, Aunt, you will be able to understand why I have made this decision."

"Oh, I know full well why—because you are a selfish, ungrateful girl!" Aunt Augusta swatted her napkin against the table. "You think you know better than anyone else how the world should be organized, and you consider nobody else's concerns but your own. Think of poor Mr. Littleton! The man is heartbroken. How can he ever hold his head up in society after such a public disgrace?"

In a fluster, the plump woman pushed herself away from the

table and paced behind Helena. "I would wish nothing like it on my worst enemy. And have you given any thought to how this scandal will affect your uncle's business? The livelihood we all depend upon? I daresay you have not." She pressed a handkerchief to her nose, and a sob broke her voice. "And I shudder to think of what this scandal will do to your cousin's chances of making a suitable match when word is out. *Selfish.*"

Amelia stiffened at her aunt's biting words and finally found her voice. "Edward will recover—of this I am certain. There is no reason why my decision should affect any business dealings."

Her uncle huffed, and she turned to find his small eyes fixed on her. "Edward is about to be, or at least is supposed to be, a partner of mine—that is how my business will be affected. Once trust is broken, Amelia, it is not easily repaired. I gave Edward my permission to court you. I gave him my blessing to marry you. Now he has been betrayed in the vilest of manners. I shouldn't blame the man if he never spoke to any of us again."

Amelia's ears flamed, and she tried to swallow. She wanted to tell them that though Edward appeared amiable, he was actually a treacherous man. Couldn't her uncle see he was only interested in a partnership because of Winterwood's fortune and would turn on his partner as quickly as he would on his intended? But such arguments would all be for naught. They were determined not to listen.

Uncle George continued, jowls trembling. "Edward is staying at the village inn. I plan to go to him later today to sort out this fine mess and try to salvage what is left of the family name. You may care little for your reputation or that of Edward's, but this scandal will shed negative light on all of us."

Amelia's pulse quickened. "Edward is still in Darbury?"

"He departed from Winterwood in the black of night, Amelia." Aunt Augusta stared down her nose. "Where did you expect him to go?"

Amelia felt as if the air had been stolen from her lungs. How could Edward remain in Darbury after being refused? What if he planned to stay?

Augusta stepped behind Helena and rested her hand on her daughter's shoulder as she stared at Amelia. "If you are fortunate, by some miracle Mr. Littleton will be willing to look past your lapse of judgment and reconsider a future with you."

"No." Amelia jumped up from her chair. Her skirt caught on the table, and she stopped to free the flowing fabric. Tears gathered in her eyes, and she quickly blinked them away. She refused to give them the satisfaction of making her cry. "I am determined to marry Captain Sterling and to raise Lucy. No amount of—"

Her words broke off as horse hooves pounded outside the window. She skirted the table and rushed to the window. A thought clenched her mind, and like a wild dog violently shaking its prey, it refused to loosen its hold.

What if Edward returned to Winterwood? What would he do?

Helena jumped up from the table and joined Amelia at the window. "Who has arrived?"

Amelia's tense shoulders relaxed as Graham's strong profile became clear. Her confidence surged at the very sight of him. Her knees nearly buckled with relief.

Helena said the words that Amelia's mouth could not yet form. "It's Captain Sterling."

"Despicable man," huffed Aunt Augusta. In a swirl of pale blue muslin, she returned to her seat at the table. "And arriving at this early hour? Ridiculous."

The wind billowed the captain's black greatcoat as he pulled his horse to a stop. Amelia watched as the groom came round to take his horse. She was happy to see him, and was even more grateful to see that he had come alone. The fact that his brother accompanied him the previous night had surprised her, but William Sterling's repeated visits to Winterwood confirmed her suspicions that he'd been too intoxicated on the occasion of his impropriety to recall it later. If he did remember it, he did not seem ready to acknowledge it, and she would not remind him. She only hoped that the captain would never find out. It was a secret she did not relish keeping. But for the sake of those involved, she must.

Unwilling to wait for Captain Sterling to be properly announced, she hurried from the breakfast room to meet him in the hall. She arrived, breathless, just as he was stepping through the threshold. He swept his beaver hat from his head and handed it to James in one fluid movement. His stormy gray eyes met hers. Her breathing slowed, and something fluttered in her heart—an emotion she did not understand.

He forewent a formal welcome. "Are you all right, Amelia?"

She flushed at the informality with which he addressed her. The only men to call her by her Christian name were her uncle and Edward. But why should he not? "Yes, I am well, thank you."

"And Lucy?"

"She is well. I spent some time with her in the nursery earlier this morning."

"Good. Any sign of Littleton?"

"He has not returned to Winterwood, although I have just learned from my uncle that he is still in Darbury."

"I cannot say I am surprised." The captain's every word conveyed purpose. His eyes darted about, as if searching for something. "Is your uncle at home?"

She nodded, purposely diverting her gaze from his split lip. "He is in the breakfast room, with the family."

"I will speak to him, and then I believe we should call on the vicar and explain the situation. In light of what has happened, the sooner all is finalized, the better."

He spoke as if checking items off a list, but with every word Amelia relaxed. He was as committed to this plan as she was. His determination boosted her confidence.

"Will you take me to your uncle?"

She nodded. "If you'll just follow me."

Amelia would not have thought it possible, but upon her re-entering the breakfast room, accompanied by the captain, the room's oppressive atmosphere grew even colder. Helena stared at something in the middle of the table. Aunt Augusta glared at the captain, and Uncle George continued eating, ignoring them completely.

Amelia's voice cracked as she spoke. "Uncle, Captain Sterling is here to speak with you."

Captain Sterling bowed toward Aunt Augusta before turning to her uncle. "Mr. Barrett, I was hoping to have a moment of your time."

Her uncle's lips disappeared into a thin line. "You said quite enough last night. I think you should be on your way, sir."

"That is not an option, I'm afraid. We need to speak. In private."

"You'll find my opinions have not changed."

"I supposed as much. Still, there are matters to discuss."

As if suffering from a great inconvenience, Uncle George pushed back his chair and stood. He said nothing, but pursed his lips and tucked his paper under his arm, then pointed to the threshold and walked through it. Graham followed.

Amelia rubbed her neck and rested her hand on her shoulder as she watched the men disappear. Unable to endure the breakfast table any longer, she withdrew to the drawing room to wait.

Outside the window, the sun's white light caught on the edge of the silver clouds and reflected to the ground below. The frost shone like diamonds on the expansive lawn. Everything looked so calm. So peaceful. Why couldn't it storm to match the restless turmoil churning within her?

❧

Graham tapped his fingers on the carriage windowsill on the short ride to the vicarage. His conversation with George Barrett echoed in his mind like a noisy gull. He'd hoped to smooth things over for Lucy's sake as well as Amelia's, but the old man had proved every bit as stubborn as his niece.

He watched Amelia as she fussed with the fur lining of her pelisse and adjusted her cap. Only when she looked at him with those bright blue eyes did he realize he was staring.

"You seem lost in thought, Captain Sterling." Her voice seemed tranquil, though her shadowed eyes and tightly laced fingers told another story.

He shifted in his seat and braced himself as the carriage lurched forward into motion. "I hope last night's events were not too disturbing for you."

She shook her head. "'Tis a shame it happened, but I daresay it was to be expected. I knew Edward was of a passionate bent, but I would never have expected him to strike you."

"I've taken my fair share of blows in my days. This was little different."

"Be that as it may, he had no right to do so." She fiddled with the lace trim on her reticule, her eyebrows drawn. "What did Uncle George say when you spoke?"

Graham looked out the carriage window. How could he tell her the truth—that if she proceeded with this marriage, she was as good as dead to her uncle? "It was . . . in keeping with what he said last night."

"Did he tell you any more of Edward being in town?"

"He did." Graham's jaw twitched. If this had been purely a case of a jilted lover, the wounded beau would retreat and nurse his wounds. But this had nothing to do with affection . . . and everything to do with greed.

Graham swayed with the carriage as it jostled down the rutted road. He studied the profile of the woman who would be his wife very soon.

Wife. The very word denoted intimacy. And yet Amelia was still a stranger to him.

He knew she was intelligent. Loyal. Kind. Impulsive. Loving with children, terrible with watercolors. But what of her past? Her dreams? He wanted to know more about her. No, wanted to know *everything* about her.

His coat seemed to tighten as the carriage's comfortable silence closed around him. He pulled his gloves from his hands and tucked them in his pocket.

Keep to business.

16

Jane Hammond didn't wait for her butler to announce Amelia and Graham's arrival. She met them at the door herself, her brow furrowed. "Edward Littleton was just here. I've never seen a man so beside himself."

Edward, here? Amelia's stomach clenched. The Hammond house had always been a refuge for her, and Edward's visit felt like a violation.

"I need to talk with you and Mr. Hammond." She gestured toward Captain Sterling, who followed her through the door. "*We* need to talk with you."

Mrs. Hammond winced as her gaze fell on the captain's lip. "For mercy's sake, what happened?"

Amelia didn't give him a chance to respond. "Edward struck him."

Jane shook her head and ushered them in. Amelia handed her cap and reticule to a somberly dressed servant and attempted to remove her kidskin gloves. She hadn't realized her hands were trembling until she tried to unfasten the tiny ivory button at the base of her palm. She bit her lip, determined to free her hand from the glove's grip. Why couldn't anything be easy?

So focused was Amelia on the glove that she nearly jumped when Jane touched her shoulder. "Here, dearest, allow me."

Amelia sighed and extended her wrist to Jane, keeping her eyes downcast. What had Edward been thinking to come here? What right did he have?

Amelia swallowed as she watched Jane's long, graceful fingers work the button through the loop and then gently pull the glove from her hand. She released a shaky breath and stretched her fingers. "Thank you."

Jane called for tea, then ushered the party into the drawing room where her husband waited. Thomas Hammond's kind, familiar smile should have soothed Amelia's nerves, but it had quite the opposite effect.

Jane directed Amelia to the settee. "Do be seated, Amelia. And you too, Captain Sterling." Amelia followed Jane's bidding and sat down, but the captain crossed the room and stood next to the fireplace by the vicar.

Amelia's eyes tracked Captain Sterling's every movement. How she wished she could read his thoughts. The farther away she was from him, the more exposed she felt, even in the sanctuary of the Hammond home.

Jane took the empty space next to Amelia on the settee and took her hand. "Now, tell us what has happened."

Amelia looked down to hide her trembling chin. She feared that the moment she opened her mouth, her every thought, every secret, would spill out.

Captain Sterling's strong voice filled the empty silence. "We wish to be married."

Mr. Hammond drummed his fingers on the mantel. "I gathered as much from our visitor this morning."

The captain reached inside his satchel and produced the license. "You'll find that everything is in order. We wish to marry as soon as possible."

Mr. Hammond took the extended document and held it to the light. His gaze shifted from the document to his wife. Their exchange made Amelia feel like a child. Heat rushed to her face. She didn't want to be questioned, and she was tired of feeling judged.

Mr. Hammond folded the document and handed it back to Captain Sterling. "Why don't we leave the ladies to their discussion? We can talk privately in my library." The captain looked over at Amelia before nodding at the vicar and following him from the room.

Amelia rubbed her hand against her forehead before clasping her hands in her lap. She had tried so hard to keep her tears from falling. To be strong, like Katherine or Jane. But as the men took their leave, a shudder escaped.

"Amelia?"

She opened her mouth to speak, but no words came, just a choking sob. For the first time in weeks, honest, unbridled tears flowed freely. Jane wrapped her arms around Amelia and stroked her hair. "What is it, dearest? Tell me."

Amelia's thoughts raced. Where could she start? What should she tell?

Jane gently pushed Amelia away from her shoulder and looked at her. "Is it Mr. Littleton?"

Amelia wiped her face with the palm of her hand. "Yes. No. I mean—not just Edward."

Jane frowned. "Is it Captain Sterling?"

Amelia hesitated. But what did she have to lose by telling Jane? The news of her and Captain Sterling would be all over Darbury by nightfall. She didn't want Jane to hear any details from another source, and the weight of her situation threatened to pull her under.

Amelia squeezed her eyes shut, drew a long, shaky breath, and forced the words. "It started when I . . . when I proposed to Captain Sterling."

She paused, waiting for Jane's gasp of shock. It didn't come. She waited for the reprimand. Nothing. Amelia slowly opened her eyes, fearing her friend's expression, but Jane's eyes were soft.

Amelia swallowed, mustering courage to continue her confession. But once she started, there was no stopping. She shared everything from her proposal to their time alone in the graveyard to her family's wrath.

Jane's silence during it all unnerved Amelia, and she was glad when her friend finally spoke. "Oh, Amelia, this is news, indeed."

"Do you disagree with my decision?"

Jane dropped her eyes as if carefully selecting her words. "You know my feelings about the Sterling family, William Sterling in particular."

"But the captain is not his brother. You yourself pointed that out."

"Be that as it may, Amelia, you barely know the man. At least, with Mr. Littleton, you know his nature and have your family's blessing. Are you quite certain this is the path you wish to take?"

"I am. I know it seems imprudent, but I am convinced. Lucy is part of me, and the captain is very kind. And I have come to believe that Edward Littleton is quite unsuitable, perhaps even unscrupulous."

Jane's eyebrows drew together. "I do not like to see you in such a situation, Amelia. If only there was another way."

"I have considered every possible course, Jane. You must believe I have."

"And you have prayed about it?"

It was Amelia's turn to hesitate. Yes, she had prayed. Perhaps she'd even experienced some answers. Then why did the topic make her so uneasy?

She stood and began pacing. "Aunt Augusta says I am selfish. I am beginning to wonder if she's right. Yes, I love Lucy and want to raise her. But part of me, if I am completely honest, is also happy to be free from Edward. What if I just told myself that marrying the captain instead of Edward is God's will, when in fact I am just trying to please myself?"

Jane looked up from where she sat. "God does not trick us. If you believe God called you to raise Lucy, then he will provide a way."

"Even if it means bringing pain to those I love? My aunt and uncle are furious, Helena all but hates me. What I have chosen will cause them many difficulties."

"It is impossible to get through life without facing such dilemmas. All we can do is seek guidance, do our best, and trust our Father for the outcome."

Jane's words should have comforted Amelia, but instead they sliced her conscience. She sniffed, not caring how unladylike it was. "I do believe this is the best course. With all of my heart I believe it."

Jane squeezed Amelia's hand. "I do believe you have more faith than you think."

Amelia looked at her hands and sniffed again, wanting to change the subject from her faith—or lack thereof. "What did Edward say when he was here?"

"He wanted me to use my powers of friendship to persuade you to change your mind."

Amelia wiped the traces of a tear away and sighed. "I dread what will happen when word of this becomes public—and it will. When the gossips learn I have broken my engagement at this late date and am to marry Captain Sterling, I shudder to think what they will say."

"I would counsel you not worry much about them. They are all prattle, and soon there will be new rumors to divert their attentions. Now, sit and have some tea. You are making me nervous."

Amelia complied, perching next to Jane on the settee. "But you know how quickly such things spread. People may get a false impression."

"Well, we will just have to intervene." Jane poured Amelia a cup of tea and handed her the dainty cup. "It's simple. Mr. Hammond and I will host a dinner to welcome Captain Sterling back to the neighborhood and to celebrate the engagement. You know how all of the gossips cling onto Mr. Hammond's every word as truth."

Jane was right. If Mr. Hammond showed favor to Captain Sterling, his parishioners likely would as well. At the very least, that should help control the local gossip. "You are clever, Jane. Clever indeed."

A playful smile curled Jane's lips. "I didn't survive being a vicar's wife for almost thirty-five years without picking up a trick or two along the way." She poured a cup of tea for herself, took a sip, then sighed. "We'll schedule it soon. I should think that if we have it within the week it will show my husband's blessing. The rest will follow. I fear that there is no way around inviting your betrothed's brother, is there?"

Amelia simply gave her a look.

"Well, too bad about that." Jane took another sip. "Nevertheless, all shall be well, my dearest. You will see."

❧

Amelia stood in Winterwood's vestibule, watching through the window as the carriage returning Captain Sterling to Eastmore Hall clamored down the drive.

My plan is proving to be successful. So why do I feel this way?

It just didn't make sense. With Lucy safe at Winterwood, the conversation with the Hammonds behind her, and her wedding scheduled for the following Friday, she should be excited, filled with plans. Instead, her back muscles ached, her temples throbbed, and she couldn't seem to make her feet move any farther.

Oh, Lord, please help me make it to Friday. She straightened and started for the stairs. But then a sharp noise echoed, and she froze. She peered down the hall to her left. A light shone under the library door. Someone was home.

Desperate to go unnoticed, she hurried across the vestibule just as James appeared in the hall. "Welcome home, Miss Barrett. I trust your outing was enjoyable."

Amelia's heart hammered in her chest at the volume of the man's voice. She raised a hand to silence him, but too late. The library door flew open, and her uncle filled the doorway.

He came toward her. "Amelia, you have a visitor."

A prickling sensation climbed her spine. "I am not feeling well. I think I will—"

"Not this time, Amelia." He reached out and wrapped his pudgy fingers around her arm. "It's time you faced the consequences of your actions."

She shifted her weight backward. "But I still have my outside things on. Give me a minute to tidy up and I—"

"It would be rude to keep your guest waiting."

He yanked on her arm, causing her to stumble forward several steps. Only when she almost fell did he loosen his grip. "Take off that coat and hat. I'll wait."

His eyes were hard under wiry eyebrows as she removed her outer garments. She threw a pleading glance at James, as if he could in some way help her, but her uncle was the master—for now, at least.

Slowly she freed herself from the pelisse.

"Come on, girl." Uncle George walked ahead of her down the hall and stepped back to give her room to enter. She handed her items to James before stepping into the sunlit chamber.

She scanned the room. Her aunt and cousin sat on the settee. Aunt Augusta regarded her with a haughty sneer. Helena would not look at her. Instead, she stared toward the far corner of the room.

Amelia's breath caught as she followed Helena's eyes to see Edward Littleton standing there. Jane had been correct—his appearance was much altered. Red rimmed his dark eyes, and his complexion, usually vibrant, was sallow and pale. A day's worth of stubble blackened his strong jawline. A crumpled cravat hung loosely about his neck, and his wrinkled tailcoat hung open over dirt-smudged fawn breeches. She gaped at him in stunned silence.

Aunt Augusta stood abruptly, pulled Helena to a standing position, then half dragged her to the doorway.

"Wait! Where you are going?" To her own ears, Amelia sounded like a bewildered child. She took a step to follow them, but they ignored her. Uncle George opened the door just wide enough for his wife and daughter to slip past, then followed them out and slammed the door behind him.

Amelia turned slowly to face Edward. She clenched her fists with such intensity that the nails dug into her palms.

His dark eyes flicked from her to the door and back to her again. "Is this what it has come to, Amelia?"

He took an unsteady step toward her. She clasped her hands protectively in front of her and stepped back. He advanced on her again.

And then something shifted within her.

She thought of Captain Sterling's bravery. His strength. He might not be here, but she could be strong on her own.

She must be strong.

She stood her ground, daring him to come closer. "Why did you visit the Hammonds?"

Edward extended his palms toward her. "Look at me, Amelia.

I haven't eaten. I haven't slept. You've driven me to desperation. Please release me from my misery. I—"

"You have not answered my question."

"Why do you suppose I went to the Hammonds?" His short laugh sounded almost like a sob. "Regardless of what you think of me, Amelia, I am not a fool. I know you hold Mrs. Hammond's counsel in high regard. I thought if she talked to you—"

"That I would what? Change my mind?"

He smoothed his ebony hair, then tugged at his striped waist-coat, the same one he had worn the previous evening. "One could only hope. Do you think I like this? Pleading for your uncle to let me into his home so I can beg you to reconsider? I admit that I've behaved poorly. I said things I shouldn't have. But I love you. That has not, nor will it ever, change."

"It's too late, Edward. What's done is done. My decision is made."

He took another step toward her. She tensed but did not back away. "I know you, Amelia. You don't mean that."

"On the contrary, Mr. Littleton. You don't know me at all."

"*Mr.* Littleton?" His head jerked back as if she had slapped him. "Such formality. Is that how it is to be?"

"It is."

A flash of anger sparked in his eyes, but then his expression softened. "Apparently I did not realize how much you cared for the child. I can admit I was wrong. If you'll reconsider, she can stay with us as long as you like. Please, darling Amelia, reconsider."

"I'm sorry, Edward."

Another laugh. "So I am to believe the captain has truly caught your fancy, hmm? What line of lies has he fed you? Or perhaps he's showing you the ways of the world?"

He took yet another step in her direction. Every muscle in her body poised to move quickly if need be. "Mr. Littleton, I want you to leave."

He lunged forward, grabbing her hands and pulling her toward him. "No, I will not leave. By my honor, I will continue to fight for you, Amelia."

Amelia had heard enough. "I believe you mean you will fight for Winterwood."

Edward dropped her hands. "What?"

"I heard you and Uncle last night in the library, before I came in. You were talking about Winterwood, about the money. About my father's will."

"You misunderstood."

"No, I do not believe that I did."

He staggered back. "And do you think this man—this captain—is any different? Of course he wants to marry you. You are beautiful. Wealthy. And you will take care of his child. He is manipulating you."

Amelia shook her head. "I am sorry if I have caused you pain. I truly am. But circumstances change. People change. I have grown to love Lucy as if she were my own. Her happiness and security are my happiness and security. And I have no faith that either of us will be happy or secure with you as master of Winterwood. So you must understand. My decision is final."

"This is preposterous." Edward's voice escalated. "Do not think for a minute that I—"

"James!"

Confusion fell across his features, then a wary smile. "Oh, come on, Amelia. You don't think—"

Her second cry was louder. "James!"

The older man popped his gray head through the door, his expression concerned. "Yes, miss?"

"Mr. Littleton is leaving. Immediately. Please call for his carriage, or horse, or however he came."

James stammered. "But Mr. Barrett said—"

Her voice hardened. "I am my father's daughter and heiress to Winterwood Manor. Please see that Mr. Littleton has his coat and have him escorted to the gate."

Edward rolled his eyes. "Amelia, this is ridiculous."

Ignoring Edward, she turned to the butler. "Thank you, James. And when you are done, please send Elizabeth up to my chamber." She gathered her skirts and brushed past James without so much as a glance back at her guest.

❧

After a nap and a warm bath, Amelia dressed in a gown of brown cambric embroidered with small white roses along the hem. She sat at her dressing table as Elizabeth worked to brush the stubborn tangles from her hair. Every stroke aggravated her aching head, so she dismissed Elizabeth and decided to perform the task herself.

As the minutes ticked, her reflection in the glass grew murky. Now that autumn had slipped into winter, night fell early over the moors. She abandoned the task completely and shifted her attention to the window, which framed the purple twilight blanketing Sterling Wood. A chill traveled along her spine. She stood, crossed to the window, and told herself to draw the drape, but couldn't resist looking for a shadow outside. She'd never actually seen Edward leave.

She returned to her dressing table and lifted the note that had arrived from Jane that afternoon. Her friend was planning to host a dinner on Wednesday night to celebrate Amelia's forthcoming union with Captain Sterling. Amelia shook her head in amazement. Only Jane could organize such an event on such short notice.

Would it accomplish its intended purpose? No doubt news of her dissolved engagement with Edward had already spread to every corner of the village. She imagined every idle tongue wagging outside the dressmaker's and butcher's shops. But surely Jane was right. If Mr. Hammond gave the union his blessing, others would follow.

Amelia rubbed her hands over her arms, hoping to generate a little more warmth. The dress seemed pitifully thin for the weather, or perhaps it was the dampness of her hair on her back that made her shiver. She pulled a thick woven shawl from her wardrobe and wrapped her fingers around the candlestick. A visit with Lucy was just what she needed.

Amelia made her way through the labyrinth of stairs and hallways to Lucy's room, where a cheery fire danced in the wide stone fireplace and bathed the room in a warm glow. Two rocking chairs flanked the ornately carved mantel. In the chair to the left sat Mrs. Dunne, her back facing the door, her figure shadowy against the fire's glow. She sang softly as she rocked. A lullaby! Amelia searched her memory, unable to recall anyone singing such a song to her. She stepped closer, straining to hear.

"Sing hushabye loo, low loo, low lan. Hushabye loo, low loo—"

Mrs. Dunne turned with a start. Lucy was nestled in her arms, her eyes closed in peaceful sleep.

"Forgive me, Mrs. Dunne. I've no wish to disturb you."

"'Tis no trouble, miss." A welcoming smile dimpled Mrs. Dunne's rosy cheeks. "Just singing to young Miss Lucy here. It's tired out, she is."

Amelia pulled the other rocking chair closer to Mrs. Dunne and sat down. "That was a beautiful song you were singing."

"Me mam sung it to me many years ago. I sang it to my own sweet babes, and now I'm singin' it to this little mite."

Amelia leaned over and brushed Lucy's curls from her forehead. "You must miss seeing your own children every day, Mrs. Dunne."

"Aye, that I do. But this angel won't be needin' me too much longer, and then I'll be back to my own. I daresay they've managed well enough without me, what with my oldest girl almost grown herself."

Amelia looked down at her hands, a familiar guilt tugging at her heart. How much had Mrs. Dunne sacrificed to care for Lucy? "We'll miss you, Lucy and I, when the time comes."

"Oh, we'll see each other from time to time. 'Tis but a short walk from our farm to here." The older woman stared into the fire, her round face rosy in the firelight. "When we love someone, we do what is necessary to provide for 'em. I know ye'll do that for Miss Lucy here."

Amelia leaned back and began to rock, feeling peaceful for the first time all day. From their first meeting, the nurse's pleasant attitude had drawn Amelia in. And they would never have met if not for Katherine. Mrs. Dunne's reputation for midwifery was unparalleled, and when the difficulties arose with Katherine's pregnancy, Mrs. Dunne had offered advice and guidance. Then when Katherine died and Lucy required a wet nurse, Mrs. Dunne, having recently weaned a child of her own, had filled the role seamlessly. Despite the differences in their stations, these days she sometimes felt Mrs. Dunne was her only friend in the house.

"Speakin' of returning to family." Mrs. Dunne looked down at the sleeping baby. "Might I ask if the captain's made any decisions with regard to Lucy's future?"

Amelia blinked. She'd assumed Mrs. Dunne had heard her news from the other servants. But the woman appeared totally unaware. Amelia leaned back in her rocking chair. "Perhaps you've not heard, but my plans have shifted. I have parted ways with Edward Littleton and will marry Captain Sterling this Friday. So your position is secure here at Winterwood Manor if you can continue on."

Mrs. Dunne nodded. "Aye, miss, I'll be thinkin' on that."

SARAH E. LADD

An awkward silence hung in the air, so Amelia promptly changed the subject.

"I cannot believe Lucy is asleep already. Do you think she will wake if you hand her to me?"

Mrs. Dunne's throaty chuckle brought a smile to Amelia's face. "I'm of the mind the Lord himself could come with the wind an' the fire, and it wouldn't wake this little one. Here."

Amelia took Lucy in her arms, leaned back slowly, and nestled the child in the crook of her elbow. Nothing compared to the serenity of cradling a sleeping infant. Her rhythmic breathing and soft scent carried away every trace of the day's troubles.

"Would ye like me to read to you, miss?"

Amelia pulled her gaze away from firelight dancing on copper curls. "That would be lovely."

"Maybe something from God's book?"

Amelia tensed, then exhaled. "From the Psalms, please."

"Of course." Mrs. Dunne leaned over the side of her chair and pulled a worn leather volume from a lopsided reed basket.

"Blessed is the man that walketh not in the counsel of the ungodly." The cadence of the woman's brogue sounded sweet as any song. Amelia closed her eyes to listen.

"His delight is in the law of the Lord; and in his law doth he meditate day and night. And he shall be like a tree planted by the rivers of water, that bringeth forth his fruit in his season; his leaf also shall not wither; and whatsoever he doeth shall prosper."

I want to be like that, Amelia mused. *Fruitful. Like a tree by the water.*

"The ungodly are not so: but are like the chaff which the wind driveth away. Therefore the ungodly shall not stand in the judgment, nor sinners in the congregation of the righteous."

The words rang like poetry, but their meaning sliced deeper than words intended to merely entertain.

162

What makes a person righteous instead of ungodly?

Lucy shifted in Amelia's arms, and she looked down at the soft curve of the baby's lips.

I want to be godly. For Lucy. For myself. I want God to be pleased with me.

"For the Lord knoweth the way of the righteous: but the way of the ungodly shall perish."

You do know my ways, don't you, Lord? Amelia thought back over the past weeks. When she strung the painful events together in her mind, she could see that none of it had happened by accident or her own doing. Minute by minute, God had indeed been faithful to her.

Hope sparked, glowing at first like a tiny ember. Each word Mrs. Dunne uttered fanned her desire to know more.

Lucy grew hot as she slept, and Amelia shifted the babe in her arms. Her sleeve was damp with Lucy's perspiration. Fiery locks clung to her forehead, and Amelia sobered. The memory of Katherine's hair clinging to her forehead flashed before her. The same titian hue.

At the memory a particular passage came to mind. "Mrs. Dunne, would you please read the Twenty-Third Psalm?"

Mrs. Dunne didn't need to turn the page. The words, memorized, slipped from her lips in perfect rhythm. Amelia straightened. She'd not heard nor read the words since Katherine's last day. Then she had spoken them without faith. How would she receive them now?

As the familiar verses washed over her, she realized she had a choice. She could continue stumbling forward in unbelief, or she could accept that she had a shepherd—and be grateful.

"Surely goodness and mercy shall follow me all the days of my life; and I will dwell in the house of the Lord for ever."

Jane believed it. Katherine had believed it.

In that moment, Amelia chose to believe it too.

17

Graham sank down into the office chair in the library and rested his forearms on the leather inlay of the desk. He studied the gold embossment adorning the edge. He hadn't noticed the detail before. The desktop, which only hours ago stood littered with papers and books, was now clear.

He leaned back to open the desk drawer. No ledger either. What else was William hiding?

He reached forward for the writing box on the corner. He needed to write Carrington a note about his intention to anonymously buy the land back from Littleton, whatever the cost, then respond to Lieutenant Foster's letter regarding the additional ship repairs.

The note to Carrington took minutes. He dried the ink, folded the parchment and sealed it, and set it aside for a courier, then pulled Foster's letter from his satchel. As he reread the assessment of damages, Graham cupped his hand behind his neck and rubbed the tight muscles, willing the memories of smoke and screams to retreat from his mind. Would he ever be free of them?

With the wedding scheduled for Friday, he'd make the long trip to Plymouth the following week to oversee the repairs personally. The success of his missions was entirely on his shoulders. It was his ship, his responsibility.

Plymouth. Another rush of memories bore down upon him. He'd said good-bye to Katherine in Plymouth, but the place stood out in his mind for another reason.

Graham rubbed his hand against the rough stubble on his chin. Stephen Sulter. How long had it been since he'd seen the man? Four years? Five? As a lad he'd learned from Sulter everything he knew about running a ship and being a fair leader. And more. He stared at the blank paper, but his quill refused to scratch across the smooth surface. Why had he avoided contacting his former captain for so long?

Graham knew the answer to that question. Pride. He didn't want Stephen Sulter to know he had failed.

Sulter no longer lived in Plymouth, of course. The man had left the navy for the church and now served as vicar for a parish in Liverpool. Graham knew he should go see Sulter. But if he did, what would he say to the man? That he'd relapsed into old habits? That as a result, nine men died and almost a dozen had been wounded? The thought of admitting that failure to anyone made him cringe. But to tell Sulter, the man who had helped him turn his life around and become a man of God? How could he face that?

He rubbed his face with his hand as memories of that time in his life overtook the others. Such peace had covered him then. Was it too late to get it back? Would God even forgive him after so much time?

Perhaps he would visit Sulter before returning to sea. Or perhaps it was still too soon.

Graham decided to save his letter to Foster for the morning. He retired to his bedchamber. But try as he might, sleep eluded him. He tossed one way, then the other, unaccustomed to such a struggle.

Graham folded the pillow in half and tucked it under his head. If only he were on his ship. The gentle roll of the sea usually rocked him to sleep, lapping waves serving as a soothing lullaby. This incessant ticking of the mantel clock was enough to drive anyone mad.

He yanked the pillow from beneath his head and hurled it to the ground. During the day he possessed greater control of his thoughts, but at night, in complete silence and darkness, his worries magnified.

After pushing himself up from the bed, he snatched the candle from the nightstand and carried it to the fireplace to light the wick. The flame danced in the drafty room. He moved to the window and lifted the curtain to peer into the night. The outlines of the main stable and the groundskeeper's shed could barely be seen under the cloak of darkness. A few more hours needed to pass before Eastmore's grounds would awaken.

He dropped the curtain. Reading would distract him for an hour or two.

He knelt before his wood-and-leather traveling trunk, which had arrived at Eastmore Hall a few days after he had, unlatched the brass lock, and propped open the lid. Inside, his belongings were packed into tight, neat rows. On top lay his uniform jacket and buff breeches, tucked away until he returned to his ship. He smoothed the jacket's lapel and placed it on the ground, along with his breeches, then grabbed a stack of books. As he did, his gaze fell upon a small tortoiseshell trinket box with ivory inlay.

Katherine's box.

Gingerly he set the books aside. He picked up the box and turned the key in the delicate lock. Inside, every memento told the story of their romance, and just looking at them transformed his frustration into sorrow. He had not looked inside it since placing

Katherine's letter there two weeks ago. But for some reason, tonight, he felt the need to look at them all, to hold them in his hands. To be reminded. As he anticipated another marriage, even a marriage of convenience, he must find a way to say farewell.

The tiny box was packed as tidily as his traveling trunk. Graham lifted out the pocket watch Katherine had given him on their wedding day. It had belonged to her father. The candle's light caught the metal surface and flashed into the chamber's darkness. One day he would give the watch to Lucy, perhaps on her wedding day. He laid it down carefully atop the other items in the trunk. He needed to give it to Amelia for safekeeping. If he never returned, he didn't want it to find a final resting place on the ocean's bed.

His heart raced as his rough fingers brushed a tiny parcel secured with brown paper. He loosened the twine and carefully unfolded the stiff wrapping to reveal a long lock of Katherine's hair, tied with gray ribbon. He flexed his fingers, so awkward and unworthy of touching something so beautiful. If he allowed himself, he could recall the feel of the silky locks sliding through his fingers. Ever so carefully, he held the lock of hair up to the light. The candle's glow caught the still-vibrant color.

The last trinket in the box was the most precious. Graham lifted out a small portrait in a gilt frame. The passing of time had made it difficult to recall the nuances of Katherine's likeness, but looking at the miniature brought the memories rushing forth.

He pinched the bridge of his nose, willing his breathing to stay slow. Steady. How he wished the hands of time could be reversed. But no amount of wishing could undo the past. He must care for Lucy now and provide for her welfare once he returned to sea. Would Katherine approve of his marriage to Amelia?

Words from her letter echoed in his mind. *"Do not let your heart grow cold."*

Eighteen months had passed since last he held her. Since he whispered farewell. He had not imagined that time would be the last.

With an impatient jerk of his hand, he swept the moisture from his eyes. With great care he rewrapped the lock of hair, pausing to whisper as he lowered it back to its resting place.

"Farewell, darling Katherine."

❦

Amelia smoothed her emerald velvet cape as she stood in the darkened hallway outside Helena's bedchamber. She mustered her courage and rapped her knuckles across the closed door. No response. She knocked again. "Helena, are you in there?"

She waited a few moments before knocking again. Helena had to be inside. Hadn't she just seen Elizabeth exit this very door? Amelia turned the handle and stepped into Helena's chamber for the first time in several days.

Helena turned from her dressing table. "What do you need?"

"I came to see if you have changed your mind about the dinner at the Hammonds'. Jane says everyone will be there, and I—"

"I have other plans."

"What other plans?"

Helena stood. Her amethyst satin gown hugged her figure, and only a gathering of lace at the bodice prevented it from being scandalous.

Amelia gawked at the dress. "That's a new gown, is it not?"

"I was just about to ask the same of yours."

Amelia looked down at her deep rose satin and ran a hand down the front.

Helena reached for her shawl. "I remember handpicking that very fabric for your trousseau. What was it you said? Something about how you thought Edward would like the hue? That Edward always complimented you when you wore that color?"

The insinuation brought a flush to Amelia's cheeks. "Helena, what's done is done. Please say you will not make me go to the Hammonds' alone."

"You made your decision alone, Amelia—with no consideration of anyone else." Helena reached down to the dressing table, removed the stopper from an etched perfume bottle, and dabbed it behind her ear. "It seems fitting that you should deal with the consequences alone, does it not?"

Amelia blinked. "Am I to lose you too, Helena?"

Helena moved from the dressing table. The lilac fabric swirled around her legs as she took a few steps toward the window. "I asked you not to make me choose between you and my family."

A wave of nausea seized Amelia, and her lungs refused to expand. She understood Helena perfectly. "Well, if you change your mind, you know where we will be."

Helena glanced out the window. "Your carriage is here. You'd best be on your way. You wouldn't want to keep your *betrothed* waiting."

Amelia forced herself from Helena's room. Tears burned her eyes, and she struggled for control. The captain had already done so much for her. How would it appear for her to be a blubbering fool on the way to their engagement dinner?

She should have brought a candle. The sun had long since set, and the hallway grew darker with each passing moment. A sliver of moonlight through the window afforded barely enough light to illuminate the staircase's curve. Desire to be away from this dark, cold mansion and into the warmth of the Hammond house fueled her descent. If she was honest, though, it wasn't the Hammonds' company she longed for so much as another's.

Captain Sterling.

They would marry in just two days. How strange to realize they hadn't even known each other three weeks. At first, she'd regarded the captain as merely a means to an end. But in those few weeks, how many times had he defended her? Protected her? His qualities were noble. She could do worse than to combine her destiny with such a man. Perhaps after—

Lost in boundless thought, she didn't notice the person waiting at the foot of the stairs until it was too late. Unable to slow her momentum, she ran right into him. She gasped. Steadying hands grabbed her upper arms.

Edward.

She tried to shrug out of his grasp. "Why are you here?"

"Are those tears I see?"

"Let go of me."

"Not until you tell me why you've been crying."

A knock sounded on the heavy front door, and James walked to open it. Edward looked over his shoulder, his hot hand remaining on her arm. She stared at the door and wriggled again to free herself.

"Expecting someone?" Edward's words strained through his teeth. "Oh yes, now I recall. I did hear something about a dinner at the Hammonds' tonight. I never did receive my invitation, though."

She put her hand on his chest and pushed. "Why are you here?"

"Your uncle invited me." He chuckled. "Oh, I see. You think the only reason I would visit here is you. I am here to dine with my business partner and his family."

She attempted to wrench herself from his grasp just as the captain entered with Mr. Carrington, who had recently returned from Sheffield. Graham's cool gray eyes immediately locked on Edward's. His nostrils flared in irritation.

Edward released Amelia. Breathless, she clutched her cape at the neck and stepped backward. A gust of wind whipped through the open door. No one spoke.

"Please, let's go." Amelia walked over and clutched Graham's sleeve with her hand, noting the twitch of hard muscle beneath the fabric.

It was as if he didn't even hear her. Her hands slipped from his sleeve as Graham took two steps into the hall. "I thought I told you that you were no longer welcome here."

Edward chuckled. "You can relax, Sterling. I am not here for Amelia. Barrett, as you well know, is my business partner. We have matters to discuss."

"Then discuss your matters with George Barrett and keep your distance from Miss Barrett."

"The master of Winterwood Manor has spoken. Or should I say the master-to-be?" A shrug lifted Edward's shoulder, and he shifted his gaze. "I see you brought Carrington along. Nicely played, sir. It is always wise to engage those who know the most about the object you are trying to secure."

Amelia had her eyes on Edward, so she jumped a little when Graham took her elbow. "If you have business with Barrett," he said, "I suggest you be on about it."

"Oh, I'll not keep you from the festivities, Sterling. I know all too well the desire of a man to be alone with the woman he loves."

He nodded toward Amelia, his false smile making her blood run cold. "Give the Hammonds my best."

18

Candlelight illuminated every corner of the Hammonds' drawing room. Tiny flickers of light danced on every surface, from the oil paintings to the polished silver. And everywhere Graham looked, he encountered another stranger.

He knew Amelia, of course, as well as the Hammonds, Carrington, and his own brother. Beyond that, he was at a definite disadvantage. The cream of Darbury society—minus the Barretts—surrounded him, and he could not remember a single name. Yet they knew all about him. His occupation. His late parents and wife. His daughter. His betrothed. And all seemed to feel that the details of his life were their personal business.

With artful tact and quick words, Graham had escaped the clutches of two women, Mrs. Bell and Mrs. Trewell. Now, as he moved toward the door, their pointed questions rang in his memory. He would readily discuss the war or life at sea or whether he was enjoying his stay at Darbury. But he was not prepared—nor willing—to answer questions about Katherine or Lucy. And fifteen minutes of fending off such questions had left him wearier than a long watch in wartime.

If memory served him correctly, there was a nook with a window seat just down the hall, on the way to Mr. Hammond's study. He would slip away there for a moment's peace.

After inching along the wall and squeezing behind an oval-backed upholstered chair, Graham rounded the doorpost into the darkened corridor and quickly found the niche he remembered from when he and Amelia visited the vicarage a few days past. Cold air seeped in around the window's cracked casing and cooled his agitation. He sank down on the window seat and stared out over the lawn, intent upon clearing his mind.

"Captain Sterling." Graham started, then relaxed when he realized it was Amelia who'd found him—not Mrs. Bell or Mrs. Trewell. The faint moonlight falling through the window highlighted her features and glistened upon her hair.

"Whatever are you doing here?" she asked.

He stood slowly. "Hiding."

"From what?"

He nodded in the parlor's direction. "Don't you mean from *whom?* You were right. These people are insatiable. I've never seen the like of it."

A smile curved her lips. "Did I not warn you that it might be difficult?"

He straightened his waistcoat and nodded. "I have faced battle, cannon fire, and the sword, and believe me when I say that nothing has frightened me quite so much as Mrs. Bell."

Even in the shadowed corridor, he could see amusement in her wide eyes. Her soft laugh was a soothing balm to his ruffled spirit. He stood a little taller when she was around him.

Blond curls danced about her face as she looked this way and that, then stepped into the nook where he stood. "I have a question I must ask you."

The nearer she drew, the warmer his place of refuge seemed to grow. His pulse quickened. A darkened corridor. Hushed tones. The setting was almost . . . romantic.

His cravat seemed to tighten about his neck as he leaned in closer to listen. She spoke so softly he had to strain to hear. "Are you angry with me?"

"With you?" His voice was much louder than he intended. "Why would I be angry with you?"

"Shh!" She looked around to make sure no one was about. "It's just that because of . . . that is to say, with Edward at Winterwood, and . . ."

He lowered his voice to match hers. "Of course I am not angry with you. Littleton's desperate. I'll not allow him to take advantage of this situation. Or you."

Was she leaning in toward him? Her golden head came dangerously close to grazing the bottom of his chin. The slightest tremble shook her words. "I shudder to know what you think of me."

Graham indulged himself and studied the long, black lashes that fanned her cheeks as she stared at the ground. What did he think of her? He thought a great many things . . . some of which would not be appropriate to verbalize.

She continued. "Please do not misunderstand me. I am grateful—thrilled—to have my Lucy. But everything else I find . . . I mean, I do not wish to—"

"There is no need for explanations. And as for what I think of you, I think you are brave. Loyal. Determined. Those are admirable qualities, Amelia. This will all pass. And you will be an excellent mother to Lucy. However, I am concerned for you."

Her lips parted in surprise. "Me?"

Graham nodded. "When all this is passed, when your family

departs and I return to sea, you will be alone at Winterwood. What then?"

Her voice sounded confident, but the expression in her eyes suggested otherwise. "I will not be alone. I will have Lucy. I will have the Hammonds . . . and my family. They may be angry, but they will come around, to be sure. And Carrington will be a help, of course."

But you won't have me.

Amelia stood so close that all he would have to do is take a half step closer and she would be in his arms. If he did that, would she pull away? His gaze drifted from the top of her golden head to her creamy shoulders.

She seemed so delicate, like a feather. And she was so close. How wrong would it be to touch her cheek or press her hand against his palm? Almost without thinking, he extended his arm to her. She stared at it, then flicked her eyes up to meet his gaze. His blood pounded in his ears as he waited to see if she would take it. She lifted her hand, hesitated, and then rested it on the sleeve of his jacket. At the touch, fire surged up his arm and through his body. Her lip quivered.

A nervous smile played on his lips. He could not control it. Like a puppet master, his emotions seemed in control of his every thought and action.

Amelia looked down at her hand and then away to the ground. With her other hand she brushed the curls from her face, something he'd noticed she did when uncomfortable.

He needed to say something. His words were far from brilliant. "Please, do not worry."

She nodded and smiled, but he could not guess at what thoughts swirled in her pretty head.

She looked at his lips and then his eyes. "We'd best rejoin the party. We already know the danger that has befallen my reputation as of late. No need to give them any more fuel for that fire."

"Must we go?"

Each smile she offered renewed his energy. "No doubt we've been given a certain leeway as we are soon to be wed, but still it would not do for us to be missing for dinner. I heard Mrs. Hammond and Mrs. Bell discussing our situation. It appears the masses are on our side, for now. No need to tempt fate."

"Very well. But I give you notice, Amelia Barrett. You have the temptation part right, but my fate has nothing to do with it."

❧

Across the dinner table, plump Mrs. Mill whispered something to Mrs. Bell, who tittered in response. Jane sat next to Amelia at the end of the table. Mr. Hammond sat at the other, eating his venison soup. Even though nearly fifteen guests separated the long-married vicar and his wife, their expressions connected them. They seemed to communicate with a secret language.

Captain Sterling sat to Amelia's right, patiently answering Mr. Mill's questions about how long the war with America might last and whether Napoleon was really secure in his exile on Elba. His head had been turned from her for practically the whole dinner.

It was hard even to imagine that she and the captain would be married in two days' time. Would she ever enjoy the kind of connection with him that the Hammonds shared? She shifted her eyes from the plate to her intended's sleeve, not daring to look at his face when such a thought spun itself in her mind.

Her plan to persuade the captain to marry her so she could fulfill her promise to Katherine was successful, or at least it would be in mere days. What right did she have to expect—or even think about—anything more? Captain Sterling had married Katherine for love. He was marrying her out of obligation. But then again, there had been a certain attentiveness to their interchange in the hall that made her believe he could, at some point, develop feelings for her. Her heart gave a little lurch. She was prepared to live a life free of romance if it meant she could care for Lucy. Dare she even hope for more?

She knew she was not well schooled in the intricacies of a relationship between man and woman. Without a mother to guide her, her sole education in matters of love came from romantic novels and poetry. And from Aunt Augusta, who had told her, "Love comes later, sometimes not at all. But you are a wealthy woman, so with love or without it, you at least will always be secure . . ."

Still, it seemed to her that something had sparked between the captain and herself. And what she felt now was like nothing she'd experienced before. She felt comfortable yet nervous. Safe but vulnerable. Protected but exposed.

But even as the memory of her hand resting on his sleeve brought a flush to her cheeks, she couldn't help remembering more of Aunt Augusta's love advice. "Men will be after you for your money, so you should trust no one."

Can I trust Captain Sterling?

Someone's hand brushed her shoulder. "That's Jonathan Riley, is it not?"

Amelia nearly jumped from her seat.

Captain Sterling leaned closer. "I didn't mean to frighten you." He put his spoon down and continued. "The man on the other side of William? Jonathan Riley, correct?"

Amelia followed his gaze to a tall, brown-haired man. "Yes, to be sure." She noticed right away that both Mr. Riley and William Sterling had already indulged in too much wine. Their laughter interrupted the conversations around them. She looked over at Jane, whose irritated gaze was fixed on the captain's brother. Amelia glanced back to the captain. If anything, he looked more agitated than Jane.

Amelia winced as Mr. Riley pounded his fist on the table and spilled the remainder of his wine. Silence fell over the room, and a servant hurried to blot up the wine. Graham's stormy eyes narrowed on his brother. She could feel his frustration just as clearly as she could smell the mild scent of sandalwood that always seemed to accompany him. She glanced over at Jane, who was glaring at William Sterling.

It was going to be a long evening.

⁂

At the conclusion of dinner, the women retreated to the parlor for tea and coffee, and the men remained in the dining room for port and brandy. But Graham worked his way over to William, grabbed his brother by the arm, and pushed him from the dining room, out the front door, and into the night.

The night had grown markedly colder since they first arrived. Frigid air gusted down from the home's pitched roof, and spattered flurries of snow played in the night wind. Graham tapped the door closed with the heel of his boot before speaking. "What are you doing? You're making a mockery of yourself."

"What?" William looked at him through glassy eyes. "I was just trying to amuse myself a bit. Deadly dull evening, I'm afraid."

"Then you need not stay."

Graham turned to rejoin the men, but William grabbed him by the arm. "Did you speak with her about the money?"

Graham jerked his arm free. "This is neither the time nor the place to speak of this. We'll talk tomorrow."

"This cannot wait."

"Why?"

William licked his lips, glancing about as if to ensure nobody was within earshot. His clumsy words slid into one another,

178

making him difficult to understand. "I'm in trouble, brother. Do not make me recount details. Let's just say my creditors are growing impatient. If you don't want to give me the money outright, so be it. A loan, then. I will pay you back."

"Even if I had the money to give, I could hardly get it tonight."

"You had Carrington purchase the west fields back from Littleton, did you not? How did you get that money?"

"I did ask Mr. Carrington to oversee the purchase—anonymously, of course—but I used my own funds, not Miss Barrett's."

A sneer distorted William's face, and the effect of drinking wobbled him from side to side. "Convenient for you to be absent all these years, marry a wealthy woman, and return to whatever it is you do without a thought to the family you came from."

Graham should ignore him. His brother's words, if he were in another state, would take on a different meaning. Graham made no attempt to hide the contempt in his voice. "But you forget one important detail. The debt's not mine. It's yours."

"But what if it had been yours?" A challenge weighed in William's voice. "What if you'd been the one saddled here? You've been free to live your life; I have been bound to this. So I have made a few bad decisions. Am I to pay for them the rest of my life?"

"You make no sense, William. We'll talk about this tomorrow."

William grabbed his shoulder, preventing him from turning. "I owe a great deal of money. You have more than enough. Am I to understand that you will turn your back on your own flesh and blood?"

Flesh and blood indeed. That was where their relationship began, and that was where it ended. If anything, *pity* described his attitude toward William. His brother was so like his father. Same light eyes. Same light hair. And same bad habits.

Graham shook off his brother's hand. "Go home, Will. You're foxed. We'll talk in the morning."

William grabbed him again. "We'll talk now."

Graham whirled around to face William. "Even if I did have the money, and even if I were willing to give it to you, there is nothing I could do about it tonight. This is an engagement dinner. *My* engagement dinner. Believe it or not, I have concerns other than the mess you've made for yourself."

William pointed an unsteady finger at him. "Talk down to me if you will. What kind of man—what sort of *honorable* man—uses a woman, his late wife's friend, to further his own interests?"

"I'm not using Miss Barrett for her money."

"You're using her to ease your conscience, as a means to find suitable care for your Lucy. Explain it to me—how is that different? How—"

"And what if I am?" At the mention of Lucy's name, something snapped in Graham. He had to force his fists to remain at his sides. "What if I am using her? What business is it of yours? I can hardly return to the sea without finding suitable care, and you have been no help whatsoever. But then again, I've managed to survive the past eighteen years without answering to anyone in this family, and I do not intend to start now."

William threw his head back and laughed. "Oh, I forgot. You're the mighty Captain Sterling, hero of the seas. But the fact is, you are no better than I. We're cut from the same cloth, are we not? My offense regards money. Your offense regards taking advantage of women. Neither of us is quite as we seem."

Graham hissed through clenched teeth. "You are making an idiot out of yourself. Go home."

William stepped close. Heat radiated from his intoxicated body. Graham refused to waver or step away. He stared hard at his brother, and he could swear he was staring straight into his father's eyes.

William finally spoke, his brandy-laced breath hot against Graham's cheek. "I saw the way you looked at her. Don't think I did not see it, that everyone in attendance did not notice. But you are a fool if you think she will ever return the regard, for it is your daughter she wants, not you. You see, we all have an angle, even the charming Miss Barrett."

"I'm warning you, William. Step back."

But his brother was not willing to let it go. "She is not what she seems either. You are not the only man to sample her charms."

Now Graham leaned in at the odd statement. "Make yourself clear."

"I've held her in my arms myself. Oh, does that surprise you, brother?"

"You're a lying drunk." Graham snatched his brother's coat by the collar.

"No need to become so angry." William's eyes were now nothing more than slits over his sloppy grin. "It was one kiss. One little, passionate kiss. And she did not mind, I assure you, not one bit. Seems you're not the only Sterling worth having."

Graham released William's collar with a bit of a shove. The older Sterling stumbled backward, fell to a knee, and struggled to stand. A slack laugh slid from William before he waved a finger in the air. "You will regret not helping me in my time of need, brother."

They stared at one another, William swaying slightly, Graham frozen to the ground. Then William broke eye contact and stomped down the path in the darkness.

Graham watched him, doubting the foxed fool could find his way home in his current state. But then again, he didn't really care.

He looked up at the black night. Only a few stars twinkled through the thickening clouds. Strange how the sky looked the same from the middle of the country as it did on the sea. Same sky. Same man. Different trials.

He turned to a trickle of light spilling onto the path. Strange, he thought he'd closed the door. He looked up and caught a glimpse of Amelia's retreating form.

19

Amelia had not intended to eavesdrop. When she saw Graham and his brother go outside, she should have kept herself planted firmly next to Jane. She shook her head, regretting her indiscretion. But her punishment for curiosity was steep, for now she knew the truth.

She'd been mistaken when she thought she'd seen a glimmer of affection in Captain Sterling's eyes when they were alone in the Hammonds' hall. The captain was marrying her for Lucy's care. Nothing more. And why should that sting? That had been the plan all along, had it not? A marriage of convenience. But she cringed to realize the captain now knew of the incident between her and his brother. She should have told him before. What must he think of her?

Amelia nodded to Mrs. Mill's account of her daughter's baby and managed to ask perfectly timed questions without paying real attention. She praised the beauty of Mrs. Bell's silver dress and admired the detailed tambour work on Mrs. Dyer's reticule.

She smiled. Laughed. Performed all of the tasks required to win their approval. After all that Jane had done to protect her, how could she let on that the evening was anything other than perfect?

On the other side of the drawing room, Captain Sterling, Mr. Carrington, Mr. Hammond, and a handful of other men clustered around a game of whist. Their laughter rose above the ladies' chatter and the fireplace's merry crackle.

Amelia shrank back against her chair and stole a glance at Graham. Again. His sable hair curled over the high collar of his black tailcoat. His military posture and bronzed skin set him apart from the rest of the men in the room.

Without warning, he turned and looked in her direction. A corner of his mouth tugged upward. She jerked her head down.

The conversation between William and Graham played once more in her mind. What were the west fields, and why were they talking about Edward? And why had they been talking about her inheritance? Why was William challenging Graham on matters of character and loyalty? And heaven help her, William did remember their kiss. And now the captain knew of it too.

She'd be a fool not to acknowledge the obvious. She had let her mind go somewhere it shouldn't, and now her heart would pay the price.

Amelia wanted to believe the romantic love stories she and Helena had devoured. She wanted to share a love like that of Jane and Mr. Hammond. But perhaps Aunt Augusta had been right. Love didn't come to a girl whose only asset was her fortune.

A pat on her hand drew her attention.

Amelia glanced down at Mrs. Dyer's hand resting on her own. With great reluctance she met the woman's eyes. A knowing grin creased the older woman's puffy face. "You're staring, my dear."

The women giggled like schoolgirls. Mrs. Mill held up her hands to quiet the group. "Now, ladies, who among you could blame young Miss Barrett for not being able to take her eyes off of the dashing Captain Sterling?"

Fresh snickers circled the group.

Let them believe it. Let them all believe this is a match made of love. Keep what little dignity you have intact.

⚜

Snow clouds obscured the moonlight, and trees blocked the flickering light from the torches in front of the vicarage as the carriage rumbled down the path to Winterwood. The journey would be a short one and the hour was late, so if Graham was to make his apology, he needed to do it quickly. He needed to speak with Miss Barrett alone. He was uncertain of how long she'd been present for his discussion with William, but her distant expression made it clear she hadn't liked what she had heard.

He chided himself for not keeping command of his words. They could have been easily misconstrued. The last thing he wanted her to think was that he was taking advantage of her kindness.

To intensify his discomfort, he could not shake the memory of William's words. Had his brother and Amelia shared an intimate moment?

Before the carriage carrying him, Miss Barrett, and Mr. Carrington even pulled to a complete stop, Graham thrust open the carriage door and jumped down. He cast a warning glance at the footman, daring him to step closer, then extended his hand to Amelia.

Miss Barrett hesitated, then took his hand and stepped down. The moment her skirt was clear of the door, she tried to pull her hand away, but Graham squeezed it.

Her eyes widened when he wouldn't let go. Graham slammed the carriage door closed with his other hand, just in case Carrington entertained a notion to join them.

"I need to talk about what you heard."

She shook her head. "You owe me no explanation."

"Then I need to talk to you about what *I* heard."

Amelia diverted her eyes. "I had no business listening to a private conversation."

The flurries falling around them increased. Silver flakes danced about her, landing on her eyelashes and melting when they kissed her cheeks. He took her by the arm and directed her closer to the house, away from the footman and driver. "We are to be married in two days, Amelia. I hardly think it wise to begin our union with secrets or doubt between us."

She pursed her lips and yanked her hand from his. "Very well." She jutted her chin out. "What are you buying from Edward?"

The honesty in her upturned face unnerved him. "Before you broke the engagement with Edward, he bought Eastmore's west fields from my brother. The west fields are the pastures that join with Winterwood's northwest corner. I asked Carrington to purchase them back anonymously."

She frowned. "Why would he do such a thing?"

"Why would that man do a great many of the things he does? All I know is I am not comfortable with him owning property next to you and Lucy while I am gone. He's a rogue, and the farther away he is from you, the better."

"Why did you not tell me?"

"I thought not to burden you with such a detail when Carrington could handle it quickly and discreetly."

She lifted her fur-lined cape hood and draped it over her head. Only the tip of her nose and chin remained visible. "I am quite capable of managing any and all issues related to Winterwood Manor, and I wish to be notified of such things, little or great."

"I shall keep that in mind."

"Good." She pivoted toward the door.

He reached out his hand and wrapped his fingers loosely around her arm, stopping her. He could not get William's words out of his mind. He had to hear her response. "While we are asking questions, I have one of my own."

Even through the heavy fabric of her cloak he could feel her muscles tighten. "Very well."

He hesitated, realizing full well the indelicacy of his question. "William says that you shared a kiss with him. Is this true?"

In a sudden burst of motion, she jerked her arm free and removed the hood's cloak. She looked him square in the eye. He had angered her—or embarrassed her. The tight line of her lips indicated nothing less. He did not regret his question. He wanted to know—needed to know—but he had not anticipated the fire in her response.

"I did not kiss your brother, sir. He forced himself upon me during one of his all-too-frequent drunken episodes. I managed to escape with my dignity intact. Until now, that is."

The instant she said it, he regretted his words. The coldness in her treatment of his brother the afternoon they'd visited Lucy suddenly made sense. He felt like an inconsiderate fool. "I apologize. I should have known otherwise." He softened his tone. "Why did you not tell me?"

She cut her eyes toward the footman, no doubt making sure the man could not hear. "Do you really think I would admit such an indiscretion to anyone if I could help it? Your brother humiliated me, and you ask why I never spoke of it?"

The words were out of his mouth before he could consider the ramifications. "I do not wish to appear indelicate, but we are to be married. I have a right to know of such things."

"A right? What exactly are you insinuating, Captain?"

"I insinuate nothing. But keep in mind that I have known you for less than a month. How am I to know your, well, your—"

"Is *reputation* the word you seek?" She did not wait for him to respond. "I assure you, sir, that you'll find no finer reputation in all of England." She pinned him with her stare. "Keep in mind that I could ask similar questions of you."

Graham shrugged. "Go ahead. I've nothing to hide."

"Your private life, such as it is, is your business. As I told you the day you arrived at Winterwood, ours is a business agreement. I will care for Lucy, and you are free to do as you have been doing."

He raised his hands as if to declare innocence. "What exactly is it that you think I do?"

She ignored his question. "I have no expectations of you in regard to a romantic relationship. I assure you, I have done nothing to tarnish my reputation with your brother, but in light of our arrangement, I hardly feel the need to defend myself."

"Our arrangement, hmm? Is that what we are calling this?" Graham did not know whether he should be angry, defensive, or offended. He stepped away from her. Perhaps he had misinterpreted her intentions while they were in the corridor. He could attribute her anger to embarrassment or exhaustion. Or perhaps he had imagined she had been warming to him because he wanted it to be true. After all, had she not made it very clear from the start that her priority was Lucy?

He straightened his shoulders. He needed to keep Lucy his priority as well and not get distracted by those lovely blue eyes. "Very well, Miss Barrett. Thank you for clarifying your expectations."

She lifted a hand to brush her hair from her face, and her lashes fanned against her cheek as she looked to the ground. "Will we see you tomorrow, Captain Sterling?"

"Yes, I'll be by to visit Lucy."

"Very well. Thank you for sharing your carriage."

She stepped toward the door, and he followed her. She stopped and looked back at him. "What are you doing?"

What did she think he was doing? "I'm coming in."

"Why?"

Why? Had she forgotten that just a few hours earlier Edward Littleton had paced these very halls? He wasn't about to take the chance that he was inside, waiting for her to return. "I need to make sure Littleton's gone."

She looked toward the window. "Everything appears to be dark, and the hour is late. Surely he has departed."

"But I don't think—"

She raised her hand to silence him. "Allow me to be perfectly clear, Captain Sterling. I appreciate your efforts on my behalf, but I can handle myself."

He had no idea how to answer that. So he just said, "Very well, Miss Barrett."

She turned, her face impassive, and disappeared inside. James closed the door behind her.

Graham stared at the empty space where she had been.

What just happened?

He turned to the carriage, unlatched the door, and climbed inside. He yanked the door closed behind him and dropped against the tufted leather seat.

He didn't look at Carrington nor did he wish to talk about it. But the weight of the older man's eyes bored into him. He glanced up.

A smirk crept across Carrington's withered face. "Don't worry, she'll come around."

※

Amelia brushed the snow from her cape and leaned her back against the closed door. She squeezed her eyes shut and exhaled in a slow, steady stream. She had not meant to speak so harshly. And if she'd had any hope at all of a romantic future with her husband, no doubt her words, spoken in the heat of embarrassment, had squelched that hope.

She opened her eyes to see James standing next to her with a lit candlestick. "Shall I send up Elizabeth, miss?"

"Yes, please." Amelia handed him her cape and took the candle. "But tell her to take her time. I am going to go see Miss Lucy for a few moments."

"Very well, Miss Barrett."

Amelia followed the aging man with her eyes as he withdrew down the corridor. When he was gone, eerie silence settled over the house. To her left was the window. Craning her neck, she watched the carriage disappear into the darkness. Her chin shook, and as hard as she tried to steady her hand, the candle trembled in her grip. Her arrangement with Captain Sterling had seemed so simple when first conceived. Now nothing was simple about it.

As she turned, light seeping under the closed door to her uncle's study caught her eye. Was Uncle George still awake? Was Edward in there too? A bolt of anxiety surged through her. Perhaps she'd been unwise to send the captain away so quickly. Holding her breath, she listened. Nothing.

She gathered her skirt in her hand and hurried toward the stairs. Muted moonlight slid in through the windows that lined the main stairwell, and wind seeped in around the window casings. Shivers coursed through her. She shouldn't have given her cape to James. Her slippers, still damp from the gathering snow, made no sound as she climbed the curving staircase to the third floor and made her way to the west wing, where the nursery was.

How many sleepless nights had she trod up these stairs for a visit with Lucy? Even just watching the child slumber brought her peace. Now she was so close—to Lucy and to a myriad of other things.

Once at the nursery door, Amelia paused. The light from her

candle danced on the brass knob. She grabbed it and turned. Her eyes adjusted to the dying fire's soft glow. Other than the crackle of coals settling, all was still.

She moved from the main nursery to Lucy's sleeping chamber. Even in the shadows, Amelia knew the small room's layout by heart. A chest of drawers next to the door. A small chair in the corner. The crib opposite the window. She lifted her candle in the air to light the way.

She leaned over the crib's edge, expecting to see Lucy's dimpled, round face. But Lucy was not there. Amelia frowned and stared. Where could the baby be? She snatched the blanket and shook it as if the child would magically appear from beneath.

Dumbstruck, she turned a complete circle, searching every corner of the room. Her heartbeat quickened. She stepped from Lucy's sleeping chamber and tiptoed toward the six-paneled door to Mrs. Dunne's room. It creaked open a little when she knocked.

"Mrs. Dunne?"

She waited for a response. None came.

She called again, louder this time. "Mrs. Dunne?"

Amelia pushed the door open the rest of the way and hurried to the bed. Empty. With her free hand she grabbed the bedsheets and yanked them around. Panic crept up from her soul, but she quickly pushed it down.

There's a logical explanation.

She placed the candlestick on the small table next to Mrs. Dunne's bed, propped her hands on her hips, and looked around the darkened room. Everything seemed to be in place. Mrs. Dunne's shawl draped over her chair, and the door to her wardrobe chest gaped open.

Where could they be? The kitchen?

Without a second thought she grabbed the candle, gathered her skirt, and hurried from the room.

Everything will be fine. Amelia repeated the words to push out the mounting anxiety tightening her chest. The tiny flame from her candle flickered and sputtered in the drafty hall. In her haste, her shoulder clipped the corner as she turned from the hall to the servants' stairs. She winced as hot candle wax splashed her hand.

She flew down the narrow, steep stairs as fast as she dared. But her foot slipped on the first landing, and her candle slipped from her hand. The flame sizzled when it hit the stone floor. Pitch blackness surrounded her. She searched for and snatched up the broken candle and candlestick and felt her way down the remaining flight of stairs.

When she reached the bottom, she fully expected to be met with the warm glow from the kitchen, but cold darkness assaulted her at the threshold. She ran past the cellar door and the pantry and peered into the kitchen, just to make sure she hadn't missed them.

Fear crept into the place in her heart where anxiety had been. Her blood roared in her ears. She couldn't swallow.

Where could they be?

20

Amelia's chest heaved with the exertion of running from the kitchen to her uncle's study.

"Can I help you, miss?"

Amelia jumped at the voice. Intent on her path, she hadn't even noticed Elizabeth coming from the shadows. "Have you seen Mrs. Dunne?"

"Is she not in the nursery?"

"No, I've just returned from there. I checked the kitchen too." Amelia retrieved the broken candle from her pocket and lit it with the flame from Elizabeth's. "Check the library, the dining room, the drawing room. I'm going to my uncle's study."

Elizabeth curtsied and took off down the hall in the direction from which she'd come. Amelia continued down the wide corridor. With every step her anxiety grew. She ignored the terrifying voice in her head, refusing to jump to a tragic conclusion. Mrs. Dunne was an intelligent, responsible woman and a very capable guardian. There was a logical explanation.

She held up her free hand to guard the flame and turned into the vestibule. The sliver of light still shone from under her uncle's door, so she ran to it. Without stopping to knock, she gripped the oval iron doorknob and flung open the door.

Her uncle, who sat behind the desk, jerked his head up. "Amelia Barrett, are you aware of the hour?"

She had to pause to catch her breath. "Have you seen Lucy or Mrs. Dunne?"

"Aren't they in the nursery?"

Amelia shook her head and attempted to swallow. Her throat was so dry she feared no words would escape. "No, they are not."

Uncle George furrowed his brow and placed his quill on the desk. "You must have overlooked them."

Amelia pulled herself up to her full height and met her uncle's eyes. He would not make her feel like a child, not now. "I searched the room, and I checked the kitchen as well. They are not there."

Uncle George's gaze shifted from her to the fireplace, and then she saw him. Edward. In her concern for Lucy, she'd forgotten he might still be here.

Edward stepped forward. "I'll go get James." Edward crossed the room to her, making no attempt to hide his lewd assessment of her. He stood so close that his booted leg brushed the fabric of her skirt. His whisper tickled her ear. "Don't worry, Amelia dear. I'll find them for you."

She looked away, refusing to flinch, and waited for him to leave before speaking. Her uncle picked up his quill and resumed writing. How could he be so nonchalant? She walked over to the desk. "What if something has happened to them? I really think you should—"

A grunt cut her off, and he looked up from the paper. "Do not overreact, Amelia. Where could they have gone? Edward will find them, rest assured."

"How do you think I could rest with her whereabouts unknown?" She blew out her stub of a candle, dropped it on a nearby table, and boldly snatched a sturdier candlestick from his desk. "I don't care what you think of me, Uncle George, but how could you care so little about the safety of a child? There is a baby in our care, and right now nobody seems to know where she is. If you don't think this is serious enough to disturb your letter writing, then so be it."

"She's not in my care. She's in yours, Mistress of Winterwood Manor."

Amelia quitted the room, unwilling to waste her time with the man. Edward, at least, had done what he'd said he would do. The butler and two footmen, roused from their sleep and in various stages of dress, scurried about lighting candles and fires. The main hall echoed with hushed voices, and Edward stood at the foot of the stairs, calling out directions. He pulled on an oilcloth coat and took his hat from one of the maids.

"Has anyone found them?" Her desire to find Lucy overcame her impulse to shrink away from Edward. If he could help her, then she could stomach his presence.

Edward looked up from the buttons on his coat. "No, you were right. No sign of them indoors."

Just hearing the words shot a fresh wave of panic through her. People now swirled around her, but alarm froze her to her spot.

Edward's tone was almost gentle. "I'm going to check outside." He jammed the wide-brimmed hat over his dark hair. "People do not simply disappear."

"Thank you for your help."

Edward leaned in close, his warm breath tickling her ear. "You see, my dear, I am not nearly the monster you believe me to be."

She didn't flinch as he moved past her. The door opened, and a blast of wind ruffled her skirt. Then the door slammed closed.

Amelia turned. She'd personally search every inch of Winterwood, and if she failed to find them, she'd search the grounds as well. With blind determination she took the steps two at a time, paying no heed to the servants bustling around her.

Someone grabbed her arm. When she whipped around, she saw Helena next to her on the landing, clutching a shawl around her body. "What in heaven's name is going on?"

Amelia's words spilled forth in jumbled chaos. "I cannot find Lucy or Mrs. Dunne anywhere. They are missing. Edward is searching the grounds."

Helena jerked. "Edward is still here?"

Amelia sniffed and nodded.

Helena patted her arm. "You know Edward, Amelia. You may find him tiresome, but you know his heart is good. If he says he will find them, then he will."

Amelia didn't even have the energy to argue. She wouldn't rest, nor close one eye, until she had the baby back in her arms, and from that point forward she would never let the child from her sight.

She waited for Helena to put her arms around her. How she needed a comforting embrace. But the embrace never came. Slowly, surely, the words spoken earlier in the evening revisited Amelia's mind.

What was wrong with everyone? It was as if an evil trance had befallen every soul within Winterwood's walls. Her uncle had never been a warm man, but she never would have imagined he'd ignore the needs of an infant. And Helena—they'd been like sisters. But Helena's demeanor tonight was void of any sisterly sympathy.

Helena spoke. "I'm going to call for some tea. Let's go to the drawing room and wait for Edward together."

Amelia shook her head, a little surprised at the calmness in her voice. "I cannot just sit. What if something terrible has happened?"

Her voice rose. "What if Lucy is in danger and we are just sitting, waiting?"

Helena withdrew her hand as if Amelia had just bitten it. "I am only attempting to help, Amelia. I am calling for tea; join me if you will. Edward has everything under control, I have no doubt." She paused and pinned Amelia with her stare. "Does Captain Sterling know you cannot find his child?"

Captain Sterling. He would know what to do. Amelia ignored her cousin's snide words and turned to run down the hall.

"Elizabeth!"

Amelia waited for a response but heard none. She cried louder. "Elizabeth!"

After the second cry, the lady's maid poked her head from the library into the main hall. "Yes, miss?"

"See that someone is sent to Eastmore Hall right away. Get word to Captain Sterling that his daughter is missing."

⅋

Graham awoke with a start. He jerked his head up and listened. Did he hear hoofbeats?

Had William finally returned?

Jumping off the bed, he pulled on his buckskin breeches, the closest item of clothing he could find, and ran to the window, not bothering to tuck in his linen shirt.

A muffled voice shouted from below. "Hello! Ho, there!"

His brother would not bother to call a greeting. That fact alone and the lateness of the hour gave him reason for alarm. Graham grabbed his candle and left his room, running barefoot down the hall and taking the stairs two at a time. He pushed past Eastmore's butler, who'd also awakened to the calling, and flung the main door open to find a young boy sitting bareback atop a massive horse.

"I have news for Captain Sterling," the boy announced.

The bitter wind ripped through Graham's shirt. "I am he." Graham watched impatiently as the boy slid awkwardly from the animal's back. "It's William, isn't it? What has he done? Where is he?"

The boy shook his head. "No, not Mr. Sterling. It's Miss Lucy, sir."

Graham winced. "Lucy? What's the matter with her?"

"She's missing."

Fire surged through Graham's chest. "Missing? What do you mean, missing?"

The stable boy shrugged and cocked his head shyly to the side. "Miss Barrett says she got home and the nurse and baby weren't in the nursery. Everyone's searching the grounds. Miss Barrett wanted that I should fetch you."

Graham didn't wait to hear more. He darted up the stairs to his bedchamber. After securing a coat, boots, and his hat, he reached into his open trunk, grabbed a pistol, and tucked it into the waist of his breeches. He sprinted to the stable. Every minute's delay meant one more minute his daughter could be in danger. He retrieved a bridle from the peg on the wall and flung open the stall gate. After bridling his nameless horse, he led him to the yard.

No. Not Lucy too.

He refused to think about the child's sweet expression. Her dimpled cheek. Her wispy red curls. Instead, he concentrated on formulating a plan. He would search the massive estate himself, call in the local constabulary if necessary. Using the muted moonlight as his guide, he swung the saddle into place. No-Name pranced and threw his head back, offering a whinny into the night mist.

Graham's fingers fumbled with the girth. By now a groomsman had heard the commotion and tried to offer assistance, but Graham refused. Beads of perspiration dotted his brow despite the chill in the air. His mind churned, trying to make sense of what he had heard as he stepped into the stirrup and flung his other leg over.

The horse shied and veered to the right, but Graham pulled the animal's head straight and gave him a kick.

He narrowed his eyes on his task as they galloped out of the yard. At one time in his life, he would have prayed for guidance when a disaster happened. But not now. Strength and resolve would locate Lucy. Hadn't he proved his worth time and time again in battle? He'd find his daughter himself, not offer halfhearted prayers to a God who may or may not remember him.

❧

The voice in his head told him to be careful. But his heart told him to press on.

Harder.

Faster.

Every minute was vital, every second, crucial. Graham urged his nameless horse into a faster gallop, and for once the horse obeyed without a protest.

They flew over the fields with little more than the filtered moonlight as their guide. Thundering hooves pounded the frozen ground. The wind whistled in his stinging ears. He leaned low. The horse's mane smacked against his face as icy bits of snow stung his eyes.

Ahead, a smattering of lights twinkled through the black boughs of Sterling Wood. If he weren't aware of the situation, he would guess a celebration was being held at Winterwood, a ball for the entire county to attend. Torches dotted the landscape. People darted to and fro. Had it really only been three weeks since his first dinner at the estate? It looked much the same now as it had then. But everything had changed. *He* had changed.

No-Name sensed his urgency. The beast didn't let up until his master pulled him to a stop. Gravel slid and crunched beneath the animal's weight. Graham swung from the saddle, tossing the reins in a stable boy's direction.

Several people lingered outside. Some faces he recognized as belonging to servants at Winterwood. Others he didn't know.

Graham stomped up the steps. The butler met him at the door. "We've been expecting you, sir."

"Where's Miss Barrett?"

"She is in the drawing room, sir."

Graham jogged across the vestibule, giving no heed to the trail of dirty snow in his wake.

He spotted Jane Hammond first. The vicar's wife sat next to the fireplace. After stepping into the room, he saw that Amelia sat next to her. Motionless and pale, she stared unblinking into the flames, the light casting vibrant shadows on her tearstained face. Always before her posture had been pristine—shoulders straight, head high. Now she sat hunched like the rag doll he'd seen in Lucy's nursery a few days past.

Graham didn't hesitate. He swept his hat from his head and strode toward Amelia. "Who are all these people?"

She licked her lips before speaking. "The man in the yellow waistcoat is Mr. Singleton, the constable, and the men with him are from the village." He followed her eyes to a small cluster of men gathered by the window that included George Barrett. She dabbed the corner of her eye with a handkerchief. "Edward is here."

Under any other circumstances, Graham would have been furious. Now concern for Lucy dominated every thought. He scanned the room and saw Littleton seated in the far corner of the room with two other men. The scoundrel reclined in the settee with one leg crossed over the other and his arm extended across the furniture's back.

Littleton looked up and nodded. Graham's jaw twitched. "What is he doing here?"

"You were right." Amelia lowered her voice and leaned in. "He was still here when we returned from the vicarage."

"Who's that?" Graham nodded toward a middle-aged man who stood alone near another window.

"That is Mr. Charles Dunne, Mrs. Dunne's husband." She wrapped her shawl tighter around her shoulders. "One of the footmen rode out to his farm as soon as we discovered that Lucy and Mrs. Dunne were missing."

Missing. The word rang in his head. The word made it sound like they were looking for a lost trinket or animal. But they were searching for a person. Persons. *Lucy and this poor man's wife.*

"Are there any signs of them at all?"

Amelia didn't answer, just shook her head and looked down. Her hair, which earlier in the evening had been pinned up so elegantly, now curled wildly around her face. He wanted to offer her comfort, but the memory of their argument earlier in the evening gave him pause. But still he stepped closer, not wishing their conversation to be overheard. Propriety would say he stood too close. But what did it matter? She would be his wife in two days. And since when did he even care what these people thought? "We'll find them, Amelia."

She wrung her hands together, intertwining and then releasing her fingers. "But what if . . . ?"

Her words faded before she completed her sentence, but with a little imagination he could finish the sentence for her. The same thoughts raced through his mind. Perhaps she was right to not verbalize the possibilities. To do so would only make them all the more real.

Laughter burst from the men by the window. Graham grimaced. The sound of amusement was salt on a wound.

He took Amelia's arm. "Will you accompany me to the nursery? I need to inspect it."

21

Amelia led the way up the broad staircase. Graham followed closely, holding the tin lantern up high enough to light the path for both of them. With each step the voices below faded.

He'd been up to the nursery once before, but the visit had been brief. He'd accompanied Amelia to fetch Lucy for an afternoon in the drawing room. But everything appeared different at night. Graham recalled snippets of a conversation when William had told him of the labyrinthine twists and turns of Winterwood, especially in the west wing . . . the oldest wing. He could only assume that was where they now were.

The stairwell jutted and arched at strange angles, and once they reached the landing, narrow alcoves and window wells notched the stone walls. If someone abducted Lucy and Mrs. Dunne, that person would need to know where they were going in this maze.

"How many stairways lead to this floor?"

Amelia responded without looking back. "Just the stairs we came up and the servants' stairs."

Graham paused at a window and looked down to the ground below. The climb would be treacherous, if not impossible.

He had to duck through the low exposed beam of the door frame to step into the nursery. After his eyes adjusted to the fire's glow, he lifted his lantern to survey the room. A long, narrow space served as a common area for a suite of three or four additional rooms. A rectangular table sat in the middle of the space. Two rocking chairs flanked the fireplace. Bookshelves lined the opposite wall. Across a threshold to the right there appeared to be a neglected classroom. To the left were two open doors.

"Everything is as you found it?"

Amelia nodded, stepping forward to place her candlestick on the table. "Both of the bedchamber doors were open. The fire was about out, but it has since been stoked. Other than that, everything appears as it ought."

"Which chamber is Lucy's?"

Amelia pointed to the farthest doorway. His pulse quickened as he approached it. How many times had he rushed headlong into a dangerous situation? Summoned courage for a bloody battle? None had prepared him for what he faced now.

An empty room. An empty crib. The eerie absence of a child in such a room overwhelmed him. He stepped closer to the crib. This was where his daughter was supposed to be sleeping. This was where the darling redhead slumbered and dreamed.

He jogged to Mrs. Dunne's chamber, lantern in hand. He sensed Amelia behind him and turned.

"There doesn't appear to be any sign of a struggle, but see there?" He pointed to a book that appeared to have been knocked off the table. "And look at this."

Her eyes widened. "Do you think someone, I mean, that someone—"

"Kidnapped them?"

He finished her sentence but didn't answer the question. "Look in the wardrobe. Does anything appear to be missing?"

Amelia dropped her shawl on the bed and pushed the wardrobe open farther. The candlelight glowing on her long, bare arm distracted him, but the alarm on her face when she turned around snapped him back to the present. "No, it all seems to be in place." She moved to a chest, pulled open the top drawer, and stood on her toes to peer in. "Her reticule is here. Letters too."

Graham rubbed his hand over his face and behind his neck and stared at the book on the floor. He needed to go talk to the constable and see what he knew. George Barrett too. And he would interrogate Littleton. The fact that the man was here in the building didn't make him innocent.

"Where's your brother?" Amelia asked. "Did he come with you?"

Graham lifted his head. William. He had been desperate. Drunk.

Would he? Surely not.

He swallowed and adjusted his collar. No need to alarm her unnecessarily. "Will you lead the way back down? I'm not sure I could find my way out."

He scanned the hall as she led him out. Could someone be hiding here? Ahead, a door stood open. "What's that room?"

Amelia stopped so abruptly he almost ran into her. "It was Katherine's room."

The words rang hollow and empty in the damp, cold hall. The air around them grew still.

She lifted the candle. "Lucy was born there."

And Katherine died there.

Graham couldn't resist the temptation. He took the candle from Amelia and stepped inside. The room was dark. Dusty. Cold. He moved to the window. Below and across the lawn torchlight flickered on the terrace where he and Amelia had talked during her engagement dinner to Littleton. An eternity had slipped by since that dinner. He was no longer the same man, and he would venture to assume Amelia had changed as well.

He was no stranger to difficult times, to situations that tried his mental strength and physical endurance. But the thought of Lucy, perhaps alone and frightened, and the image of his wife buried in a cold grave proved to be almost more than he could endure. His soul was empty, and he hadn't even recognized it until the people who filled it were gone.

He felt Amelia's presence as she stepped closer. He didn't want to look at her for fear that even in the darkness she'd read his thoughts. Mutual grief bound them now. He wanted to reach his arm out and pull her close. To feel her warmth. Her goodness. If she took one step closer, he would do it. But she stood still.

Amelia brushed a tear away with the back of her hand. "We should return to the drawing room. Someone may have news."

Graham shook emotion from his limbs and stretched his hand toward the door. "After you."

He was a captain, was he not? He knew how to organize men in times of fear, in times of chaos. He'd do so now. He knew his charge, to find his daughter and Mrs. Dunne. He'd not be distracted again.

※

Amelia bolted upright on the drawing room settee. How long had she been asleep?

She turned to look around the room, and a sharp pain shot down her neck. She grimaced and lifted her hand to massage the spot.

The drawing room was empty. As the recollection of the night's events emerged from sleep's fog, she sagged in grief.

Lucy. Mrs. Dunne.

A shout echoed from the lawn. At the sound, she jumped up and hurried to the window, her limbs still sluggish. Outside, the first long rays of dawn peeked from over Sterling Wood and filtered through the bare trees. It was not the yellow light of a pretty morning, but a dull gray light as mournful as the emotion churning within her. Last night's snow had turned to a chill drizzle.

A dozen or so men were clustered on the lawn in caped greatcoats and low, wide-brimmed hats. The light from their torches and lanterns swayed in the wind. Hunting dogs barked as they circled the group, tails wagging.

She snatched her shawl from the settee and hurried from the room to the front door. A gust of wind whipped her hair wildly around her face as she stepped outside.

Ignoring the rain and the bitter cold, she scanned the grounds. As she did, two men ran past her to the group, followed by more hunting dogs. Two men broke away from the cluster and jogged toward the stable.

Her heart leapt at the commotion. Perhaps by some miracle, they'd found Lucy and were surrounding her now. But as she drew closer and pushed her way into the gathering, she saw that a young boy, not her darling Lucy, had drawn their attention. The dirt-covered lad sat on the ground, his eyes wide in sheer terror as he stared at the men towering over him. Captain Sterling knelt on one knee next to him, and the constable knelt behind him, his hand fixed firmly on the lad's collar.

Amelia found her voice. "What's going on here?"

The constable thumped the boy on top of his soiled cap. "This boy knows who kidnapped the child and the nurse, don't you, lad?"

The boy shook his head, tracks from his tears cutting white streaks down the dirt on his face. His wide eyes darted from face to face. "'An' how would I know? I ain't done nowt', I'm tellin' ye!"

The constable jerked the boy's collar. "Do you, now? Where'd you get that letter, then, boy? Answer me that!"

"That's enough!" ordered Amelia, disgusted at the constable's rough treatment of the child. She stepped forward and brushed past two men. "That boy knows no more about who kidnapped Lucy and the nurse than you do, Mr. Singleton. Can't you see that he is frightened?"

The constable smirked. "He's not frightened. Are you, boy? He's just mad he got caught."

Captain Sterling stood and stretched to his full height, towering over the boy. "I'll know if you are lying, so don't try it. Who gave you this letter?"

The boy tugged away from Mr. Singleton and scowled when the man jerked him back. "I done told ye. A man on the road give it to me. Don' know who he were. He just give me money and told me to take the note to the kitchen, quick, like I done. So let me go!"

Amelia pushed even closer. "What letter?"

They all ignored her question. Singleton stood and pulled the boy to his feet. "You're going to show us right where you saw this man, am I clear?" He motioned to the other men to bring horses around.

Amelia chimed in again, louder this time. "What letter?"

After Singleton mounted his horse, Captain Sterling flung the boy up on the saddle in front of the constable as if he weighed no more than Lucy. He waited for Singleton to secure him before walking over to Amelia. She searched his face for any indication of emotion, but the lines of his tanned face were hard, determined, and his turbulent gray eyes were cold. Dark whiskers covered his chin and cheeks, his very presence intimidating.

But Amelia would not be intimidated, not where Lucy was concerned. "I demand to know what is going on."

"The boy has delivered a ransom letter."

She positioned herself in front of him, insisting on his attention. "What did it say?"

"Whoever has them is demanding money. Stay here. We'll be
back."

"But what if the boy tries to mislead you?"

"He won't; you can rest assured of that. I need you to wait here
in case there is another attempt at contact. Carrington will stay
with you and help keep an eye on things."

She glanced at the older man before returning her eyes to the
captain.

"I need you to stay calm," he said, "and I ask you to trust me."

Trust him? Amelia didn't trust anyone at this point.

But how could she tell him that his request was for more than
she could give?

❧

A cheery fire crackled in the drawing room fireplace, the flames
hissing and popping.

Amelia tightened the rough wool shawl around her shoulders and lifted the edge to wipe the rain from her face. Even with
the fire, damp cold permeated everything, and she indulged in a
shiver.

Jane stood next to a small table to Amelia's left, poured a cup
of tea, and handed it over. The steaming liquid heated the delicate china cup and warmed Amelia's trembling fingers. The curling
steam heated her face. Normally a cup of hot tea would soothe her
nerves and calm her agitated spirit. But today her stomach turned
at the very thought of swallowing anything at all. Amelia placed the
teacup back on its saucer.

A frown crossed Jane's face. "You must eat or drink something,
Amelia. You'll be of no use to anyone if you faint dead away."

Amelia shook her head and stood. "I'm fine, Jane, really." She rubbed the ache in her temple and stared toward the window. The rain increased, icy drops hitting the wavy glass like small pebbles. Her chin trembled. What if her baby was out in this weather? What if Lucy was hungry, or scared? Or worse?

Amelia pushed herself up from her chair and began to pace. "They should have allowed me to accompany them. If they do find Lucy, she will need me."

Jane laid a gentle hand on her shoulder. "You don't need to be traipsing around the countryside. Leave such things to the men. They will find her, I know."

"But what good am I here? So useless, sitting here, waiting."

A shout from Mr. Carrington at the far window startled Amelia. "Ho there!" he said. "They've returned."

At the words, Amelia darted from the room. She flung herself through Winterwood's entrance and out into the cold, damp morning.

A throng of horsemen lined the horizon. The thundering hooves pounded the soggy landscape, flinging up bits of dirt and sod. She lifted her hand to guard her eyes against the elements and strained to make out the figures on horseback.

Mr. Tine. Uncle George. Edward. Mr. Singleton. One by one she identified the men. *Captain Sterling. Mr. Dunne.* Her heart dropped. No Mrs. Dunne. And if Mrs. Dunne wasn't with them, neither was Lucy.

The rain ran down her neck and drenched her hair, but she didn't return to the house. She searched the faces of the returning men, looking for clues, but saw only severe, stony expressions.

"What did you learn? Where is Lucy?"

No one responded. Exasperated, she freed the wet fabric of her skirt from clinging to her legs and hurried toward the approaching horses.

Captain Sterling pulled his horse away from the group and dismounted. He tossed the reins over the animal's head and gathered them in his gloved hands. "What are you doing out here? You'll catch your—"

"Please tell me you found something. Anything." She stepped closer and grabbed at the horse's bridle. "Please, I must know."

His response was short. "We found nothing."

"But where's the boy?"

"We let him go."

Blind panic surged in her heart. "You let him go? Why would you do that?"

Captain Sterling fiddled with his saddle, the gathering rain streaming down the folds of his coat. "He knew nothing."

He wheeled his horse and started toward the house. She wished he would stop walking. She wished he'd look at her. Anything. But his eyes stayed focused straight ahead.

"How can you be certain? Someone paid him to bring a letter here. How could he not know anything?"

Captain Sterling wiped his cheek with the back of his hand, further spreading the dirt that had been flung onto his face during the ride. "He didn't. He was just a boy trying to earn some money."

If only they had let her go, she would have gotten the answers out of him. With every step and every word uttered, her irritation increased. "Well, perhaps if Mr. Singleton hadn't been so cruel to the child, he would have been a little more accommodating."

He shook his head, still not looking at her. "Mr. Singleton did what he needed to do to get an answer."

Amelia almost had to jog to keep up with the horse's gait. She lifted her sodden skirt to keep from tripping. "But to let him go! He knows what the man looked like. He knows where the man was last seen, he knows—"

Finally Captain Sterling stopped the horse and turned the full brunt of his steely gaze onto her. "Listen to me. Pursuing that boy further would have gotten us nowhere. So what would you have proposed? That we continue to question him until he was beside himself and confessed to a crime he did not commit? Gave us false information that would take us down a wrong path and cost us hours of valuable time? I daresay I have dealt with a few more questionable characters in my day than you, so I suggest you leave this to me."

She stood dumbstruck as he gave the animal's reins a yank and continued to walk. She didn't know whether to be offended at his curt reply or ashamed for questioning him. Finally she tugged her soggy, cold shawl about her shoulders and trotted to catch up with him. "So what do we do now?"

He tossed the reins to a stable boy and let her enter Winterwood before following her in. "First, you need to change clothes. The last thing we need is for you to fall ill. Then come back down, and I will share my plan."

22

Graham downed a dram of brandy, hoping the amber liquid would warm his insides. He couldn't remember the last time he'd been so cold. He recalled one black night in the dead of last winter when he'd sat out with his watchman, looking for enemy ships in the opaque fog. He had been so alert, so certain that the enemy would try to use the fog to conceal their location. But he'd been wrong. That night had been a waste, just as this morning had been.

The boy knew nothing. He was just a frightened child trying to earn a shilling. Nearly two hours later they were no closer to finding Lucy than when they had left.

Graham carried a chair over to the fireplace and sat down. He knew what he needed to do. He'd informed Singleton of the plan to go to Liverpool and managed to keep Littleton and George Barrett as far at bay as possible. But now he needed to tell Amelia.

The fire was welcome, but no amount of heat could ease the iciness gathering around his heart. His soul. His body ached from the ride, and his eyes protested the lack of sleep. No matter. Sleep was not an option.

Where was Lucy? Who had her?

He reached into the pocket of his coat and pulled out the ransom letter. He'd already read it a dozen times, though each reading sent blind rage through every fiber of his being. He unfolded the letter. It was addressed to him. Strange that the boy had delivered it to Winterwood's kitchen entrance, though Graham was staying at Eastmore Hall. What did that mean?

Graham scratched his head and slicked back his damp hair, contemplating the unfamiliar script.

Sterling,

Your daughter and her nurse are safe and well, for now, but that will not be the case for long. Deliver two thousand pounds to George's Dock at dawn on Sunday. I've no doubt you know the location. Be warned I've no patience for heroics. Upon my honor, I will not hesitate to make good on my threat should anything go wrong.

He flipped the note over, looking for more clues, but that was it. No signature. No other information. Nothing more than messy marks on a crumpled piece of paper. He smoothed the note out on his knee, then folded it as neatly as his still-numb fingers could manage.

George's Dock. Liverpool. Yes, he knew the place well, and the very thought of his daughter in such a place made his blood run cold.

He eyed each man in the room with suspicion. Someone was after a fortune—either his prize money or Amelia's inheritance—and would clearly stop at nothing to obtain it. His instinct was to discover the man's identity, hunt him down, and bring him to justice. The thought of giving in to the demands of a lunatic and simply handing over money went against the grain. But in this case, his daughter's safety trumped his need for justice. He would gladly surrender his last farthing if it meant holding his daughter in his arms once more.

Across the room, Singleton signaled his departure and called to Graham. "You know where to find me, should you need me."

Graham nodded and stood. "Thank you for your help, Singleton. It was much appreciated."

The man shoved his hat on his wet head and stepped toward Graham. "Wish I could have done more. Best of luck." He turned to leave, then hesitated. "You're sure you're not in need of further assistance?"

Graham shook his head. The last thing he needed was someone else slowing him down. "I have a connection in Liverpool. He'll give me all the help I need. I'm sure of it."

The heavyset constable shifted his weight and glanced around the room. "Surely your brother will accompany you."

"No, I'll go alone." Graham didn't miss the older man's surprised expression.

Singleton took his leave and Graham returned to his chair, content to be alone with his thoughts. To his left, Carrington and Mr. Hammond recounted the events of the day. Near the door, Miss Helena Barrett sat conversing with Edward Littleton. Graham scowled at the sight of Littleton. Despite the man's help this morning, Graham's instinct to avoid him was as strong as it had been the day he met him. Perhaps Littleton's efforts to help find the child were sincere. Perhaps not. But something seemed amiss.

He tore his gaze away just in time to see Amelia enter the room with swift and determined steps. He stood when she entered, and from the corner of his eye he saw Littleton do the same. But he was the one Amelia's eyes sought out, and she was by his side in seconds.

The expression flushing Amelia's face was anything but congenial. "Tell me. What is going on?"

He'd hoped to come up with a softer way to deliver the news. The room fell silent, as if all anticipated his response. She had not yet read the letter, so he extended it to her, watching as she devoured the contents. Her face paled, and her free hand flew to her mouth.

"George's Dock. Where is that?"

"Liverpool."

After a moment of agonizing silence, she spoke. "We must do as they say. We must go to Liverpool."

"*I* must go to Liverpool," he corrected. "You must stay here in case they return."

"I think not! I have every intention of accompanying you. Lucy will need me once you find her." She turned to Carrington. "How soon can you retrieve the money?"

Graham shifted his weight. "Listen to me. The letter instructs me to come alone, and come alone I shall."

"But I know I can be of assistance. And if I remain here, I shall go mad."

Though her voice was firm, he saw tears in her eyes, and he felt himself weakening. But he wouldn't risk disregarding the kidnapper's instructions. "It's a long journey to Liverpool, and I can travel faster alone." He turned to Carrington. "You say you have access to the amount requested?"

Carrington nodded. "I do."

"Good." Graham fidgeted with his glove. "I do not think I could gather so large a sum in such a short period of time, at least without a visit to London first."

Amelia's face flushed. "If you think for a single moment that I am going to stay here and do nothing while some barbarian holds my child and my friend captive, then—"

"Liverpool is no place for you. Trust me."

"But I—"

"No."

She opened her mouth with an obvious intent to protest further. Graham silenced her by holding up his index finger. "One mistake. That is all it takes for us to never see Lucy or Mrs. Dunne again. I do not like those odds, so I plan to comply with this lunatic's request. Am I clear?"

Amelia moved and blocked his path. "I'm not unreasonable. I promise, once we are there I will leave the rescuing to you. But I cannot stay here and wait. I simply cannot."

He glanced around the room at their audience. Mr. Hammond and Carrington stared. Looks of shock plastered the faces of Amelia's aunt and cousin. Even Littleton, who had not ceased talking and sharing his opinion the entire morning, was quiet.

Graham snatched his hat and jammed it on his head. "I am sorry. My answer is no."

❦

"Amelia, put those down this instant."

Amelia ignored Jane's plea and handed Elizabeth a pair of slippers. Captain Sterling had told her before he left for Eastmore Hall that he would return in a few hours to retrieve the money from Mr. Carrington. When he arrived, she'd be ready to go too.

Amelia pointed to the wardrobe. "No, not that dress, Elizabeth. The blue sprigged muslin. It's lighter and will take up less room." Amelia tossed Elizabeth a shawl and rolled her stockings as tightly as she could get them. She didn't travel often, but when she did, it was never without several trunks. But this was an extreme circumstance, and she needed to travel lightly. She needed to prove to Captain Sterling that she would not be a hindrance.

Jane took the rolled stockings from Amelia's hand. "This is

ridiculous, and right now I am questioning your sanity. This is not a pleasure trip. These are real, dangerous people. Not only will you be putting Lucy's and Mrs. Dunne's lives in further danger, you'll be risking your own as well, and your presence could well endanger Captain Sterling in his efforts to retrieve them. I cannot stand by and allow you to do this."

Amelia concentrated on the task of gathering her comb and lavender water. "I'm sorry, Jane. This is something I must do. If the captain refuses to allow me to accompany him, I will take the carriage on my own."

Jane removed the items from Amelia's trunk as quickly as she could pack them. "This entire situation is beyond you, Amelia. You cannot resolve every issue on your own. Do not try. Right now you need to spend your time in prayer and let Captain Sterling do what he needs to do to retrieve Lucy. He's a strong man and a brave one. He's battled people like this before. He knows what to do."

Amelia refused to look Jane in the eye. "But Lucy will need me."

"She will need you just as much when she returns. And think about Captain Sterling. He will have quite enough to worry about without watching over you as well."

"I don't care. And before you begin lecturing me about prayer, God doesn't seem to be listening to me much of late, now, does he?"

Amelia regretted the words as soon as they left her mouth. They were not true, and she knew they would hurt her friend. But at this point, she didn't know what else to do. She turned toward Elizabeth. "Help me change into the gray traveling dress, will you?"

Despite Amelia's biting words, Jane continued with her protest. "It's not just that, Amelia. You simply cannot travel alone with Captain Sterling. You are not yet wed, remember. And the thought of taking the carriage alone is simply absurd!"

Amelia turned to allow Elizabeth access to her buttons. Her words were half-sarcastic, half-serious. "It will not be entirely improper. We shall have the footmen and the coachmen, after all. But if it concerns you so, then come with me."

※

Graham shoved an extra pair of deerskin breeches into his satchel and looked around his bedchamber. What had he forgotten? He'd grabbed extra clothes. All the money in his possession. His pistol. Ammunition. A stack of papers and letters. The marriage license. Anything that was of any importance to the situation, he'd stuffed into his drawstring sack. If successful, the trip to Liverpool would not be a long one, but he wanted to be prepared. If he hurried, and if the weather and roads cooperated, he could arrive in Deerbruck by nightfall. And then, if he left at dawn, he'd reach Liverpool by tomorrow afternoon. In two days' time, he could have Lucy in his arms and be on his way back to Darbury.

When everything he would need was neatly packed and ready for the journey, he slung the cinched sack and satchel over his shoulder and pulled the bedchamber door closed behind him. His footsteps echoed in the empty corridor.

He had not seen nor heard from William since they'd argued the night before. Where was his brother? And could he possibly have had a part in the kidnapping? Graham hated to even consider the idea, but William had been so angry, so desperate. So drunk. And Graham had to consider all the possibilities, no matter how repugnant.

At the moment, however, he needed to be on his way. He could wait no longer for his brother to find his way home and explain himself. The day's light would not last forever.

Outside, the brisk wind disrupted his hat and tugged at his greatcoat. The threat of yet another downpour hastened his steps. He could not lose any time because of the weather.

The groom had readied his no-name horse, and the pair was waiting for him just behind Eastmore's gravel drive. "He's ready."

Graham patted the horse's flank with his gloved hand. "Do you think he'll make it?"

The groom tilted his head and studied the animal. "I think so. Deerbruck's not so far, and Liverpool's but a half day's ride beyond that. And this horse is dependable enough once you get him going. But if you're unsure, I can saddle another. No sense wondering."

Graham shook his head. He didn't like the idea of taking another horse. This unnamed beast was his, and the two of them had formed a bond of sorts. He'd done well on the journey home to Lucy, and with any kind of luck, this animal would carry him to her again. "No, I'll take this one."

The groom flipped the horse's reins over the animal's head. "As you wish."

Graham tied his sack behind the horse's saddle and filled the saddlebags. "Any sign of William?"

"I have not seen him, sir. His horse isn't in his stall."

Graham looked around. "Is this normal for my brother?"

The man shrugged, obviously unwilling to comment on his master's habits, and returned his attention to the animal.

Graham tightened the leather strap to secure his pack to the back of the saddle. Above him distant thunder growled. The horse shifted as Graham stuck his booted foot in the stirrup and swung his leg over.

Graham settled himself in the saddle and leaned toward the animal's ear. "We've a long journey. You aren't going to let me down, are you?"

The horse flung his head and pawed at the ground, a contrary expression in his eye, but Graham had learned over the past weeks that the animal's protests usually came to nothing.

"If you are to be my partner, you must have a name. So . . . what'll it be?"

The animal didn't answer, except to swish his tail and nod his big head once more toward the right.

"That's it, then. You're a seaman's horse. We'll call you Starboard."

With a click of his tongue and a kick of his heel, the pair departed for Winterwood Manor.

꧁

This sensation of urgency was a familiar one. Before every battle it pushed Graham to be braver. Stronger. Faster. But today he was not fighting an enemy ship. Today the battle engaging him was much more personal, the risk far greater.

He rolled his neck and arched his back to loosen the knotted kinks that had formed. The noon hour had not yet arrived, and already his body felt weary. With a slight tug of the reins he guided Starboard around the curve to the shortcut through Sterling Wood. Ahead, at the forest's edge, the trees parted to a clearing. He paused at the hill's crest to survey the Winterwood estate below him. Clouds cast a patchwork pattern on the shadowed landscape and dimmed the south gardens. Soon he'd be master of everything as far as he could see. But none of that mattered—not without Lucy.

Poised on Winterwood's main drive was a black coach with two pairs of matching bays in harness. He urged his horse forward, his eyes fixed on the carriage. As he drew closer, he saw Amelia, cloaked in a scarlet cape, talking to a coachman. The coach dog circled the horses, barking and wagging his tail.

Graham didn't stop the horse until he was next to Amelia. She pushed back her fur-lined hood and looked up at him. "Oh, thank goodness. You've arrived."

He slid from the horse and nodded toward the carriage. "What's this doing here?"

Her gaze flicked from him, to the carriage, and back again. "The carriage? For our journey, of course."

"Our journey?" Had she heard nothing he said earlier? "No, Amelia." He stepped toward her, eyed the coachman, and lowered his voice. "You cannot go with me."

"I must."

"I told you earlier, it's too dangerous."

"And I told you earlier that I do not mind. I am going."

Determination stained her cheeks with a vibrant flush made even more intense by the bright hue of her cape. Did he really expect her to act any differently? Her actions had already proved her a resolved, headstrong woman. But this teetered on the edge of reck-lessness. If she wouldn't regard her physical safety, then he would.

"Where do you want this, miss?" A maid approached with a bag.

Amelia pointed. "Give it to the coachman."

Graham nodded toward the bag. "What's that for?"

"For the inn, of course."

"The inn?"

"We'll have to sleep somewhere tonight."

This had gone on long enough. He leaned in and lowered his voice. If he couldn't reason with her, he'd appeal to her sense of morality. "We are not yet married. We can hardly go on a trip alone."

"Ah, but we won't be alone. Mrs. Hammond has kindly con-sented to accompany us. And of course we'll have the footmen and the coachmen."

Graham opened his mouth, but before he could protest, she added, "Oh, I almost forgot."

She fished around in the fold of her cloak and produced a green velvet drawstring purse.

"What's that?"

Her eyes were innocent. "Uncle George was reluctant, but Mr. Carrington was able to get him to come around. After all, how would it look if he did not agree to pay for the ransom when the kidnapping took place here at Winterwood?"

"Am I to understand that you have two thousand in there?"

"Well, not entirely, but Mr. Carrington should be back directly with the balance."

He took the money from her, surprised—yet grateful—that they had such a sum on hand. Then he placed a hand on her shoulder and bent down to look her square in the eye. "Listen to me, Amelia. I understand your desire to accompany me, but you must stay here. The journey is long, and I'll not risk another life that I—" He hesitated, choosing his words. "I cannot risk anything else happening."

He turned to walk away, but Amelia grabbed his sleeve and stopped him. He drew a deep breath and turned, preparing to repeat himself, but the fear in her eyes halted him.

"Captain Sterling, Lucy may not be my natural daughter, but I love her as if she were. Like you, I will not rest until I hold her in my arms and she once again sleeps in her own bed here. I don't know why this happened. All I know is that I will do anything, go anywhere, to have her back with me, and I simply cannot stay here and wait when there is the slightest chance that I could help. I'm telling you, I *will* go. The only question is whether I will go with you or make the journey on my own."

Graham swallowed and stared into her blue eyes. What spell did this woman cast over him? He wanted to let her have her way. But could he allow her to risk her own safety? Before he left, he'd sent a letter to Stephen Sulter to inform him that he was coming to Liverpool. Sulter had a wife and grown children. Perhaps Amelia could stay with them while he searched for his daughter.

A movement over Amelia's shoulder caught his eye, and he glanced to the drawing room window. Framed in the paned glass, Edward Littleton looked out, watching them.

Graham nodded toward Littleton. "How long does he intend to stay?"

Amelia shrugged. "Until my aunt and uncle depart for London."

"When will that be?"

She looked down at the ground. "Their plans were to leave after I wed, but now, with the changes, I—"

She didn't need to finish her sentence. He understood her meaning.

He looked down at Amelia, and something inside him began to soften. He quickly checked himself. Romantic whims only led to weakness and heartache, and he could afford neither at this time. But the blond tendrils blowing in the wind, the pink curve of her lips, and the determination in her expression all contributed to his growing desire to keep her close.

It wasn't just that she was hard to refuse, though she was. The reality was that someone was willing to do almost anything for money—even kidnap a baby—and that person could easily be in this house. Right now everyone was a suspect: George Barrett, Edward Littleton, even his own brother. With that in mind, how could he possibly leave Amelia here alone?

Blast it all. What other choice did he have?

23

melia awoke to the sounds of shouts outside the carriage. The vehicle jerked and started to slow, but she didn't open her eyes until the carriage stopped and its wheels settled in the ruts. Amelia sat up, straightened, and rubbed her hand over her face. She reached over to Jane and shook her arm. "Jane, Jane, wake up. We've arrived."

After indulging in a yawn and a catlike stretch, Amelia tightened the traveling blanket around her shoulders and leaned to look out the window. A two-story, U-shaped building stretched to the night sky. Freestanding torches flanked the main entrance, and cheery lights flickered in the numerous windows, spilling their yellow glow onto the freshly fallen snow.

She felt Jane lean over her shoulder. "Is this where we are staying, or are we just changing the horses?"

"It's too dark to go any farther. Not a bit of moonlight." Amelia squinted to read the words carved into an aged, rectangular sign. "Eagledale Inn."

The outlines of horses and men passed in front of her view, painting shadows against sides of the building. Muted music and laughter floated on the night air. The sound seemed to be coming from outside and to the left. She craned her neck to see if she could find the source, but none was visible.

The carriage door unlatched and swung open, and an icy blast swirled through the opening. After hours in the jerky carriage, the wind's wintry bite invigorated her. A ripple of excitement tickled her stomach. The inn marked the halfway mark on their journey to Liverpool. They were that much closer to Lucy.

Captain Sterling removed his hat to duck inside the coach. He had decided to ride his horse alongside the carriage. When his hand rested on hers, Amelia jumped.

He clasped her fingers. "I'm going to go check on rooms. Don't move or talk to anyone. The coachmen will stay with you." Captain Sterling closed the door behind him, and she heard the click of the latch. She watched his form turn to a silhouette against the window light and then disappear through the door.

Amelia leaned back against the seat. Her eyes burned from crying, her muscles ached from several hours of jerky travel, and her body cried out for sleep. She thought of Lucy and Mrs. Dunne. Were they cold? Hungry? Uncomfortable? The very thought made her stomach turn. She closed her eyes and leaned her head back against the tufted brocade. Now not only was Lucy heaven knows where, but she herself was hours away from home.

Jane and Amelia sat in silence until Captain Sterling opened the carriage door again.

"The inn is pretty full, but I was able to get us two rooms. You ladies will share one on the second floor. One of the coachmen is already taking your things up. Come, I'll escort you."

He extended his arm, and Amelia took it. Her legs were unsteady and stiff after hours of sleep and travel, and she almost stumbled on the narrow carriage steps. With her free hand she looped her cape hood over her head and then clung to his arm with both hands. The air carried pungent scents of horses, manure, and straw, causing her nose to wrinkle. The icy snow crunched under her half boots as they walked to the door. For once she was grateful that her feet were practically frozen; otherwise she might protest the pain of the sharp gravel beneath her thin soles.

Some of the inn's male guests exited the building as they walked to the front door. Feeling their stares, Amelia cast a quick glance back at Jane and tightened her grip on Captain Sterling's arm. He walked as if unconcerned, his breath fogging the cold night air. Amelia swallowed a lump of trepidation and tried to ignore the questionable-looking people they passed. She was far from Winterwood Manor indeed.

Once inside, Amelia was grateful for the heat, but the smell was not much improved. The scent of burnt meat and stale straw met her nose. The sounds of voices and music were louder.

She leaned toward her escort. "Where is all the noise coming from?"

He finally looked down at her. Dark circles underlined his tired eyes, and the start of a beard shadowed his cheeks and chin. "There's a dining hall through that door, but it is no place for you. I've ordered something for you and Mrs. Hammond to eat. It should be brought up shortly."

Still clinging to his arm, eyes wide, she allowed him to lead her up a narrow staircase and down a dimly lit hallway. The smell of stale straw was worse here, and she held a handkerchief up to her nose. Six doors lined the dark corridor, and he led her to the one on the right at the end. He stuck a key in the lock, turned it, and gave it a good shake. The lock popped, and the door swung open.

She stared at her sparse surroundings. The room, barely large enough for the three of them to stand in together, felt dank and dark.

Captain Sterling knelt at the fireplace and poked at the kindling with the poker. "I had them start you a fire—if you want to call this a fire." He added more kindling and blew on it. "But at least you have a little light and warmth, which is more than I can say for the other patrons."

Amelia's eyes widened. "You mean some of the rooms don't even have a fireplace?"

He shook his head. "I told you this would be different from what you are accustomed to."

She watched silently as he coerced the sputtering fire to a healthy flame. Once the fire allowed for a better look at the room, she removed her hood and surveyed her surroundings. One bed with a lumpy mattress butted up against the far wall. A single wardrobe chest stood next to a skinny window. Two wooden chairs and a rickety table edged close to the fireplace, and beneath her feet stretched a minuscule, well-worn rug. Nothing hung on the walls, with the exception of two wooden hooks next to the door.

Minutes later a kitchen maid appeared with a tray of food and tea. She set the tray on the table, bobbed a curtsy, and left. Amelia removed her damp cape from her shoulders and hung it on a hook to dry. Every part of her was cold.

She moved next to Captain Sterling at the fire. He poked the coals again and looked up at her. "I know this is not ideal, but there isn't another inn within an hour's travel."

"Thank you. I'm sure Mrs. Hammond and I will be quite comfortable here." Amelia hesitated, chewing her lip. The candlelight highlighted the strength in his jaw. The muscles in his neck twitched as he tended the fire. She wanted to grab his arm again, just as she had when he escorted her to the room. Being near him made her feel safe. Protected.

He stood and dusted his hands together to shake off the ashes from the fire. "The coachman set your things over by that chair, and if you are all settled, I will leave you ladies to rest." He walked toward the door. "Make sure you lock the door. Don't let anyone in, for any reason."

Amelia almost reached out to keep him in the room. "Where are you going?"

"To finish tending the horses. I'll be staying in the room directly above this one. If you need anything, stand on the chair and tap on the ceiling. I'll be sure to hear you."

"But surely you will eat something and get some rest too?"

He nodded. "I will knock on your door tomorrow morning. We'll leave at dawn. I want to arrive in Liverpool as early as possible."

He gave a short bow, and the smile he offered sent a flutter through her heart. But she was tired. Emotional. She needed to keep those two things in mind and not let her thoughts turn to fantasies.

Jane closed the door behind Captain Sterling, and Amelia strained to hear their retreating footsteps over the fire's hiss and the shouts from the courtyard below.

Jane hung her cape on the hook next to Amelia's and turned to survey the tiny room. "Your Captain Sterling is a very kind man. He seems quite concerned for your welfare."

Amelia ignored the subtle tease in her friend's voice. She moved to the small table and sat down. "You'd better eat this, er, stew before it gets cold."

She eyed the dubious dinner, recognizing carrots and potatoes but not much else. She picked up a loaf of bread, but it was so hard she could barely tear it in two. Sighing, she dropped the loaf back onto the pewter plate and reached for the tea.

It would have to suffice.

❧

Graham exited the stable and crossed the courtyard. With the horses secure and bedded down for the night, Amelia and Mrs. Hammond settled, and arrangements made for tomorrow's journey, he could try to get some sleep. He would need to be rested for his search for Lucy once he arrived in Liverpool. One of the coachmen had offered to tend to Starboard, but Graham had been unable to rest until he'd checked on the animal himself. He found himself wondering at that. As a captain, he gave orders daily, if not hourly. Why could he not release such a minor chore?

The noise from the pub was louder now than it had been when he walked the ladies in. Laughter and shouts peppered the night air. He shoved his fists in his pockets and forced his gaze on the door. How easy it would be to indulge in a drink or two to take the edge off of his fears over Lucy. What did he have to lose? They couldn't travel until light broke anyway.

But he knew exactly what he had to lose. It had been a long time since he'd used drink as a means to escape, and his exhausted, susceptible state made it especially important to steer clear of the temptation. But a temptation it remained. He glanced up toward Amelia's window. Indeed, it was not the only temptation.

After entering the inn's main door, Graham climbed the stairs with his bag. The key weighed heavy in his pocket, and he fumbled in the dark to unlock the door. A stale stench assaulted him. He kicked the door closed with his foot and leaned against it to turn the lock. The room was identical to Amelia and Miss Hammond's. Its simplicity did not bother him. He'd slept in much worse. But he couldn't help but wonder how Amelia, a woman used to the finest surroundings, was faring.

Graham hung his coat and hat on the hook before moving to

stoke the fire. It was a cold night, made colder by the dampness clinging to his coat, and he leaned in to let the flames warm his face and chest.

Amelia was so close. Just a floor below. Was she asleep? So much had transpired since their argument after the dinner party. With his concern for Lucy, he'd had little time to give it thought. But now, in complete solitude and relative quiet, he allowed himself to recount her words.

An arrangement, she had called it, reminding him that her interest was in Lucy, nothing more. He rubbed his arm as if to rub away the memory of what her touch had felt like when she had clung to him. He wasn't sure he could believe her words, for her expression had told him something completely different.

Amelia was a strong woman. Indeed, he'd underestimated her again and again. At every turn they'd taken in these few short weeks, she'd proven loyal, resolute, and resourceful as well as beautiful. And she loved Lucy like the child was her own. Could a man hope for a better companion?

Tomorrow would have been their wedding day. In the days and nights since he'd agreed to marry Amelia, he'd come to believe it was a good idea. But something more had developed during the course of their interactions. His concern for her had deepened. His regard for her had broadened, his affection intensified. He no longer regarded her as a woman using him as a means to an end. She was a person he cared about, and she was slowly but surely becoming the woman he loved.

Amelia had awakened something in him. Denying that reality did not make it any less true. But was it right to love again so soon after Katherine's death—or to marry another woman and promptly leave her as he had left Katherine? Guilt, swift and sure, swept its familiar pall over him. How long would he fight this battle between the past and his future?

He stood abruptly, realizing he could no longer afford the luxury of regret. Time was short. He had work to do. And a good captain always kept his priorities straight.

Priority one: Retrieve Lucy at any cost. Priority two: Make Amelia want to marry him, for more than just Lucy's sake. Because the longer this intricate dance continued, the more certain he became: Amelia Barrett needed to become Amelia Sterling.

He removed his waistcoat and slung it over the back of the chair. In a bag next to the fireplace were the clean linens that Amelia insisted they bring. Looking down at the rumpled bed, he was grateful for her insistence. He folded the fresh-smelling pillow under his head, stretched out on the smooth sheet, and covered himself with the wool blanket. He stared into the fire. It had been awhile since a prayer passed his lips, but he couldn't help the one that came upon him instinctively.

Dear Father, I don't deserve Lucy, and I don't deserve Amelia. But if it be your will, deliver them both to me.

24

Amelia had no idea if twenty minutes or two hours had passed. She lay on the lumpy bed, trying to ignore the straw poking through the rough canvas, and curled close against Jane in an attempt to keep warm. The tattered curtains hanging at the window blocked light from the lanterns in the courtyard below, but they did little to suppress the raucous sounds coming from the pub next door. Somehow she'd managed to sleep in the carriage despite the rough roads and wild winds. Now, when sleep should arrive, it refused to come.

She looked over at Jane, whose slender form sank into the mattress. The fire illuminated the rhythmic rise and fall of her shoulders under their brought-from-home blankets. As softly as she could, Amelia pushed herself from the bed and stood.

The pitiful fire did little to fight the chill in the room. Shivering, she reached for her cape, pulled it from the hook, and drew it tightly around her shoulders. With soft steps she inched close to the fire grate and poked futilely at the coals. Giving up, she sat on the rough wood floor, tucked her knees to her chest, and leaned her head on them, her mind, as ever, on Lucy.

Where was she tonight? What had happened to her? Possibility after possibility commandeered Amelia's mind, each scenario more terrifying than the last. She reviewed everything she knew, trying to figure out who could be responsible.

William Sterling had been angry with the captain, and he was known as a drinker and a gambler. According to what she overheard at the Hammonds', he was in debt and short of funds. But surely the man would not kidnap his own niece.

Would he?

Then there was Edward. Could he be guilty of such a cruel, devious act? Until recently, she would not have thought it possible. Now she was not so sure. But Edward had been present for the entire episode, even assisting with the search efforts.

And then, she had to acknowledge, there was an entire world she knew little about. Graham's world. A mysterious world of ships and warfare. Could he have enemies? Could there be others wishing to do the Sterlings harm?

Footsteps from the room above them drew Amelia's attention. Graham's room. Heavy boots paced from one end of the room to the other and back again. She'd been so engrossed in her own pain, concerned with her own plans, that she had not stopped to consider how he must feel. Her own pain at losing Katherine was great, and her fear of losing Lucy was intense. But he was Katherine's husband, Lucy's father. Back and forth he paced. He was so close, only a few wooden planks above her.

A rustling from the bed drew Amelia from her reverie. "What are you doing?"

Amelia sniffed and wiped her eyes. "I'm sorry. I did not mean to wake you. I was cold."

Jane sat up and swung her legs over the side of the low bed.

"This has to be the draftiest room I ever set foot in. Thank heavens we shall only be here one night." She reached down to pull on her slippers.

"I hope Lucy and Mrs. Dunne are in a better place than this. I cannot bear the thought of—"

As the footsteps passed directly overhead, Amelia stopped talking, and Jane looked up at the ceiling. "Sounds as if sleep is eluding someone else of our acquaintance." She fetched her own cloak from the peg and joined Amelia at the fire. "I must say, I believe I have misjudged Captain Sterling."

Amelia started at the abrupt change of conversation. "Why would you say that?"

"His behavior has been selfless. The manner in which he has handled this entire situation has impressed me." Jane settled down next to Amelia, a mischievous smile on her lips. "He appears to be quite taken with you, my dear."

Amelia tried the poker again. "We both care for Lucy, but you must not think there is anything else to the relationship between myself and Captain Sterling. We simply have an arrangement."

"Oh, I am not so sure about that."

"It is true that I have a very large fortune—or I will once I marry. No doubt the captain finds that attractive as well."

"Most men would, yes. But I believe that the captain may need you as much as you need him. For reasons other than money."

Amelia looked away from Jane to hide her quivering lip. "I do not need Captain Sterling. I need his name."

Jane hesitated and reached for Amelia's hand. "What is it, my dear, that frightens you so?"

Amelia pulled back her hand. She had no answer. Or rather, she had too many answers. Too many fears. She feared never having a family of her own. Needing someone and not being needed in return. Being taken advantage of because of her wealth. Loving intensely, only to have that person snatched away . . . again. Having to live her whole life as she had lived so many early years—with a broken, empty heart.

She couldn't tell Jane all that. She could barely admit it to herself. So she said, "The only thing that frightens me is losing Lucy. I cannot lose another person I love, Jane."

Jane's nod was thoughtful. "Fear takes so many forms. I remember back when I was still a new wife—new in Darbury too. I was so lonely in those days. I'd only known Mr. Hammond a few weeks prior to our marriage, and our new parish was far from my family in Bristol. I was eager to become a mother, thinking a baby would help me be less lonely. I prayed daily for a child. Fervently, like Hannah in the Bible."

Amelia pulled her cape closer around her. "But you never had children, did you?"

"No. And eventually I would come to terms with that. But in those early years, the fear that I would never have a child consumed me. I pulled away from Mr. Hammond and others who loved me. I could think of nothing but my own sorrow and my fear that my life would not turn out as I had imagined. It was a dark time, Amelia. I wasted so much of my youth wishing for things to be different, unable to accept the role God had given me to fulfill."

"So how did you find peace with it?" Amelia's voice did not sound like her own.

"When I finally was able to accept that God had a plan for my life, that his way is best, I began to see the world in a different light." A smile transformed Jane's face. "And then he gave me you. You became the daughter I never had. The Lord has blessed me in so many other ways as well. But I lost so many blessings while confined in the prison of my fear."

Amelia stared into the fire as the full meaning of Jane's words pressed upon her. Something within her recognized the truth in them. But a stubborn streak deep in her heart wouldn't accept it.

Jane laid a gentle hand on her shoulder. "There are seasons to every life, Amelia. God gives each of us a great capacity to love, if we will only open our minds to it. I am not a woman given to romantic flights of fancy, but even I can tell the captain has developed feelings for you. The way he fusses over you. The great lengths he is going to protect you—"

"He's protecting Lucy."

"No, Amelia, he is protecting you as well. You will have a very lonely life if you refuse to let others in because you are afraid."

Those final words stung. Amelia pushed to her feet. She didn't want Jane to see the tears gathering. Jane stood too and returned to the bed.

Above them the pacing continued. *Thud. Thud. Thud.* Amelia waited until she was certain Jane had fallen asleep before she climbed back into bed. Her eyes drooped with exhaustion, and she squeezed them shut. *Oh, God, if you really care for me, where are you?*

And in the quiet of the room, a response, subtle and low, balanced in the quiet places between sleep and a dream.

"*My child, I am with you wherever you go.*"

※

Amelia tossed. She turned. Someone was chasing her.

She bolted down a darkened corridor in her nightdress, her bare feet slapping against cold stone. The footsteps were gaining on her.

Faster and faster she ran. Hot tears streamed down her cheeks, and her lungs burned with lack of oxygen. How much longer could she keep this pace?

A menacing, angry voice kept calling her name.

"Amelia. Amelia!"

From the narrow window in the stone wall, a flash of blinding lightning pierced the darkness. A simultaneous clap of thunder boomed with such intensity the ground beneath her trembled. She opened her mouth to scream, but no sound came. Again and again she tried, but no sound, not even a whimper, passed her dry, cracked lips.

Lightning flashed again, and this time her lungs filled with air. She released a bloodcurdling scream before falling to the ground.

The footsteps drew closer. They came faster. Pulse racing, she glanced over her shoulder. By the light of a subsequent lightning bolt she could see it. A dark shadow, a mass, crept closer. Closer.

She tried to get up, but her nightdress caught on something. Desperate, she felt around in the darkness to free it but felt nothing besides limp fabric. She scrambled to her feet and attempted to rip the nightdress free, but whatever gripped it was pulling back, just as hard, just as determined. The shadow drew closer, closer . . .

"Amelia."

The mass was upon her. Its unbearable heat engulfed her.

Unable to free her dress, she succumbed to the instinct to fight. She swung at the mass. She kicked her legs. She writhed and twisted. It would not overcome her.

"Amelia, wake up."

The mass grabbed her by the shoulder and shook her. Again she screamed. Pain pressed her head, and fear squeezed her heart.

The voice grew louder. Her kicks grew stronger.

"Amelia, wake up! You are dreaming!"

A solid shake snapped her eyes open, and she bolted upright. Perspiration trickled down her neck and back. She gulped for air and dug her nails into the wool blanket.

When something touched her back, she jumped and cried out, then blinked as she looked around.

She was not in a dark corridor, but a room at the Eagledale Inn.

A black mass had not grabbed her. It was Jane touching her arm.

Nobody had chased her. The footsteps were not footsteps at all, but a knock at her door.

And Lucy was still missing.

"For mercy's sake, child, are you awake?" Jane's voice rose, and Amelia, still lost in the haze between reason and dream, jerked away from her friend's touch.

The knocking at the door grew more insistent. The knob jiggled. "Are you all right?"

Captain Sterling. *Her* Captain Sterling. He'd protect her, keep her safe.

She jumped to her feet and ran to the door. "Yes, yes." She fiddled with the lock. Still bewildered with sleep, she struggled with sluggish fingers to pull back the metal bolt. When it finally gave way, she flung the door open.

His startling gray eyes met hers. His gaze fell to her nightdress. "What on earth is going on in here?"

Suddenly conscious of her thin attire, she pushed the door closed, leaving only a crack to peer out through. "It was a frightening dream, Graham. Nothing more."

She did not realize she had addressed him by his Christian name until she saw the surprise on his face. He cleared his throat. "I heard you from my room. I thought something was wrong." He tugged unconsciously at his untucked shirt. "Last night I instructed the coachman to return to Darbury and hired a post chaise for the rest of the journey to Liverpool. I was concerned for your horses, and the post chaise will get us there faster."

Her mind slowly cleared, and Amelia nodded. With each nod the pounding in her head intensified, though the black mass slowly shrunk to the background of her mind. She stared at the broad expanse of his chest. How would it feel to be in the protection of his embrace? She caught the scent of sandalwood, he was so close.

Her Captain Sterling. Her *Graham*.

25

Liverpool. They'd arrived.

The sea breeze lured Graham like a siren's call, drawing him closer to the water. The familiar seaport sounds—men shouting, hammers pounding, gulls crying—helped him breathe easier . . . until he recollected why he was here.

All along the wide River Mersey, ship masts, dressed in canvas sails and draped with ropes, reached skeletal fingers into the sky. Frigates lined the docks, crammed tightly in a sea of rope and sails.

His heart beat a steady cadence in his chest. He was that much closer to Lucy.

Behind him, the post chaise transporting Amelia and Mrs. Hammond jostled over the cobbled streets. He turned in Starboard's saddle to see if he could catch a glimpse of Amelia. The thrill of hearing her address him with the intimacy of his Christian name had been the bright spot of his dark morning.

Graham consulted the directions he'd received from a nearby merchant and raised his hand to alert the driver that their destination was near. Across the bustling street, a tiny stone church nestled beneath ancient elms. To its left, a crooked fence encased a tidy grave-yard, and just behind that sat the vicarage. Stephen Sulter's house.

Graham drew a deep breath, filling his lungs with the salty air. *Stephen Sulter.* Their paths had been destined to cross again. He waited for a cart and donkey to clear the way before urging Starboard forward. What would it be like to see the man he'd revered as a midshipman and later as a lieutenant? The man who'd taught him how to lead others, to judge fairly, and to develop disci-pline . . . the very man who had led him to God?

His stomach tightened. God had used Sulter as an instrument to open his eyes to the wonders of what a personal relationship with him could bring.

And what had he done with that relationship?

Graham pushed the question to the back of his mind as the door to Sulter's house opened. A tall, thin man stepped outside, a grin spread across his face. Time's paintbrush had turned Sulter's dark hair gray and etched wrinkles into his leathery skin, but his long-toothed smile was unmistakable. Memories rushed Graham in chaotic disarray. Stephen Sulter knew him better than any other person, living or dead.

Sulter reached for the bridle and steadied the animal as Graham slid to the ground. Then he reached for Graham and embraced him as tightly as any father would. "Can it be? Graham Sterling!"

It was not discomfort but regret that caused Graham to stiffen a little at the affectionate greeting. "Did you receive my letter, sir?"

The other man sobered. "Just an hour or so ago. I regret our reunion must be on such difficult terms, but still, it is good to see you, my boy."

The carriage pulled up to the house just as a round little woman burst out of the house and flung her arms around Graham. "Graham Sterling!"

She squeezed him in an awkward embrace and then stepped back, face flushed and arms akimbo. "As I live and breathe, there now, let's have a look at ye." She eyed him from the top of his hat to the tips of his dusty boots. "Well, there now, see, Captain Sulter!" She turned her beaming face to her husband and flung her hand in Graham's general direction. "He's not a thing like the boy we saw last. So tall. And handsome, at that."

A smile cracked Graham's face. Mary Sulter was the closest person to a mother he'd had since he left Eastmore. How she used to fuss over him. Cook his favorite meals. Mend his clothes. Give him advice. Words didn't seem enough to express his feelings upon seeing her again. "Mrs. Sulter. I hope this visit is not an imposition."

"Imposition? Glory be!" She waved her hand in the air, her ruddy face beaming with pleasure. "You are always a welcome guest in this house, Graham Sterling, and don't you forget it. As soon as Captain Sulter said you'd be arriving today, I set about making your favorite pound cake. See, I haven't forgotten."

Graham felt his dusty sense of humor slowly returning. A sense of comfort spread from his chest to his limbs. He was home. Why had he waited so long to return?

"I knew you, of all people, would not forget."

She leaned in closer, pushing past her tall, narrow husband. "I am very sorry to hear about your young wife. And your daughter! Oh my, I haven't ceased praying since my Stephen told me the news."

Graham shifted his gaze from Mrs. Sulter to her husband.

"Don't worry, Graham." Stephen stepped forward. "This isn't the first pickle you and I have found ourselves in. We'll figure this out. Together."

❧

Amelia ducked her head out of the carriage in front of the Sulter home.

Today was to be my wedding day.

She looked behind her at the thoroughfare they had just departed. Carts darted to and fro, and seagulls swooped from the heavens. On the opposite side stood the docks, and beyond them, a broad river that just as well could be the sea. Men rushed about amid a tangle of ropes. The scents of salt and fish rode in on the nippy breeze, so different than the earthy moorland scents of Darbury.

And Lucy could be anywhere amidst the bustle.

Amelia drummed her fingertips on the leather seat. *When will we begin searching?* Graham stood talking to an older man and an animated, dark-haired woman. What were they talking about? Lucy? Her? She was in no mood for conversation.

Graham strode up to the post chaise. "We've arrived."

Today was my wedding day, and Graham should be helping me out of the carriage and into our home with Lucy at Winterwood Manor, not a stranger's house in an unfamiliar town.

Amelia forced a smile and looked over at Jane before placing her hand in his. Her feet touched the ground, and cool air swirled her skirts around her wool stockings and half boots. An unexpected thrill shot through her as Graham took her hand and looped it around the crook of his arm. The protective act of familiarity warmed her heart, but the emotion was quickly dampened at the memory of why they were here.

The timbre of Graham's voice was rich and confident as they approached the tall man and his wife. "Mrs. Sulter, Captain, I would like for you to meet my betrothed, Miss Amelia Barrett of Winterwood Manor in Darbury."

Captain Sulter bowed. "Welcome to our home, Miss Barrett."

Mary Sulter clasped her hands in front of her. "Welcome to our home, indeed! What a beauty you have found, Captain Sterling." She stepped forward and gathered Amelia's hands in her own. "Captain Sterling is dear to our family, dear, indeed. What a pleasure it is to have you here with us."

The hearty welcome nearly overwhelmed Amelia. Mrs. Sulter chattered on, and Amelia smiled, nodded, and stepped closer to Graham to make room for Jane to step forward and be introduced. As she did, she glanced up at Graham . . . and couldn't help staring. His expression was softer than she had seen it since the party at the Hammonds'.

Why now, in the middle of a strange street, in front of strangers, and in tragic circumstances, should she be struck by Graham's smile? The firm set of his square jaw had slacked and the hint of a smile curved his lips. Something was different about it—about him—today. *Is this Graham's demeanor in the presence of friends?*

He'd shown her a hint of this unguarded freedom, this easiness of spirit, in the fleeting moments when she imagined a romance between the two of them. But here, in this company, he seemed to share it freely, even in the midst of fear and uncertainty.

A group of young adults gathered at the home's modest threshold. They had to be the Sulters' children. The two taller young men stepped forward to help with the luggage. Two young women, one of whom could not be much younger than Amelia, scrambled out of the way as their mother ushered the group inside.

Graham put his hand on the small of Amelia's back. Optimism flicked in his steel-gray eyes, and his warm whisper tickled her ear. "We're close, Amelia. We'll find her shortly, mark my words."

⚭

Graham watched as Mary Sulter escorted Amelia and Mrs. Hammond down a narrow corridor to the bedchamber they would share. Then he turned his attention back to Stephen Sulter, who was dropping a seasoned log on the fire.

Sulter watched his two oldest boys leave the room and shook his head. "Rowdy bunch, they are. Too much like me and not enough like their mother, to be sure." He turned to Graham, his smile fading from amusement to genuine concern. "Don't worry, Graham. We'll find your daughter." He sat in a worn chair and leaned forward. "Tell me everything you know."

Graham moved over to the window and glanced at the busy street below before turning back to face Stephen. Where to start this nightmare of a story? Should he start at the beginning, with what had transpired since he arrived in Darbury? Or should he go back further and admit that these occurrences were punishment for past actions?

He pulled the ransom letter from his pocket and handed it to Sulter, who unfolded the wrinkled paper and held it up to the window's light. Graham stood silent, waiting as the man read.

Sulter finished examining the note and lowered it to his lap. "All right now. Start from the beginning."

Graham drew a long breath and began. The events of the past three weeks spilled from him with unguarded honesty. At times the tightening in his chest and the shortness of breath threatened to prevent his words, but he pressed on, omitting no detail. Sulter was safe and unbiased, just as he had always been.

When Graham finished, Sulter stood, leaned his elbow against the mantel, and rubbed his chin. "So, there are three possibilities."

Graham raised his eyebrow, curious if Sulter's assessment matched his own.

"The Edward Littleton fellow, Miss Barrett's uncle, and—"

"My brother." Graham winced as the words passed his lips. But his brother had been desperate and drunk—an ominous combination. "So now you know the situation. What's your assessment?"

Sulter refolded the note and passed it back to him. "Liverpool's a big city, a lot of people coming and going. But George's Dock— that's our key."

The glimmer in Sulter's eyes sparked a flicker of hope in Graham. "I remember that place. Used to be big in the slave trade, if I recall correctly."

"Aye, you do. Now it receives ships coming from the West Indies."

The West Indies. It wasn't until Graham repeated Stephen's words in his head that a thought formed. Weren't Edward Littleton and George Barrett partners in a shipping business? Memories of the very first dinner at Winterwood Manor rushed his mind. Yes, Barrett had announced that Littleton was joining the family business.

Graham leaned in close to Sulter. "Have you heard of the Barrett Trading Company?"

⚜

Amelia clutched her cloak around her and surveyed the tiny room she was to share with Jane. Two slivers of afternoon light slid through the narrow windows flanking the fireplace.

Mary Sulter scurried around the bed, smoothing the bright blue quilt and fluffing the pillows. She looked up from her task when one of the Sulter sons entered the room with Jane and Amelia's trunks. "Just put those over there, and then take your leave. Miss Barrett and Mrs. Hammond need to rest after their journey."

Amelia opened her mouth to reassure her that she had no intention of resting until Lucy was secure in her arms once again. But before she could respond, Jane spoke. "Thank you for your hospitality, Mrs. Sulter."

Amelia caught Jane's pointed expression and swallowed her impatience. "Yes. Thank you."

The sound of men's voices floated from outside the window. The voices were near . . . and familiar. Amelia hurried to the window and looked down. On the cobbled street below, Graham,

Captain Sulter, and one of the Sulter sons were walking toward the small stable behind the church.

"Where are they going?"

Mary Sulter looked up from the bedding. "I imagine they are going to look for the child."

Amelia propelled herself away from the window. She had not traveled all the way to Liverpool to sit and wait. "But I need to go, I need to—"

Jane reached for Amelia's arm, stopping her midstep.

Mary hurried over. "Do not fret, my dear. My husband knows everything about everyone in Liverpool. You need to rest. The little one will need you to be strong when she returns. Am I right?"

Amelia pressed her lips together with such intensity they trembled. With both Jane and Mary next to her, she felt more like a young girl than a woman on the verge of marriage.

Mary's warm brown eyes met hers. "Now, child, you and Mrs. Hammond here have had a trying day. I think it best, and I am sure Mrs. Hammond will agree, that the two of you rest after your journey. Mark my words, after you have had a cup of tea and a little time to freshen up, you will feel much better. Ah, and here is our Becky with some tea."

The oldest Sulter girl maneuvered her way into the room with a tray of tea and biscuits and set it on the table next to the bed.

Jane spoke when Amelia could not. "Thank you, Mrs. Sulter. We will be down in a bit."

Jane had barely latched the door behind their hostesses before Amelia marched back to the window. "I can't believe he would leave without me. He knows how strongly I feel about this."

Jane removed her cloak and hung it on the peg next to the door. The floorboards creaked beneath her feet as she joined Amelia next to the window. "I know you are upset, but I think you know the streets and docks of Liverpool are no place for you."

Amelia swallowed. "Yes, but I—" She stopped. That was what she wanted, wasn't it? She wanted Graham to be out searching for Lucy. She was not so much upset with Graham as she was with herself for not knowing what to do.

She looked over at Jane, who had stretched out on the bed. The sleepless night and long journey had taken a toll on her older friend.

She decided to keep her thoughts to herself and let Jane sleep. She sat on a chair next to the fire and contemplated Jane's words about losing years to sorrow. There was no way to tell what the outcome of this situation would be. Perhaps Graham would find Lucy before Sunday morning. Perhaps he would not, and they would exchange the money they'd brought for her at the docks. Or perhaps something would go wrong and—

There was nothing she could do except one thing.

She looked back at Jane, who now slumbered. She crossed over to her trunk, opened it, and pulled out her small book of Psalms, the same book Graham had returned to her with the note tucked inside that changed the course of her life. At the last minute she had tossed it in on top of her clothes. Now, after her talk with Jane, she was so glad she had.

She opened the little book at random, and the words drew her in, comforting her and compelling her to read further.

O God, be not far from me: O my God, make haste for my help. Let them be confounded and consumed that are adversaries to my soul; let them be covered with reproach and dishonour that seek my hurt. But I will hope continually, and will yet praise thee more and more.

26

Graham sat at the table in the inn and leaned his elbows on the rough wooden table. His head hung low, but his eyes scanned the lively room, searching for anything that might be useful—a familiar face, a conspicuous character. He found nothing.

A roaring fire sputtered and hissed in a wide, open fireplace. Candles and wall sconces projected flickering light, but stale air dominated the tiny space. Strange faces, foreign voices, and the strong smell of ale surrounded him. Graham looked toward the door and spoke more to himself than Sulter. "I don't think Kingston's coming."

Sulter straightened in the chair across from him. "Give him time. If Miller said he'd get Kingston here, he'll be here."

"You're certain he's trustworthy?"

"Aye. A year ago I might have spoken differently, but he's well worth what you are willing to pay him."

An entire evening scouring Liverpool's streets and docks,

and he was no closer to finding Lucy than when he arrived. How arrogant he'd been when making his promise to Amelia. The expression on her face had wrenched his soul, and he would have done whatever was necessary to restore the smile to her face. But unless something changed soon, he would have nothing to offer her tonight but failure.

He stifled a mighty yawn, the result of the long ride and sleepless nights. His nerves were raw, and every emotion teetered just underneath the surface. He wanted to sleep, if only for a few hours, but the visions that met him there might prove even more gruesome than reality.

He slumped in his chair. If only this nightmare would end.

The ale taunted him. The old vice knew its strength and mocked his weakness. He had ordered it for show and would drink in moderation. But his desire was to drink it and as many more that it took to dull the pain of his past and present. He tapped his fingers on the rough wooden table before taking the mug in his hand. His scar, purple and tight, flashed before him.

"So are you going to tell me what happened with that hand, or are you to leave me to wonder?"

Graham drew a sharp breath. He'd tried to hide the scar since he arrived in Darbury. But how long could he pretend it wasn't there? He propped his elbow on the table and held his damaged hand in the air, forcing himself to look at the disfigurement. He flexed his thumb. The purple scar pulled tight with the movement.

Sulter leaned forward to get a closer look, and Graham pulled back the cuff of his coat, giving Sulter a hint of his marred forearm. The physical pain had passed. But the real pain, the guilt that flashed into his mind every time he viewed the ruined flesh, raged with unmatched ferociousness. He let his cuff fall back.

Sulter shook his head and gave a low whistle. "That's a scar, all right. Looks like it hurt."

"It did."

The memory of splintering burning wood slammed Graham's awareness. If he thought about the accident in too great of detail, the unforgettable stench of burning flesh, sea air, and gunpowder turned his stomach. And if he dared blink, he could still see the terror on the sailor's young face just before the spar crashed to the deck.

He kept his eyes open.

"Do you know what that is, Sulter?" Graham held up the scarred hand, then let it fall back to the table. His voice did not sound like his own. "It is a constant reminder of a grave lapse in judgment."

Sulter settled back in his chair and tented his fingers. Graham grew uncomfortable under the man's assessing stare and looked down. He wanted to avoid the questions in the man's eyes . . . questions he was not prepared to answer.

Stephen filled in the gap. "Listen, Graham, it has been a long time since we talked, and I can't pretend to know what has transpired these past few years. But I'm going to tell you what is on my mind—as your friend. I have followed your career, read about your conquests in the newspapers. News travels fast when you live in a town that rises and sleeps by the stories of the sea. I know now that you lost your wife and your daughter is missing. It would be tempting for anyone, God-fearing or not, to think that God has departed. And knowing you as I used to, I would guess that is where you are."

Graham studied the table's wood grain. His body grew very warm.

Somewhere behind him glass shattered, and the resulting roar of laughter tapped his tense nerves. He twitched, unable to separate the sounds from those of the battle's ghosts beating on the door, scratching to get out. Would today be the day that he spoke the words aloud and released them from the prison of his mind?

Graham stopped thinking and started talking. "The weather was unlike anything I'd seen. The fog hung so thick we could barely make out each other's faces, let alone a ship upon the horizon. That night the crew grew raucous, and like a fool, I indulged them." He cast a glance down at his ale. "Indulged myself as well."

After a nervous glance around the room, Graham leaned forward. "The next morning, just as dawn broke, we spotted the frigate off the starboard bow. It engaged us first, but we outgunned them. I thought it would be an easy victory. Then"—he paused and drew his sleeve over his forehead—"chaos ensued. The men were sluggish. Tempered by the ale from the previous night. Nine men died." He paused, clenched his jaw, and released it. "I was responsible. It should have been me."

Stephen leaned forward, one arm on the table. "Are you God that you should decide who lives and who dies?"

Graham huffed at the ridiculousness of the question. "I am in no mood for a philosophical discussion, sir."

"But you take responsibility for their death?"

Graham grew impatient. "I was the commanding officer. I gave the orders. I made the decisions."

Stephen shook his head. "War is a terrible thing. Men die during war. But in both war and peace, every man's days are numbered by God. If God wanted those nine men with him, do you think any action by you would stop him?"

Graham tightened his fist around the mug. How could he make Sulter understand? "But it was a punishment. I knew better. I was—"

"You utilized poor judgment. Do you think you are the only man ever to have done so?"

"Poor judgment?" Graham released the mug and slammed his hand on the table. "Men are dead, and I am to blame."

Sulter leaned closer, his eyes intent. "You have a choice. You can surrender to guilt and spend your days wrapped in its darkness, or you can repent and accept forgiveness."

Graham studied the scar on his hand. God would forgive him, even though he'd failed. But could he forgive himself for the lack of discipline?

"You are a good man, Graham, a strong one. I believe God has a path for you, but how can you find it under the shadow of guilt? Instead of succumbing to guilt every time you look at that scar, you can be reminded of God's forgiveness. When you're tempted to dwell on past failures, you can pray. Ask God to continue to show you your path. He has one, I assure you."

Graham could not meet his mentor's eyes. He knew all of this. Indeed, he had asked for forgiveness many times. He had just been unwilling to accept it.

How different would his story now be if he had relied on God these many months instead of relying on his own strength to see him through?

After all, where had his strength gotten him?

☙

Graham and Sulter were about to depart when a burly, fair-haired man approached their table. The pounding of his dusty boots on the planked floor could be heard over the noisy patrons, and the scar marring the man's cheek made the one on Graham's own hand pale in comparison.

Sulter's face flashed recognition. "Ah, Cyrus Kingston. Just the man we need to see."

The man tugged a wide-brimmed hat from his head and cast a glance at Graham before answering. "Heard ye lads have yerselves a bit of a situation."

"Aye, we do. Kingston, meet Captain Graham Sterling, recently returned from activity off the coast of Halifax."

Kingston nodded in Graham's direction, his black eyes wild and intense. "You the bairn's father?"

Graham nodded. He eyed the man, assessing every detail and searching for clues as to his character. A scruffy, reddish beard darkened his chin. Dingy clothes hung limp on his massive frame. Graham kept his voice low. "Sulter tells me you're familiar with George's Dock."

The man lifted his hand to order ale before turning his attention back to Graham. "Aye. Worked the waterfront since I was a lad meself." Kingston sat down and leaned against the table. "Got a letter, do ye?"

Graham pulled the worn letter from his pocket and slid it over the table.

Kingston's expression was stone as he read. "Ye know who done it?"

"I have my suspicions." Graham was reluctant to say too much. But what had he to lose? If Sulter trusted the man, he should too. "Ever heard of the Barrett Trading Company?"

Kingston took a swig of ale and leaned with his elbows on the table. "I know it."

"Do they do much business in these docks?"

"They've contracted the *Perseverance*. Setting sail any day."

At the ship's name, Graham exchanged a glance with Sulter. The question smoldered on his lips, begging for release. "Do you know George Barrett or Edward Littleton?"

"Nay."

Graham showed no reaction to the answer and took the letter from Kingston. "You're sure it's the *Perseverance*?"

"Aye."

Graham tucked the letter back in his pocket. "I believe we are

252

dealing with one of three scenarios. One, the kidnapper is using the dock as a decoy. Two, the kidnapper will use a ship in George's Dock to make his escape. Or three, he plans on using a ship to dispose of my daughter and her nurse should we refuse to meet his demands."

Kingston's face showed nothing but blank indifference. "Could be. Or could be he jus' knows the dock and where to hide out there. Anyways, what's it got to do wit' me?"

The stranger's disinterest irked Graham. He glanced at Sulter—again. He'd never known the older captain to steer him wrong. He took a drink of ale before continuing. "I'll wager if there is an exchange planned at the dock, then someone employed there knows about it."

Kingston sneered. "Aye, but getting 'em to talk about it is a horse of 'nother color."

Graham raised his eyebrow. "That's where you come in."

Kingston cocked his head in response. "What ye got in mind, Cap'n?"

Graham pulled a leather pouch from his pocket and dropped it on the table. "One hundred pounds to the man who gives me information that leads to the safe retrieval of my daughter and her nurse. The same to you for your assistance."

The dim candlelight flickered off the worn surface. Kingston eyed the pouch and extended his paw-like hand. With rough fingers he opened it, peered inside, glanced over his shoulder like a greedy thief with a treasure, and leaned in toward Graham. "You got my attention, sir." A smile cracked his chapped lips, exposing crooked, discolored teeth, and a jeer, more like a hiss than a laugh, wheezed from him.

Graham snatched the pouch from Kingston's hand. "Good. Find out what you can and report back to me. Pay heed to happenings with the Barrett Trading Company." He pulled out half the contents from the pouch and slid it over to Kingston. "Take this now, and I'll see you get the rest when I have the child."

The smell of sea and fish clinging to Kingston wafted across the table, contesting the strong scent of the smoking fire. Kingston narrowed his eyes on Graham as he crossed his arms over the broad expanse of his chest and leaned back in his chair. "Well now, I'm not so sure about that, Cap'n." The man nailed Graham to his seat with an icy stare, all trace of a smile vanished. "See, a man can get hisself killed snoopin' round."

Graham clenched his jaw. He knew this man's angle. It was one of intimidation, one he'd not cower to. He locked eyes with the man, refusing to look away. He'd not waver, nor was he prone to negotiation. But he needed help and quickly. The image of Lucy's eyes flashed in his mind for the thousandth time. Be it the lack of sleep or pure desperation, he consented and dropped the pouch and all its contents into Kingston's outstretched hand.

Indeed, he'd give far more to see his daughter safe.

A satisfied smile curled on Kingston's face, puckering his scar and wrinkling his eyes. "Tomorrow, then." He bounced the pouch in his hand before it disappeared into the folds of his rough coat. "Can't make no promises, mind you that." He tipped his hat with mock formality. "Sulter. Cap'n."

"I'm not asking for promises," Graham muttered as the character exited the pub. "I'm asking for a miracle."

※

Footsteps outside the Sulters' door demanded Amelia's attention. She held her breath, waiting, praying, and tucked her trembling hands beneath the folds of her shawl. The rest of the house had retired several hours hence, and the clock had long struck midnight, but Amelia sat awake in the Sulters' modest parlor, unable to find any manner of rest. The agonizing day had rolled into an excruciating night. Hours had passed with no word to offer hope or comfort.

But then the footsteps stopped, a muted voice sounded, and something rubbed against the rough wooden door. Her book of Psalms fell to the cushion beside her as she stood.

The latch lifted and the heavy wooden door swung open. Blustery wind spun through the opening. At the very sight of Graham, with his hat pulled low and his cheeks red from the cold, her optimism soared. Amelia hurried toward the door and held it open. "You've returned. Thank heavens!"

Graham stepped in first, the cold clinging to his wool coat. His words were gruff, his tone made hoarse by the bitter cold. "What are you doing awake?"

"I couldn't sleep." Her words spilled forth in jumbled anticipation. "Did you learn anything?"

It was Captain Sulter, not Graham, who stepped past her to the coatrack and spoke first. "We are closer, Miss Barrett. Rest assured. We will have the little one back to you in no time. Right, Sterling?"

Graham looked up from pulling off his gloves but only nodded.

Captain Sulter removed his coat and hat and patted down his thinning hair. "We've done all we can tonight. I suggest you get some sleep." He clasped a hand down on Graham's shoulder and turned a warm smile toward Amelia. "Good night, my dear."

Amelia watched the man lumber down the corridor, leaving her alone with Graham. Her lungs refused to expand as she watched him remove his hat and greatcoat. So handsome. So strong. And he alone could help her get Lucy.

"Where are you going in the morning?" She felt her smile fade when Graham pulled a flintlock pistol from the folds of his coat and placed it on the sideboard. "What is that for?"

Graham raised an eyebrow at her. The fire's dying embers cast a russet glow on his shadow of a beard and caught on the glint in his gray eyes. "I'm going to get Lucy back."

She swallowed the lump of fear and stood perfectly still.

Graham crossed in front of her to the settee and dropped down on the tufted cushions. He pinched the bridge of his nose, squeezed his eyes shut, then opened them again and stared unblinkingly into the fire. Though weariness played on his every movement, his posture remained alert, as if at any moment he expected Lucy's kidnapper to burst through the door.

Amelia studied him, attempting to read the nuances of his expression. Was he keeping something from her? She noted the lines on his face, the tension tightening his mouth. He'd tried so hard to protect her the past few days. Would he withhold information to keep from upsetting her further?

She sat down next to him, careful to keep a respectable distance. The urge to pepper him with questions was strong, but she held her tongue. What had Jane said? *"You will have a very lonely life if you refuse to let others in because you are afraid that you will lose them."*

She pushed her hair from her face. She wanted to bring him comfort, as he had her. But what could she do?

"You look exhausted. You should sleep." Amelia's voice sounded small in the still silence.

He shifted his weight and balanced his elbows on his knees, a lock of dark hair falling with rogue defiance across his forehead. "I'll be fine."

The broad smile from earlier in the day flashed through her mind. She missed the easier tone she'd heard at their engagement dinner. His voice was heavy now. Defeated.

Graham turned his eyes from the fire to look at her, but his expression was distant. He let out a long, disgusted sigh and rubbed his hand over two days' worth of stubble. "We wasted the day. And found nothing."

At the short words, panic flooded Amelia. She tapped her hands nervously on the wool fabric of her skirt. If Graham lost hope, what chance did they have?

With the exception of the waning fire glow, the room was dark. Made bolder by the stillness, Amelia leaned toward him. She allowed her eyes to linger on his striking features. His straight nose. Full lips. And despite the worry about Lucy, her heart responded to his nearness. What would his strong arms feel like secured around her shoulders? What would it feel like to rest her hand in his, to let him share her fear? Help carry her painful burden?

The pain in his eyes hurt her, and guilt over her actions rose to the surface. "I owe you an apology."

The expression in his eyes changed to confusion. "For what?"

Amelia toyed with the fringe on her shawl and wove it through her fingers, the weight of emotions she did not quite understand pressing on her chest. "I have been so consumed with my own desires and fears that I have been blind to a great many things going on around me. It was wrong of me to get so angry that night after the dinner at the Hammonds'. You had every right to ask any manner of questions, especially considering our future. I am sorry I behaved so poorly."

Graham raked his fingers through his dark hair. "*Our* future? I thought we had a business arrangement."

A flush rushed to her cheeks, the tease a welcome release from the suffocating tension. She eyed the mystery of a man in front of her, searching for meaning in his words. "One day Lucy will be home, and we will marry, and then—"

"We shall be a family." His large hand covered hers. He squeezed it ever so gently, then laced his fingers through hers.

Amelia tried to think of something to say, but at the touch, her mind blanked. She could only stare at their intertwined hands—his so strong, hers small in comparison.

Her gaze fell on the shiny purple scar that crossed his hand

and disappeared under his cuff. In this moment of connectedness, she felt a rising courage. She lifted her other hand and ran a finger along the scar. He jumped at her touch, almost as if he'd forgotten it was there.

"When did this happen?" she asked softly.

Graham straightened but did not pull away. "Last summer."

She looked back down. "How?"

"During battle."

His clipped words made it clear he'd not discuss the topic further. She could only guess as to what horrors Graham had witnessed—horrors that she, in her sheltered world, could never imagine. She moved to pull her hand away, but he caught it in his, turned it over, and wrapped rough, warm fingers around hers. Fire exploded in her at the intimacy.

He rubbed his thumb against the palm of her hand. His words were low. "I couldn't predict it, just as neither of us could have foreseen Lucy's kidnapping."

Amelia barely heard his words over the erratic beating of her heart. She couldn't look away.

"My years at sea have taught me—and I have been reminded tonight—that we cannot control everything around us. We all will answer for what we do, including this blackguard who has taken Lucy and Mrs. Dunne. But we control how we react. And I have chosen to react to this circumstance with reason and calm." He paused before adding, "And prayer."

Prayer? His comment caught her off guard, triggering more unanswered questions about this man. Did he share Katherine's strong faith? Or was he like her, lost and desperate to find the truth?

"Do you put your faith in God?" she murmured.

He squeezed her fingers. "I didn't when we departed Darbury. But now I am trying."

27

"Sterling, wake up. You have a visitor."

Graham opened his eyes to narrow slits, just wide enough to see dawn's faint light seeping through the windows. It took a moment for the words to register. "Is it Kingston?"

Sulter's voice was hoarse. "No. Says he's your brother."

Graham bolted upright, uncertain he'd heard correctly. "My brother? William?"

"Says he's here to help you find Lucy."

Graham scratched his jawline, sat up, and looked around. He stretched the kink from his back and shook away his slumber, struggling to add this new piece to the puzzle. If his brother was involved with the kidnapping, would he dare show his face under the pretense of helping?

Sulter disappeared down the corridor, muttering something about privacy. With one determined step after the other, Graham exited the small parlor where he'd slept and moved to the main door. He straightened his rumpled waistcoat, still buttoned from the previous night, smoothed his tousled hair, and pulled open the door.

William stood in the bright morning air, a wide grin plastered on his face. A beaver hat covered his sandy hair, and a leather satchel like Graham's hung by its strap over his shoulder. Graham tugged at his sleeve and leaned across the door frame. "What are you doing here?"

"Well, that's a fine greeting." William looked past Graham's shoulder into the house. "I heard about what happened, about Lucy, that is to say, and I've come to offer my assistance. Will you not invite me in?" Without waiting for an invitation, William pushed past Graham into the warmth of the Sulter home.

Graham closed the door behind him. "How did you find us?"

"Mr. Hammond. He rode out yesterday and told me about the kidnapping." William's smile faded. "What's the matter?"

"Nothing. I just didn't expect to see you after your drunken tirade at the vicarage."

"About that." William shifted uncomfortably and let the strap slip from his shoulder. "I got a bit carried away."

"Carried away? Is that what you call it?" Graham looked over his shoulder to make sure Sulter was out of earshot, then stepped very close to William. At the very memory of the argument, the back of Graham's neck began to grow hot. He fixed his eyes on his brother and held the stare, daring William to look away. His brother may be able to pretend it never happened, but it was an offense Graham could not overlook. "I'm going to ask you this once, and I expect a direct answer. Because if you lie to me . . ." He let his threat fade and grabbed William's sleeve. "Did you have anything, anything at all, to do with Lucy's kidnapping?"

The grin contorting William's face faded. His eye twitched. "Do you jest?"

"Do not lie to me, William. Outside the vicarage you told me I would regret not giving you money. Is this what you meant? Is this a—"

"Have you gone daft?" William's eyes widened and he jerked his arm free. "No. No! Of course not. How could you think that I—"

"You told me yourself that you were desperate."

"Desperate, yes. A criminal, no." William's already ruddy complexion reddened. "How can you even suggest that I would kidnap my own niece?"

"Desperate men take desperate action."

"If I didn't think you were delirious with grief, I'd be offended." William swept his hat from his head and tossed it onto the side table next to Graham's pistol. William eyed the weapon, picked it up, and turned it over in his hand. "So this is how it is?"

Graham stepped forward and held out his palm for his brother to hand over the piece.

William let the pistol drop into his brother's hand. "I am going to forget you asked me such a ridiculous question and start over." William gave a little bow. "Greetings, brother. I am glad to see you too, and I want to help you find your daughter. Now, tell me, have you been able to ascertain her whereabouts?"

Graham eyed his brother, assessing his trustworthiness. Surely he wouldn't be here if he had anything to do with the kidnapping. But what if he was just covering his tracks? How could Graham be sure? His normally sharp senses, his keen eye of discernment, seemed muddled.

His candid talk with Sulter flashed in his mind. God had forgiven him for a much more grievous lapse in judgment. Could he not manage the same for his brother? He breathed an awkward prayer. Perhaps William's return was the answer in disguise.

Graham folded his arms across his chest, his voice low. "The ransom note instructs us to meet at George's Dock. I've engaged the services of a dockworker who has agreed to assist us as needed."

"Well then, I am at your service as well. Give me a task. I saw Littleton last night at the inn, but he was headed in the opposite—"

"Wait." Graham held up his hand to stop his brother. "Littleton, you say?"

William's eyebrows shot up. "Yes, Littleton. I saw him last night and I—"

"Where?"

William's forehead furrowed. "He was outside the inn with a group of men. I assumed he— Wait, did he not journey to Liverpool with you?"

"No. You are certain it was him?"

"Certainly." For once William appeared completely sober.

Graham would not waste time. "Show me exactly where you saw him."

※

Amelia could not sit still. One more minute spent trapped amidst the silence of the Sulters' parlor and the cage of her own fear and she'd most assuredly go mad. How she wanted to be a help in finding Lucy. To be useful. But here she sat. Waiting.

Next to her Jane mended her shawl, which she'd torn climbing down from the carriage at the Eagledale Inn. Amelia had tried to read but found concentrating impossible. How could Jane be so calm when such uncertainty swirled in the air?

The clock's incessant ticking drove her to distraction. *Eleven o'clock in the morning.* Her toe tapped against the rough wood floor. She wanted Lucy in her arms. She wanted to become Graham Sterling's wife. And she wanted it all now.

Noise in the hall caught Amelia's attention, and she arched her neck to see through the low framed door. Becky, the Sulters' oldest daughter, appeared in the narrow corridor, pulling a dark blue pelisse over her woolen dress.

Amelia straightened. "Are you leaving, Miss Sulter?"

Becky jerked her head up, as if surprised by the question, and nodded. "Indeed. Mother is sending me to the market."

Amelia's heart leaped. Finally, an opportunity! "You do not mind a bit of company, do you? I'm aching to be out of doors."

Jane's protest was immediate. "Captain Sterling asked you to stay here. I think you should respect his request."

Amelia grabbed her cloak and flung it about her shoulders. "We'll only be gone a short time. No harm will come from it, you will see. Please, Jane, I cannot just sit here and wait. I need to do something."

Without waiting for a response, Amelia donned her own bonnet. She looped the gray satin ribbon into a bow beneath her chin, then hurried to open the front door. A stunned Becky grabbed a small basket from next to the door and followed Amelia down a narrow lane and out to the busy street.

Amelia looked around from side to side as they walked, soaking in the activity around her. Carts jostled over cobbled roads. Children in tattered coats of gray and brown darted to and fro. She sidestepped to miss crates and coils of rope. Men and women of every class bustled about, carrying packs or selling wares. So different this place was from quiet Darbury. She scanned the narrow row of shops. The answer to finding Lucy had to be here.

She paid little attention to Becky's friendly chatter. Instead she searched each face as if it might possess a clue to finding Lucy. Elderly women, young men, soldiers and sailors in uniform—any one of them could know something that would help their efforts.

They reached the market, where Becky bought carrots and cabbage from a merchant's cart. Amelia had never been in such a bustling place. Wares hung from an assortment of rickety carts outside more permanent shops. Long leather leads tethered sheep and goats to makeshift fences. Shoppers jostled one another and stopped to haggle over merchandise. Horses and carriages rumbled by on the cobbled road, lined with tall warehouses, that wound toward the river. The wind carried scents of smoke and meat and river and sea.

When Becky stepped inside the butcher's shop, Amelia opted to remain out of doors. She walked to the building's edge and paced the length of the other shops, hoping to put some distance between her and the rank pile of rubbish outside the butcher's unpresumptuous shop.

Suddenly something made her pause and take notice. She turned and peered back through the throng of people and horses at a figure that was eerily familiar.

Could it be?

Amelia drew closer to the shoddy brick wall, wishing to be invisible. A quiver tugged her lip. The gait, the build, the mannerisms—she was certain. Edward Littleton was in Liverpool.

She squinted to make him out in greater detail. He stood close to a woman cloaked in black, a dark blue bonnet obscuring her face. They appeared to be arguing. The sounds of the docks and people muted their words, but their tense stances and jerky movements suggested a heated debate.

Amelia lifted her hand to shade her eyes from the sun peering from behind wispy silver clouds. The cut of the woman's cloak and the color of the bonnet looked familiar. Then the woman pivoted, and even from the distance there could be no mistake. The sun's golden light fell on none other than Helena Barrett.

Amelia gasped and fell back against the wall, her heart threatening to beat out of her chest. Her first instinct was to run to Helena. Surely she was here to assist in Lucy's rescue. But more rational thoughts prevailed. Helena was in Edward's company. And no good could come from Edward Littleton's presence in Liverpool.

By the time she gathered her wits and pushed away from the bricks, it was too late. Helena noticed her first, and her mouth fell open. Littleton, reacting to Helena's sudden change in demeanor, followed her gaze. For a moment, nobody moved. Then Helena tried to break free from Edward's grasp, and he turned and shouted over his shoulder.

Amelia forced foot in front of foot. She needed to reach the butcher's shop. She had to get Becky Sulter, and they needed to find Graham—now.

Alarm increased her pulse but slowed her steps. Edward. And Helena! She tried to tear her eyes from Edward, but his gaze—his hot, angry stare—locked on hers. He pointed in her direction. Then the two large men who had appeared at his side began crossing the street.

Amelia bolted for the butcher's door. Why had she left Becky? She hazarded a glance behind her as she ran. The men had disappeared. She slowed. But as she was about to reach the door, a thick arm cinched around her waist and a gloved hand clapped over her mouth. Before she could process what was happening, someone yanked her into the small alley next to the butcher shop.

She kicked, flailed, even tried to bite through the glove, but the arms around her were too strong. She tried to scream but managed only muffled squeaks. She looked around, disoriented. Above her, sky. To her left, bricks. In front of her, the street receded with each step her assailant took. She kicked again, even harder, but the arms lifted her off the ground.

"She's biting me!"

"Can't control a woman?"

"Shut up and give me a hand."

A second pair of hands grabbed her legs, then someone tied a kerchief around her eyes. Its smell was putrid—sweat, tobacco, and gin.

This couldn't be happening. Not now. Not when Lucy needed her the most. Graham flashed in her mind. With a grunt, bulky arms lifted her, and she fell against a hard surface. A hand pushed her down on her stomach. The overwhelming scent of moldy straw nearly gagged her. It pricked her cheek, and something sharp pushed against her side. Hot breath grazed her ear. "If ye know what's good for ye, pretty lass, you'll keep yer mouth shut."

❧

Graham adjusted the pistol at his waist for what felt like the hundredth time. More than an hour had passed, and still no sign of Littleton. "You're sure this is where you saw him?"

William nodded. "I'm certain of it." He nodded toward a pub next to the Darndee Inn. "That's where he and his comrades went last night."

Graham leaned against the pillar supporting a portico, his eyes fixed on the shabby pub and the dilapidated inn. He gritted his teeth. Now, more than ever, he was certain that Littleton was involved in Lucy's disappearance.

Another ten minutes whispered past when Graham snapped to attention. "That's him." The inn's door had flung open, and a trio of men emerged. They whispered amongst themselves. One of them shielded his eyes from the sun's bright glare. Then the two other men broke away from Littleton and started down the street.

Littleton straightened his tall hat atop his head, stuffed something in his pocket, and arched his neck to see down the street. Whatever the case, Littleton was alone. Now was their chance. Graham grabbed William's arm and pushed him forward. "Come on, let's go."

The brothers dodged through the pedestrians and carts on the walkway, weaving in and out of pockets of people, excusing themselves as they went.

"Littleton!" Graham called.

Littleton turned at the sound of his name, a shadow passing over his arrogant features when his eyes met them. His gaze darted between the approaching brothers and his departing colleagues.

Graham and William paired up shoulder to shoulder as they faced the man. Graham didn't wait for him to speak. "What business brings you here to Liverpool, Littleton?"

Littleton stuttered a response, a false smile on his lips. "Barrett Trading, of course. Busy dock, Liverpool. Ships coming in almost daily. Have one leaving in the morning, in fact. I'm here to oversee. Dockworkers can be a dastardly lot. But I'm sure I need not tell you that, *Captain.*"

His justification was too quick. Too complete. Graham forced a stare, daring Littleton to look away. "Coincidental, do you not think?"

Littleton shook his head. "What do you mean?"

"Just two days ago the three of us are in Darbury. Lucy is kidnapped. I receive a ransom note demanding that I come here. And now I find you."

Littleton's eyes narrowed. "I don't like what you are suggesting, Sterling."

Graham shrugged. "I suggested nothing. I merely presented facts."

"I had nothing to do with your daughter's disappearance, if that's what you are implying."

"Listen to that, William." Graham's words were addressed to his brother, but his stare never left Littleton's face. He stepped even closer, forcing the man to look him square in the eye. "If I find out you had any role in what happened, I will see that you pay."

Littleton's face deepened to crimson, and his chin shook. He glanced over his shoulder in the direction that the other men had disappeared. "As much as I would like to stay here with you gentlemen, I have business to attend to." He spun on his heel and headed after his colleagues.

William watched as Littleton darted across the street and into the crowd. "Where do you suppose he is going?"

Graham wondered the same question. Littleton wove through the crowd, his pace increasing. Something was not right. He could feel it as surely as he could sense a storm brewing on the seas. "I don't trust that fellow. He knows something, so I am going to follow him. Go get Sulter. He went to meet with Kingston at George's Dock. Can you find it?"

"I can manage."

"Good. Then let's all meet back here in about an hour. Oh, and, William?"

"Yeah?"

"Tell them to bring their pistols."

❦

Darkness surrounded Amelia. She yanked a coarse blindfold from her face.

Edward Littleton is behind this. Edward has Lucy.

Angry, frightened, and sore, she pushed herself off a dirty floor and sat up. She attempted to brush mud from her cloak and peeled off her soggy, soiled glove. Within seconds her eyes adjusted to the narrow stream of light filtering through a rip in the black rag covering a high window.

Where was she?

She attempted to stand, and at the movement overwhelming pain sliced through her forehead. She pressed her palm against her head. The last thing Amelia remembered was being lifted onto something and blindfolded.

She forced herself to remain calm. Her second attempt to stand was successful, and she turned in a circle to assess her surroundings. A lumpy straw mattress in the corner. A single chair against the wall. A chamber pot. A dusty planked floor. A closed wooden door.

She staggered toward the door and jiggled the handle. Locked. She struggled to make her voice confident and strong as she knocked on it. "Edward Littleton? I want to speak with Edward Littleton."

A shuffle outside vibrated the floor beneath her, and steps pounded toward her door. "Shut yer mouth, or I'll shut it fer ye!"

Her legs trembled, but sheer determination kept her voice steady. "I will not be silent. I know Mr. Littleton is the reason I am here, and I demand to speak with him."

Laughter sounded from the other side of the door, and she heard whispering. "Demand all ye want. Ye'll not be speakin' to no one."

She grabbed the door's ancient handle and shook it again, with more vigor, but something heavy on the other side prevented it from swinging open. She expelled her breath and leaned back against the wall with a thud. The scanty wall wobbled with her weight, and at the movement came a sound sweeter than any she had ever heard. A baby's cry.

"Lucy!" Joy surged through Amelia at the painfully familiar cry. Her knees threatened to buckle beneath her. She shook the door until her muscles burned with fatigue. "Let me out!"

Laughter rang out once again. She stood back away from the door and stared at her obstacle, her chest heaving with the exertion. She had to get out of there to get to Lucy. Waiting for their laughter to die down, she decided to change her tactic. "I'll stay in here and will not disturb you. You have my word. Just, please, let the baby come in here with me."

"Not on yer life, lady."

Amelia succumbed to the shaking in her legs and slid down the wall. She shivered when she once again heard the sweet cry. It was the cry Lucy gave when she was hungry or tired . . . not scared. At least she was safe. Alive.

Drawing her knees to her chest, Amelia trembled in the dark room. She leaned her forehead against her knees. Tears began, every inch of her body wracked with sobs. Why was this happening? If she ever needed an answer to prayer, it was now, and she assumed God would hear her just as well in this shabby room as in her chamber at Winterwood Manor.

And so she prayed.

28

Graham shaded his eyes with his hand and glanced up at the noonday sun. Spots of sunlight danced among the ever-present clouds. From where he stood, he could keep an eye on the location where he told William to meet him and the warehouse that Littleton had disappeared into. He scanned the wide, muddy street, looking for William. An hour had passed, and the dock was but a short walk away. What was taking so long?

He returned his attention to the warehouse. As far as he could tell, Littleton had been inside the entire time. To his knowledge, no one had entered. None had exited.

People swarmed the square and wagons lined the streets, making it easy for Graham to remain unnoticed in broad daylight. He leaned against the abandoned cart he had chosen for cover. Had it been a mistake to trust William to get Sulter? His brother hadn't proved himself to be very trustworthy in the past, but surely he could be trusted on such a simple mission.

Graham pulled his hat low over his eyes. He couldn't think about that now. It was time for action. He'd prefer to have assistance, but he'd act alone if necessary.

Just as he was about to move toward the building on his own, he saw them. William approached from the right, Sulter following closely, their black and gray coats and low hats blending them into the crowd. Graham straightened as they approached and made room for them behind the cart, looking about to make sure no one saw them gather. He was about to greet them when their expressions made him stop. He straightened. Something was wrong.

"What is it?"

Sulter gave a quick glance over to William before speaking. "It's Miss Barrett, Graham. She's gone."

The words didn't make sense. "What do you mean, gone?"

Sulter pressed his lips together before speaking. "She and my Becky went to the market. When Becky came out of the butcher shop, Miss Barrett wasn't there. She asked around and was told by an onlooker that two men grabbed Miss Barrett. But nobody saw where they took her."

Fierce panic seized Graham as Sulter's words scorched his ears. Amelia? If it had been any other man besides Sulter, he would not believe the words. His eyes darted to his brother, whose somber expression confirmed what he'd heard. Graham sucked in a sharp breath. "I told her not to leave."

Sulter stretched out his hands as if to calm Graham. "We went to the scene, but we found nothing."

Graham had seen many battles. He was no stranger to danger and fear. But he also knew it was crucial to stay calm in the face of the enemy. But never before had an attack been so personal. First Lucy. Now Amelia. His heart was unversed in how to react. "Littleton's behind this."

Graham cast a quick glance back at the warehouse where Littleton had disappeared. Lucy, Mrs. Dunne, and Amelia were all in danger—if not worse. He flexed his scarred hand, and then he noticed it. Someone was absent. "Where's Kingston?"

Sulter and William exchanged an uncomfortable glance. Graham knew their answer before they said a word. "I searched everywhere." Sulter's voice was low. "He was not to be found."

"Blast!" Graham slammed his fist against the wall next to him. His cravat grew unbearably tight as thoughts fired at him in rapid succession. He needed to fight the sinking feeling and stay calm. For Lucy. And now, for Amelia.

"Sorry, Graham." Sulter spoke with utter sincerity.

"We don't need him," Graham blurted, giving rise to his own confidence. "Littleton's in that warehouse. I'll get Lucy and Amelia back if I have to rip it down brick by brick."

Sulter's voice, as ever, was calm. "Consider, Graham. We do not know how many men are in there. May I suggest we wait un—"

"No!" Graham would not hear of waiting. Not now. Not when he was so close. He'd made a mistake trusting Kingston, and he would deal with the rogue later. But he would not make another mistake and risk losing everything. He whirled around. "Do you have a firearm?"

Sulter opened his coat just enough so Graham could see the flash of metal tucked in his waistband. William nodded, his face flushed. The thought of William fumbling to clean the pistol in the library flashed into Graham's mind. He eyed William. "Do you even know how to fire that thing?"

"Well, I told you I'm more of a horseman, but I'm not ignorant. I can shoot well enough." William's nervous laugh did little to convince Graham. He needed everyone to be confident. Disciplined. And William's experience in this type of pursuit was limited at best. But what choice did he have? He had these two men willing to help, and he needed each one. He slapped his hand on William's shoulder.

"All right, men. Here is what we are going to do."

⚘

Amelia tucked her feet below her as she watched a beetle scurry along the wall's edge and disappear in a crack. A shiver pulsed through her limbs, and she bit her lower lip. The lengthening shadows slipping in from behind the curtain hinted dusk was about to fall. Not since she demanded to speak with Edward Littleton had she heard so much as a peep, save for a whimper from Lucy. How much time had passed? Six hours? More?

She wrapped her cape around her, grateful for the little warmth it provided. Her thoughts turned to Helena. The shock of seeing her in Liverpool with Edward had not worn off. The argument Amelia witnessed had been heated indeed. Had Helena been helping Littleton with the kidnapping, or had she been trying to intervene?

Amelia scanned her surroundings, now barely visible in the dying light. How long would she be kept here? How on earth would Graham find her? Jane had said that God would never leave her nor forsake her. Was he watching her now, protecting her? Was he watching Lucy and Mrs. Dunne?

A tapping on the wall startled her. She scrambled to her feet and searched anxiously for the source of the noise. The tapping continued, then a finger poked through a small hole at the bottom of the wall. Amelia's heart leapt to her chest, and a cry escaped her lips. But the whisper that followed had a familiar Irish lilt. "Miss Barrett. Miss Barrett, are you there?"

Mrs. Dunne! Desperate for contact, she fell against the filthy floor and grabbed the finger with her own. "Mrs. Dunne, are you all right?"

The older woman's pudgy finger wrapped around hers, and its warmth seemed to spread through Amelia like hot tea on a frosty day. "I'm fine. And Lucy's fine, praise be to God. It's Mr. Littleton who's behind this. None other."

Amelia's heart raced faster than ever. "What else do you know?"

"Shhh . . . you'll need to stay quiet now. The man who's keeping guard—Jack's his name—he's finally nodded off."

"My door is closed. Locked. I can't see a thing."

"From what I heard, they're planning on exchanging us in the morning for money. But if Captain Sterling doesn't deliver it, then they'll put us on a ship bound for Barbados."

"Barbados?" Amelia had heard lurid tales about orphans being kidnapped and sold in the islands where abolition had created the need for cheap labor. She never imagined the stories could actually be true. Fear trailed down her back as a scene played across her mind.

She squeezed Mrs. Dunne's finger. "Is Lucy all right? Is she frightened?"

"She is doing just fine. Doesn't seem to know a thing is different. She's asleep right next to me, she is."

"Do not worry, Mrs. Dunne. Captain Sterling will find us." Her words were directed to herself as much as to the nurse. "He's been out looking all day."

"Does he have enough to pay the ransom?"

"He does. Let's just pray it all goes well." She hesitated, but her desire for the truth outweighed the need for discretion. "Are you aware of Helena being involved?"

"What, Miss Helena Barrett?"

"The very same."

"No, ma'am, not at all. Surely you do not think—"

Without warning, a crash thundered from outside her door. Amelia gasped and jumped to her feet, and Mrs. Dunne's finger disappeared through the hole in the wall. A distant door creaked on its hinges, and boots stomped the planked floors. The blood pounded in her ears with such intensity that she feared she wouldn't be able to hear a thing.

Two, perhaps three male voices echoed, but her heart lurched when she heard one voice in particular. Edward.

"Where is she?"

Amelia stiffened. She knew he was talking about her. Her hair, which had long since fallen free of her ivory comb, hung limply over her shoulders. She combed her shaky hands through the tangled curls. She might not feel confident, but by the grace of God, she would appear so.

Something was dragged away from the door. Amelia held her breath as the latch turned and the door swung open. Light from a lantern stung her eyes. Determined to show no weakness, she forced her eyes wide.

"What is she doing in the dark?" Edward hissed at the men behind him. "Is this any way to treat a lady?" He shouted his reprimand over his shoulder as he stepped into the dingy room, a lit tin lantern in hand. Dark shadows hid his features, but she could imagine the smirk he used to give her when he believed he had the upper hand. Well, those days were in the past . . . and they had taken a very dangerous turn. She had to be strong now—for Lucy and for herself.

She jutted her chin in the air. "I demand to know what is going on, Edward."

"I think you know exactly what is going on, Amelia dear."

"You are mistaken. Perhaps you had better explain it to me."

He chuckled. "Oh, Amelia, do not be coy. It doesn't suit you. You understand perfectly."

Even in the dark, she saw the outline of his firm jaw. High cheekbones. How had she ever thought him handsome? Charming?

His customary scent of port and tobacco assaulted her senses. She winced as his forefinger traced down her cheek, but she refused to allow her gaze to falter. "You're a liar, Edward Littleton." Her pointed accusation reverberated from every surface in the room. "I know you are angry with me, but how could you do this to an innocent child?"

Her statement seemed to amuse him. His white teeth flashed in the darkness. "You forced me to. Do you not see it?"

"I forced you to do nothing."

"On the contrary." With slow, deliberate steps he began to circle her, like a hawk circling its prey. She straightened her posture and stared forward. She would not give him the satisfaction of showing any fear.

He continued in hushed tones. "You betrayed me, Amelia, and see where that has gotten you?"

Amelia winced as he leaned close to her, his thick fingers caressing her shoulder. "Where's Helena?"

"Helena?"

"I saw you with her. Where is she?"

"Do not trouble yourself with Helena. She is not your concern." He dropped his hand and called back over his shoulder, "Get the baby and the nurse and get ready to head to the docks." He turned his attention back to Amelia. "And don't think I have forgotten you."

Amelia gritted her teeth. She glanced around, searching for a means of escape, but Edward's large frame blocked the door, and behind him stood at least three other men. "Where are you taking us?"

"That would spoil the surprise, wouldn't it? No doubt you expect your dashing Captain Sterling to rush to your aid. But we shall see about that, shall we not?"

Amelia balled her fists at her sides. But suddenly, it all faded when she caught sight of what she had been waiting for days to see—a glimpse of Lucy, her Lucy. The baby's face was dirty and tearstained, and she squirmed in the arms of a strange man.

Amelia's nostrils flared, but she forced herself to remain controlled. This was a game to Edward. She could play it too. "I know what you are after. I'm no fool. Let Mrs. Dunne and Lucy go free, and I will give you whatever you want."

A lewd sneer twisted his face. "Whatever I want?"

She ignored his innuendo. "I'm talking about money. That is what this is about, is it not? Name your sum, and I give you my word, I will make arrangements to get you what you want."

He snorted. "You give me your word? Ha! I seem to remember that you gave me your word on another matter, and look how well that came to fruition. Your word is useless to me. If you had made that proposition a few days ago, I might have been able to accept your generous offer, but now I have another score to settle."

He didn't need to explain. *Graham.*

Amelia jumped as Edward leaned back and shouted, "Bring her in." Then she gasped as a broad-shouldered man pulled Helena into the doorway. Helena's chestnut hair hung loose about her shoulders, and tears wet her face. A rip in her cloak caused it to hang on her at an awkward angle, and her hands were bound behind her back.

"Helena!" Amelia tried to push past Edward to get to her cousin, but he grabbed her arm and held her tight.

His lip curled in a sickening smile. "You don't mind, do you?" Producing a slender length of rope from somewhere, he stepped behind her and began to tie her hands.

"Tell me, dearest Amelia, are you fond of the sea?"

29

Edward took hold of Amelia's elbow, just as gently as he had dozens of times at Winterwood. Except they were not at Winterwood, and instead of her arms swinging freely by her sides, a coarse rope bound her hands together at the wrists.

She winced as Edward's grasp tightened. From the corner of her eye, she noted his discomfort. Perspiration dotted his brow. His jaw clenched, unclenched, then clenched again. She looked straight ahead down the dark corridor.

"Please, Edward, reconsider this insanity."

"Oh, it's Edward now, is it? Not Mr. Littleton? I've never known you to be so fickle."

"Uncle George will find out about this. Do you really think he will continue as your partner when he learns how you have treated his daughter and niece?"

"Barrett's a fool. Besides, where we are going, we will not need his help."

She swallowed. She feared his answer. "And where is that?"

An answer did not come. He merely pushed her down the hall, and once at the end, he jerked her to a stop.

His fingernail dug through her muslin sleeve, jabbing her arm's soft flesh. "It would be in your best interest, Miss Barrett, to keep your mouth shut." He looked out the door, gave a low whistle, nodded, and gripped her arm. She followed him through the door. Night, black and cold, surrounded her. The wind whistled around the corner, carrying with it bits of icy rain that made her eyes water.

Outside the warehouse, shadowed men darted to and fro. Three carriages were lined up in a tight alley. Steam rose from the horses' backs. One of the black beasts nickered, sending a plume of hot breath into the freezing air. Where was Lucy? Helena? Mrs. Dunne?

He tugged at her arm, and she dug her heels stubbornly into the muddy street. "Where's Lucy?"

He did not answer, and when another man came up behind her, fear dragged its fingers down her spine. Edward yanked her, nearly pulling her off her feet, toward a carriage, lifted her by the waist, and all but tossed her inside. She landed awkwardly against the seat. A timid cry startled her already tense nerves. She struggled to sit up and looked at the carriage's other occupant: Helena.

Edward cursed and looked in the carriage, his eyes wild, black hair disheveled. The wildness, the desperation in his eyes struck a chord of pure fear within Amelia, and she thought better of protesting. She straightened and sat back against the seat, hands bound behind her.

Edward pinned her with his half-crazed stare. He pointed at her and hissed through clenched teeth. "This is your fault, Amelia. Look at how your poor decisions have hurt so many."

He slammed the door. Urgent, muted voices circled the carriage, and she waited for the sound of footsteps to retreat before she turned to her cousin.

Amelia faced her cousin, who was in the corner, sobs wracking her body. She wanted to feel compassion, wanted to comfort her, but instead eyed her warily. Had Helena played a part in all of this? Or was she merely a victim of Edward's cruelty?

Helena sniffed, her sobs echoing in the tiny space. It was the first time the women had been alone since their capture.

Suddenly Amelia saw Helena as she had when they were children, with her hair in plaits and ribbons. Her mind was rich with memories of a happy time when they would whisper secrets and share dreams. Regardless of how she had come to be here, the pain in Helena's eyes tugged at her heart. Amelia scooted close, until her cloak brushed Helena's. "Tell me, how did this happen? How did you get here?"

Instead of an answer, another cry escaped from Helena. Frustrated, Amelia repeated her question, this time louder. "I know you are frightened, but now is not the time to be hysterical. You must be strong, Cousin. You must. We haven't much time. Do you know where he is taking us?"

Helena shook her head, her cloak carrying with it the scent of tobacco. Her whisper was barely audible. "You were right. About Edward. You were correct from the very first day Father brought him to Winterwood."

The carriage lurched forward, and with an awkward flounce, Amelia fell against Helena. She was torn between her desire to comfort her cousin and the desire for truth.

Helena wiped her cheek on her shoulder. "He told me he loved me, Amelia. Said it was me he loved, not you. And like a fool, a stupid fool, I believed him. I *wanted* to believe him."

Amelia chewed her lip. Right now was not the time to right past wrongs. They needed to find a way out of their predicament. Amelia spoke quickly to forestall another flood of tears. "Think, Helena. We must get out of here."

But Helena ignored the question, seemingly unaware of the danger of their situation. "He told me to play the part. Told me that he was going to put an end to the engagement with you when the timing was right and marry me."

Amelia winced in shock from the words. The reality of what Helena was saying nicked its way into Amelia's conscience. What relationship had Helena and Edward developed? And how had she not noticed? Edward had betrayed her in every other way, so the news hardly surprised her. But the admission of betrayal by her cousin, her own flesh and blood, cut like a blade. She reminded herself to breathe. Of the need to stay calm and controlled. Nothing of the life she knew seemed clear. She held her breath. All would be revealed. Soon.

Helena's whisper continued to tremble under the weight of her emotions. "When you announced the end of your engagement to Edward and your new engagement to Captain Sterling, I was optimistic, but then Edward changed. He grew angry. Distant. I never thought him capable of such coldness."

Amelia frowned, trying to follow her cousin's strange string of words. "Please, be clear."

Helena adjusted, and a sliver of light slanted across her face, shining on the tears tracking down her cheeks. She looked away from Amelia. "I—I'm with child."

Amelia jerked. The unexpected lurch of her stomach made her light-headed. She stared at her cousin in sheer disbelief, momentarily forgetting about the coldness of the carriage. The dirt caking her dress and hands. The fear clawing her chest. Amelia's voice was lost between shock and dismay, and pity for her cousin at the dire situation she found herself in. She was not sure she wanted to hear more. She slowly swung her head from side to side and stared at Helena's midsection. "I do not understand."

Helena's words were sharp. Short. "What do you not understand?

I am with child, Amelia. Everyone will know soon, for I cannot hide it much longer."

The carriage seemed to slow, and she heard voices shouting outside. A tremor of panic shot through her. "Quickly—we need a plan of action if we are to again see the light of day. You must tell me, how did you come to be in Liverpool?"

Helena's words were frustratingly—nay, maddeningly—slow and limp. Did she not comprehend the urgency of their situation? "I told him of the child after the altercation he had with Captain Sterling. I thought it would bring him joy. We could finally be together. But instead his countenance grew dark. Gloomy. He left shortly after you and the captain departed for Liverpool in foul spirits. I thought he was angry with me, angry about the baby. He said he had some affairs to tend to and he would send a carriage for me. I had no idea where he had gone or where the carriage was taking me, but when the driver told me we were bound for Liverpool, I began to grow suspicious. Then when I arrived and met Edward, it became apparent what he had done—that he had taken Lucy. We were arguing about it, and that is what you saw on the street."

Amelia struggled to separate her emotions from the story. "You had naught to do with the kidnapping?"

"No. Nothing. Upon my honor. How could I have known what he had planned? He never trusted me."

Amelia fell back against the seat, trying to absorb all she had heard. "Edward is a snake, a scoundrel."

Helena's face crumpled, as if torn between the desire to defend Edward and acknowledging her mistakes. Tears once again began to flow. "My life is ruined, Amelia. What have I left? If Captain Sterling does not deliver the money, Edward is going to take us to the West Indies, and heaven knows what he will do with us there. Father and Mother will never know what happened to us and—"

"Are you sure, Helena?" Amelia interrupted, unable to prevent the sharp edge in her voice. "Are you sure that your father knows nothing of this? He would have as much to gain and—"

"No! I am certain Father knew nothing. Edward even told me as much." Helena sniffed. "Poor Father. And Mother will be heartbroken. It will be as if we simply vanished."

"Well, that will not happen." Amelia forced as much confidence into her whisper as she could muster. "Captain Sterling has the money. He will not leave us. Mark my words."

"And if he does recover us, how can I ever show my face in society again? I am such a fool!"

"What's done is done." Though compassion for her cousin's situation pricked her, she fought a rebuke. Helena was entrenched in her own pain. Did she not see the more immediate threat, not only to herself but to Amelia, Lucy, Mrs. Dunne, and Graham? But Helena's actions were consistent with her nature. "Come now. We must stay strong. Tears will not help us one bit."

Helena gave another big sniff. "But what are we going to do?"

Unable to hug her cousin due to the rope around her wrists, Amelia leaned her head on Helena's shoulder. For once, the path she needed to take was unwaveringly clear.

"Pray, Helena. We will pray."

❧

Despite the cold air, Graham felt a trickle of perspiration run down his neck. The purple shadows of dusk blanketed the streets, and yellow candlelight spilled from dirty windows onto the cobblestones below.

Graham squinted in the fading light to see across the marketplace. On the other side of the square, Sulter leaned against the warehouse wall, smoking a pipe. He tipped his hat in Graham's direction. *The signal.* His plan was working. He was one step closer to bringing Lucy, Amelia, and Mrs. Dunne to safety.

Graham nudged his brother's arm. "Let's go." Sure-footed and determined, he crossed the street, keeping his hat pulled low.

William struggled to keep up. "What will we do when we get there?"

"Just keep your eyes open and wait for my lead."

Sulter withdrew to the alley, as planned, and Graham and William followed him.

Sulter waited until both brothers were in the alley's safe shadows. "I took a turn around the building and spied in a few windows. Didn't see Miss Barrett but heard a woman's voice awhile back and a baby cry some time past. Whatever we do, we best be quick about it. A carriage pulled in the alley as I came round."

Graham narrowed his eyes. He surveyed the dilapidated building, noting the broken window and crumbling façade. Every instinct within him screamed that Lucy, Amelia, and Mrs. Dunne were within this building. He wanted to rip it down stone by stone to get to them. But he had to be smart. He flexed his scarred hand. He knew better than to be impatient. The price of failure was far too steep.

Graham returned his attention to Sulter. "What are we dealing with?"

Sulter drew another puff from his pipe and looked down the dark alley. "Three doors into the place. One locked; it appears to be a cellar. The other is the main entrance where Littleton went in. There's a third door behind the building, off another alley. If we go in, that door's the one we should use."

Graham flipped his collar up around his chin. He knew the answer to his question before he asked it. But stubborn hope pushed the words from his lips. "Any sign of Kingston?"

Sulter's silence provided the answer.

Graham pressed his lips together, then opened his mouth to speak, but the sound of a carriage stilled him. In quick response, the men lined up against the wall in the shadows, waiting for it to pass. But instead of rumbling by the warehouse, it groaned to a stop somewhere to the side.

Graham motioned for Sulter and William to stay still. A carriage stopping at the warehouse at this late hour could only mean trouble. He held his breath and waited, each second sliding into the next.

The sound of the carriage door opening was followed by hushed voices. Above the normal sounds of evening, the men heard the warehouse door open, then slam shut. The voices ceased.

Sulter's whisper was rough. "Saw three men already inside earlier. Littleton and two others. If I was one to gamble, I'd wager the carriage is there to transport 'em to the docks."

Graham immediately began to adjust his plan, growing nervous. "Can we get in that third door?"

Sulter nodded. "Aye."

"Good. Any idea of the layout of this building?"

Sulter shook his head. "Never been inside, but it's a warehouse. Likely 'bout the same as the others—storage in back, office up front. If they have them in there, they probably have them in one of the office rooms. Like I said, I didn't see them but heard the babe crying."

Just the knowledge that Lucy had been crying revived Graham's fury. "We'll go in the back way, then. Ready, William?"

William swallowed and nodded, but did not speak.

Graham pointed at the handle of William's pistol. "You really know how to use that?"

His brother hesitated, then nodded again.

"Use it only if you have to. Our objective is to get all of us out safely."

286

Graham looked hard at his accomplices. Sulter's eyes held focus. William's barely contained his fear. Graham wished there was time to come up with a better plan, but he wasn't about to risk letting his quarry slip away. He removed his pistol from his waistband, checked it, then nodded toward the back alley.

"Let's go."

But as he turned down the alley, the sight he saw sickened him. The carriage was not arriving, but departing. Disbelief momentarily froze his feet to the spot. And when he regained his senses, he ran to the warehouse door, still open. He entered with reckless abandon, weapon brandished, only to be met with an empty room. A dying fire. And the impending sense of failure.

Footsteps entered behind him.

Graham let his weapon fall to his side. He'd misjudged—miscalculated the plan. "We're too late."

William's voice echoed. "What do we do now?"

With renewed vigor, Graham spun on his heel. "We go to the docks."

❧

The carriage door yanked open, the force of which jostled the entire carriage, and Amelia pressed back against the seat. Edward filled the opening, but behind him, the moonlight shimmered on waves, and a great ship settled on the water. The gull's cry met her ears. Edward grabbed her and lifted her down. She swung her head around, desperately searching. Surely Graham would rescue them. This couldn't be the hour it would end. The feel of Edward against her sickened her, and as soon as she found her footing she pulled away. She searched hungrily, slightly relieved when she saw Lucy in Mrs. Dunne's arms . . . until she saw them boarding a great wooden ship.

Edward lifted Helena down and then took Helena's arm in one hand, Amelia's in the other. Two other men swarmed around them. Amelia searched the landscape for Graham, hoping, praying he had figured out where they were. But only the sight of crates, rope, and smoke met her. As Edward yanked her toward the ship, she was overcome with a new fear: neither she nor Helena had ever been on a ship. She stared down at the churning water as she stepped across the wooden walkway to the frigate's upper deck. In front of them, Lucy and Mrs. Dunne disappeared through a companionway.

Amelia imagined she heard a breath of relief before Edward spoke. "Welcome to the *Perseverance*, ladies."

As night deepened, clouds rolled in, thickening the sky and obscuring the moon's glow. Graham paused only long enough to fill his lungs with air.

He was close to them. He could feel it in every fiber of his being.

Above him, the clouds hung thick and low, and at his ankles, a night's mist swirled at his feet. He stood in the shadows, watching the ship rock. The choppy water pulled it, testing the tether of the ropes. Through a tiny window an unsteady light wavered.

Even in the black of night, the docks were never quiet. A man ran past. Two others came from the opposite direction, their voices no louder than whispers.

Graham felt William approach. "What are we going to do?"

"We are going to wait."

"Wait?"

"Patience, brother."

Graham was as eager—if not more so—and checked his timepiece, though he already knew the time. The moon's location in its path across the night sky gave him all the information he needed. Dawn would arrive soon and shed its cool light on the docks and sleeping ships, rousing all from their slumber.

To Graham's best guess, Littleton had left the warehouse with five men. The odds of being able to board the ship were unfavorable. After all, the entire crew could be aboard. He spotted one sailor. Then another. But his options were waning. A hired crew would likely offer little loyalty and protection to Littleton, and he'd already missed one opportunity to free the women and Lucy. He'd not miss another.

Minutes slipped by at a sluggish pace, and the moon crawled along its path in the night sky, illuminating the low-hanging clouds. With every passing moment, his senses heightened just as they had in an impending battle. The hair on his neck stood straight. He was on constant alert. But never before had a battle been so critical—never had so much been at stake.

Sulter's past and long-forgotten words of God rushed to the forefront of his mind. Suddenly they seemed clear. His own strength was not sufficient. Even though he did not know what awaited him in the wooden confines of the *Perseverance*, God did. Graham knew well the dangers of boarding an enemy ship, docked or not. But tonight he would not board the ship of his own strength. He would not cower in fear at the unknown. Tonight he would pray. He would put his faith in the God who had offered him forgiveness. Offered patience. Offered him a future.

A cloud covered the moon, shadowing the docks still further. But just then, a lantern's light appeared on deck. Then another. Two darkened forms accompanied the lights. Graham's jaw twitched. Now was the time.

Sulter leaned close, his gravelly voice low. "Thou, O Lord, art just and powerful: O defend our cause against the face of the enemy."

Graham recognized the prayer. It was from the Book of Common Prayer, often spoken at sea when facing an imminent battle. The words had been long memorized and often quoted. But tonight they took on new meaning and infused him with humble confidence.

He finished the prayer. "O God, thou art a strong tower of defense to all that flee unto thee: O save us from the violence of the enemy. O Lord of hosts, fight for us, that we may glorify thee. O suffer us not to sink under the weight of our sins, or the violence of the enemy." His voice shook with the final words. "O Lord, arise, help us, and deliver us for thy Name's sake."

Graham's heart pounded as erratically as the waves lapping the side of the *Perseverance*. After instructing William to stay behind and keep watch, he and Sulter turned toward the ship. Even though the ship itself was unfamiliar, his confidence surged. They were on his turf now, and with God's help, they would persevere.

❦

Sure-footed, with weapon brandished, he boarded the frigate with Sulter close behind.

But then he heard her. Lucy.

The babe's sharp cry punctuated the night's sounds, followed by an angry voice that could only be Littleton's. Graham adjusted his grip on his pistol and with his other hand reached down to make sure his blade was still tucked in his boot.

The vessel creaked and rolled beneath them. With his feet firmly on the deck, he looked up. The mainmast stretched into the starless sky, and coupled with the vessel's gentle movement, a myriad of memories flooded him. But it was the sounds of voices Graham listened for. They could be anywhere in the dark maze of lower decks. When a cry pierced the night, he looked at Sulter. They followed the cry down a ladder. A dangerous decision, really, for once below deck, they would be trapped if they were not successful.

The sound led them to the wardroom. How many times had he entered a wardroom? In times of relaxation, to dine with officers. In times of battle, when it served as a makeshift surgery room. But never would he have thought he would be entering one to rescue his daughter.

Time was limited. The crew would be on to them soon, and what match would two men have against a crew? Sputtering light flashed from behind a drawn door. Graham looked back at Sulter, pressed his finger to his lips, and leaned closer, desperate to hear anything above the thudding in his brain.

From within the wooden walls he heard a woman's voice, soothing, soft, and low. He heard a harsh whisper. A baby's whimper. Graham held up one finger, then another to indicate the distinct male voices that met his ear. Their best hope was to catch the men off guard.

He waited through the silence until the murmur of men's voices once again sounded from within. Good. The men were distracted. He signaled Sulter, and then with all of his weight, he rammed the door with his shoulder and slammed it against the wall. Women screamed. He saw one man. Two men. And then his eyes narrowed on Littleton.

Pistol pointed straight at Littleton's chest, he pushed him and one other man past a table and against the paneled wall.

Littleton's struggle for composure played on his dark features. Flickering light from one of the hanging lanterns glimmered off of the perspiration trickling down the sides of his face. His voice rang with imperious bravado. "Ah, the mighty Captain Sterling, come to claim his bride. I'd wager this is not what you expected to find, is it?"

Graham fought the urge to look back at Amelia and Lucy and

kept his eyes focused on Littleton. He pressed the pistol against Littleton's chest.

A sinister smirk curved Littleton's lips. "You'd best kill me, Sterling," taunted Littleton. "Because mark my words, if you are fool enough to let me live, I'll have my revenge yet."

Graham gritted his teeth. "Nothing would give me greater pleasure, but unfortunately it isn't up to me when your miserable life will come to an end."

"Then you're a greater fool than I thought." Littleton's squeaky laugh dripped with the desperation of a caught man. He licked his lips and shifted his eyes to the man Sulter was tying to the table leg. "You may think that you will have your way by simply barging onto this vessel, but you are sorely mistaken."

Graham narrowed his eyes on the man, his chest tightening at the pure evil lurking in Littleton's expression. But suddenly, a woman's scream pierced the air. He glanced back toward the sound, and in that split second, the man who'd been standing at Littleton's right lunged, pushing Graham backward against the long table situated in the middle of the room.

Graham gulped for air as the man struggled to pin him down. But the smaller man was no physical match. After taking a few blows to his side, Graham adjusted his grip on his pistol, righted his opponent, and landed a solid blow to the man's jaw, sending him staggering against a sideboard. Candlesticks and decanters crashed to the ground at the impact, and Graham whirled back to face Littleton. To his surprise, Littleton had locked his arm around a woman's waist and held a knife to her throat. At second glance, he saw it was not Amelia or even Mrs. Dunne whose eyes were wide with terror. It was none other than Helena Barrett.

Graham did not have time to figure out how this woman had found her way into this mess. He raised his pistol. At the movement, Littleton tightened his grip on Helena, and she squeaked in fear.

The pitch of Littleton's voice increased. "I would not recommend that, Sterling."

Graham's was steady. "Let her go."

Littleton sneered. "I want my money."

Graham licked his lips. He was not dealing with a sane man. "And if I give you the money, will you let her go?"

He laughed. "You can take them when you leave." Littleton nodded toward Amelia, Mrs. Dunne, and Lucy but tightened his grip on the horrified Helena. "But I'd be a fool to let this one go."

Graham's pistol itched in his hands. His coat might as well have been made of fire. Perspiration poured down his temples, burning his eyes. He was a man of swift decisions. And a swift, sure decision needed to be made. In addition to saving his daughter and Amelia, he needed to get Mrs. Dunne and now Helena Barrett to safety. The desire for justice bubbled up within him. If it took his last breath, he would not allow this man to terrorize another.

Graham glanced as Sulter, who nodded. With a swift motion, the older man kicked a chair across the floor, the commotion of which was enough to distract Littleton. Graham lunged forward and pushed the blade away from Helena. Graham shoved Helena away and grabbed Littleton by the coat, pulling him to the opposite corner of the narrow room away from the women huddled next to the scullery door. A fistfight, a pure battle for physical domination, ensued. Littleton still fisted the blade in his hand. Graham's gun had fallen by the wayside. The men were unevenly matched. Graham tried to reach for his own blade tucked in his boot, but he was forced to call on every bit of energy to keep Littleton's blade away from his body.

He thought he was gaining the upper hand when he pinned Littleton on the planked floor, but with a sudden jolt, Littleton broke from his grasp and dove away from him. Graham seized the opportunity to jump to his feet and ram Littleton into the wall. At the motion, Littleton's blade dragged across Graham's arm, slicing through his coat and penetrating skin. The shock was so strong that he wasn't even sure if he'd been cut until a searing pain followed by a blinding heat radiated from the spot. Graham swung his other arm, pummeling Littleton's shoulder, but Littleton answered with his own punch to Graham's jaw.

Graham heaved for breath, but then, from a direction he did not know, a shot rang out. Only when Littleton's eyes widened in stunned pain and he stumbled and fell to his knees did Graham realize what had happened. He whirled around. In the doorway stood William, pistol pointed, smoke curling up from the barrel.

Regaining his senses, Graham grabbed Littleton's knife, threw it to the side, and patted him down for other weapons. Littleton cried out at the pressure, and Graham pushed his shoulder against the ground.

Graham thrust his own pistol, which was still loaded and had fallen to the ground, across the floor to his brother. He then pulled the fabric of Littleton's trousers away from his leg to reveal a raw flesh wound. He looked closer. No bullet. "You're a lucky man, Littleton. It grazed you. Count your blessings it was not I who took the shot."

Littleton groaned, his teeth clenched, and spewed a smattering of curses before dropping his head back against the planked floor.

Graham called to William, whose face was as pale as a man who'd just witnessed a murder. "Come over here. Don't let him move a muscle." He straightened, glanced over at the group of women and screaming baby, and then down at his own arm. Blood seeped through the heavy fabric, darkening the wool to nearly black.

He wiped the hair sticking to his forehead away and assessed Littleton. Now he hardly looked a threat. Pale with a smearing of crimson blood across his nose and cheek. Sulter hurried forward to assess Graham's wound.

Graham expelled his breath slowly.

Could this really be over?

He had to touch Lucy. Make sure she was real. And Amelia. His beloved Amelia.

Before he could even turn, he felt a hand on his shoulder and then caught a glimpse of blond hair from his peripheral vision. His muscles tensed until he heard a voice—more soothing and softer than his own mother's.

"You're hurt."

Amelia.

Her hand traveled his back. The tenderness of her touch was a balm. He wanted to fall against her, let her comfort him, but he gathered his senses. Pushed the pain down. They were not safe yet. They all needed to depart the ship. With Littleton's accomplices still near, they weren't safe until their feet were safely on land.

He stood and took her hands in his. He wanted to grab hold of her. To pull her to him and feel her against him. To let her very presence heal his wounds and calm his weary soul. But now was not the time. "You must get Lucy off this ship." His voice was little more than a growl.

"Sulter!" Graham dropped her hands and wove through the throng of tossed chairs and ushered Mrs. Dunne and Helena Barrett forward. "Get them off the ship. Now."

He looked back down at the other two accomplices. Sulter, who'd always been quick with a rope and stronger than his small frame would suggest, had the two men bound. Sulter nodded and took Mrs. Dunne's hand. Graham and William leaned down and lifted Littleton from the ground, each taking an arm.

"Nice shot, Will." Graham grunted as he lifted the man from the floor. "Remind me to thank you."

William huffed under Littleton's limp weight. "Do not thank

me yet." William cast a nervous glance at the man between them. "You do not think he will die, do you?"

Graham shook his head as he carefully angled himself to fit through the narrow door frame and passageway. He waited for the ladies to ascend the ladder. He winced at the cut on his arm and flexed his hand. He'd lived through worse pain. Much worse. With William's help, he managed to get Littleton up the ladder and onto the upper deck.

At first Littleton squirmed, but within moments Graham and his brother had their hands on him. "It's over, Littleton," grunted Graham. "This time, for good."

30

Graham stepped from the steamy confines of the ship. He could not recall a time when the brisk air of early dawn was so refreshing. Littleton's body grew limper with each step. The man was not in danger of dying. The shot had but grazed him. But he was losing blood, and no doubt the pain was significant.

Graham scanned the gathering crowd for Amelia. His heart ached with renewed hope when he spotted her, waiting from a safe distance. How could he miss her? Her hair, made brilliant by the rising sun, spilled over her shoulders. Her eyes were locked onto him. Boldy. Expectantly. Now that her hands were untied, she held Lucy in her arms protectively. At the very sight of them, an overwhelming sense of protectiveness wove through the fibers of his being.

His task here was almost complete. And then he would take his daughter and his beloved home. Back to Darbury. Away from the fear and uncertainty that had met them in Liverpool.

All around him, everything seemed suddenly vibrant. The sounds of the sea. The call of the seabirds. It was all alive.

Littleton stumbled, his injured leg limp, unable to sustain his own weight. Graham left Littleton in the care of William and Sulter and jogged over to Amelia. He forgot the pain of his arm. The fury of the fight. That was behind him. And his future in front.

He could almost feel Amelia's warmth. Feel the weight of his daughter in his arms. But as he drew closer, Amelia's expression darkened. Her eyebrow raised, and she sucked in her breath. The sudden change in her demeanor slowed Graham's steps. He pivoted to follow her gaze. Across the dock, the outline of a tall, burly man approached William and Sulter. Without warning, the stranger rushed up to Littleton, who was now sitting on the ground, and rammed his booted toe into Littleton's ribs.

Graham stared in disbelief. More than anything he wanted to return to the Sulters'. To take Amelia and Lucy away from the nightmare of the past few days. But what he had seen stilled his legs. Sulter attempted to stop the man from repeating the assault, but was shoved out of the way.

That was all Graham needed to see. He took off like a shot toward the perpetrator, siezing the much larger man by the arm and whirling him around.

"What is the meaning of—" His words fell flat when the man turned.

Kingston.

A flash of recognition sparked on Kingston's scraggly face. "Cap'n Sterling."

Graham squared his shoulders, narrowing his eyes on Kingston, forgetting for the moment about Littleton. "Did you forget something?" Graham's words were every bit as hard as he intended. "By my calculations you are several hours late for a task for which your services were engaged."

A rough smile cracked the man's leathery features. He shrugged. "Well now, that's an unfortunate oversight. But see here, my business right now's not w' you. It's w' 'im." He kicked at Littleton again.

Graham put his arms out to push the man back. He did not begrudge the man anger toward Littleton, nor was he surprised to learn Littleton had more enemies. But he was not about to watch Kingston beat a man who was too weak to stand.

Before Graham could speak, Kingston leaned forward and hissed in Littleton's direction. "I think you owe me something, Littleton. I don't want to tear your limbs off in front of your friends here—"

"Be on your way, Kingston," demanded Graham, pushing his own body between the two men.

Kingston ignored Graham. "This man's comin' w' me. He's got some blokes what wants to see 'im."

Kingston reached down as if to grab Littleton, and both Graham and William blocked his path.

"I do not know what your business is with this man, but he is guilty of kidnapping. I'm taking him to the magistrate."

Kingston sneered. "Magistrate, you say? I got my own brand of authorities. Get outta my way." The man lurched forward and shoved against Graham with his forearm.

Graham couldn't care less what happened to Littleton. He wanted to nurse his own wound, return to the comfort of Amelia's arms, and hold his daughter. But whatever had transpired between Littleton and Kingston, Littleton was not fit for a fight. Graham had come to Liverpool with the intent to save his daughter and bring about justice. Justice was not handing the pitiful Littleton over to the likes of Kingston.

With every muscle still tense and alert from the previous skirmish, fresh fire surged through his veins. Within moments, fists were once again flying. But as corrupted as Littleton was, Kingston's fight was more savage. More vicious.

And then Graham saw his opportunity. He took a punch that pushed him back several feet, which gave him just enough room. He lifted himself from the ground, kept him body low, and thrust all of his momentum into the middle of Kingston's body. Kingston flailed back, tripped on the coils of rope behind him, and fell off the dock into the frigid sea.

With near expert timing, William threw his pistol to his brother, who peered off the dock to the man treading water.

"Get out!" Graham shouted as Sulter secured a rope to the dock so Kingston could climb up. Graham stared down at Kingston with steely reserve. It was over. There was no way he could fight. Nowhere he could go. When the man floundered, Graham fired a shot into the water. "Get out!"

Kingston, wet and shivering, climbed the rope. Once he was on the dock, Graham whirled around, half expecting another attack. But aside from the gathering crowd watching the incident, all was quiet. His arm throbbed. His head pounded. But he would continue to fight, if need be—for justice. And, more importantly, for his family.

Littleton lay on the dock, pale and unconscious as Sulter made quick work of tying up Kingston. Graham leaned over their new enemy.

"Wait. Before you do that—" He reached in the man's coat and felt the lumpy contents of his pockets until he found what he sought. The act of retreiving the waterlogged money, for what it was worth, brought little satisfaction. "Hmm. I do not believe you held up your end of the bargain, did you, mate?"

Sutler tsked. "And after all the trouble I went through recommeding you."

Kingston's chest heaved, his scraggly hair plastered to his face.

Graham straightened. "Sulter, see that the women are taken care of. William and I can take it from here."

But before the words were even out of his mouth, Amelia was at his side. Brave, impulsive Amelia. The very sight of her both weakened him and infused him with a strength—and dedication—he'd never imagined before now.

By the dawn's light he saw the dark shadows gathered beneath her eyes. The straw in her tangled hair. He reached out to smooth a smudge of dirt on her cheek, relishing the sensation of the petal-soft skin beneath his rough hand.

Motion caught his eye, and he glanced up to see a constable walking in their direction. No doubt the gathering crowd piquing his interest. He felt a tremor of relief at the sight. It was almost done. The end was in sight. He'd deliver Littleton and Kingston and then be free of them both. He looked back down at Amelia. Her eyes held questions, but the strength he saw in them renewed him.

He pressed his lips to her forehead, noting how she trembled beneath his touch. "This is the end. I promise. I will take care of this, but I need to know you and Lucy are safe." He leaned close, his lips touching her ear, and whispered, "I love you, Amelia Barrett. You are a part of me. No one will keep you from my side. *No one.*"

❦

In the stillness of her room at the Sulters' house, Amelia lay propped on her side, watching her cousin sleep. With Helena's hysteria finally coming to an end, exhaustion had set in.

Amelia lay her head on the pillow and tucked her hands underneath it. The sheets felt cool against her cheek.

The events of the last few days haunted her, and she did not doubt they would do so in the days—nay, years—to come.

Next to her, Helena stirred. She did not even want to think how close she had come to losing her. When Edward held the blade to her cousin's throat, the depth of her affection became clear. How it must hurt Helena to know the father of her child could treat her in such a way. The thought of Helena as a mother seemed surreal. But perhaps knowing what it was like to love another more than herself—just as Amelia loved Lucy—would help Helena, in time, understand why Amelia made the choices she did.

She smoothed Helena's nut-brown hair against the pillow. It no longer mattered what had caused the rift between them. All that mattered now was repairing what had been broken.

Helena's eyelashes fluttered open, and Amelia sat up, waiting for her to speak. Helena's words were barely more than a mumble. "Lucy and Mrs. Dunne. They're all right?"

Amelia grabbed Helena's hand. "Yes, dearest, they are well. Mrs. Hammond is preparing a bath for Lucy now."

"I'm sorry . . . so sorry." Helena's eyelids almost drooped closed and her words slurred. "This is all my fault."

Amelia shook her head. "This is all on Edward's shoulders. He took advantage of you, me, Aunt and Uncle—and to put a child through this . . ." She shivered. "But it's all over now, and the captain will see that Edward pays for what he has done."

"Captain Sterling is a good man."

The words echoed in Amelia's heart. A flush rushed to her cheeks at the memory of his hand caressing her cheek. "He is a good man. He is indeed."

Helena's head rolled to the side and slumber replaced consciousness. When Amelia was certain Helena was asleep, she sat up from the bed, her muscles protesting the movements. She rubbed her raw wrists as she walked down the hall and headed toward the modest kitchen where Jane was bathing Lucy.

Tears pooled in Amelia's eyes at the sight of the baby. Fewer than two hours had passed since Graham freed them and Sulter returned them to the safety of his home. Even though they were now out of danger, her heart still seemed to rattle in her chest. How close she had come to losing her darling Lucy! The child appeared happy and content, as if the kidnapping had never happened. But the recollection of her in that warehouse, dirty and scared, still lingered in Amelia's memory. She suspected it would haunt her dreams for years to come.

Lucy dunked a chubby fist into the water and giggled with delight at the resulting splash. Pleased, she turned her round face to Amelia and smiled, revealing three tiny teeth. The baby's laugh was sweeter than any sound, her smile more beautiful than any painting.

Amelia picked up the linen cloth, dipped it in the warm, sudsy water, and brushed it against Lucy's soft cheek. Jane stepped aside so Amelia could care for Lucy. Three days' worth of filth rolled off with the water. Amelia drew a slow breath to combat the tightening in her chest. Tenderly, she rubbed soap in the child's hair and poured water to rinse it clean. Desperate to be free from the memory, she washed the child's hair again. It could not be clean enough.

Jane's voice was soft. "I'll tell Mrs. Sulter we'll need more warm water."

Amelia swiveled to face her. "No need, Lucy is almost clean."

A smile eased across the older woman's face. "Not for Lucy. For you, dear. You need a bath just as badly, if not worse."

Amelia lifted her hand to wipe the hair from her face, and for the first time noticed the layer of dirt covering her forearms.

Jane's face scrunched as she picked something out of Amelia's hair. "What is that? Straw?"

"Most likely."

"Well, Captain Sterling will be home soon. You must wash the dirt away."

Captain Sterling. Graham. Her heart beat an erratic cadence as she turned back to lift Lucy from the tub.

"Amelia, you're trembling." Jane stepped forward. "Here, let me help you."

Frustrated at her own vulnerability, Amelia shook her head. "I don't need help, really. I—I . . ."

Ignoring Amelia's protest, Jane reached for the child, wrapped her wriggling wet body in a blanket, and snuggled her close. Amelia's shoulders sagged as she watched Lucy play with Jane's necklace. She wanted to be the one to care for Lucy, to hold her and never let her go. But her strength was gone. A sob caught in her throat, and her words spilled forth in uncontrollable fervor.

"I came so close to losing her."

Jane placed Lucy down in the cradle and returned to Amelia's side and drew her into a tight embrace. Days of pent-up frustration found release as Amelia sobbed against Jane's shoulder.

"You were right about so many things, Jane."

"Hush now, dearest. It's all over."

Amelia pulled away from Jane and wiped the back of her wet hand across her eyes. "God did just what you said he would. He was faithful." Amelia sniffed and diverted her gaze. "And you were right about Captain Sterling. Graham."

She searched for the words that would accurately describe a feeling she didn't quite understand. "He told me loved me, Jane." She could barely force her words above a whisper as the depth of their meaning took hold in her heart. "I hadn't dared think it could be true, but at the dock, when he rescued us, there was something in his voice. In his eyes." A warmth swelled within her at the memory.

Jane reached forward and wiped Amelia's hair from her face. "And do you love him in return?"

Amelia pressed her hand to her cheek. A little surge of excitement ran through her as she realized the truth.

"I do, Jane. I love him with all my heart."

Satisfied that Littleton and Kingston were secure, Graham fell in step next to his brother. A brief rain had rolled in and rolled on, and the clouds parted, allowing the sun to once again shine and reflect off the wet streets. Graham yawned and ran his hand through his hair and down his face. He was exhausted. His body ached. His arm throbbed. Despite the discomfort, anticipation soared within him, increasing his pace.

"Now that we've got Lucy, Mrs. Dunne, and Miss Barrett back, we can go home to Darbury and everything will be as it was before," murmured William, stifling his own yawn. "Everything will be normal."

Normal? Not a single thing had been normal since Graham had arrived in Darbury, and judging by the changes stretching before him, Graham wondered if he ever would know normality again.

Graham threw William a sideways glance. His older brother looked worse for the wear. Mud and soot darkened his cheek. Blood streaked across his coat. Surely he'd judged William too harshly. Yes, his brother had experienced a serious lapse in judgment—perhaps many lapses. But had not Graham done the same? If God could forgive him, could he not manage to forgive his brother in turn?

And not only that, but Graham had seriously underestimated William's ability to rise to the occasion when duty called. If the man had failed to take the shot when he had the opportunity, the night before might have turned out quite differently. That relationship, too, had changed and was no longer what it had seemed. William had risked his life to help save another, and there was honor in that action. What kind of brother would he be if he did not respond in kind? "When we get back to Darbury, I'll talk to Carrington to see what can be done to help with Eastmore's debt."

William released a shaky sigh. "I appreciate that." William

cocked his head and straightened his hat, which had, miraculously, managed to survive the night's chaos.

Graham clapped his brother on the back. "Now that I know you're such a marksman, I'll depend upon you to watch over and protect Amelia and Lucy while I am at sea."

William snorted. "Marksman indeed. It was a lucky shot. I think I'll stick to dealing with horseflesh in the future."

Graham laughed, and it felt good. Finally, after weeks of turmoil and uncertainty, after months of holding on to regret, he felt the weight lift from his shoulders. He could barely wait to hold Lucy in his arms, to see Amelia.

"And what of you?" William seemed to know his thoughts. "I trust you are to be a married man in but a day's time."

Graham nodded, the very thought sending waves of anticipation through him. "If she will still have me."

"And your duties. When will you return?"

Graham almost stopped short. After all that had transpired, how could he leave Lucy? Amelia?

Even just a few short weeks ago, the sea had been his world. He breathed by the rise and fall of the tide. Its rules were his rules. But now, another reality was just as real. One of family. Of love.

He was honor-bound to return to his duties and did not have long before his responsibilities called him back to the sea. The thought of separation from Amelia and Lucy made his chest ache. Always before his love of the sea and his sense of duty had eventually pulled him back to his ship. Now the promise of a family secured him like a welcome anchor dropped at his final port, his destination.

But when fighting ceased, when war was done and battles won, could he leave the sea? The only thing he'd ever known? He thought of Amelia and Lucy and let the question linger in the air. The answer came with resounding clarity, for Amelia and Lucy were his future.

Yes, he could leave the sea. And he would give up much more.

31

G raham paused outside the front door of the Sulters' house, his hand hovering over the latch. He had parted ways with William, who opted to secure a room at a nearby inn. The frosty air soothed his heated spirit, but something in him still felt restless.

Leaning to the left, Graham peered through the window. Amelia sat in a chair next to the fire. Lucy, looking more like a cherub than a child, slumbered on Amelia's chest, her curly head tucked tightly under Amelia's chin.

Graham let himself in and closed the door quickly behind him, fearing the cool air would disturb the pair. Even though the morning sun was already climbing the sky, the house was quiet. All were asleep, worn out. He tried to be quiet, but as the door fell closed behind him, Amelia jerked her head up. As her eyes met his, a warm smile curved her lips. Inviting him in, drawing him closer.

The fire's cordial glow bathed the small room in warm light, playing on Amelia's golden strands and Lucy's copper curls.

Graham's chest swelled with unexpected emotion as he touched his fingers to Lucy's sleeping head.

He swayed from foot to foot, hesitant to speak lest his voice break the peaceful spell. "Is she all right?"

"She's fine, Graham." Amelia's words were soft. "Do you wish to hold her?"

Graham held his breath. He *did* want to hold her, but he hesitated. "I've no desire to wake her."

"Nonsense." Amelia stood from the chair, her movements gentle, and slowly extended Lucy toward him.

Graham gathered his sleeping daughter protectively in his arms and inhaled her scent. His little girl was perfect, from the copper curls to her dimpled hands. And she was his. "She smells sweet."

"It's lavender."

His gaze met hers. He already knew that. It was the same scent Amelia wore.

She stood close and adjusted the blanket around Lucy, and as she did her hand brushed his chest. Warmth surged through him from her touch, and he heaved a deep breath. At this close range, the fire reflected on the tracks of dried tears down Amelia's cheeks, a sobering reminder of the day's events. He glanced around and found the cradle next to the settee. He gently laid Lucy down, pulling the blanket over her and tucking it around the edges. Then he returned his attention to Amelia, aware of a tremor beginning somewhere deep within him.

Her chest heaved with a shallow breath. Her eyes fell on his arm, and she reached out and touched his forearm with timid fingers. Such a simple touch, yet he felt it to the very core of his being.

She whispered, "Does it hurt?"

He shook his head. Indeed, he felt no pain.

Amelia's expectant eyes held his and refused to let him look away. He didn't miss the flush of her cheeks, the shallowness of her breath. "I should have listened to you," she said. "You told me not to leave the Sulters', and I did. I am so sorry. Please don't be angry with me. I know I—"

He lifted his hand to her cheek and rubbed his thumb tenderly over her soft lips, silencing her. Now was not the time for words, for what words could describe what he felt for her in that moment?

Fierce longing commandeered his senses as his gaze lingered on her full, parted lips. He tipped her chin upward with his forefinger, his face hovering just inches above hers. She gasped as he pulled her tighter, but she didn't look away.

Desire for the woman he loved pulsed through his veins. He cupped the back of her neck, splaying his fingers aggressively through the damp golden tresses.

Slowly he lowered his mouth to hers, intending to be gentle. He didn't want to frighten her, not after what she'd been through. But every fear, every emotion from the past three days transformed into possessive passion at the velvety touch of her lips. Discipline of will, his constant companion, fled, leaving behind a yearning unlike any he'd ever known. Boldly, without apology, he deepened the kiss, pressing her body closer to his.

Beneath his touch her body trembled, but she didn't resist. Instead, she wrapped her arms around his neck, trailing her fingers through his hair.

His lips left hers to move to her ear. His whisper was rough. Desperate. "Marry me, Amelia. Not for Lucy. Not for your inheritance. But for *me*."

He couldn't wait for her answer before his lips again captured hers. Reveling in the intoxicating scent of her, he buried his face into her neck. He needed to hear her say it. He was a man desperate for the words. Perhaps at one point he could have been satisfied to be her husband in name only. But now, after he had tasted her lips, after his hands had memorized the feel of her skin, it would be impossible.

Her body weakened underneath his touch, and she pulled back. Large eyes regarded him with curiosity, but not fear. Even in the shadows he could see the flush of her cheeks, the smile curving her lips. Her breath came in shallow gasps, and her chest rose and fell with emotion. A single word sealed his future happiness: "Yes!"

He released the breath he'd been holding, wrapped his arms tighter around her waist, and lifted her up off the floor. A giddy giggle bubbled from her, and he lost himself again in the wonder of her kiss.

Amelia now belonged to him. He belonged to her.

And heaven help him, he would endeavor to deserve her.

READING GROUP GUIDE

1. In this story, Amelia risks everything—her future, security, and reputation—to keep a promise to a loved one. Have you ever had to give up something to keep a promise?

2. Amelia was forced to choose between following the will of her family and keeping a promise to her friend. Do you think Amelia handled her situation in the best way? If you were Amelia, what would you have done differently?

3. Initially, Graham is unable to forgive himself for some of the mistakes in his past, but over time he learns to accept God's forgiveness and, in turn, forgives himself. Is there something in your past that you have had a hard time forgiving yourself for?

4. Do you think that Edward ever really loved Amelia as he claimed? Why or why not?

5. Amelia grew up without a mother, and when she needed advice, she often turned to Mrs. Hammond. If you had been Mrs. Hammond, what advice would you have given Amelia?

6. At the end of the novel, Helena is pregnant and comes to realize that her impressions of Edward were false. How is Helena different at the end of the novel than she was at the beginning? What lessons do you think she learned?

7. Why do you think Captain Sterling is so reluctant to give his horse a name?

8. Growing up, Amelia and Helena were very close, but over time, circumstances drove a wedge between them. Have you ever had a relationship in your own life take such a turn? How were you able to repair the relationship?

9. At the beginning of the book, instead of turning to God for guidance, Amelia relies on her own wisdom to concoct a plan of how she can keep her promise to Katherine. In the end, she realizes that her own strength is not sufficient and learns to rely on God. Has there been a time in your life when you learned a similar lesson?

10. In what way is Amelia different at the end of the story? In what way is she the same?

ACKNOWLEDGMENTS

No relationship is by accident, and I am so thankful for the people God has brought into my life. Words cannot express the extent of my gratitude for those who have supported and encouraged my writing.

To my husband, Scott, and to my darling daughter—the two of you are my greatest joy and inspiration. Thank you for believing in my dream and going on this journey with me. I am richly blessed.

To my parents, Ann and Wayne, who have prayed for me and cheered me on through every endeavor, and a special thanks to my mom, Ann, and my sister, Sally, who were my very first readers. Who knew editing could be such fun?

To my friend and agent, Tamela Hancock Murray, whose guidance has been a blessing on my writing career. Your passion is truly contagious.

To my editor, Natalie Hanemann, and my copyeditor, Anne Buchanan. Your insight is impeccable, and you both taught me more than you could ever realize. And to the design team, the editorial team, and the marketing folks at Thomas Nelson . . . you guys are amazing.

ACKNOWLEDGMENTS

To my fellow historical authors Kim Taylor and Carrie Fancett Pagels, who offered advice and friendship while I was writing this book, and to the TG5 ladies, who encouraged me when this story was just a whisper of an idea. Each one of you is a blessing to me.

ABOUT THE AUTHOR

Photo by Forever Smiling Photography

Sarah E. Ladd has more than ten years of marketing experience. She is a graduate of Ball State University and holds degrees in public relations and marketing. *The Heiress of Winterwood* was the recipient of the 2011 Genesis Award for historical romance. Sarah lives in Indiana with her amazing husband, sweet daughter, and spunky golden retriever.